The
Wild
Ways

TANYA HUFF

The
Wild
Ways

DAW BOOKS, INC.

DONALD A. WOLLHEIM, FOUNDER

375 Hudson Street, New York, NY 10014

ELIZABETH R. WOLLHEIM

SHEILA E. GILBERT

PUBLISHERS

www.dawbooks.com

First Printing, November 2011
1   2   3   4   5   6   7   8   9

DAW TRADEMARK REGISTERED
U.S. PAT. AND TM. OFF. AND FOREIGN COUNTRIES
—MARCA REGISTRADA
HECHO EN U.S.A.

PRINTED IN THE U.S.A.

For Heather Dale,
who sang about Selkies and inspired the whole thing.

ONE

AMELIA CARLSON'S OFFICE was large and the wide window overlooking Halifax Harbor kept it well lit in spite of the traditional dark woods of the paneling and furniture. Nothing in the room screamed money, but everything said it quietly, well aware—given the quality of the furnishings—that shouting wasn't necessary to make the point.

All right, *Algoma Hill*, the Lauren Harris painting hanging across from her desk, screamed money but only because the price paid during the Sotheby's auction, while unfortunately not a record, had been high enough to make the front page of even the American papers. She'd purchased it anonymously, of course, but the people it had been bought to impress recognized it and exhibited the expected sticker shock. So much easier to attract investors when her personal salary allowed her to purchase a painting by one of the Group of Seven.

And *they* said that when her father died, the company had died with him. She may have been a competent Vice President of Exploration and Development, but *they* didn't hesitate to announce that a fort . . . *thirty-six*-year-old woman with a twent . . . *fifteen*-year-old engineering degree couldn't run the second largest oil company in the Maritimes. She wasn't a member of the old boys' club and she wasn't a hot, young Ph.D who'd picked up an MBA on the way to a petrochemical doctorate. Worst of all, at least to those running the *largest* oil company in the Maritimes, she had no extended family to help her. *They* said she'd run the company into the ground in two, three years at the most. Several of them had offered to take the company off her hands.

A year later, a year of betting everything on one roll of the dice, and she was on the verge of gaining the rights to one of the biggest fields in the North Atlantic. After that debacle in the Gulf, no one else had the balls to try for it, to spend three hundred and sixty-five days quietly working behind the scenes convincing the decision makers to make the *right* decision. And they all had. The moment the Minister of the Environment stopped faffing about, appearing to weigh the potential of spilled oil against jobs and tax income, and issued the drilling permit, the barges would be out of Sydney Harbor so fast they'd look like jet skis.

Granted, even given near guarantees of five hundred million barrels accessible of a three billion barrel potential by the best geophysicists in the business, there was no oil at all until drilling replaced science. Which was why the drilling platform had to be in place as soon as possible. Once they started production, they'd quickly surpass Hibernia's fifty thousand barrels a day.

The board of directors had given her until the end of the year to get the permit. She'd been promised it by the end of the summer.

They could shove their sexist, patronizing, dumbass . . .

When the door opened, she raised her head, her expression neutral, and met the worried gaze of Paul Belleveau, her executive assistant.

"It's happened," he said, "just like she told you it would. The Ministry of the Environment is being pressured by *Two Seventy-five N*, the same Hay Island group that stopped the seal hunt."

"Nice to have so much free time," she muttered. *Two Seventy-five N* were a group of crazy environmentalists run by an old Cape Breton family. The name referred to life jacket buoyancy. Measured in newtons, one newton equaling one kilogram of flotation, a two seventy-five newton life jacket was intended for extreme conditions. Amelia admitted it was a clever name and despised the anti-development, anti-growth rhetoric the group clung to. Until recently, she'd believed the group's successes could be laid at the door of deep pockets and an underemployed membership with time to meddle, but new information had revealed they were so much more.

"We're front page in the *Herald*," Paul continued. "There's articles in both the *Globe* and the *Post*, and their objection to the well was the lead on Canada AM's business report. Mr. Conway isn't returning my calls, but his aide . . ."

"The chatty one?"

"Yes. He says that the minister is talking about a class two environmental assessment or even asking for a Royal Commission on offshore drilling, so he doesn't actually have to make a decision."

Royal Commissions could take years and were the traditional way politicians avoided handling hot topics while still looking like they gave a shit. With the investment Carlson Oil had already made in this well, they'd never survive the delay. She could feel the edges of her very expensive manicure cutting half moons into the equally expensive wood of the desk.

"Rallies and protests against the drilling are in the planning stages," Paul finished, "although reports from the legislature say Mr. Peterson has already added us to his inventory."

Gandalf Peterson—he'd had his name legally changed—sat in front of the provincial legislature Monday to Friday, eight thirty to five thirty, protesting the Sable Island wells with a rotating series of sandwich boards. He was out there rain or shine, whether the legislature was in session or not, reasonably well behaved unless he recognized one of the industry players; then all bets were off. One of the most recognizable, Amelia made it a point to walk directly past him whenever she had to enter the building, accepting his vitriol as evidence of a job well done.

"All right." She took a deep breath and forced her fingers to release their hold on the edge of her desk. "*She* told us what was going to happen and she was right about everything up to and including Mr. Peterson. That leads me to believe her when she tells us she can fix things in our favor."

"Ms. Carlson . . ."

"You don't believe her?"

"Believe her?" Paul shook his head. "I'm not sure I believe *in* her. Or them. Or any of this."

"Any of this?" Had the Botox allowed her to arch a brow, she would have. "And yet, you still cash your paycheck."

"I believe in you."

"I'm pleased to hear that." When he smiled, Amelia took a moment to admire the effect. While undeniably gorgeous, with the shaved head and neat goatee she felt only black men could successfully pull off, Paul's good looks were surpassed by his skill at the job which was surpassed in turn by his extreme discretion. He'd been with her just over two years, cut from the herd of brand new MBAs the company employed, and she didn't know what she'd do without him.

Beyond the obvious: work twice as hard and get half as much done.

"All right," she said again, although it wasn't. "She's proven her point. Turn her loose."

"No love, we're from Cape Breton."

"But you say *b'ye* like you're from Newfoundland. How's it going, b'ye. You want another beer, b'ye? What's up with that?" Charlie glanced around the tiny table at the four men who'd asked her to join them for a drink between sets—Fred Harris, Tom Blaine, Bill Evans, and Bill McInna, although Bill McInna had told her to call him Mac. Not that it really mattered what she called him since after tonight's gig, she'd never see them again and they all seemed like the type to think *call me anything you want but don't call me late for supper* was a lot funnier than it was.

"They got the b'ye from us, didn't they?" Frank grinned and raised his beer. The other three returned the salute. "I mean, yeah, this here's the Newfoundlander's Bar . . ." The bottle became a pointer—at the flags, at the photos, at the fish mounted on dark walls barely visible behind the Friday night crowd. ". . . but it ain't just the b'yes from the Rock heading west looking for a way to keep body and soul together, is it? Economy's in the shitter all through the Maritimes. DEVCO's closed the coal mines, steel mill's been shut in Sydney . . ."

"Used to make good money there," Tom sighed. He was the oldest of the four, late thirties Charlie figured, and the one with the strongest family ties to the east. She could almost see them stretching out and away, linking him with the people he'd left behind. It was one of the reasons she'd sat down. Her family, the Gale family, understood those kind of ties.

"Used to make good money," Frank repeated. "That's my point, isn't it? And those suits in Halifax are telling us we should just be quaint for the tourists; like the Rankin family can put a roof on the house and oil in the furnace of the whole God damned place. Freezing our asses off in Fort McMurray, paying nearly three grand a month rent on a shithole apartment north of the downtown, complete with a leaky ceiling and rotten windows, that's the best option we've got left."

"And now they're talking layoffs." Bill glared at the wet ring his bottle had left on the tabletop. "Investments are down, aren't they? Gotta cut the costs of getting' the oil out of the tar sands, so they'll find guys willing to work for less."

"It's how they built the fucking railroads," Mac growled.

Frank rolled his eyes. "Jesus, Mac, you're a welder; you're good. They bring in cheap labor from overseas and it's the rest of us poor buggers that'll be heading home and back on the dole."

"Don't be giving him any sympathy now,"Tom said before Charlie could speak. "B'ye just bought himself a brand new F250."

"Needed something that'd fit the new ATV in the back, didn't I?" Frank laughed. "And who knows, maybe it won't be so bad going home. I hear rumors offshore oil's expanding again, and we've got mad oil field skills."

Bill laughed with him. "Yeah, and the fishing's already for shit, so when the drilling platforms break up and dump a few million gallons of crude, who'll notice, eh?"

"How long can you tread water?" Tom snorted. Charlie knew he was quoting, but she didn't know what.

"When my brother called . . ." Something in Mac's voice said this was important and Charlie wasn't the only one who'd noticed. Frank and Tom and Bill turned toward him, closing him in the circle of their attention, closing out the rest of the bar, their silence pushing back the ambient noise. They'd have closed her out as well, but Charlie refused to go. "When he called, he said he heard Carlson's trying to get permits to drill near Hay Island." Mac picked at the label of his bottle. The other three watched him watch his moving fingers.

Hair lifting off the back of her neck, Charlie froze in place, breathing slowly and quietly through her nose so as not to spook them. If they remembered she was here . . .

"Hay Island. That's the seal rookery,"Tom said at last.

Mac nodded. "My brother says there'd be a couple hundred jobs on the rig and more in the refinery they say they'll build by Main-a-Dieu, but his wife, well, she's against it."

"Yeah, well, she would be, wouldn't she?" Frank's grin twisted into a curve that hinted of secrets.

Charlie had a Gale girl's objection to secrets she, personally, wasn't keeping, and it struck her that this particular secret wouldn't be pried loose by smiling and looking interested—no matter how few women there were in Fort McMurray. Prying free this particular secret would require a completely different skill set. She'd drawn her finger through a puddle of condensation and sketched out the first curves of a charm when a familiar hand landed on her shoulder.

"Charlie, come on!" Tony, the drummer for *Dun Good*, had to lean forward and shout as the noise of the crowded bar rushed back in to fill the space around the table. "Break's over!"

Wiping out the half drawn pattern with one hand, Charlie set her empty bottle down with the other and shoved her chair back to a chorus of protests from her companions. "Sorry, boys, music calls."

The music was, after all, why she was here.

By the time she picked up her guitar, grinning at the raucous welcome the band's return to the stage evoked, she'd almost forgotten how that secret had licked a frisson of *strange* across her skin.

Almost.

Later that night she almost asked Mac what he'd meant, but, by then, they were trading other secrets.

The drive south from Fort McMurray to Calgary took almost nine hours. Theoretically. They'd managed it once in nine and a half but only by keeping rest stops to an absolute minimum. Fortunately, in the last fourteen months of intermittent touring, they'd become old hands at covering the less well traveled parts of the western provinces and had two coolers of food stuffed in between the stack of amps and the box that held the snow chains and the twenty-kilo bag of clay kitty litter no one wanted to remove in spite of it being almost the end of July and nearly thirty degrees. Why tempt fate? They had six drivers—the band plus Tony's wife Coreen and Taylor's girlfriend Donna, who'd joined them at Provost just after they'd crossed back from Saskatchewan—and, of the six, Charlie was, by no means, the most disdainful of posted speed limits.

Since Donna'd had no actual obligations during their last gig at the Newfoundlander's Bar, she'd drawn short straw as first driver.

They were on the road by eight, five of the six passengers completely unaware of the charms sketched under the grime covering the old school bus, charms that had ensured an almost miraculous absence of mechanical difficulty considering the vehicle's age. Charlie'd done what she could for the gas mileage as well but suspected it'd need a full circle of aunties to drop it from *Oh, my God* to merely appalling.

Of the three aunties she had available out west, Auntie Gwen had suggested they switch it to bio diesel, Auntie Carmen had sighed damply, and Auntie Bea had said, *"If you choose to ride in that death trap, Charlotte Marie Gale, rather than Walk the Wood as any sensible person with the ability would choose to do, do not assume we will ride to the rescue after the inevitable fiery crash."*

The aunties were big believers in *you made your bed, you crash and burn in it.*

And, while Charlie was one of the family's rare Wild Powers, it wasn't as if she could take the whole band through the Wood. Of course she'd thought about it, even worked out the charms she'd need to handle the remaining iron in the bus, but had balked, in the end, at explanations. They were a country band; beer and Jack did not set the stage for the truly inexplicable.

"They told me this road was only busy on Thursday nights," Donna muttered as half a dozen tanker trucks roaring north on 63 nearly sucked the bus over to the wrong side of the two lane highway. "They needed to define *busy.*"

Sitting in the first seat back—Board of Education back-cracker seating having been replaced by the bench from a wrecked Aerostar—Charlie picked out a complex pattern nearly at the top of her fretboard and said, "Yeah, well, what do *they* know."

"Excellent point. What're you playing? It sounds familiar."

What was she playing? She had to pick out another four bars before she recognized it. "'One.' It's *Metallica.*"

"I know it. I hold my breath as I wish for death. Oh, please, God, wake me." Donna met Charlie's eyes in the rearview mirror, and grinned. "Trapped in a broken body, begging for release. And I thought country music was depressing. Problems, chica?"

"No, everything's good. It's just where my fingers fell." Because everything was great. The band was getting some solid recognition, their EPs selling well enough that Tony was talking about them taking it full time and touring outside of Alberta and Saskatchewan. More Gales were moving west to Calgary and, as much as she enjoyed staying with Allie and Graham, Charlie'd been thinking of getting her own place. There'd been rumors that the apartment over the coffee shop next door to the Emporium would be available sometime in the fall and she couldn't think of anything more perfect. She'd gain a little privacy while changing almost nothing about how she lived.

"Broken Wings?" Donna's question jerked her out of her thoughts. Apparently, her fingers had moved on without her. "Chica, I wasn't suggesting you *play* depressing country music. I mean, sure, there's nothing like starting the day with a song about a woman trapped in a . . . Shit!" Swerving onto the shoulder, she somehow missed the car suddenly in their lane trying to pass an oil truck headed north.

Charlie hit a quick A minor 7th and managed to get all four wheels back on the pavement.

"Know any songs about assholes on the road?" Donna wondered after they'd spent a moment or two remembering how to breathe.

Charlie could feel a faint buzz under her skin. As though the adrenaline rush had plucked a string with its action set too low. "I know a few . . ."

Almost eight and a half hours and an uncounted number of assholes slowing them down later, they reached Edmonton. An hour after that, pulling out of a gas station onto highway 2 on the south side of the city, Charlie gripped the bus' steering wheel and smiled. She could feel Calgary, feel the branch of the Gale family newly anchored there tugging at her. Anticipating home, she could almost ignore the lingering buzz.

"Fifty says I can make it to Tony's place in less than three."

Before anyone could point out that a legal speed would take closer to four hours, Jeff, the bass player, took her up on it.

Two hours and forty-seven minutes later, they unloaded the essentials off the bus in Tony's driveway.

"If I hadn't seen it," Jeff muttered, handing over a twenty and three crumpled tens, "I wouldn't have believed this hunk of junk could make a lateral move across four lanes of traffic at one twenty."

"I didn't think it could *do* one twenty," Tony grunted, loading the last of his drum kit onto the bus' old wheelchair lift. "All right . . ." He straightened and stretched, twisting the knots out of his back, damp streaks of darker gray staining his pale gray T-shirt. " . . . since I'm pretty sure you lot are as sick of the sight of me as I am of you, let's give it a couple of days, and say Tuesday evening for the debrief at Taylor's place."

Taylor waved a finger but allowed the offer of her apartment to stand.

Weighed down with two guitars, her mandolin, her banjo, and a duffel bag of dirty laundry, Charlie waved an entire hand and then staggered down the driveway to where one of the younger members of the family had left her car.

"Allie, it could easily be stupid o'clock in the morning when we get in."

"Yeah, and they have these things called phones, you know. You could call when you're close."

Gale family phones began as the cheapest pay-as-you-go handset available, spent quality time with the aunties, and finished as free, reliable cell service—where reliable meant the aunties saw no reason to allow an absence of signal to interfere with their need to meddle. In the right liver-spotted hands, tech sat up and begged.

Charlie'd rolled her eyes in her cousin's general direction. *"Or you could just have one of the kids drop my car off at Tony's Sunday afternoon."*

Given that their younger cousins considered the car theirs while Charlie was touring, they'd gone with the second option.

Embracing the clichés of playing in a country band, she'd intended to buy a pickup, but safely transporting more than one instrument at a time turned out to be more important than a faux redneck image. Sitting behind the wheel, everything securely stowed, Charlie sighed and glanced up at her reflection in the rearview mirror. "I have a station wagon."

Her reflection wisely did not point out that the amount of crap she'd accumulated required a station wagon.

She used to store her extra instruments at her parent's place, dropping by to grab what she needed when she needed it.

She used to travel with her six string and a clean pair of underwear stuffed into a pocket on her gig bag. Some days, the underwear had been optional. The roads she used to take had no traffic, no GPS location . . .

"No idiot driving like a gibbon with hemorrhoids!" she snarled, finally managing to get around the SUV driving 10K under the limit while hugging the center line.

No Gale ever said *driving like an old lady*. Old ladies in the Gale family drove like they owned the roads. And the other drivers. And the local police department. And the laws of physics.

Roaring up the ramp onto Deerfoot, Charlie felt the city tuck itself around her. It was nice. There was nothing wrong with nice.

Glancing over at Nosehill Park, she searched the curve of the hill for the silhouette of a ten point stag. Even passing at 110K, she could feel the power radiating from both the ancient and current ritual sites, but there was no sign of David. It wasn't like she'd *expected* to see him. He'd been spending more time on two feet lately and, for all she knew, he'd headed into town for a beer.

With the change under control, he'd been talking about finding some consulting work. Everyone felt a job would help him regain the scattered pieces of his Humanity where everyone, for the most part, meant Allie, who still felt irrationally guilty about her part in her brother's transformation into the family's anchor to this part of the world. Charlie figured it had been a fair trade for saving said world, but David wasn't *her* brother and Allie . . . Well, Charlie loved her, but Allie had a habit of holding on just a little too tight.

Three weeks ago, just after the Midsummer ritual and before the band had left on this latest mini tour, Charlie'd spent some time with David in the park and he'd seemed fine to her. He'd been managing weekly dinners with Allie and Graham at the apartment over the Emporium, with Katie at Graham's old condo, and with Roland and Rayne and Lucy at Jonathon Samuel Gale's old house in Upper Mount Royal. *Plus variable members of the family* being a given in each case. Over the last year, three sets of Gales—couples of Charlie's generation—had transferred from the Toronto area to equivalent jobs in Calgary, and bought houses next to each other on Macewan Glen Drive. It wouldn't be like it had been back in Darsden East when Charlie was growing up, when the Gale girls had run the schools from kindergarten to college, but it was a start.

Gale boys were too rare to be allowed out alone, but they couldn't run a ritual without at least one in the third circle, so Cameron, now heading into his second year at the University of Alberta, had been sent west with six of the girls on his list, carefully picked by the aunties to be distant enough cousins to eventually cross to second circle with him. Charlie hadn't bothered keeping track of the girl cousins who'd come and gone and returned and reconsidered. Cameron's list, Roland's list, David's list—Gale girls flocked around Gale boys like bees around flowers.

Fortunately, only three aunties were required for a first circle. Although nine short of a full circle, three were enough to keep things going, particularly when backed by Allie's second circle *why yes, I can do scary things* level of power. After that whole saving the world thing, Auntie Bea and Roland's grandmother, Auntie Carmen had gone back to Ontario only long enough to pack up the essentials and have an extended meeting behind closed doors with Auntie Jane. No one could tell Charlie what had been said, but no one doubted Auntie Bea and Auntie Carmen were Auntie Jane's eyes on the ground.

When they'd returned to Calgary, they'd been the first to buy property on Macewan Glen Drive as two of the twenty-five houses overlooking the park had gone on the market the moment they'd made it clear they were interested. They currently lived together in the smaller of the two and rented the other to Cameron and the girls. Cameron had the basement apartment and got in a lot of practice recharming the lock on his door.

Auntie Gwen remained in the apartment over the Emporium's garage, refusing to share her leprechaun.

Charlie'd spent most of the time she wasn't with the band helping the family get settled in and agreeing, as graciously as she could, to retrieve treasures forgotten in Ontario.

The buzz returned, running across her shoulders. She nearly spun out on the off ramp trying to scratch the itch it left behind.

At nine thirty on a Sunday night, 9th Avenue was empty enough that Charlie could make the left turn onto 13th Street without pausing. She parked in the alley behind the Emporium, noted what looked like a new scorch mark on the wooden siding, grabbed her guitar, charmed open the small garage door, and squeezed through to the inner courtyard. Extending the space to put Graham's truck and Allie's car under cover without collapsing the loft upstairs had required impressive charm work.

Charlie couldn't have done it.

But then Charlie *wouldn't* have done about eighty percent of what Allie'd been up to lately even if she could have. Second circle, Allie's circle, was by definition appallingly domestic and Charlie considered showing up in time for dinner to be quite domestic enough, thanks very much.

Not that there was something wrong in always showing up at the same place for dinner; Allie was one hell of a cook. All the Gale girls could cook— Charlie herself being the exception that proved the rule. Her sisters claimed that Charlie's single attempt at lemon meringue pie still gave them citrus-themed nightmares. The grass never had grown back.

Attention caught by a familiar sound, Charlie glanced up at the loft over the garage and grinned. Auntie Gwen and Joe were home. Her grin broadened as the rhythm and intensity increased. Joe was full-blood Fey; he'd survive.

As Charlie crossed the small courtyard between the store and the garage, leaves rustled. All three of the dwarf viburnum in the center bed leaned toward her, creamy white flowers trembling.

She could step into the Wood right now. Step out anywhere she wanted to.

Anywhere.

This was where she wanted to be.

There was nothing wrong with that.

The back door to the Emporium was never locked. It stuck a little, though. The buzz now making the muscle in her right calf jump, Charlie jerked the door closed behind her, turned, caught sight of her reflection in the huge antique mirror hanging in the back hall and said, "I'm happy to see you, too, but I've never met Paul Brandt and I'm not double jointed."

The mirror had belonged to Allie's grandmother, Charlie's Auntie Catherine. They'd found it up and running when Allie'd inherited the Emporium and, given that magic mirrors were rare on the ground, the odds were high Auntie Catherine had activated it. Problem was, she'd been banished from the city before providing an owner's manual. Although they had no proof, what little evidence they had suggested that, for Auntie Catherine, the mirror had been a full orchestra. Metaphorically speaking. For the rest of them, it was more a twelve year old with a kazoo and a dirty mind. Almost literally.

Auntie Catherine was, like Charlie, one of the family's Wild Powers, but if that had given her an edge with the mirror, Charlie couldn't seem to get her own ducks in a row. The mirror reacted to her the way it reacted to everyone else—with juvenile lechery and vague affection. It reminded Charlie of Uncle Arthur, only without the persistent pinching.

Resting her palm against the mirror, fingers spread, Charlie watched as her reflection's hair color cycled through various blues, reds, greens, purples, paused on the short cap of turquoise she currently wore, and finally finished with the dark blonde/golden brown that was the Gale family default.

"You're right," she sighed, suddenly very tired. "The hair's become shtick." She sagged forward until her whole body pressed against the glass and wondered, yet again, how Auntie Catherine had slid inside. What had she seen inside the mirror? Had she been Alice or the Red Queen?

Stupid question.

She'd been the Jabberwocky.

Because Auntie Catherine had done what every Gale with Wild Powers did. She'd gone Wild. The *we know best* of the aunties had become a much less restrained *I know best* and anything that made the aunties seem restrained, was pretty freakin' scary.

In the mirror, Charlie's reflection aged, hair graying, gray eyes darkening to auntie black.

"Yeah, I know." She straightened, feeling every kilometer of the drive south from Fort McMurray in a retired school bus with no air-conditioning. Her reflection continued to lean against the inside of the glass. "You're not going anywhere and I've still got plenty of time to work out how Auntie Catherine did it."

Halfway up the back stairs, the door to the apartment on the second floor slammed open, slammed shut, and Charlie suddenly found herself facing a seriously pissed-off teenage boy—the smoke streaming out of his nostrils a dead giveaway of his mood. He rocked to a stop and glared, hazel eyes flashing gold, pale blond hair sticking out in several unnatural directions, wide mouth pressed into a thin line.

"Jack."

"Oh, you're back." The smoke thickened. "Good. You can tell Allie I don't have to put up with this stuff!"

"She's making you listen to Jason Mraz again?"

"What?" He had to stop and think, rant cut off at the knees. Charlie gave herself a mental high five; she rocked at pissy mood deflection. "No! She thinks I'm helpless!"

"Does she? Well, she thinks Katy Perry is edgy, so . . ." Charlie shrugged, letting the wall hold her up for a while. "Where are you heading?"

"Flying!"

"It's . . ." It was too much effort to look at her watch, so she settled for general and obvious. ". . . late."

His eyes narrowed. "That's what Allie said!"

"Yeah, but *I'm* not trying to stop you. Go. Fly." She waved the hand not holding the guitar in the general direction of the back door. "It's not like you can't handle anything that sees you."

"That's what Graham said," Jack admitted, the smoke tapering off.

"He's smarter than he looks. Just try to handle it *non*-fatally, okay? I've had a long day, and you know Allie'll make me come with her to deal with the bodies."

"Bodies." His snort blew out a cloud of smoke that engulfed his head and he stomped past, close enough Charlie could feel the heat radiating off him, but not so close she had to exert herself to keep from being burned. "Jack, don't burn down the building," he muttered as he descended. "Jack, don't turn the Oilers into newts and then eat them. Jack, don't eat *anything* that you can have a conversation with. This world sucks!"

He made an emphatic exit out into the courtyard, slamming the door with enough force that the impact vibrated past Charlie's shoulder blades.

"Well . . ." Charlie lurched away from the wall's embrace and up the remaining stairs. ". . . that explains why the door's sticking."

Jack loved hockey, although he thought it wasn't violent enough. He'd spent his first season as an enthusiastic Calgary Flames fan, learning the unfortunate fact that enthusiasm wasn't enough and devouring their opponents wasn't allowed.

The new scorch mark on the apartment door came as no great surprise.

"Because he's fourteen," Allie was saying as Charlie let herself in, put down her guitar, and closed the door. "And we're responsible for him."

"He's a fourteen-year-old Dragon Prince and a fully operational sorcerer." Graham wasn't visible, but the double doors to their bedroom were open, so Charlie assumed that Graham was out of sight in the bedroom. There were other, less mundane possibilities, but he'd probably sound a lot more freaked had Jack made him invisible, microscopic, or transformed him into furniture. Again. He'd made a surprisingly comfortable recliner. "There's nothing out there that can hurt him."

"You're missing my point." Even looking at the back of Allie's head, Charlie could see her eyes roll. "He's a fourteen-year-old Dragon Prince and a fully operational sorcerer."

"That's what I said." Graham sounded confused.

Charlie snorted. "Dude, she's not worried about *Jack*."

Allie spun around and Charlie had a sudden armful of her favorite cousin.

At five eight, Allie was an inch taller, but she was in bare feet and Charlie's sneakers evened things out.

"Don't you ever knock?" Graham asked, coming out of the bedroom, charms covering more skin than the shorts. Most of the charms were Allie's, a couple were Charlie's, and one was David's. And wasn't that interesting. "Never mind," he continued, crossing toward her, "stupid question."

He didn't bother pulling Allie out of the hug, just wrapped his arms around both of them and squeezed. Graham wasn't exactly tall—Charlie knew damned well he lied about being five ten—but he was strong. Even working full time at the newspaper, he'd managed to hang on to the conditioning his previous part-time position had required. Although, why an assassin needed muscle when the big guns did all the work, he'd never made clear to Charlie's satisfaction.

"Did we know you were coming in tonight?" he asked, dropping a kiss on Charlie's temple.

"I did," Allie gasped, crushed between them. "Charlie, sweetie, you stink." A judicious elbow broke Graham's hold.

"Yeah, twelve hours on the highway in a bus without air-conditioning will do that."

Graham snorted. "Even to a Gale?"

A quick pit check suggested *stink* was an understatement. "Please, we sweat flowers."

"Seriously?"

"Occasionally." Charlie patted Graham's cheek and Allie's ass on the way to the bathroom. "If Jack starts another apocalypse while I'm in the shower, fix it without me."

"He's a teenager." Washed, dried, and wearing black silk boxers under a faded *Dun Good* tank, Charlie snickered into her mug of tea and added, "He has to spread his wings."

"Wow, that's original." Allie poked her in the shoulder as she set a piece of strawberry pie down on the table and handed her a fork. "You should put it to music. And he's been spreading his wings plenty. They had to stop mail delivery in Bayview because a *hawk* . . ."

In the three weeks Charlie had been gone, Allie's air quotes had gotten a lot more emphatic.

". . . kept attacking the postal worker."

"Big difference between a hawk and a dragon, Allie-cat. And Jack's a big dragon."

Allie dropped in the chair next to Charlie and prodded her in the thigh with her bare feet. "Jack's a sorcerer. And we know his uncles played with their sizes, so it may be a Dragon Prince skill and have nothing to do with sorcery."

Too tired to make the obvious *played with themselves* comment, Charlie waved her fork, bits of pie crust speckling the tabletop. "Yeah, but no teenage boy would willingly make himself smaller. Dragon. Prince. Sorcerer. Doesn't matter which, it's not going to happen. It's all bigger is better at that age. Actually . . ." She frowned thoughtfully as she chewed. " . . . bigger is better at any age. Ow! Allie!"

Graham sat down across the table with his own piece of pie. "Somewhere in there you have a valid point, but the attacks on the postie stopped when Gwen threatened to clip Jack's wings."

Jack had spent his first thirteen years under the tender care of his uncles. Tender care when referring to Dragon Lords meant no need to marinate. He knew a legitimate threat when he heard one.

"So if the attacks have stopped, what's the problem?"

"He's working twelve hours a week at the *Western Star* this summer," Graham told her.

"At your skeezy tabloid?" That was new. She leaned away from Graham's swing. "Why?"

"Why?" Allie rolled her eyes. "Because school's out and he needs to do things like a normal boy."

If anyone asked, they were home schooling Jack which had the added benefit of being the truth, even if lessons tended toward *it's a bus, you can't fight it* rather than algebra. Although Roland had also taught him some algebra. Dragons were surprisingly good at math.

"Yeah, but he's not a normal boy." Charlie flipped up a finger. "Dragon Prince." And another. "Sorcerer." And a third. "Gale. Strike three." She frowned at the sheen of turquoise on her nails, the same shade as her hair. "Oh, that's definitely too precious. What the hell was I thinking?" The buzz crawled across her forehead.

"Why is your eyebrow twitching?"

"It's a thing. Back to Jack."

"When it comes right down to it," Allie sighed, "this world isn't shiny and new anymore. No one's threatening to eat him, and he's bored."

"So send him to the farm; Auntie Jane'll threaten to eat him."

Auntie Jane made Auntie Gwen look reasonable. Auntie Jane made Simon Cowell look reasonable.

"Only as a last resort." Allie's lip curled. "I don't want to spend the rest of my life listening to the aunties go on about how I failed to deal with him."

When Jack broke through from the UnderRealm looking for his father—Stanley Kalynchuk aka Jonathon Samuel Gale—the aunties had been forced by circumstances to explain that sorcerers were Gale boys gone bad. Jack was both a Gale boy and—thanks to the magical means of his conception—a sorcerer, but Allie had argued that, as a Gale, until he turned fifteen he was too young to be judged. The aunties had agreed, and Allie and Graham had started their marriage as the de facto parents of a teenage boy with a Dragon Prince's power and undetermined sorcerous abilities, who not only smoked in bed, but occasionally set fire to his pillow.

The first few months had been fun. Allie had overreacted, Charlie had underreacted, and Graham had hit the roof about the marshmallow roasting over the coals of an empty industrial building by the airport. Somehow or other, mostly because Jack absorbed new information like a sponge, they'd muddled through.

Charlie swallowed the last mouthful of pie and pushed her plate away. "So send him off to eat a bison and sleep for week while he digests. Works while the Stampede's on."

Horses and cattle at the Saddledome, barely two kilometers away from the Emporium, were more temptation than anyone expected Jack to resist.

"Unfortunately his cave was a little to close to Drumheller." Graham stacked his empty plate on hers. "Couple of dinosaur guys from the Tyrrell found his scat and nearly had kittens. I had to cover the story in the *Star* to discredit it. I'm not saying it *isn't* a skeezy tabloid," he added when Charlie snickered. "I'm just saying I don't need anyone else calling it that."

"Sensationalist rag?"

"That's better."

"He's been so moody lately," Allie explained. "I miss how he was in the beginning. You know, minus the whole burning things down and using sorcery to jump the line at the Apple Store."

"He's fourteen. That's the definition of moody." Charlie at fourteen had a brief, intense flirtation with *Three Days of Grace*. "And now that I think of it, isn't fourteen a little young for a job?"

"He can't exactly join a soccer team, can he?"

Stronger. Faster. Liable to eat the opposing strikers. It was like raising Clark Kent had Clark Kent been likely to make a meal of Lana Lang.

In spite of the imagery, and the sugar she'd just ingested, Charlie found herself suddenly unable to keep her eyes open. "As much as I'd love to keep discussing your crappy parenting . . . Ow!" She rubbed her thigh where Allie'd kicked her again. " . . . it's past eleven, I've had a long day, and I need to fall over. You going to wait up for him?"

"I'm not." Graham pushed his chair back and stood. He sounded pretty definite, but then he'd spent thirteen years killing nonHumans for Kalynchuk and while he'd made his peace with the Gales, that didn't mean he gave a half-eaten rat's ass for a half Gale/half dragon.

Tonight, Allie was more concerned for her city than for Jack in a teenage snit, but she'd fought to have Jack regarded as a Gale boy and Gale boys, vastly outnumbered by the girls, lived in a bubble of protected indulgence. Her view of Jack was as skewed as Graham's.

Charlie, who'd spent more time than either of them with his uncles, had trouble seeing Jack as a special snowflake.

As Graham put the dirty plates in the sink, Allie leaned against Charlie's shoulder and murmured, "Coming to bed?"

Before Graham, she wouldn't have asked. Nor would she have asked right after Graham had chosen, but about six months in, while acknowledging that Graham was both family and not exactly subject to the obligations of blood, the three of them had worked out an effortless arrangement.

Nothing wrong with effortless.

The buzz had spread out, defused by whatever charm Allie had baked into the pie. Charlie yawned. "No, I'll open a sofa bed and talk to Jack when he comes in."

"What makes you think he'll listen?" Graham asked, arms wrapped around Allie's waist.

"Novelty. It's been three weeks since I told him anything he didn't want to hear."

When the wind was from the north, like tonight, Jack liked to hang out by the big concrete dinosaurs at the zoo because it only took a minimal glamour to make him look like he was part of the display. When the wind was from the south, he didn't go near the place because his scent made the animals go a little crazy—okay, a lot crazy—and he'd stopped thinking that was funny when Allie'd gone up one side of him and down the other.

Even without fangs or claws or fire, she could be way scary.

Sometimes, she reminded him of his mother.

He didn't miss his mother because his mother was like his mother all the time, and Allie was only like that sometimes. When she was like that, then he missed his mother. Only not in a good way.

He frowned at the small flock of Pixies fluttering around the pole light.

His mother didn't care when he went flying or what he destroyed or who he ate. In the UnderRealm, he'd been expected to take care of himself.

He kind of liked being taken care of. Most of the time, he liked knowing he'd survive the day. But it had been more than a year of days in this world's time and he knew Allie assumed he'd stay and he liked being a Gale, but he also liked being a Prince and a Sorcerer and they were fine with him being a dragon as long as he was careful, but he didn't have subjects and . . .

"Highness?"

Okay, maybe he had a few subjects.

The Courts came through all the time, more than even the Gales knew—not that the Gales cared if it didn't affect the family, they were like dragons that way—but the lesser Fey slipped through with the Courts, and it turned out there were a lot of them here.

He looked down and frowned. Right here. At his feet. Looking familiar. "What?"

The Brownie bowed. "I bring a petition asking that you roast . . ."

"Hold it." Jack folded his neck and peered down his muzzle—it was never easy focusing on things so much smaller than him. "You're that Market

Mall Brownie who's totally baked about the outlets, right? Dude, for the seven millionth time, I'm not destroying your competition. Have a sale or something."

"It's a matter of quality, Highness."

"Still not going to happen."

"You fear the old women, Highness."

"Well, duh." The aunties could send him back to the UnderRealm. Okay, he wasn't sure they could do it without Allie—they'd needed Allie to send his mother and his uncles back—and Allie didn't like to do what the aunties said, but they were all so stupidly weird about the sorcerer thing—even though he almost never used it—that they'd probably send him back anyway as soon as he turned fifteen and their rules said he wasn't a child anymore, but . . .

"They are keeping you a child, Highness."

Was it reading his mind? No way was that allowed. Jack reared back. "You want me to roast someone? I could always roast you."

The Brownie turned slightly green. "Highness!"

Snorting out a cloud of smoke, Jack watched the little weasel scurry away, sent a silent apology to weasels because they were actually pretty cool, and thought that maybe if he was gone long enough, his mother would clutch again and he wouldn't be able to go back. He'd have to stay.

If they let him.

Why weren't there ever any easy answers? Questions sucked.

He spread his wings and launched himself into the sky, a sweep of his tail knocking the head off the concrete Apatosaurus.

Crap.

When the charm jerked her awake, Charlie blinked at the familiar shape sneaking past the end of the sofa bed. Blinked again as the night-sight charms sketched on her eyelids kicked in and Jack came into focus. "Have fun?"

He spun around to face her. "I didn't destroy anything!"

The sudden billowing cloud of white smoke seemed to argue differently. A wave got rid of the smoke although the scent of dragon lingered. "I didn't say you did."

"And I only ate a goose. It tasted like old french fries," he added sounding disgusted. "Even the food here sucks."

"There's a reason no one eats those things. And remember . . ." She sat up, legs crossed, sheet pooling in her lap. " . . . if you're not happy here, you can go back to the UnderRealm any time."

"I never said I wanted to go back!" Jack's eyes flared gold. "I like . . ." He waved a hand, searching for the words. " . . . you know, stuff."

Charlie liked stuff, too. The band. Allie. Family. Calgary. They wrapped around her warm and comforting. She twitched.

"You okay?" Jack saw fine in the dark without charms.

"Yeah, I'm good." Nothing wrong with warm and comforting. "So what brought on today's rebellion?"

"They won't let me do anything."

"At all?"

"Nothing . . ."

Charlie thought he was going to say *fun*—obvious response—and was a little surprised when he shrugged and didn't finish.

"I want to *do* something," he said after a moment.

"What?"

"I don't know!" Another small puff of smoke. Charlie let this one dissipate on its own. Jack glanced toward the double doors leading to Allie and Graham's bedroom and lowered his voice. "It's just . . . it itches under my skin."

Fingers curled to scratch at her shoulder, Charlie dropped her hand back into her lap and didn't ask him what itched. Or if he could also call it a buzz. "The job at the newspaper . . ."

"Is lame."

About to explain that pretty much everything seemed lame at fourteen, Charlie reconsidered. It wouldn't help. And Jack was . . . well, more than just fourteen that was for damned sure. "No promises, but I'll see what I can come up with."

"Vague much?" Jack snorted.

"Butt munch!" Charlie shot back.

"That makes no sense."

"What does?"

He stared at her for a long moment. "You used to be cool," he muttered and stomped off to his bedroom, the faint whisper of wings following behind him.

Amelia stared at the pelt draped over Paul's arm. "Is that . . ."

Paul nodded, holding it out toward her as though he was handling a dead animal instead of just the useful, external bits. "It was on my chair when I got back from setting up the board room." She could hear a hint of hysteria seeping out around the edges of his voice. "No one saw her come in. Or go out."

"Well, they wouldn't, would they?" Beckoning him forward, she hoped he'd reward her trust by postponing his reaction to this evidence of just what exactly they were involved in until he left the building. Only the two of them knew about the arrangement, and she'd like to keep it that way. If he said too much, she was willing to declare *the stress of the job pushed poor Paul into a breakdown,* but she'd rather not. Who had the time to find a new assistant who was both attractive and efficient?

"This proves they're vulnerable," she declared as he reached the desk. "And now they know who holds the cards."

"Card," Paul amended, nodding at the pelt. Her lack of reaction seemed to have helped to stabilize him.

"There'll be more. She knows my needs and she's being paid very well to fulfill them. As for our suddenly pelt-less opposition, they've been informed that they're to give their full, and fully visible support to our well off Hay Island. Once drilling has begun, they'll get their property back."

"They've been *informed,* Ms. Carlson? She's dropping off ransom notes?" When Amelia nodded, he shook his head. "Writing this kind of thing down . . ."

"Means nothing. They can't exactly go to the police, can they?" The fur was surprisingly soft under the longer, coarse, and oily hairs on the surface. This was, Amelia realized, the first time she'd ever touched a seal pelt. "A pity they stopped killing the white coats back in 1987. If they'd kept it up, we wouldn't have this problem. Not to mention, I'd have an upgraded winter wardrobe." She pulled the heavy skin from his hands, draped it around her shoulders, stroked it thoughtfully, and looked up to see Paul staring at her, brows up. "A little too Cruella de Vil?"

He held his thumb and forefinger about a centimeter apart. "Just a bit."

Charlie's phone woke her at eleven the next morning. Graham, Allie, and Jack had already woken her at seven, eight, and eight-thirty, further convincing her that she had to get her own place. A "Ride of the Valkyries" ringtone modulated her greeting to a fairly neutral, "What?"

"There's no need to be rude, Charlotte."

That, she'd expected. The particular voice, not so much. "Auntie Catherine?"

"How nice your current lifestyle hasn't entirely rotted your brain," Allie's grandmother confirmed. "I have a proposition for you."

"A what?" Charlie rolled over and blinked at the ceiling, scratching under the edge of her boxers where the elastic had dug into the skin. Easier to blame the elastic for the itch. "I mean, what kind of proposition?"

"You and I are not so different, Charlotte . . ."

Given the shit Auntie Catherine had put them through, Charlie wasn't inclined to jump on the Wild Powers *all together now, rah rah, go us* bandwagon. "What kind of proposition?"

"One that will get you out of Calgary."

"I'm happy here."

"Please." That was possibly the most definitive eye roll Charlie had ever heard. "Meet me in Halifax and we'll talk."

"Of what?"

"Ships and seas and sealing wax, tentacles and kings. As if I'd risk the others overhearing."

"Is that what's causing the buzz in the line?"

"Have a coffee and jumpstart your brain, Charlotte. I don't have time for this."

Auntie Catherine had a distinctly emphatic way of hanging up a cell phone.

"Dude!" Charlie smacked the mirror frame on her way by. "Tighten things up. It looks like my skin doesn't fit."

In the store, Allie and Joe stood staring at something on the glass counter. Their expressions suggested a hazmat suit might not be a bad idea.

"A nail?" Charlie asked when she got a little closer.

"The nail," Allie replied glumly. "For the loss of a nail," she continued when Charlie shook her head. "Horseshoe, horse, battle all lost. This is the nail."

"It's rusty."

"Don't think that matters," Joe muttered. He wore a mid-thirties glamour these days. Young enough for Auntie Gwen's ego, old enough that public PDAs had stopped attracting dangerous attention. The aunties' response to people stuffing their noses in where they didn't belong was not subtle by several fairly terrifying degrees of *not*. "It was in a jar with a bunch of screws, nuts, bolts . . ."

"Nails?" Charlie offered.

"Yeah."

"What's it do?"

"Nothing until you lose it. Then you lose everything else."

"So put it back in the jar and sell it."

Allie looked disapproving. "That's a bit irresponsible, don't you think?"

Charlie shrugged. "Depends on how you're defining irresponsible. Seems like the responsible thing would be to get it the hell out of here. It's not like family's going to pick it up."

"Tony, your drummer, he builds stuff, doesn't he? Suppose he came down and bought the jar with the nail in it because he needed some cheap screws and then he took it home and somehow lost the nail and lost his wife and his house and . . ."

"Yeah." Charlie cut her off. "I get it. It's dangerous. So what are you going to do with it? Lock it up with the monkey's paw?"

"No . . ." Allie reached under the counter and came up with a hammer. ". . . I'm going to put it where it can't get lost." She turned, lifted the signed photo of Boris off the wall, used the claw to pull the more mundane nail, and slammed the lost nail in about two centimeters higher.

"Gale girls know where the studs are," Charlie said.

Joe snickered.

"Why don't you go next door and get coffee," Allie muttered, hanging the Minotaur's photo back up.

*   *   *

Kenny Shoji looked up as Charlie came through the door of the coffee shop, muttered something that sounded uncomplimentary even at a distance, then moved to the row of urns behind the counter to start filling the tall red mugs he kept for the Emporium staff.

"So," he said without turning, "you're hanging around again. Wasting your life."

"I like my life."

"So you say."

"I don't feel trapped!"

He turned then. "Who said anything about trapped?"

"No one. You just . . . I mean . . . Look, whatever." She frowned purposefully at the small TV next to the cash register. The mute was on, but the banner across the bottom of the screen announced CBC *News at Noon* was showing visuals of the Hay Island Seal Rookery. Why did that sound familiar?

She jumped a little when Kenny set the three mugs down in front of her.

He looked from her to the television and shook his head. "Bad deal that. Some oil company's been pushing the Nova Scotia government for permits to drill just off the island. All hush hush. Some group that works to protect the seals found out, just about at the last minute, and there were a couple days of protest but they seem quiet now. Lots of oil, the company says, and no one's arguing that, but too close to shore and way too close to the seals if anything goes wrong."

"What could go wrong?" Charlie snorted. The visuals changed to an attractive woman speaking earnestly to a reporter. The banner now read *Amelia Carlson, CEO of Carlson Oil*. She wore the glamour money provided in order to look in her mid-thirties, plumped lips lifted in a smile equally as unreal. "I met some guys up in Fort McMurray . . ."

"Good for you!" Kenny's face pleated into a thousand wrinkles when he smiled. Even when it was a sarcastic smile. "I hear that's what happens when you hang out in bars. You should watch the news more."

". . . they were from Cape Breton," Charlie continued, ignoring him. "They talked about Carlson Oil trying to get offshore drilling permits. Said the company'd build a refinery and everything."

"Lots of jobs," Kenny sighed. "That's hard to argue with. It's always been tough going in the Maritimes. I know money was tight back when I was surfing off the north shore."

"Wait." Charlie moved her attention from the television to the very old man behind the counter. "You used to surf the north shore of Nova Scotia?"

"That's where I met Robert August." He pointed to one of the framed photographs on the wall of the shop. It was a signed, black-and-white shot of a young man in board shorts, cutting a sweeping line down a wave. "That was in the summer and the ocean was still cold enough to freeze your manhood off. And speaking of freezing . . ." He pushed the mugs toward her. ". . . take these before they get cold. Oh, and the apartment's free end of September. You can have it if you want it."

Sleeping in without interruptions. Practicing without silence charms. Still close enough to Allie's cooking. And bed. Charlie opened her mouth to say she wanted, but nothing came out.

Kenny shook his head. "I'd cut you off if I hadn't already poured. Your lip is twitching."

Auntie Gwen, Auntie Bea, and Auntie Carmen were waiting by the counter when Charlie got back to the store. Joe had left. Apparently Kenny's uncanny ability to know who wanted what coffee could be thrown out of whack by the presence of the aunties. Hardly surprising; whole civilizations could be thrown out of whack by the presence of the aunties. And if some of the stories were true, had been.

Auntie Bea looked stoic, Auntie Carmen looked concerned, but Auntie Gwen's expression lifted the hair off the back of Charlie's neck. She shot a silent *What's up?* at Allie, who shrugged an equally silent *I have no idea.*

"We just got off the phone with Jane," Auntie Gwen said as Charlie put the mugs down. "And we decided you should be told this in person."

"I should be told?" Charlie asked, licking at the coffee slopped on the back of her hand.

"Everyone here in Calgary needs to be told," Auntie Bea announced. "We're just starting with the two of you."

Auntie Carmen shook her head, concerned expression morphing to mournful. She took a deep breath, opened her mouth . . .

And Auntie Gwen cut her off. "Alysha, your grandfather . . ."

Charlie moved to Allie's side. Alysha's grandfather, Charlie's Great Uncle Edward, held the same position back in Ontario that David did here in Calgary. Allie adored him.

". . . wavered during the ritual at Midsummer. It has been decided, there will be a Hunt."

TWO

"A HUNT?" Behind the shield of the counter, Allie wrapped her fingers around Charlie's. "Because Grandfather *wavered?*"

"Weakness at the heart of the family cannot be tolerated, Alysha." Auntie Bea's dark eyes narrowed. "You know that."

"But there hasn't been a Hunt for generations." Allie's grip tightened past the point of pain. Charlie gritted her teeth. "Why hasn't one of the uncles just challenged him?"

"*Just* challenged him?" Auntie Bea snorted.

"David's tied here," Auntie Carmen sighed, thin fingers twitching at the hem of her pink polyester blouse. "I'm sure it was the only solution at the time, but no one else is strong enough."

Auntie Gwen shook her head. "Even if one of the others could defeat Edward . . ."

"And we're not saying anyone could," Auntie Bea interjected.

"If they could," Auntie Gwen continued, "they couldn't do it easily."

Auntie Carmen sighed again. "Not easily."

"David could have," Auntie Bea snapped.

Auntie Gwen turned on her. "David had a different destiny."

"Without David . . ." Auntie Carmen's voice trailed off.

"Without David," Auntie Gwen continued, "it has to be a Hunt."

"Without a Hunt, the center will be too damaged to hold," Auntie Bea pointed out, as though that, at least, should be obvious.

"If the center doesn't hold . . ." Auntie Carmen's eyes glistened and Charlie tried not to think of crocodiles and tears.

"If the center doesn't hold," Auntie Gwen said definitively, "then the family falls."

Outside the store, an SUV roared past, bass thumping, two kids walked by arguing about a television show, and half a dozen pigeons muttered amongst themselves as they wandered desultorily around the sidewalk directly outside the door looking for food.

Another moment passed, another SUV, and Charlie realized the aunties were waiting for a response. They'd finished talking. Good. The three of them had been very close to starting in on the eyeball swapping thing and that never ended well.

"So let me see if I can sum up." When no one objected, Charlie continued. "Uncle Edward wavered. That makes him weak, and we can't have a weak anchor. Unfortunately, David was the only male strong enough to take him out without taking the kind of damage in return that would keep him from doing his . . ." It wasn't exactly a job. " . . . thing. Duty. Under those circumstances, in order to put a strong male at the center of the family, there has to be a Hunt. That it?"

"That, Charlotte . . ." Auntie Bea folded her arms over a large, glittering image of a gossamer winged fairy distorted into caricature by the shelf of her breasts. " . . . is what we said. Edward's replacement will, of course, be temporary. *He* will be replaced by challenge and that replacement will last for a while longer."

Charlie borrowed an eye roll from Allie. "Of course."

Auntie Bea ignored the sarcasm. "As you've grasped the situation, we'll be off. We need to tell the others who've relocated." She made it sound as though the family had relocated to dirt roads, wooden sidewalks, gunfights at high noon, and saloons with sawdust floors. Auntie Bea made no secret of having come west to keep an eye on things.

"You're not telling David," Allie growled.

Auntie Carmen reached over the counter and patted her on the arm. "Of course not, dear. You anchor second circle; that's your job."

The expected protest never materialized. Allie merely closed her eyes for a moment and, when she opened them, asked, "When?"

Not when should she tell David, Charlie realized, but when was it happening. Second circle made connections. Allie was upset not surprised. She was part of the process now.

"Full moon's tonight," Auntie Bea sniffed as she headed for the door. "No time like the present."

"No time for second thoughts," Auntie Carmen sighed, following.

Auntie Gwen lingered a moment. "We'll take to the air and head out beyond the city limits. We don't want to be on territory David holds when we get caught up. Yes, we will," she said in response to a sort of cough from Allie. "We spent years with Edward; we're too connected not to react. But we'll find something to . . . take the edge off. David will be . . ." She bit her lip and tapped French-tipped nails against the counter.

"In a state?" Charlie offered. "Freaked? In no danger from the three of you but likely to trample you flat anyway?"

Auntie Gwen ignored her. "He'll be agitated. It might help if you were with him, Alysha."

"I plan to be."

"I'll be there, too," Charlie pointed out. Allie squeezed her hand a little tighter.

"Of course you will." Auntie Gwen frowned, sharing her disapproval equally between the two of them, and opened her mouth, but, before she could speak, Auntie Bea stuck her head back in through the door.

"I'm not paying for this cab to sit at the curb, Gwen!"

"You're not paying for the cab!" Auntie Gwen pointed out acerbically. The aunties needed a cab—a cab appeared. Never the same cab twice, so at least they spread the free rides around. Charlie wasn't sure if it was a result of the family's tie to the city or the aunties being cheap, but both were likely. Also, Auntie Bea's lime-green Capris were terrifying when seen through the door's clear-sight charm.

Auntie Gwen took a couple of steps away from the counter, paused, and pinned Charlie with a look that suggested a conversation involving the words, *we need to discuss your future* was in the offing. "Just to be on the safe side, Charlotte . . ." *And I shouldn't have to tell you this,* added the subtext. " . . . stay out of the Wood tonight."

"I'll be with Allie."

Her expression shifted, but before Charlie could define where it ended up, a car horn sounded. "Who tied Bea's sensible cotton briefs in a knot,"

Auntie Gwen muttered. Her rubber sandals made less of an aural impact than she'd probably intended as she stomped out of the store.

Still clutching Charlie, Allie stood in silence. Watched the cab drive away. Watched the traffic pass.

"Allie-cat," Charlie said at last, "could I have my hand back? I can't chord with broken fingers."

"You're not going because you could put Allie in danger!" Charlie snapped at last, stepping between Allie and Graham and waving a flip flop, first at Graham . . . "Sure, you married in, but the whole seventh son of a son of a thing gives you gnarly powers of your own and you know that." . . . and then at Allie. "He anchors ritual with you; stop treating him like he doesn't know what's going on." Back at Graham. "You want to be there to protect her." Back at Allie. "You want him not to be there to protect him. Oh, joy. True love. Stop making me nauseous and consider that we don't know how Graham would be affected and that could put Allie in danger and so you're not . . ." She slapped him on the chest with the flip flop. " . . . going! End of discussion."

After a long moment, Graham sighed. "If music doesn't work out for you, you could go into marriage counseling."

"Music is working out just fine," Charlie muttered, yanking her crushed flip flop from his grip. "Thank you."

"No way!" Jack folded his arms, brows nearly touching over his nose. "You can't make me stay in tonight, that's not fair! And, it's totally . . ."

"The aunties are Hunting."

" . . . totally the night I'm gonna kick Graham's ass at Madden."

Hand in the small of her back, Charlie pushed Allie toward the apartment door. "Told you *he'd* understand."

*   *   *

Charlie kicked at a chunk of dirt by the boulder that marked a hidden cache of David's clothes. Nose Hill Park was deserted. At seven, it was two and half hours until sunset, but there were no runners. No cyclists. No dog walkers. No surprise really; the air felt heavy, thick, and hot. Body temperature. Blood temperature. The moon would be full at seven thirty-seven— nine thirty-seven Ontario time. "He's not going to come, Allie. He knows what's happening; all the Woods are joined, and he's going to need to run."

"Nothing's chasing him." In spite of the heat, Allie had her arms wrapped around her torso.

"Even if nothing's chasing him."

"I wanted to tell him . . ."

"What?" Charlie suspected Allie wanted to tell pretty lies. *I won't let this happen to you.* David probably knew they were lies as much she did and wanted to hear them even less.

Finally Allie stopped scanning the visible acres of the park, and sighed. "He's strong. So many lives in the city, and I can feel every one of them through him. Not just the bright, clear touch of family, not just the land, but every little . . ." She flicked her fingers, right hand, left hand, right hand.

"That's weird." Charlie slid down the boulder, sat with her back against the rock, and repeated the movement. "Because Calgary never struck me as a jazz hands kind of city."

Allie sat beside her. "You'd be surprised," she said, tugging the hem of her shorts back into place, her voice tight. "Things are happening here."

Charlie bumped her shoulder. "Let's not start that again."

The grass on the hill was gold, the sky a heated silver blue. Leaves hung motionless on the trees. Charlie could feel the way into the Wood through them, feel the point where Jack and his mother had broken through from the UnderRealm, the ancient site sealed with modern ritual. She felt the city beyond the park only because her family was a part of it now. But Allie . . .

"Every life? Isn't that distracting?"

She felt Allie's shrug where their bare shoulders touched. "When you're listening to music, do you hear every note?"

"Sometimes."

"Sometimes it's distracting, but mostly it's just an awareness. It's what second circle does. Here, we tend our bits of the city the way the older piece of the family tends their land."

Although, because she'd been the primary conduit, Allie *tended* on a deeper level than any of the cousins who'd joined them. *Her*, Charlie corrected hurriedly. *Joined her.* In fact, Allie likely tended on a deeper level than any of the second circle back east. Odds were, she wasn't even aware of how often her attention drifted away from conversations, eyes unfocused slightly as she twitched a bit of the city back the way she wanted it. The whole uber *connectedness* freaked Charlie out a bit. Personally, she needed to have her options just a little more open than that.

Open enough to go all the way to Fort McMurray with a bar band?

Wow. Her inner voice had gotten sarcastic of late.

"You'd know if you crossed," Allie began but Charlie cut her off.

"Not going to happen, Allie-cat. I don't care how much the aunties want a seventh son of a Gale. I'm not crossing to second circle—it's express lane all the way to first—and I'm not splitting Graham's mystical lineage with you."

Given the way Gales skewed to girls, producing a seventh son of a seventh son of a seventh son in the Gale family meant approximately thirty-five babies. Gales liked babies, hell, Charlie liked babies, but that, that was heading into rodent territory even if Allie's unusual sibling situation—one brother, no sisters—helped adjust the numbers.

Allie snorted, sounding more like herself than she had at any time since the aunties had dropped the bombshell about the Hunt. "I'm not suggesting you split Graham's mystical lineage with me. I'm not even starting on Graham's mystical lineage until Jack's . . ." She waved a hand. " . . . resolved and even then, since it's not the aunties knocking me up, we're talking four or five tops—not fifteen or sixteen. But that doesn't mean you can't cross."

"Have the aunties been chewing at you about this?" That could definitely explain Auntie Gwen's expression. Every now and then, opinions shifted from *don't waste a Gale boy on* her *to breed the Wild Power back into the lines* and at nearly twenty-eight, Charlie knew she was reaching the age where the nagging started in earnest. "Second circle ties you down. I need the open road, the wind at my back, and a new horizon out in front of me."

"It's quite possible you also need to sing a little less country music," Allie muttered.

"Not to mention," Charlie continued, ignoring her, "that the Wild Powers usually skip right from third circle to first."

"Gran didn't."

"Yeah, well . . ." Kicking off a flip flop, Charlie used her toes to comb the dead grass into parallel lines. If the aunties hadn't been chewing at her, then Allie had brought the second circle stuff up on her own and that freaked Charlie out a bit, too. " . . . if your grandmother had been a boy, the aunties would have taken her out by now."

"Not telling me something I don't already know," Allie sighed.

They sat quietly for a few minutes. Charlie buried her toes in pale dirt, uncovered them, buried them again, until she couldn't stand it anymore and glanced at her watch. "Ten minutes left to kill."

Allie stiffened.

"Sorry." Charlie pressed closer, but Allie didn't relax.

Eight minutes.

Five minutes.

Two minutes.

The leaves shivered. A faint line of dust feathered off the top of the hill.

When the wind reached them, it smelled of the dark hollows under tree roots and the sharp, bitter scent of fear.

Allie shivered. Charlie wrapped an arm around her shoulders.

Between one heartbeat and the next, the moon was full and Nose Hill Park went wild.

Back in Ontario, the aunties would be crossing the cornfield behind the big white-and-green farmhouse and gathering on the edge of the wood. Uncle Edward would be out of sight, racing through the deepening shadows under the trees, antlers catching at branches. If this were a modern story, there'd be an out if he survived until dawn. But this was a much older story than that.

Blood would be spilled.

Bonds would be renewed.

The Hunt would feed.

Charlie could hear Allie's heartbeat, or maybe it was her own. Or David's hooves slamming into the hard, packed dirt as he ran because he couldn't not run. Not tonight.

She thought she could hear baying in the distance. Wild laughter beyond that.

Except it wasn't so much wild as self-satisfied.

The sun had reached the edge of the mountains when Allie jerked and said, "First blood."

Charlie hadn't felt it. Third circle clearly wasn't connected enough and that was fine with her.

It was dark when it ended. Darker than it should have been in the center of a major city under a full moon.

Charlie felt it end. Through her bare feet and legs pressed against the dirt, through her back pressed up against the rock, through all places she and Allie were touching.

Breathing heavily, she turned when Allie did and saw David silhouetted against the light bleed from the city. It was exactly what she'd been looking for driving in from Tony's house, although she wouldn't have felt such a wave of irrational relief had she seen him then. He stood for a moment, sides heaving, pelt streaked dark with sweat, then he half reared and ran for the trees.

Allie let out a breath she'd probably been holding the entire time.

They didn't speak on their way down to the car. There wasn't a lot to say. Charlie's stomach growled. They both ignored it.

"You okay to drive?" Charlie asked as they stepped over the low barrier into the gravel parking lot.

Allie threw her the keys.

"I wonder who . . . ?"

"Probably Uncle Evan," Allie answered before Charlie could finish.

Uncle Evan had the Canada Post contracts for two rural routes. Someone else would be covering them now.

"You know . . ." Leaning on the open door, Charlie frowned into the shadows at the edges of the wood. " . . . we only have the aunties' word that Uncle Edward wavered. You ever wonder?"

"If they lie?" The quiet question drew Charlie's gaze across the top of the car to meet Allie's, the pale gray of her eyes darker in the moonlight. "We'll be aunties one day."

To anyone outside the family, that wouldn't have sounded much like an answer.

*   *   *

"Evan," Auntie Gwen confirmed the next morning. She'd stumbled in at five past eight, brushed her teeth twice, then had three glasses of water and a glass of orange juice. Her eyes were still mostly dark from lid to lid; there were unidentifiable stains on her sleeveless blouse, and a scratch up the length of her right arm. Graham had taken one look at her, and his fingers had twitched toward the weapons he no longer carried. Jack had taken a slightly faster look and decided to go into the office with Graham even though the job sucked and Tuesdays were usually a day off. Joe had come over from the apartment but stayed in the store.

"She knows where I am if she wants me," he'd pointed out when Charlie'd gone down to ask if he was coming upstairs. *"And if she doesn't want me, I'd rather not be in her way."* Joe, Charlie decided, was smarter than he looked.

"Turn the pancakes, Alysha, or they'll be overcooked on that side."

Auntie Gwen had poured the pancakes herself, charms were too easy with a ladle of batter and a hot grill, but she'd seen no point in standing over the stove in midsummer when there were younger members of the family available.

Any other morning, Charlie knew Allie would have turned the command into a test of will; this morning, she flipped the pancakes.

When they came to the table, Auntie Gwen buttered each one carefully, poured syrup over the whole stack, chewed and swallowed two dripping forkfuls, and pushed the plate away.

Cradling a mug of coffee between both hands, Charlie could feel the buzz traveling under her skin, trying to get out. She'd spent the night sitting cross-legged on the sofa bed, quietly picking out the melody lines to songs she couldn't quite hear. A glance at the abandoned pancakes, and she heard herself say, "Still full?"

Allie gasped. Charlie thought she caught a whiff of decaying leaves, saw Auntie Gwen lift her head, and was most definitely not feeling reckless enough to look her in the eye. After a long moment of weighted silence, Auntie Gwen's fork hit the table at the edge of Charlie's peripheral vision.

"I'm sorry, Charlotte, I didn't quite catch that. Would you care to repeat it?"

"Not fucking likely." When the silence grew more weighted still, she realized she'd answered out loud.

But Auntie Gwen merely sighed and said, "I could use a coffee, Alysha."

Charlie watched Allie move around the kitchen, watched her walk up and set a full mug on the table, and finally looked at Auntie Gwen because Allie's path had put the older woman in her direct line of sight. "Are you okay?"

"Me?" Allie asked, frowning.

Charlie shook her head and watched Auntie Gwen wrap her fingers around the mug. They all pretended to not see them shake.

"It was hard not to be there," she said at last. "Bea and Carmen and I, we have years of ritual tying us to Edward." She took a long swallow of coffee and added another spoonful of sugar, the spoon rattling against the sides of the mug. "And we lost Janet, Abby, Betty, and Dot."

"Those horns aren't just for show," Allie said softly.

Charlie stared at her cousin. "Well, duh! You knew we lost four aunties and you didn't mention it?"

"We didn't lose four. They did."

"We are them!"

"We were them."

"Is she still them?" Charlie demanded, nodding at Auntie Gwen.

"She is the cat's mother." Auntie Gwen flinched. "Oh, dear God, I sound like Jane." She took a deep breath and stared at her coffee. Charlie had to bite her tongue to keep from asking if she was scrying, maybe checking the box scores while she gathered her thoughts. Auntie Gwen had a touching belief that the Jays would pull it out of their collective asses after the All Star Break. A long moment later, she exhaled and squared her shoulders, clearly having come to a decision. "New branches of the family separate, Charlotte. Given modern technology, connections won't be entirely severed this time—beads on a string is the inane analogy Meredith is using given that there's only two beads."

"This time?"

"Don't be stupid. You don't honestly think the entire family, from the bright beginning, is there in rural Ontario?"

Charlie glanced up at Allie who didn't seem surprised. "You knew?"

She shrugged. "Seemed kind of obvious."

Auntie Gwen sighed. "You haven't thought about it at all, have you?"

"Why would I?"

"Why, indeed." This second sigh held subtext Charlie ignored. "To answer your question, Carmen, Bea, and I will always be at heart a part of *them*—we have too much history there to ever break entirely free. As for the younger members, with every ritual the emphasis will shift until their ties are entirely here. As for you, Charlotte . . ."

"Me?"

"The assumption was that you were too wild to settle. We've been reassessing."

"I haven't settled!"

"Easy to say." She smiled a familiar self-satisfied smile and finished her coffee as Allie made faces at Charlie suggesting she disengage. "Bea's right. Evan isn't strong enough to hold for long," she said, putting her mug down.

The aunties didn't bother with graceful segues.

"There will be challenges. Multiple challenges. We'll have to tell the county we're extending the family plot—Ruby's talking dahlias. Things will be topsy-turvy for a while."

"Topsy-turvy?"

"Jane again. Remind me to fight that. The point is, we're looking at uncertain weather patterns, more boys being born, cakes not rising, unnaturally tough pastry, and cabbages shaped like Elvis."

"Elvis? Seriously?"

"Oh, for pity's sake, Charlotte, why would we get cabbages shaped like Elvis?" She stood and stretched, her shirt riding up enough to show a bruise just above her hip and a scrape rising up from the blotch of purple-green.

Charlie scratched at the buzzing under her left forearm and showed teeth in what wasn't even trying to be a smile. "So, since you couldn't go home, what *were* you hunting last night, Auntie Gwen?"

"None of your business, Charlotte. Alysha, you'll need to cover the store. Joe's leaving."

Allie paused, about to remove the rejected pancakes. "Auntie Gwen, we talked about this. He's my employee."

"And he's my . . ."

"Never mind." When Allie cut her off, Charlie nearly applauded. Auntie Gwen's descriptions of what Joe was to her made it difficult to look Joe in the eye. And Gales weren't exactly shy. "I'll be right down."

"Good." She paused at the door and swept a dark gaze over both of them. "There's a chance Jane engineered this whole thing because she's afraid Catherine might decide to spend some time at home. Your grandmother always had a frightening amount of influence on your grandfather. The last thing we need is a Wild Power playing at being domestic."

"Worked out the last time," Allie muttered at the closed door.

"She wasn't talking about your grandmother." The buzzing under Charlie skin revved up.

"Yes, she was. She said . . ."

"She meant me. She thinks I've settled."

Allie smiled, the curve of her mouth an invitation. "Would that be so bad?"

Before Charlie could respond in a way that wouldn't get her cut off—the sofa bed was a choice not a necessity—she remembered Auntie Catherine's call. "So, a funny thing happened . . ."

"It could be a coincidence," Allie allowed a few minutes later, leading the way downstairs.

Charlie snorted. "We don't believe in coincidence."

Their reflection showed them joined at the hip.

"Still not double-jointed," Charlie muttered as they passed.

The store was empty, the door was locked, and there was a note from Joe on the counter. *"I sold a yoyo. We're going to need another box of rhinestone p . . ."* The shape of the "p" suggested Auntie Gwen had waited as long as she intended to.

"So . . ." Allie unlocked the door, flipped the sign, and turned to stare measuringly at Charlie. Charlie had no idea what was being measured but had a funny feeling she was coming up short. "Are you going to take the apartment over the coffee shop? It wouldn't be hard to put in a connecting door."

Charlie clenched her jaw to keep her teeth from chattering as the buzz reached a crescendo. Before she could answer, before she knew what she was going to answer, her phone ran. "Looks like things are getting back to normal," she muttered digging it out of the pocket of her shorts. Normal in the Gale family *wasn't* over twenty-four hours of phone silence.

"Hey, Chuck! Got a minute?"

"Mark?" *It's Mark*, she mouthed at Allie who mouthed back *no shit* as Charlie moved in between two sets of shelves and made herself comfortable. Back before Calgary, and *Dun Good*, she and Mark had spent the Nova Scotia summer festival circuit in a band called *Wylde Chylde*. The spelling had made

Charlie's eyeballs ache and the band itself had been a high-energy mix of styles that had never quite jelled. When *Wylde Chylde* blew apart, Charlie and the bass player had headed for Toronto and the *blink-and-you-miss-it* punk revival movement while Mark had formed and re-formed the remaining pieces into something closer to east coast traditional. Their friendship had survived time and distance and step dancing. "What's up?"

"Aston got bit by a seal."

"He what?"

"He was out in his cousin's boat, saw a seal swimming by, and reached overboard to pet it."

About to poke her finger into a box of plush toys, Charlie reconsidered. "He's an idiot."

"Way to state the obvious, Chuck. Fucking seal bit off two of his fingers. Clearly the stupid fucker isn't going to be playing much for a while." Mark seldom swore. He considered it the sign of a weak vocabulary. Things must be bad back east. "We need you."

"I'm already in a band."

His sigh was deep enough she nearly felt it against her cheek. "Look, Chuck, I wouldn't ask, but we've got five weeks of festival coming up, a good chance of taking top prize, and I know you'll mesh. You're at the same e-mail, right? I'll send you the set list; you'll be covering guitar and mandolin and you've got range enough to sing backup vocals without key changes left, right, and center. You take Aston's lead; we can change the pronouns on the fly."

"I don't . . ."

"Think it over, that's all I'm asking. Okay, that's not all I'm asking, I'm totally asking you to ditch the band you're with for us, but you don't have to tell me right away. What time is it there?"

She stopped running a die-cast tractor along the edge of the shelf and checked her watch. "Almost ten."

"Where the hell are you?"

"Calgary."

"Why? Never mind. Look, get back to me by four, four oh five, four ten maybe your time and we can figure out the best place for us to hook up. We're in Cape Breton, but you'll fly into Halifax, right?"

"Mark, I don't . . ." He'd hung up.

Allie was perched on a stool behind the glass counter, the yoyo ledger open in front of her, when Charlie emerged from between the shelves. "So?"

"So Mark's guitarist lost two fingers to a seal, and he wants me to head east and finish the festival season with him."

"Seals bite?"

"Apparently." Charlie waited while Allie recorded the latest sale, put the ledger away, and straightened.

"Your hair's blonde."

Okay, not what she'd expected. "What?"

"Your hair . . ." Allie gestured at the top of Charlie's head. " . . . is blonde. It was blonde when you woke up this morning."

"It was turquoise when I went to sleep," Charlie muttered pulling an orange plastic hand mirror off a shelf. One of those trick Halloween mirrors, it substituted a skull for her face, but the hair above the empty sockets was definitely her natural ash blonde.

"You're leaving, aren't you?" Allie's tone made the question almost more of a statement.

Cape Breton seals in Fort McMurray. Then on the news in the coffee shop. Then eating Aston's fingers. That was three.

Meet me in Halifax and we'll talk.

Okay, four.

The last thing we need is a Wild Power playing at being domestic.

Fine, five. But who was counting.

The buzz under her skin made it hard to stand still.

"Yeah, I'm leaving."

And the buzz stopped.

Oh, really? she thought, putting the mirror facedown on the shelf. *Subtle much?*

The thing was, *Dun Good* had only made it as far as it had because of Charlie. It wasn't ego and it wasn't like she'd done it on purpose, but sometimes she wasn't as careful as she could've been with the music. Charm a set of broad shoulders here, a rounded cleavage there, don't stay on top of the way it's spreading and, well, it was no surprise people loved the band.

Literally.

Without her, things wouldn't go as well.

Not ego. Fact.

All right, fine; a little ego.

She didn't owe the other members of *Dun Good* anything. They weren't family. But they *had* been together for over a year, and breaking up via text seemed like a bad high school cliché, so Tuesday evening found Charlie at Taylor and Donna's one-bedroom basement apartment, guitar slung on her back, fully aware she might have to charm the lot of them if things got ugly.

Noise spilled out through the open door. Charlie'd arrived last by intent. She stepped over a grubby gray backpack, moved down the short hall to the living room, and saw a natural redhead she didn't recognize. Strange. The apartment was so small, even Donna usually vacated the premises when the band met there.

"Charlie!"

"Tony!"

Tony grinned a little too broadly. "This is Kristie!"

Charlie nodded at Kristie and glanced around the room. Taylor stood in the doorway to the kitchen, arms crossed. Jeff straddled a chair over by the television. They were both watching Tony. The redhead, Kristie, gave a little wave.

"You replaced Kristie, you know when you started, last um . . ."Tony's voice trailed off, then his smile broadened back out again. "She had a baby! Uh, anyway, she was thinking of coming back and well, me and Jeff have known her since high school and . . ."

"You're kidding, right?"

"I know this is . . ."

Charlie raised a hand and cut him off again. "I'm talking to the universe, Tony. But thanks for playing."

Allie twisted the end of her braid around her finger, perilously close to pouting. "I don't want you to go."

"I've left before," Charlie reminded her, checking to make sure she'd put a couple pairs of underwear in the outside pocket of her gig bag.

"Sure, a week or two touring with the band . . ."

"Before that."

"That was before this." Her gestured somehow seemed to take in the entire city of Calgary. "This is the first time after this. And the first time since this when I don't know when you'll be back."

It took Charlie a moment to parse that. Since Calgary, she'd toured on a schedule, out and back like an Emporium yoyo. This trip, no string. She wanted to say, *I always come back to you,* but the words got stuck, so she wrapped a hand around the back of Allie's head, pulled her in close, and kissed her instead.

"Yeah." Allie's smile looked bittersweet as they pulled apart. "That's what I thought. Are you going to talk to Gran?"

"No, I don't think so. I'm feeling manipulated enough."

"It hardly counts as wild when the whole universe is telling you to hit the road," Graham muttered. His arms were crossed and his brows drawn in, but odds were he was reacting to Allie's mood not Charlie's imminent departure.

"That's what I'm saying." Charlie moved in close, waited pointedly until he unfolded his arms, then kissed him, too, tracing a quick charm on the damp skin behind his ear for Allie to find later. "You'll have to be the man of the house while I'm gone," she said, as she stepped away. "Think you're up to it?"

"At the moment, I can't think why I let you hang around."

Charlie grinned. "Takes a village to raise a dragon. And speaking of . . ."

"He won't come out of his room." Allie half turned toward Jack's door.

"Then I'll just have to go to him."

"He slammed the door and a power grid went up."

"Sorcery?"

"You think? He knows he's not supposed to do sorcery in the apartment."

"He was angry. He probably didn't do it on purpose."

"You're always making excuses for him." Allie tossed her braid behind her shoulder. "He won't let you in."

"He won't let *you* in," Charlie corrected, crossing the living room. So what if she occasionally made excuses for Jack; she knew what it was to be the odd Gale out.

The power grid flashed gold when she knocked. Charlie leaned in as close as she could without getting singed and said quietly, "Open the door, or I tell Allie about . . ."

The grid vanished, the door swung open, and a voice muttered out of the smoke, "I never thought you were a snitch."

"Dude, empty threat. If it happened in Calgary, Allie knows about it." She slipped in as the door closed again, waving a hand in front of her face. The temperature was in the high thirties, making the sulfur smell stronger than usual—could be dragon, could be teenage boy. Impossible to tell for certain. "What do you have against open windows?"

"Stupid neighbors keep calling the fire department."

"All right, one last freebie before I go." Right hand on the outside wall, Charlie came farther into the room, only tripping twice over the debris on the floor before she found the window. "Back in the day," she grunted, forcing the casement up, "there was a time or two I didn't want my parents to know what I had going on." Pressing only enough to lightly etch the weave, she dragged the edge of her thumbnail over the exposed screen. "This will filter everything coming out of your room. No visible smoke. No . . . uh, nosable smell."

"Nosable?"

"Shut up, I'm doing you a favor."

"You're leaving."

The smoke had already started to clear. When Charlie turned, she could see Jack sprawled on his bed, wearing a pair of shorts and an award-winning sulky expression. "Yeah, I'm leaving. So?"

"So, nothing." He scratched at the gold scales scattered over his chest and stomach. "Go ahead. Leave."

"They have these things called phones in this world." Jack wouldn't get his family phone until fifteen, but even considering Canada's crappy cell coverage, there were other options. "You want me, call me."

"Why would I want you?"

She kicked a pair of enormous, glossy, red board shoes to one side and leaned against his dresser. "Maybe because you can't stand how uncool it is around here without me."

"You're in a country band." He balled up a dirty sock and threw it at the poster of *Inner Surge* taped to the back of his door. "That's not cool. And cool's not cool, it's sick."

"Okay, point one, not in a country band anymore; I'm in an alt Celtic band."

"Wow. So much better." Teenagers did sarcasm almost as well as the aunties.

"And two, what's really up with you?"

Jack threw another sock. After a long moment he sighed, a gust of smoke wafting toward the open window. "I'm trying really hard to be what they want me to be."

"Allie and Graham?"

"Them, too." Another sock. "There's too many stupid choices here. You're the only one who gets that."

"Thanks. I think. For what it's worth, being fourteen is all about making stupid choices."

"Not for me."

"Are you lying on your dirty laundry?" Charlie asked as another sock hit the poster.

He turned to glare at her. "What if I am?"

"Then you're doing better at being a fourteen-year-old boy than you think. Look . . ." She crossed the room, shoved his leg out of the way, and sat on the edge of the bed. " . . . Allie's not going to send you back if you don't want to go, no matter what you do." The bed quivered as he stiffened. Bingo. "She fought the aunties for you. She sends you back, she's lost the fight."

Those were the kind of power dynamics Jack understood. His eyes narrowed thoughtfully, showing a glimmer of gold.

"Don't waste energy worrying about Allie, just concentrate on finding who you are here. And that advice was so tree-of-life tote bag, I think I'm going to hurl."

He snorted. "Yeah, I didn't want to say."

"I promise I'll keep trying to come up with something more interesting for you to do than working Graham's skeezy newspaper."

A pair of underwear hit the poster and slid to the floor. "Push pins melt."

"Good to know. Remember, I'm only a call or text away because I'm so totally sick you're going to miss me like crazy." She closed her hand around his knee. The skin under her fingers was just on the edge of scorching. "Pretty much the way I'm going to miss you."

He had enough white showing around the gold to make the eye roll obvious. "You won't miss . . ."

"Call me a liar again, and I *will* use the charm of disgusting backney I created for my sisters."

"Gross."

"Exactly." She shook his leg. "We good?"

"I guess," he admitted reluctantly. He stood when she did, kicking a stack of old comics under the bed.

"If those are Graham's, I'd be a little more careful. He doesn't carry them anymore, but he didn't actually get rid of his weapons. Now, come're." Dragging Jack into a hug, she found his skin had cooled to as close to Human body temperature as it got. Always a good sign.

"If you just drew a charm on my back, I'm telling Auntie Gwen who ate that rhubarb pie," he snarled, jerking away.

"You shared it."

"You cut it. And I'm just a kid, remember? You led me astray."

"That's part of my job." Reaching behind her for the doorknob, she sobered. "Be careful with the sorcery. I know it usually just happens," she cut off his protest. "But that's part of the problem. The aunties think you have no control."

"Yeah, but they don't want me to do it on purpose or practice." Jack scratched at the old crescent scar on his cheek. It looked like a hockey scar but had probably been a near miss by one of his uncles. "They say practicing accumulates power. They can't have it both ways."

"How long have you been here? The aunties have it any way they want it." She opened the door about two centimeters then closed it again. "Keep an eye on Allie for me, would you? Graham's cool, but he's not blood."

Her reflection in the mirror was so close to how she actually looked— jeans, sneakers, tank, gray eyes, short blonde hair, three gold rings in her left ear, one in the right—that it took her a moment to find the changes. Change. Probably.

Just in case, she checked her gig bag. Guitar tucked safely away, mandolin case piggybacking, small pockets on both cases stuffed with the essentials—nothing matched the image in the mirror where *something* was struggling to get out.

"I hope you're telling me to free the music," she murmured patting the edge of the frame. "Because if my underwear were any freer, it'd be illegal."

She had to put her knee to the door to get it open. Given that Auntie Gwen was in the window of the loft, glaring down into the courtyard, it was possible that the weight of her gaze had been holding it closed.

Charlie waved, then laughed delightedly, as Auntie Gwen flipped her off. If they'd wanted her to cross, if that's what all the *we have to talk* eyebrow waggling had been about, it wasn't going to happen now. She didn't look up to see if Jack was standing by his window, he'd only be embarrassed to be caught. There was no reason to look for Allie and Graham because she knew damned well they were watching.

The shrubs leaned toward her, leaves quivering.

"Hang on, kids." Freeing her guitar, she hung the gig bag on her back then settled the guitar strap over her shoulders and checked the tuning. A flat G had once resulted in a detour through a bed of decorative plantings at the Illinois State Fair and a fast dive for cover while she figured out what had gone wrong. Like many celebrities, the Budweiser Clydesdales were shorter up close. She'd had to throw out her shoes. And socks.

Tuned and ready, Charlie gave her assembled audience her best Ahn-old . . . "Ah'll be back." . . . started the melody line that would take her to Mark, and stepped into the shrubbery . . .

. . . and stepped out again in a fringe of trees about a hundred meters from a red-roofed building in the middle of an acre or so of mowed lawn. She could smell the ocean, but given that Cape Breton had more coastline than the interior geography could account for, that didn't give her much of a clue. Recent rain had stopped, but the cloud cover was still too thick for her to even pick up a direction from the sun.

"Guess we'll do it the easy way then." Guitar stowed safely back in the bag, she crossed the wet grass to the sign.

"Celtic Music Interpretive Center. Wednesday Ceilidhs 7:00 PM to 9:00 PM, five dollar admission. July 27th starts the Samhradh Ceol Feill." Charlie traced a charm over the sign and the letters rearranged. "Ah, Summer Music Festival. Makes sense. And as today is July 27th, the only question remaining is, where's . . ."

"Chuck! Where the hell did you arrive from? If you hitched over from the airport, I'm going to slap you silly. It's not the summer of love, baby. Well, not officially anyhow."

Charlie turned to watch Mark charge down the path toward her, wearing a CIJK-FM T-shirt over a black utility kilt barely held within the bounds of decency by his blue fake fur sporran. He had a set of drumsticks shoved through his hair just above the elastic that held his ponytail.

As soon as he was close enough, he pulled her into an enthusiastic hug, then pushed her back to arm's length and said, "I don't suppose you've learned to play the fiddle since we talked?"

"Another two waiting for you in the Sydney office? Good news. I haven't seen much in the way of support from them yet, but this should certainly encourage more active participation in the process." Leaning back against the butter-soft leather, Amelia glanced down at the papers spread out on the seat beside her. "I'll be done at the studio by seven, but I expect there'll be a bit of necessary socializing with the producer to keep his opinion sweet, so there's no point in me leaving Halifax tonight. I'll head out in the morning and meet you at the office at eleven. That'll give you plenty of time to find off-site storage unconnected to the company in case they get desperate enough to try something. Better to be safe than sorry," she continued before Paul could speak. "I leave the details in your hands."

She switched her attention to her notes as she hit the disconnect. The moment Two Seventy-five N had taken them public, Paul had done his usual excellent job and put together an inarguable list of facts that supported their position as well as a number of anecdotes that sounded inarguable but had no factual support at all. All she had to do tonight was hit the emotional beats and start swaying the voting public onto their side. Sway the voting public, sway the politicians they voted for.

In a just world, the honorable minister would have gotten his shit together and issued the permits before the application for the well had been thrust into the public eye by a group of environmental extremists. Amelia, well aware the world was far from just, believed in contingency plans.

"Ms. Carlson." Her driver flicked open the communication hatch. "We're five minutes out."

"Thank you, Val."

The papers, edges parallel, went into her briefcase; she wouldn't be referring to them again. Paul had provided a printout of the facts, not only clear, concise, and bulleted but available for the station to copy and give to their researchers.

Well, *researcher*, the CBC budget being what it was.

She slid her phone into her Italian leather bag. It was starting to look genteelly worn, but then she'd had it made to her specifications right after she'd gone to work for her father and it had rarely left her side since. The craftsman had included enough interior sections and outside pockets that she'd never be caught rummaging about like a north shore granny looking for a lozenge.

Yes, I have an assistant who could handle my minutiae, but I prefer not to waste his talents dealing with the sort of thing that every other woman in the world manages on her own.

The purse told the world that she wasn't helpless. She was aware of her privilege. She was of the people.

It was a killer shtick.

The car slid into VIP parking under the studio.

Showtime.

Earbuds in, music loud enough to rattle the scales on his tail—if he had a tail right now which he didn't because it wouldn't fit in this stupid room and yeah, okay, it didn't suck that he could let down his guard because he didn't have to worry about his uncles sneaking up on him—Jack dragged another one of Graham's old comics out from under the bed and propped it up against his knees. Earlier, he'd tried to make issue seven, *Crisis on Infinite Earths* hover in the air above his eyes and two hours later still wasn't able to get it down off the ceiling. That was the stupid sort of thing that happened when he actually tried to do sorcery instead of just letting it happen. If Graham saw what had happened to one of his precious comics, he'd be grounded for a month. He wouldn't have even tried, but he wanted his hands free to deal with a bag of frozen cookies with his name on it.

After the first time he tried claiming food the way he would have back home, Allie'd put his name on everything he was allowed to eat.

And bought a new freezer.

Those things really stank when they melted.

"Find out who I am here," he muttered, around a mouthful of gingersnap. "I don't even know what that means."

He was a dragon. But no one outside the family was supposed to know that. He was sorcerer, but even some people inside the family weren't supposed to know that. He was a Gale and that was all about family who weren't trying to eat him.

That was cool.

Maybe Charlie'd meant he should work on being more of a Gale.

Turned out that Mark's fiddle player wasn't missing, just very late, arriving as the band before them took their bows.

"Look, it was an emergency," he snapped before Mark could actually articulate all the jumping around and hand waving he was doing. "Tanis, my girlfriend, couldn't find a family heirloom and she's a little hysterical. I left when her sisters showed up and I'm here, so calm down. Hey." He waved the hand not holding his instrument. "You must be Charlie. Bomen Deol. You might as well call me Bo, I can't get Mark to stop, and before you tell me I don't look like a fiddle player, I'm ethnically Indian. The Romany came out of India, and some of the best fiddle players in the world are Roma, QED."

Charlie grinned. "You get asked that a lot?"

"You'd be surprised." He took a deep breath, shook out his shoulders on the exhale, and nodded toward the now empty stage. "Okay. I'm calm. Let's do this."

Tim Waters, the keyboard player and the underreaction to Mark's over-reaction since they'd met playing soccer in university, led the way out onto the polished maple half circle, accordion slung around broad shoulders. Shelly Simpson followed, wrestling her upright bass into position before the stage got any more crowded, muscles moving smoothly under the golden freckles covering her bare arms. *"I use the electric a lot of the time,"* she'd told Charlie earlier, *"but this place seemed to cry out for the all-natural sound."* A few people in the audience cheered when Bo took his place—this was a crowd that appreciated fiddlers.

To keep things moving, all the bands used the Center's drums and key-boards. Mark had a set of sticks in his hands and two more plus a penny-whistle tucked in behind the waistband of his kilt.

"So," Charlie said as they stepped out of the shadows, "I forgot to ask; this band got a name?"

"*Grinneal!* Scot's Gaelic for bottom of the sea." Mark grinned and saluted her with the sticks. "It's sink or swim time, Chuck!"

THREE

THE PELTS SMELLED like fish. Paul hadn't noticed it before, but piled on the backseat of his car, tucked into suit bags that made fine camouflage but terrible filters, the scent was unmistakable. Technically, he supposed they smelled like the ocean, like brine and kelp rotting on the shore, but the signature, the grace note, was definitely fish. And not fish the way he preferred it, filleted almost transparent and lying on a bed of sticky rice next to a serving of sake; this was fish the way he remembered it from meeting his dad at the docks and nearly gagging on the stink rising off glistening piles of guts speckled silver with scales. It stank of barely getting by and wearing his cousin's hand-me-downs and being expected to never achieve his full potential because if kids like him went to work for Carlson Oil, it sure as hell wasn't in the office.

The odor anchored the skins in a pungent reality that removed any lingering disbelief. Why worry about the hard left his worldview had recently taken when his time could be better spent worrying about getting the smell of the docks out of his car. It was the first new car he'd ever owned and he really didn't want the past he'd worked so hard to shake to take up residence in the upholstery.

He cranked up the air-conditioning another notch and thought about how he'd never have been expected to transport sealskins while working in Toronto. He'd been thrilled when Ms. Carlson had gone from VP to CEO and wanted him to remain with her, but he'd been significantly less thrilled about returning to the Maritimes and his family's incessant: "Why don't you drop by, Paul." "We never see you, Paul." And the ever popular: "Well, if you're not gay, what's wrong with meeting Mrs. Harris' daughter for lunch? You're not getting any younger and your grandmother, who'd like to see you settled before she goes, won't live forever."

His grandmother had every intention of living forever.

He'd nearly cheered when Ms. Carlson had decided it would be good public relations to temporarily relocate to the Sydney office. It wasn't out of the province, but at least it was out of Halifax.

"You have reached your destination."

The voice of his GPS was bland, generic North American; entirely unremarkable for a businessman using a tool. He'd downloaded the Darth Vader program but never installed it, well aware it would give the wrong impression should Ms. Carlson ever need to ride in his car. She hadn't needed to in the two years, four months, and twenty-seven days he'd worked for her, but that didn't mean she never would.

Dewie Center Self-Storage consisted of long, beige rectangular buildings with red roofs and doors, bordered by just enough asphalt to get trucks in and out. Paul had already stopped by the office—shared with the local U-Haul rental—to sign the papers and pick up the key. Fake name, fake address, paid in cash.

The middle-aged man behind the counter had looked down at the money and up at Paul. "You hiding a body?"

Paul had looked down at the man's left hand and the tan line on the empty ring finger, did the math, and said, "No. Just hiding some stuff from my ex-wife."

There'd been no further questions.

Forty square feet of storage had seemed like a lot when he'd rented it, but Paul had no idea how many pelts Ms. Carlson would eventually need him to store, and moving pelts between units if the space he'd provided turned out to be too small would only attract attention. They didn't need any more of that. In spite of everything they'd done over the last year to keep the permit process out of the news, Two Seventy-five N had shone the bright light of public opinion on Carlson Oil. Even years later, BP's adventure in the Gulf of Mexico continued ramping the reaction to maritime wells up to hysterical levels.

Stacked against the back wall, the three bulging black suit bags that had so dominated the backseat of his car looked slightly pathetic, dominated in turn by all the surrounding concrete.

If there was a descriptive phrase more depressing than "surrounding concrete," Paul didn't want to hear it.

The bags, or more specifically their contents, didn't look like they'd provide the leverage necessary to silence the Hay Island group, but appearances could be deceiving. Ms. Carlson gave no outward indication of how entirely ruthless she could be although a growing list of people—and evidently other things—had discovered the inner Amelia. To her credit, she'd never tried to hide it from him. After the other two young men who'd made it to the final job interview had emerged from her office, mere shadows of the arrogant MBAs who'd gone in, Paul had decided he didn't need to prove how smart or ambitious he was, but how useful. It was, after all, better to stand beside the devil than in front of her.

When he turned and saw the slender figure silhouetted in the storage unit's open doorway, he had to bite his tongue to keep from shrieking.

"This isn't good enough," she said.

"What?"

"Storing them off-site is a good start, but this . . ." Silver bangles clanged together as she gestured. ". . . isn't good enough."

Without the sun behind her, the figure became a woman on the downhill side of middle age. Tall and slender, with thick gray hair in a long braid, she wore an ankle-length, sleeveless dress, a mix of blues and greens and yellows, in a batik pattern that had been popular a few years ago. His mother had one but didn't wear it nearly as well. The legs flashing through the slits in the skirt as she walked toward him were in great shape. This older woman had been a looker once and hadn't entirely left it behind.

"I'm sorry," he said politely. "I have no idea what you're talking about."

Her dark eyes narrowed, and he had the strangest urge to run. Then she smiled. "Where are my manners? You're Paul Belleveau." It wasn't a question. She knew who he was. "I'm Catherine Gale."

He felt like a butterfly pinned to a corkboard. "These . . . those . . ." He nodded toward the back of the unit and fought to get a grip on his reaction. ". . . are yours."

The second and third pelts had appeared as mysteriously in the Sydney office as the first had in Halifax. Delivered mysteriously by Catherine Gale.

"Mine? Don't be ridiculous. They're yours now. I'm *merely* the intermediary," she added before he could protest.

Paul didn't need the emphasis to know that the woman in front of him had never been *merely* anything.

"However," she continued, the curve of her lip suggesting she knew exactly what he'd been thinking, "it turns out I need to become more involved in order to keep my plans from being disrupted."

"Plans?"

"You don't think items like these can be picked up without planning, do you?"

He didn't. He also didn't believe that was what she'd meant, but he had no intention of challenging her on that. He liked his balls right where they were, thanks very much, and anyone who thought Catherine Gale wasn't following her own agenda had never met her. He'd been in a storage locker with her for barely three minutes and it was entirely clear to him. "I'm sorry, go on."

"You can't leave the items here." Her tone suggested here was the equivalent of a damp cardboard box. "I've found them."

"Why were you looking for them?"

"To see if I could find them."

"Ah. So you think they'll find them?" It was the only logical conclusion.

"Oh, please, tradition suggests they can't find the damned things if they're wrapped in a shawl and stuffed in a box under the marital bed. No . . ." Catherine Gale ran a hand down the drape of her dress, reminding Paul of a cat smoothing its fur. ". . . there's a new player in the game, and once she realizes she's playing, she'll need to prove something by returning these to their original owners."

"Prove what?"

"That has yet to be decided." The last time Paul had seen that smile, it had been on a shark. "You have a short grace period while this new player gets up to speed."

"I see." Paul suspected the new player was yet another thing he'd prefer not to believe in. "How long is short?"

"I have no idea. But the number of angels who can dance on the head of a pin depends entirely on the dance."

"What?"

"You wanted to know how long short was."

"That's not what . . ." She knew it wasn't what he'd meant. He bit off the rest of his protest and took a deep, cleansing breath. It smelled of fish. Not entirely reassuring. "Not to presume, but can't you deal with the new player?"

"I can." *But I won't* came through loud and clear.

"All right." Given where they were in the suburbs of Sydney, it took a moment to lock his phone onto a wifi signal. "I'll need as much information as you can give me."

"You have as much information as I'm going to give you."

"But . . ."

"The rest is no business of yours."

"No offense, but it sounds like it's very much my business." No point in mentioning that Carlson Oil had bet everything on this roll of the dice. If they hadn't already invested so much that sinking this well was an absolute necessity, they wouldn't have accepted Catherine Gale's impossible offer.

"It's only your business if she finds the pelts, which she won't if you put them somewhere safer." A business associate had once declared Amelia Carlson had a smile that could flay small animals. Current evidence suggested that business associate had no idea what that particular smile looked like.

Thankful he'd emptied his bladder before leaving the office, Paul considered his options.

What was safer than an anonymous storage locker? A vault would require a lot more paperwork and, even if he could get access to one, there was the whole fish stink to consider. It would have to be an empty vault and emptying one would also cause the kind of attention they wanted to avoid. On the other hand, Carlson Oil owned a lot of property in Nova Scotia.

"We have mines. Closed mines," he expanded.

A steel-gray brow rose. "Are there still open mines? Rhetorical question," she added. "Dropping them down a shaft is not . . ."

"I'd secure them in a cross tunnel. It would be impossible to stumble over them by accident and difficult to find them on purpose. The link between Carlson Oil and the mine is well hidden inside a number of shell companies," he added reassuringly. "Coal gets no respect."

Catherine Gale frowned thoughtfully, drawing the fingernail of her right index finger along the bracelets on her left wrist, head cocked as she listened to them chime. "Do any of these tunnels extend out under the water?"

"Of course. It's not that large an island."

"Excellent. Water will slow her down."

"Her?"

The shark smile returned. "The new player. She'll work around it but, fortunately, you only need a short-term solution. I believe you were promised a decision on the permit by the end of August?"

"Now the public knows . . ."

When Catherine Gale snorted, Paul half expected smoke. "Given what's in those bags, Two Seventy-five N will issue the requested retraction and, in this province, where Two Seventy-five N stands on environmental issues, so stands the public. If the potential for public embarrassment leading to an election loss is all that's holding back the permit, you'll have it by the end of August."

"Before the legislature breaks for Labor Day."

"That would be the end of August."

"Right." Paul fought the urge to apologize for stating the obvious. He knew he could maintain a perfectly neutral expression regardless of the patronizing, sexist, and racist comments tossed his way by the old school oil men he dealt with on a daily basis. He was young, he was attractive, and he was black. Even worse, he worked for one of the few women who played with the big boys and won. He knew he could maintain that neutral expression indefinitely, because he had.

Catherine Gale looked right through it.

"Relax, cutie, or your face'll freeze that way and you'll never get laid."

"Hey, you got a new van." Charlie patted the side of the big silver box. "What did you do, mug a soccer mom?"

"I did not so much mug a soccer mom," Mark said, sliding the bags holding his cymbals in along beside the snare, "as I charmed a lovely woman into giving me an excellent price provided I got TIM TO CALL HOME on occasion."

Charlie leaned away from the sudden increase in volume and grinned at Tim. "Your youngest sister went away to college and your mom wanted to unload the mom-mobile?"

Grunting under the weight of one of the amps, Tim managed a single, abrupt nod.

"How do you remember that family shit?" Shelly asked. Her own vehicle crammed full, she leaned against the hood and watched them tesseract the van.

"I'm good at family shit," Charlie told her. "And trust me, next to my family, remembering a couple of sisters and a mom with a van is nothing much."

"As I recall from our previous time together, Chuck's family is large and enthusiastic. Largely enthusiastic. And a bit weird." Mark jumped out of the van, examined the odds and ends still piled on the gravel and then, head cocked, mentally measured the crammed interior. He beckoned to Charlie without turning and she handed over her gig bag, watching not exactly nervously as he slid it into a space with about a millimeter to spare on all sides. It had been charmed against every possible type of damage she could imagine . . . but this was Mark.

Shelly snorted as the remaining spaces began to fill. "Good thing Bo travels light."

"And speaking of the one man we can't do without because Lord knows an accordion, a bodhran and a pennywhistle can walk into as many bars as they want, but they won't win shit in a Celtic festival without a fiddle. Where the hell is Bo?"

Tim smacked Mark on the shoulder and pointed at the ancient pickup truck pulling into the parking lot. It paused long enough to disgorge their missing fiddler and an old hockey bag before roaring off in a cloud of dust.

It wasn't Bo's girlfriend behind the wheel, unless she had what looked like a '70s pornstache attached to her upper lip. Not that Charlie was judging.

While Shelly, Tim, and Mark argued over who was to ride with whom—although as usual Shelly and Mark were making most of the noise—Charlie joined Bo, who'd taken over Shelly's spot slumped against the hood of the car.

"You look like shit."

He scratched at stubble and yawned. "Gee. Thanks."

"You get any sleep last night?" They'd closed up the ceilidh around three when the poor women who'd had to lock the Center behind them had finally kicked the last musicians out. Charlie'd crashed in a cheap motel room walking distance from the Center with the other three but Bo lived in Port Hastings, close enough to go home.

He yawned again. "Not much."

"Girlfriend still upset?"

His fingers drummed out a tune Charlie nearly recognized. "You know the phrase weeping and wailing and gnashing of teeth? Multiply by ten."

"By ten? What the hell did she lose?"

"It's a . . . thing. A family heirloom . . . thing."

To Bo's credit, he was a terrible liar. He knew exactly what the "thing" was. Charlie wondered if he was embarrassed about the actual object or embarrassed because he'd agreed not to identify it to anyone and that made venting awkward.

"She actually thought I'd taken it. I mean, I was there the night she lost it. With her the night she lost it, so how . . ." He slapped his hand down against the hood, loud enough for Shelly to turn and yell at him to fuck off or he'd be riding with Tim and Mark. "Okay, she didn't mean it, not really, but her and her sisters, they're talking Gaelic now, like they don't want me to know they're still suspicious of me, but I feel like I . . ." He sighed, shoulders sagging. "Fuck it."

Charlie filled in the next bit of the lyric line. Who knew that year playing country music would come in so handy. "You feel like you failed her even if she doesn't blame you."

"You don't know her." Both hands pushed thick, dark hair up into spikes. "How do you know she doesn't blame me?"

"Dude, you're here while Tanis is still freaking about what she lost, so she obviously told you to go. She gets that the festival is important to you. If she really blamed you for taking her . . ." Air quotes. ". . . thing, she wouldn't care how important it was to you. And, while she might have told you to get out, you'd have shown up acting all defensive." Charlie slapped him in the chest. "Which you're not."

Bo's eyes widened theatrically. "I'm not? Okay," he added after a moment, "I'm not. I feel guilty for leaving, though. Even if she didn't want me there." He managed half a grin. "I miss her, you know? I just left her an hour ago, but I really miss her. Is that pathetic? Because it sounds pathetic. She says she'll join us up coast," he continued before Charlie could agree that, yeah, it sounded pathetic. "She has more family up there and . . ." His laugh held little humor. "I think she thinks she's going to need to defend me when they find out."

"Even though you didn't take and/or lose the thing?"

He snorted. "Even though. It's just . . . we're amazing together, but it hasn't been that long and maybe her family disapproves of the brown. Or the itinerant musician thing. Or that my family moved here from Toronto."

"Toronto? Damn. Around here, that's definitely going to count against you."

"Tell me about it."

"She have overprotective parents?"

"I don't think so but lots of cousins. And her family, it's tight."

"I hear you." Charlie stared down at her bare toes for a moment. The raised voices across the parking lot blended with the cries of the gulls wheeling overhead and came out sounding like half a dozen aunties arguing in the kitchen. "Could it have been stolen?"

"What would be the point in someone who wasn't family stealing a family heirloom? And it sure as hell wasn't someone in her family."

"You sure?"

He was staring out toward the sea now, never very far away in this part of the world. She could feel the force of his gaze reaching for the distant horizon. "I'm sure."

And *that* was no lie.

"They're my cousins, right? You like spent all your time with your cousins growing up; that's a Gale thing. Family. The cousins out here, they think I'm pretty cool and it's not like I'm going to be playing soccer with them or anything." Jack still didn't understand the point of chasing something and not getting a meal out of it. Sure, let it go a few times, have a little fun running it down, but in the end, eat it.

Soccer balls tasted like farts.

And the yelling afterward had gone so long, he'd gotten bored and flown away.

"Anyway . . ." He folded his arms, looked Allie right in the eye, and tried very hard not to smoke. "Either I'm a Gale, or I'm not."

"He's got you there." Graham sounded like he was smiling around a mouthful of cereal, but Jack didn't dare check. Gale girls were tricky. He'd learned that in his first twenty-four hours here. If Allie had a countermove, he needed to stay on top of it.

But Allie only looked thoughtful. "What did you have in mind?"

"Just, you know, spending time with my cousins. Like a Gale."

"I had no idea you were interested in doing that."

"I wasn't." Dragons spent time with relatives for two reasons, politics or food. Okay, technically, one reason. "Now, I am."

Allie wanted him to be interested. That helped convince her. "No sorcery."

Jack snorted. "Gales don't do sorcery."

"Not and survive it," Graham muttered from the other side of the smoke.

"All right, this is ridiculous." Charlie grabbed Bo's arm and dragged him over to the van. She had no idea what Shelly and Mark were arguing about beyond passenger seating, but it clearly went deeper and just as clearly had no resolution. Odds were, it was left over from Aston, his love of cheese, and his lactose intolerance. "It's past noon, we're playing at four, and we're still not on the road. Bo!" When he pivoted to face her, she held out her fist. "On three."

"The original or liz . . ."

"The original. One. Two. Three. Scissors cuts paper, I ride with Shelly. Let's go!"

"Well, that works, too," Mark observed philosophically.

Riding with Mark and Tim meant listening to Mark expound constantly about nothing much for the duration of the trip. But the odds of arriving in one piece were higher. Charlie settled in with her bare toes on the dashboard and a bottle of ice-cool plum nail polish in her hand. Between the aunties and *Dun Good*'s old school bus, she'd used up all fear of dying in a fiery car crash.

"Uh, Shelly, it's a twenty-minute drive to Port Hood. Is warp drive really necessary?"

"You wouldn't ask that if you were hauling Moby Bass. I want parking as close to the stage as possible and there's eight other bands who want the same thing. Bump."

"Thanks." Charlie lifted the brush as the car went momentarily airborne. The flight wouldn't mess things up, it was the landing. Good shocks, though.

However, since the car was pre door airbags, she painted a quick plum charm on the gray vinyl interior.

"What're you doing?"

"Just a little insurance."

"Right, Mark says you're into something like that Wicca thing."

"Like," Charlie allowed, "but not." Wicca was a religion. The Gales were a family. "We've gotten kind of far ahead of the van."

"Yeah, that's because the van's so top-heavy. Mark gets up any kind of speed and he splats the curves." Yanking the wheel hard to the right, Shelly tucked in front of a trailer of openmouthed tourists just before a slightly larger trailer filled the space they'd been occupying in the other lane. She fishtailed on the gravel shoulder for a moment, then got all four wheels back on the asphalt and accelerated.

Port Hood, the self-proclaimed step-dancing capital of Cape Breton, was the first stop on a festival circuit that would, over the last of July and through all of August, cover the island, knitting together various fairs and community celebrations, as well as the varying and ubiquitous Highland Games. Music was a huge part of the Cape Breton lifestyle, and every summer it became a huge part of the Cape Breton economy as tourists flocked to the island to tap along to the jigs and reels, gawk at the men in kilts, buy tartan-covered kitsch, and create traffic jams that made some of the most scenic coastline in the world the most frustrating to drive. With the mines closed and the fishing heavily regulated, the locals were well aware they needed tourist dollars to survive, but most of them would prefer said tourists stop about midpoint on the causeway, toss their wallets over, and then go the hell home.

And speaking of home . . .

Charlie fished her ringing phone out of her bag and checked the caller ID. "My mother. . . ."

"Say no more." Shelly turned the radio up. "I'll be listening to the local maritime weather report."

"Thanks." Years spent with bands that never quite made it big enough to get out of each others' space, made faking privacy a necessary skill. Charms not needed. Charlie thumbed the connect and pitched her voice below the earnest CBC announcer listing wind speeds coming in off the Northumberland Strait. "Mom?"

"The twins want to spend three weeks traveling through Europe before school starts."

"Okay." If they wanted to go badly enough, there'd be a last minute seat sale for exactly what they had saved; that was how the family worked. "So they go after the second of the month; what's the harm?"

"Do you honestly think it's safe?"

"Mom, it's Europe."

"Cultural differences . . ."

Personally, Charlie thought Europe could handle it. However, based on the way Montreal had survived the twins' freshman year at McGill . . . "You want me to check on them occasionally, don't you?"

"If you wouldn't mind popping in and out. Don't tell them I sent you. And speaking of the second . . ."

Had they been?

". . . I know you're based in Calgary now, with Allie, but her circles are very small and Cameron will likely have at least a dozen girls to cover . . ."

"He's young. He'll survive."

"It's just that you won't have many options, not for years, and . . ."

"Maybe."

"And the aunties say you're traveling again, so . . ."

"I said, *maybe*, Mom. Gotta go." She cupped the phone in her left hand and said, "My mother wants me home for a family thing." Faking privacy included sharing enough information to soothe unavoidable curiosity.

"Your family's tight, right?"

New branches of the family separate, Charlotte. And then they evidently get into a pissing match over who gets the Wild Power at their ritual. The phone rang again, the tag of a commercial jingle for a children's cereal repeated over and over. Charlie didn't bother glancing at the screen before she answered. "I didn't tell my mother which ritual I'd be at, Auntie Gwen, and I certainly didn't tell her I was going back to Ontario. Auntie Jane's poking you with sticks." This time after disconnecting, she dropped the phone back into her bag. They'd chew at each other for a while now and leave her alone. "Oh, yeah," she sighed, "we're tight."

"Cool. Now, me, I have cousins I haven't seen since I was twelve."

"They move away?"

"No," Shelly laughed as she reached for the radio, "we just don't like each other."

Frowning at a half-heard introduction, Charlie blocked her hand. "Hang on a minute."

". . . in many ways it's actually safer to drill in close to shore. Should, God forbid, anything go wrong at a well off Hay Island, equipment to contain a spill can reach the site much more quickly than it could in a deepwater situation. And it wouldn't take weeks to cap the wellhead."

"So you believe certain other companies took too long . . ."

"I believe that Carlson Oil has plans in place to cap a wild well off Hay Island in less than twelve hours regardless of weather conditions. Less if we can move some of our operations onto Scatarie Island."

"Scatarie Island is a protected wilderness area."

"And we'd be there to protect it."

"So you agree that things could go wrong."

"Of course things can go wrong."

Charlie was impressed. The aunties couldn't have thrown in a more obvious subtextual, *What are you, an idiot?*

"And because we acknowledge that," the entirely reasonable woman's voice continued, "we're prepared. Because of the proposed location of the wellhead, we can put our preparations into action quickly and efficiently. We have people on our team, local people, who know how to work these waters. People who've survived only by making the right decisions. But putting a well out in the deep water? Well, I think experience has proven that in deep water, sooner or later, the ocean always wins."

"She doesn't say much, but she says it loud." Shelly snorted and turned the radio off as a used car commercial attempted to raise the ambient noise about seventy decibels. "Amelia Carlson, taking care of the seal problem by dipping them in crude."

"There's a seal problem?"

"There is if you're in the bullshit department at Fisheries. I mean, Jesus Christ . . ." The car rose up onto two wheels. Drifted down again. ". . . dudes in Halifax only just shot down a motion to reopen the Hay Island seal hunt. Bo met Tanis at the protests."

"Protesting for or against?" It was never wise to assume. If Tanis' family were fishermen . . .

"Against. Tanis' whole family's big in the environmental movement, run this high-profile group called Two Seventy-five N. Funky ass name, but they've got some weight to throw around. You, though, you haven't been back east for any length of time in a couple of years . . ." Shelly braced the steering wheel with her knee as she fixed her ponytail. ". . . what's your interest in Carlson Oil's line of bullshit?"

"Besides thinking that dipping seals in crude is a bad idea?" Charlie frowned down at her half-painted toenails. "I don't know yet." She'd been ear wormed by the chorus since Fort McMurray—seals or oil, rinse, repeat—but still had no idea of the verse.

The last coal mine in Cape Breton closed in 2001, but when a Swiss mining consortium won the right to develop an abandoned mine site in Dorkin, Carlson Oil had taken notice. If coal was set to make a comeback, Amelia's father had reasoned, it wasn't coming back without them.

As a result, Carlson Oil owned two small abandoned collieries in Inverness County and a much larger old DEVCO mine in Lingan. Hedging their bets, they'd also invested in the wind turbines erected along the cliffs outside of Lingan—the later investment significantly more public than the former. As Paul had told Catherine Gale, local coal got no respect in the media in spite of the fact that coal imported from the United States and South America powered the Lingan Generating Station at the same time as unemployment hovered perpetually around 16 per cent and the economy of Cape Breton tried to fiddle its way into solvency.

While the collieries across the island in Inverness County were more isolated, the mine in Lingan, the Duke, had gone much deeper with lots of damp, extended cross tunnels perfect for making terrifying old women happy and, more importantly, it was half an hour away from Sydney. About at the limit Paul was willing to have those pelts stinking up his car.

"You want to take the sealskins from an anonymous storage locker and drop them down the *Duke*?" Leaning back in her chair, mourning the loss of the ergonomic wonder in her Halifax office, Amelia almost thought she saw *here we go again* cross Paul's face.

"No," he said, so carefully it convinced her she had indeed seen that flicker of impatience, "I'd descend into the *Duke* and place them carefully in a cross tunnel. They'd come to no harm."

"I was being facetious, Paul." She steepled her fingers. "Carlson Oil owns the *Duke*. The . . . creatures behind Two Seventy-five N are going to be looking for those pelts, so they're going to be looking at Carlson Oil holdings. Particularly those holdings a convenient distant from the remarkably ugly office we're now spending our time in."

"They'd have to be high-level hackers to get through the shell companies between the *Duke* and Carlson Oil."

Amelia waved that off. "Why shouldn't they be computer wizards? They're already impossible. You haven't said anything to convince me that dropping the pelts down a mine . . ." Deliberate phrasing so she could enjoy how well he hid his annoyance. ". . . is safer than anonymous off-site storage. We only have her word for it that there's a new player, after all."

"We only had her word for it that they existed," Paul reminded her.

"Point." Leaning back far enough to cross her legs, Amelia indicated he should go on.

"When Catherine Gale introduced the new player, she began by reminding me that she, Catherine Gale, had found the pelts and then pointed out that the previous owners of the pelts wouldn't be able to do the same. She then told me that the pelts wouldn't be safe in the storage locker. Because she, Catherine Gale, had found them, the new player, whoever the new player is, could also find them. We don't know *what* Catherine Gale is, but I doubt there's only one of her."

"That's a thought to give a person nightmares," Amelia murmured. Catherine Gale reminded her of the nuns who'd taught at her primary school—only with the powers that terrified children had always assumed the nuns could manifest. Two of whatever Catherine Gale was, well, that was two too many.

"The conclusion that best fits the facts we have," Paul continued, "is that Two Seventy-five N have hired something like her to retrieve the pelts. We therefore know they can find the storage locker. Catherine Gale believes the mine will hide the pelts from the new player long enough for the permit to clear if they're in a tunnel that extends under water."

Amelia tapped her upper lip, wondered if it was time for more collagen, and said, "Do we believe her? She could want the pelts in the mine for her own reasons."

"Does it matter? For whatever reason, she doesn't want them found, and that works in your favor."

A significant part of Paul's job description involved shoveling through the details to find the bottom line and, bottom line: Catherine Gale, seal pelts, and the availability of the *Duke* all came back to keeping imaginary creatures the hell out of her business. Carlson Oil had everything tied up in this well. In order to pay for the platform, the refinery, a new rail line—not to mention bribes and "entertainment" of local officials—she'd sold what she could and borrowed against what was left. If she had to hire a character from a fairy tale to stop a character from a fairy tale in order to finally get that oil out of the ground, then so be it.

"Take the pelts to the mine." A raised hand held him in place. "Tomorrow," she told him after a moment spent appreciating the way he'd instantly responded to her gesture. "The rest of today is booked solid and I need you here."

"Tomorrow, then. Catherine Gale did say it would take a while for the new player to get up to speed," he added making a note on his phone.

"How convenient her information dovetails with my needs." When Paul ducked his head in silent apology, reminded of which *she* he worked for, Amelia pushed a government file folder across her desk. "Right now, we've kept the honorable member of parliament for Cape Breton South waiting long enough." Long enough he knew her time was valuable but not so long as to devalue his. "Send him in on your way out to find me a chair exactly like the one in my Halifax office."

"That particular chair won't fit behind the desk, Ms. Carlson."

"Then replace the desk." The Gale woman had obviously rattled him; she shouldn't have had to tell him that. "Oh, and have the room painted. I can't work in this shade of green."

Jack's family lunch turned out to be a picnic in Nose Hill Park with an aunt, an uncle, and seven cousins. Aunt Judith and Uncle Randy weren't married to each other, but both of their mates were at work.

"We don't say mates," Aunt Judith corrected.

Jack cocked his head and frowned. "Why not?"

It was another one of those things no one had a good answer for, so he let it go. Maybe Allie would explain later.

When he'd decided to be more Gale, he'd forgotten that he was pretty much exactly in between the cousins who'd come west for university and the cousins who'd come west with their parents. The older cousins were all working . . .

Jack stared down at his vanilla-glazed, custard cream doughnut with sprinkles and snorted. "You know this isn't actually food, right?"

"You can't smoke in here," Melissa sighed.

. . . so today was all about the kids. He didn't mind. He'd been youngest for so long, it was kind of cool being the oldest.

"I think you should take us flying."

Jennifer, who was part of Aunt Judith's clutch, was eleven and closest to him in age although Wendy, who was Uncle Randy's, was only a few weeks younger. Even after a year, it still kind of weirded him out that Gale fathers were so . . . alive. Female dragons ate their mates.

"Jack!" Jennifer poked him in the chest with an imperious finger. "Did you hear me? I think you should take us flying!"

He caught her hand, careful not to hurt her. "Why?"

"Because you aren't seven years older than us." Tugging free of his grip, she folded her arms. Her expression dared him to argue. "We totally can ride you. I saw the movie."

"You can carry both of us because you're so big," Wendy added. "Auntie Gwen says you're big enough to come with bar service."

"What?"

Wendy shrugged. "I don't know either, but that's what she said."

"We should go now." Jennifer grabbed his hand and pulled him away along the path. "We should go while Mom is busy with Richard."

Richard was only just hatched, smelled bad a lot of the time, and screamed when he wanted feeding, but Aunt Judith didn't seem to mind.

"How fast can you get into the air?" Wendy asked as they crested the hill.

"Why?"

The girls leaned out to exchange a look across his body that made him think of Allie and Charlie.

"You should do it fast," Jennifer told him. "Hit the air as soon as we get on. Oh, and change now. Right now."

They'd all seen him change. Allie hadn't wanted anyone relocating to Calgary who had a problem with him, although Jack had assured her he could deal with them. Turned out dealing with them topped the list of things that weren't allowed.

The moment between skin and scales burned. Sometimes, Jack wanted to get lost in the fire. Just let it burn and not worry about who he was or what he was supposed to be doing or what world he was supposed to be doing it on. He'd bet lower dragons did it, just woke up one morning, decided they'd had it with never knowing the answers, and burned away. But he was the Prince. And, right now, he was a Gale.

He shrugged, settling into scales, shifting a wing at the last moment so as not to knock down a small tree.

For all they wanted into the air right away, the girls wasted a moment admiring him . . .

"Oh, my God, so totally gorgeous."

"He gleams like real gold in the sun, doesn't he? He just gleams."

"He's definitely prettier than Connie Anderson's stupid pony."

. . . before they ducked under his wings, scrambled up his tail, and climbed until they sat together on his shoulders; Jennifer out in front, arms as far around his neck as they could reach, Wendy behind her.

"Go, go, go!"

So he went. Balancing with his tail, he rose up onto his hind legs, slammed his wings down, and grabbed sky, moving as fast as he could. He could hear them shrieking with laughter, but he tucked his legs up against his belly and concentrated on gaining altitude. At his size, he felt a lot better when he had a bit of distance between him and the ground. Leveling out at about two hundred feet, wings sculling to maintain lift, he suddenly realized he couldn't feel Jennifer's arms. Or the insignificant weight of their bodies. Or the drumming of their heels.

When he looked down, their pinwheeling forms had almost run out of sky.

He couldn't reach them in time.

There was only one thing he could do.

Standing on a riser built to look a bit like an overturned dory, Bo played "The Duke of Gordon's Birthday" as a line of step dancers formed a wall of nimble feet and nearly motionless upper bodies along the front of the festival stage. Festival rules required one traditional dance tune per set and, at just over three and a half minutes, this was the longest strathspey any of the bands had played yet. Mark and Tim had bodhran and accordion out in support, but this was all Bo.

He was good. More than just technically good, although he was that, too. Bow flying over the strings, he made an emotional connection with everyone listening—not just the dancers who smiled and moved as though it was the music lifting their feet off the floor. It was as close to magic as most of the world ever saw.

Charlie's fingers itched to take it that single step further, but she wove them together, rested them on the shoulder of her guitar, and distracted herself by watching the crowd.

She appreciated the chance. Bar lighting made it impossible to see much of anything, but outside, on a midsummer afternoon, the audience—on blankets or lawn chairs or sprawled on the bare ground—was as well lit as the bands on the stage. A number of people were up and dancing and a spirited, if spatially challenged, square dance dominated the far right. A pack of kids too old to be easily contained and young enough not to be cynical about traditional music ran around and occasionally through the more sedate groups, grandmothers reaching out to swat at them as they passed. A lot of the heads were gray and as many of them were moving to the music as not.

The other fiddlers, and there were dozens seeded through the crowd, not even counting the ten from the other bands, all stared at the stage with expressions of fierce possessiveness, claiming the music Bo pulled from his fiddle as their own. Later, they'd pick it apart like a group of aunties over a chicken carcass, but while he played, they were one.

In the open space between two spread blankets, a girl no more than three danced in place, chestnut curls bouncing, one hand clutching a fistful of her tartan shorts, the other swinging a stuffed animal over her head. It was so exactly the sort of heartwarming scene the local news loved to show that Charlie checked for the camera, half convinced it had been staged.

Apparently not.

Behind the girl, a patch of stillness drew Charlie's attention. The woman, tall, with a rippling fall of long dark hair stared at the stage with eyes so black Charlie's heart said "auntie" even as her brain said, "too young" and "not here." Charlie had never seen anyone listen with such intent. Her generous mouth was curved up into a smile that made Charlie think the word beatific although it had never been part of her vocabulary before and she'd shifted her weight forward onto the balls of her feet as though the music was physically pulling her in.

She was different. No, she was *more*.

When Bo finished, drawing out the last few bars with a not exactly traditional flourish, Charlie lost sight of her in the swirl of dancers leaving the stage. Before she could find her again, Mark called them into place for the next song.

"When I'm right, I'm right; you sounded good, Chuck, it's hard to believe you've been away from real music for so long. And hey, nice fake on the last verse of "Highland Heart"; you forget the words?"

No. The old imperfect rhyme had finally gotten to her.

"Just a little bit," Charlie lied to Mark's ass, as he bent to shove his cymbal stands in under two hockey bags. "Think anyone noticed?"

"Besides me? Not likely. Lyrics are pretty flexible even with the shit this lot's heard a hundred times. I'll put money on them noticing every extra wiggle Bo tossed in, though."

"We get points for extra wiggles?"

"Who the hell knows?"

Bands registered for the Samhradh Ceol Feill collected points every time they played. The more often a band played, the more chance for points, but that was the only straightforward part of the exercise as far as Charlie could tell. Still, Mark had managed to get *Grinneal* signed up for nearly the entire circuit, so they had a good chance of taking first prize and scoring the studio time with the MacMaster's recording engineer. The ten song EP they were already selling wasn't bad, but even Mark admitted it could use a professional polish.

"Chuck!"

"Right, sorry." She handed over her gig bag. The party'd be going on for a while, but, given the number of guitars around, she'd decided to stick with the mandolin—easier to carry and more chances to play. She could stuff everything else she needed in the pockets of her cargo pants.

Mark shifted his snare and slid the bag in on top of Tim's keyboard. "Bo's good, and fiddles rule the trad stuff, so I'm not ruling out points for extra wiggles. You know," he added, somehow backing out without losing the coverage of his kilt, "this might be the last part of the country where I'd feel safe leaving the instruments locked in the van." He straightened, turned, and dragged his hair back off his face. "I mean, this shit is our livelihood and if some asshat walks off with it, we're screwed, but this is me walking away and feeling good about it." Grinning, he slammed the door and tucked his thumbs under the strap of his bodhran case.

"You're not walking away," Charlie said after a moment.

"What?"

"You're not walking away," she repeated. "You're standing by the van."

"Yes, I am. Because I'm completely full of shit and I don't want to leave this stuff unguarded. Maritimers as a whole might be their mamas' darlings, but give it another hour. Once it's fully dark and the kiddies have been packed off to bed, half that lot hanging around will be pissed and the other half well on the way. I don't trust drunks."

"Every vehicle parked back here behind the stage has instruments in it. There's a one in seventeen chance the drunks will find ours. Less because we're buried safely in the middle of the lot."

"Less than one chance in seventeen?" His eyes narrowed. "You're blowing smoke out your ass, aren't you?"

"The numbers don't lie, Mark."

"Okay." He patted the bumper as he moved away. "I can work with those odds."

"I thought you could." About to fall into step beside him, Charlie heard a sound that stopped her cold. It ran under the music and laughter and gulls and screaming children the way the ocean did, cadence rising and falling with the crash of the waves against the shore as the tide came in.

"Hey! Chuck?" When she looked up, Mark was already at the edge of the field given over to parking. "You coming?"

"In a minute." The sound pulled at her. It was important, whatever it was. "I'm going to go down to the shore for a minute. Clear my head."

"I'll join the party without you, then. If I leave Tim on his own for too long, he makes friends with everyone under five, forgets what an asshole I am, and starts thinking about starting a family." With a jaunty wave and a flick of the kilt Charlie could have done without, Mark jogged around the stage and disappeared into the crowd.

Charlie spent a moment sifting through the ambient noise, then she followed the pull of sound out past the last car, across the road leading to the jetty, and stopped when she saw two women standing by the water's edge, so similar in appearance they had to be related. Tall and slender, with dark hair and dark eyes, they stood at the place where land met sea, looking more real in the dusk than they could possibly be in full sunlight. Water swirled around their feet and up over their ankles, but they didn't seem to care. One of the women clutched the other, clutched the woman Charlie had seen listening so intently to Bo's playing, and it was obvious, even from a distance, the first woman was on the edge of hysteria.

". . . stolen . . ."

The rest of her lament blew away on the wind.

The Gale family did not involve themselves in anything that didn't involve the family first, but the whole point of being a Wild Power was being, well, wild. Unpredictable even.

Charlie stepped forward.

Her phone rang.

FOUR

CHARLIE COUNTED TO TEN, not for the first time since arriving back in Calgary, and finally managed to slip into a break in the flow of over-lapping words. "But both girls are okay?"

"It wasn't easy gathering and then separating all the butterflies so Jack could change them back." Allie rubbed her face with both hands. "Wendy keeps trying to land on flowers, but, bottom line, they're fine."

"The point isn't that they're *okay*, Charlotte." Auntie Bea emphasized her point with the rolling pin, smacking it down on the table beside the ball of pastry dough. "The point is that he used sorcery to keep them from hitting the ground."

"That's better than letting them hit the ground."

Allie nodded. "That's what I said."

Auntie Carmen looked up from the peaches she was slicing and shot Allie a look that would have curdled cream. Had curdled cream, Charlie noted as Auntie Gwen snorted, glared at Auntie Carmen, and dumped the contents of her mixing bowl down the sink. "Gales," Auntie Carmen sniffed, throwing a peach pit into the compost bucket, "do not use sorcery."

"Gales don't bounce from a hundred feet up either," Charlie pointed out.

"They had no business being a hundred feet up." Auntie Gwen's fingers were white around the handle as she opened the fridge. "Jack should never have agreed when they asked him for a ride."

"Oh, please, what chance did he have? He had two determined Gale girls nipping at him, both well aware they're inside his seven-year break and equally aware of what that'll mean the moment they join third circle."

"Who may or may not be within his seven-year break is irrelevant."

Charlie snorted. "Yeah, right."

"We will not be breeding him back into the lines." Auntie Bea's tone froze the water in the measuring cup beside her. The glass shattered. The water rolled off the table and smashed on the floor. "We would not breed him back into the lines if he was the last Gale boy alive."

"Oh, come on, if he was the last Gale boy alive, you'd have to . . ."

"Charlotte."

Charlie teetered on the edge of ignoring the warning, but self-preservation won out. "Fine. He's different. We make use of difference, we don't embrace it."

"When have you felt un-embraced, Charlotte?" Auntie Carmen sniffed. "You're still listed with two boys who haven't chosen and another two who have, should you want a child without the inconvenience of a husband."

Auntie Bea slapped the sheet of dough over the pie plate. "Not to mention . . ." Each word came punctuated with a jab of her thumbs, pushing the dough down into place. ". . . the situation with Alysha and Graham having sons would be . . ."

"This isn't about me," Charlie reminded her quickly, before they could get tangled up in that argument again.

"You have useful talents," Auntie Bea sniffed.

"So does Jack."

"Sorcery . . ."

"Isn't necessarily a bad thing."

"Experience begs to differ."

"Experience with a dragon? A Dragon Prince?"

"What?"

"Jack is a sorcerer," Charlie said, slowly, carefully, not giving them a reason to stop listening, "and a Gale boy, and yeah, that combination always goes bad, but he's also a dragon, raised as a prince. You have no idea how he'll turn out."

"Exactly. He's unpredictable."

"Wild?"

"Precisely."

Charlie folded her arms and raised both brows.

"No Gale boy has ever been a Wild Power," Auntie Gwen stated flatly, dumping the bowl of sliced peaches into the pie.

"Or a dragon." Charlie dropped down onto the sofa beside Allie. "When will you . . ."

Hand out of sight between her hip and the sofa, Allie pinched her.

". . . understand," Charlie amended, "that Jack is unique?"

Lip curled, Auntie Bea rolled on the upper crust. "Alysha's argument for allowing him to stay . . ."

Translate *stay* as *live*.

". . . was that he was a Gale boy and Gale boys are not unique."

"We're not good with unique," Allie said quietly before the aunties could weigh in.

Yeah. Understatement. "Actually, Allie's argument was that he was a Gale under the age of fifteen and therefore could not be judged."

"His gender seems fairly self-evident," Auntie Carmen noted.

"Charlotte, stop looking like you want to bang your head against the floor and make your point."

Auntie Gwen was perceptive. "Stop thinking of him as a Gale boy and start thinking of him as a Gale dragon." She spread her hands. "New label, new rules."

All three aunties and Allie stared at her.

Given that she couldn't stare back at all four of them at once, Charlie focused on Auntie Bea. Auntie Gwen was the most flexible, but Auntie Bea was the one to convince. "Jack's not a defective Gale boy. He's a fully operational Gale dragon."

Dark eyes narrowed. "We got it the first time, Charlotte. And the sorcery?"

"He's not a Gale sorcerer . . ."

"He's a dragon sorcerer," Allie finished, one hand wrapped around Charlie's arm.

Forehead pleated into a deep vee, Auntie Carmen waved her knife like a wand. "But you just said, he's a Gale dragon."

"Ah, but all cats are not Socrates."

"Yes, Charlotte, you're clever." Auntie Gwen pointed the whisk at her, cream dripping off the wires and back into the bowl. "What do you suggest we *do* with this Gale dragon?"

We're not good with unique.

"Fine." Charlie sagged back against the cushions and went where Auntie Gwen wanted her to. "He can spend the summer with me. I can teach him how to be a Gale who colors outside the lines. And besides, we could use a roadie; Mark's got us booked into every freakin' festival on the island and I am not carrying all that beer. That last bit was a joke," she added as all three aunties stared. "Look, there's open space in Cape Breton. Deer, moose, he'll be fine."

Allie's grip on her arm tightened. "Do you remember the hamster you had when you were ten?"

"No. And ow."

"I do. It died."

"Hamsters don't live very long."

"You sat on it!"

Oh, yeah, *that* she remembered. "Dragons are tougher than hamsters, Allie, and it's pretty obvious the p . . ." Auntie Gwen's whisk scraped the side of the bowl and Charlie hastily discarded the peanut gallery. "People who make the decisions in this family don't want Jack to stay here. And as he's not here while we're discussing him, where is he?"

One final squeeze, then Allie released her. "Down in the store with Graham and Joe."

Charlie stood, tugged down the hem of her shorts, and picked up her mandolin.

"Where are you going, Charlotte?"

"First, I'm going downstairs to ask Jack if he wants to go east."

Auntie Bea cut three lines across the top of the pie so quickly Charlie wondered if she'd ever been a ninja. "If he's a Gale, as you two keep saying, dragon or boy, he'll do what he's told."

"You can get more flies with honey, Auntie Bea."

"I can get as many flies as I want, Charlotte, however I want, but I don't want flies. And second?"

"Second, I'm heading back. I've got . . ." *Tall and slender, with dark hair and dark eyes, they stood at the place where land met sea, looking more real in the dusk than they could possibly be in full sunlight.* ". . . commitments. To the band." Of course to the band.

"And these band commitments, they're more important than family commitments, then?"

"I'm fulfilling family commitments, Auntie Bea," Charlie said, and turned to go. Flip flops, not the greatest for pivoting on one heel, but she managed.

"Your pie isn't ready," Auntie Carmen pointed out mournfully.

Tempting, Charlie admitted, but pie had never been enough to keep her at home.

"If he agrees . . ." Allie caught up to her at the door.

"When he agrees. My persuasion-fu is strong."

"Fine, when. How will you get him there? He's too big to take through the Wood."

Charlie grinned. "They have these things called planes."

A dimple flashed in Allie's cheek. "Yeah, but they smell like ass and make you check your guitar."

Still licking the flavor of Allie's cherry lip gloss off her mouth, Charlie glanced over at the mirror and the reflection of her standing in the hall holding her mandolin, a small duffel bag of clothes slung over one shoulder. It seemed she'd grown out of the whole traveling with only extra underwear lifestyle.

Then Allie slowly appeared behind her. Then Katie, then Maria, then Judith, then Lynn, then Rayne, then Holly, then her sisters, her mother, her aunts . . .

Tall, with blonde hair and gray eyes. Some slight differences in shade of hair, in shape of body, in skin tone, but it was easy to see the family resemblance. Charlie had started dyeing her hair when she was fifteen, a way of saying, "*Yeah, I'm different. Want to make something of it?*" With it back to her natural color, nothing visibly separated her from the others.

Then her reflection split down the middle and a glittering dragon stepped out holding her mandolin.

"I'm different on the inside." She patted the frame. "Like Jack. A little obvious, but thanks."

The dragon rolled silver eyes and stepped forward with such assurance that Charlie stepped back, convinced for a moment that it was going to step out of the mirror.

"And I thought that whole 3D craze had died," she muttered going on into the store.

*   *   *

"Do I have a choice?"

"Sure." Charlie leaned back against the counter. "You can choose to spend the rest of the summer hanging out with a group of musicians who will very likely teach you a number of bad habits, or you can stay here where the aunties will watch you with suspicion, your cousins will continue to get you into trouble, Allie will treat you like a fourteen-year-old boy, Graham, who could teach you any number of cool things, will insist you do boring office work . . ."

"Hey!"

She ignored him. ". . . and Joe will keep reacting to that Prince thing and resenting it even though he's never actually lived in the UnderRealm."

"Wait . . . You resent I'm a prince?" Jack stopped spinning the wheels of an old die-cast tractor and turned a golden gaze on the leprechaun. "Why would you resent that?"

Joe's freckles disappeared under a sudden flush. "I don't believe your birth makes you better than anyone else."

"Yeah, right. That's 'cause you haven't met my mother."

They'd all nearly met Jack's mother, but she'd been in a hurry to destroy the world and Allie had been in a slightly greater hurry to send her home and that hadn't left much time for introductions.

Charlie straightened, leaving sweaty smudges behind on the glass. "Bottom line, Jack, being forced to wave the sorcerer flag this afternoon has gotten you a get-out-of-boring free card. So make a decision. I've got a beer back east with my name on it."

"Fine." He tossed the car back on the shelf. "I'll go with you."

"I'm overwhelmed by your enthusiasm. And technically you'll be sent after me."

"He's not flying from Alberta to the east coast." Feet shoulder width apart, arms folded, Graham's posture announced he would not be moved.

"Why not? Oh, wait, you mean *flying*?" Charlie flapped her arms. "Duh. Of course not. Put him on a plane to Halifax, and we'll work out how he'll cover the last few kilometers when he gets there."

"I'll know where you are. I mean I can find you wherever you are," Jack expanded when Charlie flashed a raised eyebrow at him. "Remember how my mother followed the blood link here? I can follow the Gale blood anywhere."

"Anywhere?"

"It's kind of loud. Obvious, I mean."

"I thought you followed your father's blood up from the UnderRealm?" Graham growled.

He shrugged. "I didn't know I was a Gale then, did I?"

They weren't getting him away from Graham any too soon, Charlie realized. Jack's tone had tottered on the edge of challenge and in any testosterone-fueled, teenage rebellion, Graham would lose. No matter what Graham thought.

"Great, you'll get to Halifax, then fly to the island to find me. You'll need to stretch out after the plane. So, we're good." She ruffled Jack's hair, moving just fast enough to keep from being burned by his reaction, then grabbed the front of Graham's T-shirt, pulled herself to him, and kissed him good-bye. "I've got to go, I was in the middle of something. Well, on the edge of the beginning of something. I think."

Charlie'd intended to follow Mark's song back to Port Hudson but ended up following a line of fiddle music that wound in and around the Wood. It wasn't music she could remember ever having heard before, but it had a Pied Piper thing going for it and when she emerged into the world, the last few notes whipped by on the wind followed by a roar of appreciation. She could hear laughter and smell the smoke of the beach fire as she stepped out between the trees, but the corner of damp sand beyond the pier was empty. No women and only one set of footprints heading up to the pier. Not really surprising they'd left—she squinted at her watch—she'd been gone for nearly ninety minutes.

One set of footprints heading up to the pier . . .

Charlie stared out into the harbor for a moment.

She lost the footprints on the hard-packed dirt of the access road, thought about using a charm to keep following, but lured by the distant sound of "Back in Black" played on a fiddle headed for the party instead. Between following a hunch and joining a gang of musicians with beer, well, she'd had enough of being responsible for one night.

On the way through the parking lot to drop off her bag, she passed two guys trying to pretend they weren't breaking into a car, tossed the first three bars of "Sail Away Ladies" at them, and didn't bother waiting around for the splash.

Given that he'd recently been forced to recognize there were significantly more things in heaven and earth than were dreamed of in his philosophy, Paul figured his reaction when he turned on the light was completely justified. By the time he realized the creature sprawled on his desk was another pelt, his extra-large black coffee was already dripping past the empty eye-holes and onto the floor. The smell of the new paint—first coat applied the moment Ms. Carlson had left for the evening, a light taupe for the outer office and a darker shade for the inner sanctum—had covered the smell of fish. The building had been locked and while the second-floor windows were open, they were securely screened in and the screens were still in place.

Granted, his office was on the twelfth floor in Halifax and that hadn't stopped Catherine Gale's first delivery.

The painters would arrive at five thirty to put on the second coat. He had fifteen minutes to get rid of the evidence or risk damaging rumors about Amelia Carlson and fur. Seal fur. By noon, people would speculate about how she wanted the seal hunt reopened. By tomorrow morning, rumor would have her out on the ice clubbing baby seals herself.

Stuff it under the table in the boardroom?

Or in Ms. Carlson's private bathroom?

No. He'd be driving out to the mine the moment the painters left, and he'd have no chance to smuggle it out while they were in the building. His morning was tightly planned: he'd shove the pelts away in the dark while the paint dried, be back in time for the delivery of the new desk and chair. Be ready for work when Ms. Carlson showed up at ten after her breakfast meeting with the local representatives of the Seafarers International Union, North Atlantic District. Unions had been trying to organize on the deepwater rigs for years, and Carlson Oil was dangling the carrot of a shallow water well. Get the unions on board and the Ministry of the Environment would think twice about blocking the permits regardless of what power Two Seventy-five N wielded locally.

Power . . .

If they had someone like Catherine Gale working for them, would they use her power to influence the government? He paused, one hand extended toward the pelt, and considered it. It would have been tidier to use Catherine Gale to directly influence the government—as they were hip deep in the messier option, clearly Ms. Carlson hadn't been able to convince her to do it. Yesterday in the storage locker, she'd warned him the new player would go after the pelts, but that was all she'd warned him about. Two Seventy-five N were the good guys. They'd use this new player to get their property back, but they wouldn't use her against the government *because* they were the good guys.

Which was why they were going to lose. Business didn't recognize the generalizations of good and evil although he'd heard a rumor they were adding ethics classes to most MBA programs.

He glanced down at his watch. Currently he wore a eight hundred dollar copy of an Omega Seamaster, but by next summer he'd have the real thing and . . . shit. The painters would be here in ten minutes!

The pelt was as heavy and awkward as the other three, but at least the outer hair had treated the coffee like the North Atlantic and repelled nearly all of it. Fortunately, he'd covered his cleared desk for the painters, so most of the coffee had spread out over the drop cloth. He wasted a moment jerking the damp canvas back into place, then another jerking it back down over the framed maps leaning against the side of his desk.

Coffee soaked into his shoulder while carrying the pelt down the stairs, but he was dressed in a golf shirt and khakis for the mine and he'd change before returning to the office, so he could ignore it.

He'd left his car parked directly in front of the building, willing to risk a bylaw officer wandering by at five thirty in the morning. By the time the first pickup truck of painters rolled past on their way to the parking lot, he had the pelt safely tucked away in his trunk.

The newspaper truck pulled up while he was having a "friendly chat" with the head painter. After talking about the weather, the price of gas, the price of coffee, and other things Paul could care less about—some days he really missed Toronto's surly, no-nonsense contractors—Paul managed to establish when and how he wanted the job finished, sent the yawning man upstairs to his crew, and took a moment to grab a *Post* from the newly filled box.

The headline above the fold read: *Hay Island Environmental Group Withdraws Objection to Carlson Drilling*

Good news, but it only meant they'd spoken to a local reporter. He'd reserve judgment until after he spoke to the minister's office although, with any luck, this would be the last disgusting piece of fish-soaked fur he had to deal with. Seriously, this was the twenty-first century; what was wrong with microfibers?

The headline under the fold read: *Fisherman Catches Not-A-Squid off Scatarie Island.*

Not a squid? Shaking his head, Paul delayed leaving for the mine long enough to drop the paper in the recycling bin by the elevator. Lots of things in the ocean weren't squid; he didn't have to be the son of a fisherman to know that. The slightly out-of-focus photograph suggested *Fisherman Catches Tentacled Mutant* might be more accurate. And this was the fishing ground environmentalists were afraid Carlson Oil might ruin; an oil spill could only improve things.

Charlie woke up thinking the world was ending. Heart pounding, she jerked up into a sitting position, fighting her way free of her sleeping bag and ready to . . .

. . . deal with Tim snoring.

Mark, head on Tim's shoulder, drooling into a dark triangle of chest hair and a half-inked tattoo of a sea serpent, had apparently gotten used to it. Tucked up on their other side, Bo had earbuds in, cords disappearing under his Ryerson hoodie. Shelly'd hooked up with someone—or someones. Charlie was a little fuzzy on the details. She vaguely remembered being asked to join in, couldn't think why she'd refused, and hoped it wasn't because the people involved who weren't Shelly were from one of the other bands. Even without Charlie accidentally charming them, that never ended well during festival season.

Technically, they were camping. Realistically, no one had been sober enough to drive, so they'd just bunked down on the flattened grass between the van and Shelly's car. Given the number of vehicles in the makeshift parking lot, and at least one set of sinuses giving Tim a run for his money, they weren't alone.

Moving quietly so as not to wake anyone, and carefully so her head wouldn't fall from its precarious perch on her neck, Charlie skimmed the sleeping bag down her body until she could kick free.

The sun was barely up and when she got to the beach, a little early morning fog still clung to the surface of the ocean—silver-gray mist above slate-gray water. Stripping down, leaving yesterday's clothes just above the dark line in the sand, she gritted her teeth and walked out until she could dive through a swell.

Northumberland Strait never got warm, but the shallow water between the mainland and Port Hood Island was closer to refreshing than profanity. By the time she surfaced, her hangover had eased and, provided she got something to eat in the next little while, Charlie felt she just might . . .

The seal looked as startled by their sudden meeting as she felt.

Gasping in surprise while treading salt water—not smart.

By the time she finished coughing, the seal was gone, with not so much as a ripple across the swells to mark its passing. Charlie peered out into the fog a moment longer, remembered why she'd replaced Aston in the band, curled her fingers into fists, and turned for shore.

The elderly man standing by her clothes was clearly a local. "You're not one of *them*, are you?" he asked as she rose to her feet in the shallows, water sluicing off her skin. "You're not one of the water women?"

Gales were connected to the land and, wild though she might be, Charlie was still a Gale. "No, I'm not."

"They're not happy, them." He jerked his head out toward the island. "I heard them at night. Wailing."

"Wailing?"

"Aye, wailing."

"What about?"

After a noise like a cat coming to grips with a hairball, he hawked a lougie into the sand. "How the bloody fuck should I know?" he demanded. "You can't go wandering around naked, then."

"I'm not."

"I'm not blind, girl!"

Charlie scooped up her clothes. "I'm not wandering."

"You think I'm so old it doesn't matter, eh? Is that it? You can just go wild?"

He'd been a strong man once, broad shoulders, large hands, skin browned by the wind and the sun and sea. No ring, so no prior claim.

Underwear dangling from one finger, Charlie dug her toes into the sand, noted the clear flecks of gold in his hazel eyes, and grinned. If he wanted wild . . . "How's your heart?"

"How's my . . ." Silver brows rose as he realized what she was actually asking and, after a moment of stunned silence, he laughed, loud and deep, his eyes crinkling at the corners, the change of expression taking years off his age.

Charlie traced a charm on the inside of his forearm anyway, just in case.

The middle-aged man who'd wandered out of the security trailer when Paul hit his horn had opened the gate with no more than a yawn and a cursory glance at the paperwork. Nearly at the end of his shift, he clearly didn't care about someone from head office arriving in the early hours to check out the mine. Paul had been counting on that. The man's lack of professionalism, however, was not in Carlson Oil's best interest, and Paul made a note of it.

It didn't occur to him until he was on his way down the hoist shaft, elevator cables grinding out protests as the cage descended, that what he was doing might be considered dangerous. Under the dome of the borrowed hardhat, his scalp suddenly prickled with sweat. Paul had been down into the *Duke* before on one of the quarterly inspections, but that had been with a half dozen other people, another dozen up top in case something went wrong.

This morning, if something went wrong, he'd be entirely on his own.

He checked his phone, feeling unbalanced without his earpiece in.

No signal.

Entirely on his own.

At one hundred and fifty meters, he reached the first transfer station, a big open area about ten, maybe fifteen meters square. On that quarterly inspection, he'd been told the miners had called it Canaveral.

The safety engineer spread his arms. "It's where they took off for the sky."

"Yeah." Paul brushed a bit of dirt off his sleeve. "I got it."

He could go deeper, a lot deeper, but it wasn't necessary and he had no intention of spending all day at this. Locking down the elevator, he dragged the pelts to one of the flat equipment carts—a negligible resale value had left them abandoned to rust—and loaded them alternately lengthwise/crosswise trusting their weight to hold them in place. After spending a moment working out how to switch the rails—the carts ran on steel lines like train cars—he pushed his loaded cart down C tunnel.

C tunnel.

It went out under the sea.

Oh, ha. He flicked on his helmet light even though the tunnel lamps threw sufficient illumination, focused on the task at hand and not the kilometers of dark, silent, empty tunnels around him or the way he was probably drawing coal dust into his lungs with every breath, and walked briskly until he reached a point where the schematic on his phone told him he was under the Atlantic. Or maybe the Gulf of Saint Lawrence. Either way, he was absolutely not thinking of the water pressing down on the rock over his head.

Sweat rolling down his sides from a combination of exertion and humidity, he stopped at the next cross tunnel, flicked on the breaker for the lights, and unloaded the pelts, stacking them against the wall about five meters in. When he returned to C tunnel and flicked the breaker off again, the pelts disappeared. The darkness filled the cross tunnel so completely that when he held out his hand, he expected to meet resistance.

"That ought to be good enough for Catherine Gale," he muttered.

The words rolled off down the tunnels, bouncing off the walls, not so much fading as disappearing into the distance, in constant motion until they finally reached a coal face and began the long trip back.

A conceit Paul knew was ridiculous.

Gale.

Gale.

Gale.

Any sound other than his own breathing or the motion of the cart or his work boots against the tunnel was a product of an early morning, not enough caffeine, and a unique situation.

About halfway back to Canaveral, returning the empty cart at nearly a jog, he stopped to drag his palm across his forehead, wiping the sweat off on his thigh.

Claws skittered against rock in the pause between inhale and exhale.

Not possible.

If he turned, he'd see C tunnel angling off until it curved out of sight.

He'd see slices of darkness marking the cross tunnels.

And nothing else.

Claws . . .

He didn't turn. He scrubbed his palms against his thighs, got a better grip on the crossbar, and kept walking. Walking. Not running.

Not running until he could see the open gate of the elevator and then he abandoned the cart, raced down the last ten meters of tunnel and across the open area ignoring how many tunnels spilled out into it. How many open, unbarred, indefensible . . .

His boots slammed against the metal grate. He slammed the gate shut. His hands were *not* shaking as he keyed in the elevator codes and slapped a palm down on the big green button the moment it lit.

His hands were not shaking because there was nothing in those tunnels but abandoned machinery, four seal pelts, three suit bags, and the death of any chance Canada ever had to produce enough coal to supply the generators that kept the Maritimes powered up.

The lights for the main lines turned off at the surface. The tunnels were *not* growing dimmer.

The elevator jerked up a half meter, then began to rise smoothly toward the surface. Pressed against the side, Paul watched the walls pass, did not look down past his boots through the grate. Concentrated on the sounds of the motor and the winches and the chains.

Had it taken this long on the way down?

At the surface, he shut the system down, hung up his hardhat, and checked his watch when he finally stepped out into blue skies and sunshine.

An hour and thirteen minutes round trip.

The gate guard barely glanced his way before opening the gate to let him out. Paul composed his expression anyway. In many respects, Cape Breton was like one big small town. People were connected in ways no one in their right mind could anticipate and gossip was cheap and easy entertainment. It wouldn't do to have the guard spread a story about how a man had left the mine, the empty mine, looking like he'd seen a ghost.

Or had heard claws against the rock.

At an hour and twenty-four minutes, his phone rang. He fumbled his earphone in, fading adrenaline making him clumsy.

"It's about time, Paul. Where were you that I couldn't reach you?"

"Dealing with *storage* at the *Duke*, Ms. Carlson."

"*Storage?*"She repeated his emphasis. "For God's sake, this is Nova Scotia; our phones have not been bugged." He could hear her ring tapping against the plastic case. "And given that, I need you to find dirt on Mathew Burke. He's with the union, he's being rude at breakfast, is very likely obstructionist, and I want him out of my way."

One hand on the steering wheel, thumb working the keyboard on his phone, Paul noted the name. "Out of the country?"

"Possibly. I definitely want him out of a job."

"I'm heading back into Sydney now." Beside Mathew Burke, Paul typed: BURY HIM. "Anything else?"

"A green tea soy latte waiting for me on my desk wouldn't hurt. I've had a morning."

"Because he's my cousin, he's having a rough summer, and I already told him he could come."

Mark stared at her for a long moment, scratched under the waistband of his shorts, and shrugged. "If you're not worried about contributing to the delinquency of a minor, Chuck, it's no skin off my knees. And, hey, maybe we'll pick up a couple of extra family friendly points."

Knees? Charlie wondered as Bo hung up his phone and glared at Mark. "We've got bigger problems than babysitting Charlie's cousin. We don't have a cottage reserved."

"Yeah, we do." Mark ducked away from Tim's swing. "We do! I called as soon as they set the festival schedule." He frowned. "At least I intended to call . . ." Tim's second swing connected with the back of his head. "Look, I'm sure I called!"

"Dude, it doesn't matter if you sent smoke signals." Bo leaned forward and poked Mark in the chest. "There's no reservation."

As Mark and Bo argued, Charlie dug her phone out of the side pocket on her gig bag, pulled Bo's phone from his hand, and dialed the last number he'd called. She had everything settled by the time Shelly wandered over to join them, carrying a box of pastry and two trays of coffee balanced one on top of the other—three to a tray—in an impressive bit of postcoital share the wealth.

"What's with them?" she asked, putting the box down on the roof of the car, the coffees beside it.

"Mark forgot to reserve one of the cottages in Mabou." The turnover Charlie plucked from the box was still warm. More importantly, the icing hadn't been swirled on with intent to make her settle down and help Allie raise boys.

"Asshole. I need to shower."

"Me, too." The salt residue from her swim made her skin feel tight. "I took care of it."

"Blackmail? Seriously," she continued when Charlie just smiled around a mouthful of wild blueberry filling, "you can't just get a cottage at the last minute."

Bands had dibs on the ten cottages—one to a band—but on the Friday of the Mabou weekend, there was zero chance of one being empty.

"I can."

"How?"

Charlie leaned out of the way as Tim grabbed for a Danish, then leaned back, snagged a coffee, and spread her arms. "The universe likes me. I want a cottage, I get a cottage."

Shelly snorted and rolled her eyes. "Fine, don't tell me, but I'm going to want the truth if I have to help hide a body."

Gales seldom bothered to lie. Unfortunately, far too many of them were addicted to bad Jack Nicholson imitations. Before Charlie could decide if Shelly needed to be told she couldn't handle the truth, her phone rang.

"Ride of the Valkyries?" Shelly's brows nearly hit her hairline.

"Not my idea," Charlie muttered. "I'll just be over . . ." She pointed toward the ocean. ". . . there." Figuring an auntie vs Valkyrie cage fight would would be an easy win for the auntie, Charlie'd never bothered changing the aunties' chosen ringtone. "What can I do for you, Auntie Jane?"

"You can tell me if you've lost what little mind you have left, Charlotte Marie Gale."

Auntie Jane was not the oldest of the Gale aunties nor was she usually the auntie who anchored first circle back with the bulk of the family in Ontario. She was the auntie who decided which of the other aunties would anchor first circle. Charlie wasted a moment feeling very sorry for Uncle Evan.

"Charlotte?"

"Is this about Jack?"

"Is this about Jack?" Auntie Jane punctuated the repetition with a disapproving sniff. "Why on earth would you think that? Could it be because you've arbitrarily . . ."

"Arbitrarily?" Charlie rolled her eyes. "Second circle anchor agreed as well as the entire first circle." All three of them.

Auntie Jane refused to budge. ". . . arbitrarily decided to pull a Gale boy from his home? We do not allow our boys to go wandering about unsupervised, Charlotte."

"I'll be with him!"

"Children trying to raise children."

"I'm nearly twenty-eight!"

"You're third circle, Charlotte."

Charlie took a deep breath. "He doesn't need a mother; he has a mother and she's a dragon. He needs to learn that there's a way to be what he is *and* a Gale before he turns fifteen and judgment is passed. And," she added, as she reached the pier and kept walking, "I'm here for a reason. Maybe that reason is Jack."

"I very much doubt it. Have you even considered what your *friends* will say the first time Jack is even a little careless letting the dragon loose?"

"Depends. If he eats that idiot from *Tumble Down* who plays 'White Rabbit' on a set of Uilleann pipes, they'll probably applaud."

"Don't be trite, Charlotte."

"I trust Jack to be discreet, Auntie Jane. And I trust in my ability to shield him if he isn't. And I'd very much appreciate it if you'd place a little trust in my ability as well." Charlie snapped the phone closed. It had been over a decade since she'd played right field for the Darsden East high school softball team, but standing on the end of the pier watching her phone sink, she figured she'd made the cutoff man.

*   *   *

"As you can see," Mark announced from the middle of the bench seat as Tim eased the van onto the Mabou causeway behind an enormous trailer with Massachusetts plates, "we're not talking a major metropolitan area. Not even for the island. Not much more than four hundred people call this little piece of maritime paradise home, but it's big-time Gaelic around here, Chuck. Big-time Gaelic. Lots of music lovers. Four-day ceilidh back in July where we kicked ass in a major sort of way even though it wasn't one of the Samhradh Ceol stages so, Christ, I hope we didn't spend it all there. Thank God we're not playing until after six—it's going to be hotter than Tim's ass today."

Shoved up against the passenger window, Charlie ducked as he pulled an elastic from his wrist and tied his hair up high off the back of his neck, nearly elbowing her in the ear and exposing the darker circles under the arms of his *world's greatest grandma* T-shirt.

"And," he continued, the hand back on Tim's thigh doing nothing to keep him from pushing her even farther into the door as they turned left onto the harbor road, "there's ceilidhs every Tuesday at the community center plus a theater slash performing arts center plus a pub owned by the Rankins, so you know what that means."

"A local crowd who knows what it's listening to," Charlie grunted, shoving him back upright. This might be her first run around this particular festival circuit, but some things were a given; an enthusiastic reaction from a crowd of tourists who couldn't tell the "Gay Gordons" from a "Dashing White Sergeant" could influence where the nine unknown judges placed their points.

Just past Larche Way, Tim turned left again into the gravel road that led down to the *Rest and be Thankful Cottages, Campground, and Trailer Sites*.

Charlie reached past Mark and poked Tim in the bare shoulder. "We're in number ten."

"Number ten?" Mark repeated, dipping his head and staring at her over the edge of his sunglasses. "Seriously?"

"That's what she said when I called." Charlie barely waited until Tim stopped in front of a large clapboard building with a wraparound porch and a view of the water before unbuckling her seat belt and getting out of the van. "You were right," she called into the car at Bo as Shelly pulled up beside them.

Bo grinned as he got out and stretched. "Come on, it was less than twenty minutes? You got off easy. Last summer, Dundee to Dingwall, he didn't shut up once."

"We're in number ten." Shelly rubbed a can of soda over her stomach as she came around the front of the car. "That's . . ."

"I told you I made reservations the moment I heard!" Mark crowed from the porch.

Beer cooler balanced on his shoulder, Tim followed him inside.

Case in hand, Bo had a foot on the stone steps when a burst of fiddle music stopped him cold. When a second fiddle answered the first, he turned and ran for the next cottage.

"Bo?"

He half turned and waved. "They just stuffed 'Pretty Peggy' into freakin' Mendelssohn!"

"That sounds kinky," Charlie said as he disappeared.

"Fiddlers," Shelly observed as though that was explanation enough. She popped open the can of soda and took a long drink. "The cottages are assigned to the bands on a first-come, first-served basis. Call early: enjoy two bedrooms, a large kitchen/living room, a view of the water from the wraparound porch, and a shower big enough to share with friends. Call late and cram the band into one rustic room with a shower slightly less wide than my shoulders that'll try to electrocute you if you touch the showerhead while wet. Aston licked it on a dare last summer, nearly melted his fillings."

"Aston is an idiot."

"I'm not arguing, but that's not my point." Shelly waved the can at number ten. "The universe doesn't like anyone this much. What did you do?"

Charlie shrugged, bumped her shoulder into Shelly's, and quickly traced a small charm on the small of the other woman's back, her fingertip skating over fine hairs and sweat slick skin. "I just got lucky."

"Okay, then."

In the next cottage, the fiddles slid out of Mendelssohn and into something wilder that lifted the hair off the back of Charlie's neck.

The shower worked off a flash heater, so everyone got hot water. Charlie would've charmed it but was just as glad she didn't have to. Gales had better luck with sand in places sand shouldn't go than most people but salt water was salt water and she felt significantly better scrubbed and shampooed.

By the time she emerged, wearing clean shorts over her bathing suit, Shelly had flaked out on one of the twin beds in the room they'd claimed up under the eaves and Mark and Tim were arguing over whose turn it was to make lunch. Charlie could no longer hear music coming from the cottage next door—although she *could* hear music coming from all over the property, not only from the cottages but also the crowded campground and the slightly less crowded trailer park. Bagpipes, accordions, guitars, banjos, drums, a lone trumpet, and through and around them all, the fiddlers, pulling the friendlier tunes together and building walls of sound to keep the antagonistic apart. Music was the whole point of the weekend and the ten bands in the Samhradh Ceol Feill only a small part of a much larger whole.

Heading out to catch a breeze on the porch, Charlie paused, one hand flat against the wooden frame of the screen door. Head cocked, she sifted through the sounds of a hundred or so people settling in, touched the bit of melody that had caught her attention, then lost it again as one of the pipers started up a medley of television theme songs.

"Hey! 'Meet the Flintstones!'" Mark pushed past her, grabbing his bodhran out of the van, closely followed by Tim who scooped up the smallest of his three accordions

"There are times," Charlie sighed stepping out onto the porch, "when playing cowboy covers in Fort McMurray looks like it might have been the better choice."

The music she'd almost heard had been passionate and unrestrained. She couldn't have held it, but she could have laid down a harmony that would have led her along new paths through the wild ways. Paths drenched in salt spray and slippery with . . . well, with that green crap that grew along the rocks down by the shore. She had no idea what it was called.

Mark and Tim had left the van's side door open, so she wandered down and slid her guitar off the stacked drum kit. With half a mind to join the jam—and given that they'd segued into a rousing rendition of the old *Animaniacs* theme, half a mind seemed to be what was required for this particular jam—she turned and caught sight of Bo and a young woman by the water's edge. Her long dark hair had been pulled back into a haphazard ponytail and in spite of the heat she wore a sweater, the sleeves stretched down over her hands. Even at a distance, she was visibly upset and Bo looked lost. Body language had essentially erected a neon sign over his head saying *HELP ME!*

"So, do I help?" Charlie wondered.

As she watched, the young woman threw herself into Bo's arms. When he caught her, the edges of the sound she made lifted the hair off the back of Charlie's neck.

"I heard them at night. Wailing."

Hurrying toward the water, Charlie thought she heard the music again. Then realized it was the cry of a gull. The waves on the shore. As she set foot on the beach, she saw three women, long dark hair whipped about by the wind, approaching from the other direction. All three were dressed for the heat; one wore an orange muslin skirt and a bathing-suit top, the other two were in shorts and tanks.

The tallest of the three looked familiar, Charlie had seen her in the audience at Port Hood and then on another bit of beach in the moonlight. As they drew closer, her eyes were black from lid to lid.

Then she blinked and they were merely dark eyes just a little too large for her face surrounded by long, thick lashes under a sable arc of brow and over a generous curve of mouth. She was the most beautiful woman Charlie had ever seen.

Except, of course, that she wasn't a woman at all. Well, a woman, yes, all three of them were women—all four of them Charlie amended, glancing over at the girl weeping in Bo's arms—but they weren't Human women.

It was hard to breathe. The music filled every space in Charlie's chest, leaving no room for anything as mundane as oxygen, barely leaving her heart room to beat. The tune sounded like "Mary's Fancy," a reel in A, played on a single fiddle. "Am I the only one who can hear that?"

The three women looked confused.

It was probably someone playing up in the campsites. "Never mind."

The other two women held back, their eyes locked on Charlie's face, but *she* stepped forward, graceful in spite of the way her bare feet sank into the sand.

"I know what you are, Wild One," she said after a long moment.

Charlie sighed. "You're completely straight, aren't you?"

"Tanis, baby . . ." Bo sounded a short hop from hysteria himself. ". . . please stop crying."

*   *   *

"All right, Shelly's out until I wake her." The weight of accumulated re-
gard stopped Charlie three steps from the bottom of the stairs. Bo and Tanis
staring up at her from the big armchair, Morag and Aisling, Tanis' sisters, sitting on the sofa on either side of Eineen who looked just as gorgeous inside
as she had on the beach. She had broad swimmer's shoulders and lithe,
smoothly muscled arms. Her breasts were small and perfectly formed under
the dark purple tank top, without a bra to . . .

"Charlie?"

"Right. What?"

Bo rolled his eyes. "Shelly?"

"Shelly? Oh, right." She spread her hands. "It's just a charm. It's perfectly
harmless."

"A charm?" Tightening his grip on Tanis, Bo frowned up at her. "What
the hell does that even mean?"

"It means she believes her decisions take precedent over Shelly's choices."

"Yes, I do." Charlie smiled at Morag, continued descending the stairs, and
dropped into the old padded rocker, draping one leg over the arm. "And, in
this instance, so do you, so let's skip the part where you try to set me up as
one of the bad guys and move onto the part where we try to get Tanis' skin
back."

The silence in the room was so complete Charlie could hear the sand
falling off her bare foot as it whispered against the pine floor.

Bo inhaled noisily and said, "Okay, I swear I didn't say anything."

Eineen raised a slender hand and pushed dark hair back off her face. "It
would be easier without him."

"Probably," Charlie agreed—as much because she actually did agree as
because Eineen had said it. "I can . . ."

"No!" Tanis lifted her face from Bo's chest and twisted just far enough
to glare around the room. "I need him! I want him here. I'll speak for his
discretion."

"*You* are not thinking clearly and as long as you are not thinking clearly,
you cannot guarantee the behavior of your man." Eineen turned to Charlie.
"Can you speak for him?"

"Me?"

"You play with him. A band is a family of a sort."

"Of a sort," Charlie agreed, "but we've only known each other since Wednesday."

"It's not like you need a lot of time," Aisling pointed out.

Charlie thought of the old man on the beach and smiled. True.

"And you know his music," Morag added.

Also true.

"All right, I'll speak for him."

All four women looked like they were in their mid-twenties, but Charlie, who knew damned well they were considerably older, couldn't tell their actual ages. Behavior put Eineen as the eldest and Tanis as the youngest. Case in point, it was Eineen who nodded and said, "Then start at the beginning and tell us how you knew Tanis' skin was missing."

"So not the beginning," Bo muttered, shifting Tanis to a dry spot on his T-shirt.

Charlie snorted. "Valid observation. But once I knew what Tanis was, and noted the level of hysteria . . ."

Tanis sniffed.

". . . what she'd lost was pretty damned obvious."

"Not lost." When Eineen shook her head, her hair rippled across the bare skin of her arms and shoulders like waves. "Stolen. And not the only one. As of last night, three others are gone."

"So I guess it's true. They are trying to start up the seal hunt again . . ." Eineen's glare made Charlie sit up straight and put both feet on the floor. "Okay, not funny. Sorry. You're sure it was stolen?"

"They left a note," Morag growled.

"Ransom?"

"Blackmail," Aisling snarled. "If you want it back, start supporting Carlson Oil's shallow water well just off Scatarie Island. Scatarie is a nature reserve, and Hay Island, right by the proposed well, is a seal sanctuary."

There was a nearly audible thud as the final piece dropped into place.

"Subtle," Charlie sighed.

"Yeah, not really." Morag echoed Charlie's sigh.

Not what Charlie'd meant, but since it was an equally valid observation, she let it stand.

"Our family are environmental activists," Eineen told her. "Since before your people knew what that meant, we've been doing what we can to lessen the damage Humans do to our habitat."

"And the waters off Scatarie have already been damaged," Morag broke in. "Ever since their test ships were out there doing seismic soundings and stuff, things have been weird. The seabed has shifted . . ."

"Okay, not much," Aisling interrupted. "But the water temperature has dropped four degrees and there's about six square meters of sea floor with nothing living on it. Not a crab, not an urchin, not lichen. Nothing."

"If a sounding can change things that much, what's a well going to do?" Morag demanded, eyes flashing black. "We have to stop it."

"We work in the traditional ways . . ." Eineen seemed calmer, but Charlie could hear the anger behind her words. ". . . informing public opinion, making legal challenges, but we find that if we can speak directly to the law-makers, we can . . ." Her lips curled into the semblance of a smile. ". . . ease them around to our way of thinking."

Charlie glanced over at Bo. He had his cheek resting on the top of Tanis' head, both arms wrapped around her. They had his attention, or as much of it as he was able to detach from the woman in his arms, but it didn't look as though he'd caught on to what Eineen had actually meant. Fiddlers. They didn't listen to the lyrics. It wasn't Charlie's place to fill him in. He'd only doubt his feelings and, besides, it wasn't like the Gales didn't do the same thing. Except that the aunties didn't so much *ease* as terrify.

And speaking of terrified. . . .

"Bo, do you know what Tanis is?"

"Hello, I play the fiddle in a Celtic band. Celtic-ish," he amended, kissing Tanis' hair. "'The Great Selkie' is on today's set list. You're singing it."

"Right." Charlie made a mental note to look up the lyrics before they hit the stage. "You told me you two haven't been going out for long, but you seem remarkably cool about this whole missing sealskin thing. Not cool about it being missing," she added quickly, "but about it being a sealskin. And Tanis being a Selkie."

He shrugged as well as he was able, given his position. "That doesn't matter. From the moment I saw her dancing in the moonlight, she was my whole life. Why should I care about unimportant details when I have her?"

"And I have you!" Tanis twisted in his arms and claimed his mouth.

"Oh, barf," muttered someone from the sofa.

"Good defense mechanism," Charlie drawled as the kiss continued, shifting her attention back to Eineen. "True love trumps the unexpected, the unexplained, and, I'm guessing, flippers."

Eineen spread her hands, the webbing briefly visible. Charlie couldn't help thinking it was the sexiest webbing she'd ever seen. "Once they have accepted us, it becomes easier for them to accept other . . . oddities."

"Oh, that's . . ." Charlie cocked her head, trying to figure out where "O, She's Comical" was coming from. Bo was the only fiddler in the room, and he was most definitely not playing—although Charlie couldn't see his left hand, so she wouldn't swear it wasn't on his instrument. If the music wasn't being played inside the cottage and it wasn't coming from outside the cottage . . . "Can anyone else hear a reel, in A? Anyone? Bueller? No?"

"If you're hearing things," Eineen began.

Charlie cut her off. "Then I'm meant to hear them. That's how we roll. Moving on." She had a fiddler in her head. Who seemed to be doing editorial commentary. That was . . . okay, that was odd. "So someone at Carlson Oil knows what you are and is using that to keep you from stopping them. The way I see it, you have two options. One, leave them to it and move. Give them free access to what they want and get your skins back. There can't be that many of you on this side."

"Some of us have children."

"Yeah, but . . ." Eineen raised a perfect brow and Charlie actually thought about it for a moment. Selkies had two forms. "Okay." She glanced at Bo again and left it at that. She didn't really want to find the point where the Selkie defense mellow gave way to irrational Human squeamishness. "Okay, then, option two. You get your skins back."

"Duh." Morag snorted.

Granted out of the water, the Selkies didn't exactly have a lot of offense. *Give us our skins back, or we'll stand around the waterfront looking gorgeous.* Unless they could arrange a one-on-one in the moonlight with someone who knew where the skins were, there wasn't much they could do.

Aisling tucked her legs under her at an impossible angle. "They're being taken from places Humans couldn't get into."

"Then maybe Carlson Oil has made a deal with other Fey. It's not like you lot all get along."

"You think we don't defend against that?" Eineen sneered. "We came here because of the infighting in the Courts."

They were waiting for her to say she'd help. But the Gales didn't get involved with the business of the Fey unless they involved themselves first in family matters.

Except for Allie. And that had turned out to be a family matter in the end.

"I have a proposition for you. Meet me in Halifax and we'll talk."

Oh, crap.

FIVE

A S MARK'S DRUM INTRO finished up and Tim took them into Brian McNeill's "Best o' the Barley" on his big, forty-five key piano accordion, Charlie stepped downstage, threw in a little mandolin ornamentation, and tried to decide if she was out of her mind. Auntie Catherine had always been considered one of the more unpredictable of the aunties by the younger generations and "unpredictable auntie" wasn't a comforting sort of phrase. Much the same way "I've never seen a rash quite like that" wasn't a comforting sort of a phrase.

Auntie Catherine embraced the Wild in Wild Power.

When Charlie came into her power the Midsummer she was fifteen and it became obvious she was Wild, Auntie Jane had asked Auntie Catherine, who'd been home for the ritual, if she had any words of advice.

"Live your own life, Charlotte," Auntie Catherine had snorted. *"Don't live the life they tell you to."*

"They?" Charlie asked.

Auntie Catherine sighed. *"I suppose brains as well would have been too much to hope for."*

She walked the Wood and she saw the future, and she'd been strong enough to bear Uncle Edward two daughters.

Uncle Edward.

Now replaced by Uncle Evan.

Charlie wondered if Auntie Catherine had gone home for *that* ritual. Seemed like one she'd enjoy.

She'd strung Allie up like a puppet and danced her across Calgary until Allie was in place to defeat Jack's mother. Her only mistake, not realizing Allie was in place to defeat her as well.

Charlie knew Auntie Catherine was involved with the missing Selkie skins. She knew it the same way she knew "La Bamba" used a I, IV, V, V chord progression. She knew it the way she knew the taste of the soft skin below Allie's ear. She knew it because Auntie Catherine was in Halifax, and four Selkie skins were missing. It wasn't rocket science.

There was always the chance that Auntie Catherine had come to Nova Scotia because she'd Seen the skins were about to be stolen. There was a chance that she was here in order to return the skins to their rightful owners and she wanted Charlie's help. There was a chance the Leafs would win the Stanley Cup, too, although it was an appallingly small chance.

Still a chance.

Like it or not, Charlie would have to talk to her.

As Tim announced that Uncle Jim *never missed a measure of the dance*, she caught back up to wondering if she was out of her mind. And then, as the crowd roared out the final couplet, she remembered she'd thrown her phone off the pier back in Port Hood.

"It's not a bad thing being one of the two bands playing on the Friday night." Mark twirled one of his sticks like a baton, both feet keeping time as four local teenagers kicked the shit out of Ashley McIsaac's "I Don't Need This" up on the festival stage. "Play Friday night and you become the standard all the others are judged by. Of course, you've got to take into account that tonight the judges are fresh and by Sunday it'll be 'fuck it, give me a beer and give them a ten just to get this over with,' but still, we play early and we can concentrate on scooping out the competition."

"Shouldn't that be scoping?"

"Does it matter? I was thinking of using a melon baller."

"Okay, then." Still pleasantly wrung out from their set, Charlie scanned the crowd for Eineen, fully aware that finding one woman amid the dark mass of bodies filling the field in front of the stage was unlikely, bordering on not-going-to-happen. Tanis said she'd stayed, but pretty much from the moment they'd stepped off the stage, Tanis had been attached to Bo at the mouth and so wasn't exactly at her most coherent. At least she wasn't crying. Charlie counted that a win.

If Eineen wanted me the way I want her, there'd be a line of power joining our . . . hearts.

No line of power. No surprise.

"Piper in Albion Rising is American. We ran into him last March down in Texas at the Dog and Duck, and Aston hated him on sight. Guy rocks a kilt almost as well as yours truly. Totally a chick magnet . . ." He grunted as Charlie elbowed him in the ribs. "Total woman magnet," he amended, but Charlie could hear the grin in his voice. "In Aston's tiny little mind, that was the reason he continuously failed to score."

"Was it?"

"Probably had more to do with Aston being a dumbass. Aston being Aston. He called this afternoon, wished us luck, and said you were almost good enough to fill his shoes, so maybe we stood a snowflake's chance in Waa Waa without him. Made so little sense that odds are he was totally looped on painkillers. Not that that's a gimme with Aston."

"Killer ax man, though."

"And if we were a death metal band, that would be relevant, but yeah, he doesn't suck. Neither do you. You're better on the mandolin."

"I know."

"And smarter."

"Hard not to be. He lost two fingers petting a seal."

"He's better looking."

"Bite me."

"Haven't bitten a girl since Jeanie Bennett in third grade. She swung at me with her backpack which, unfortunately, held a hardcover copy of *The Hobbit*. While I was stunned and reeling, she bit me back. If you're really nice to me, I'll show you the scar." Heaving himself up onto his feet, Mark scanned the crowd as he twitched his kilt back into place. "Which reminds me, I need to find Tim and remind him he's doing a workshop tomorrow morning at ten."

"Tim's doing a workshop?" Charlie tilted her head back so she wasn't speaking directly to Mark's sporran. "Seriously?"

"What? He loves kids, and we get points for community involvement.

When you see Shelly, remind her I want us all together around two to go over the new arrangement for 'Wild Road Beyond.' We get a chance to run through it a couple of times and we'll toss it on the set list at the park on Wednesday night and see if anyone salutes."

"You need to stop rewriting that thing."

He grinned as he tucked the drumstick in beside the one already in his hair. "Gets better every time, Chuck."

Charlie watched him walk away until he got lost in the dark and the crowd. A visit to the beer tent was always an option, but she was comfortable on her hillock. Sitting cross-legged with her mandolin tucked safely in the space between her legs and her body, she had a good view of the stage, and . . .

"You're in that bottom of the sea band."

The big guy had moved in quietly for someone so drunk. Charlie hadn't heard him until he'd spoken although, in her own defense, it wasn't exactly a silent night. "*Grinneal,* that's right."

"Heard you play." Three slaps against the logo on his GBS *Courage & Patience & Grit* tour shirt loosened an impressive belch and intensified the eau de brewery surrounding him. "Want me to tell you what you did wrong?"

"Not really."

He stared down at her for a moment, swaying slightly. "Okay, like to begin with . . ."

"Go away."

". . . buddy on the drums, drummer, needs to get a haircut and the other guy . . ."

Turning her mandolin, Charlie ran her fingernail along the E string, catching it just under the edge of the nail. "Seriously, dude . . . Go. A. Way."

As each of the three notes hit him, he jerked slightly back. "So, I'm going away now because I have to take a piss. Why take a piss?" she heard him say as he turned. "Why not leave a piss?"

Not a bad question, actually.

"Are you Charlie?" The girl was about nine or ten and the boy with her, with the same dark eyes and hair dark enough for the moon to paint on silver highlights, was likely a year or so older. "Our mum says Eineen says we should give you this."

There, on the palm of her hand, was Charlie's phone.

Charlie looked past them but could spot neither mum nor Eineen. She could, however, hear very faintly behind the noise of the kids on stage and the distinctly less melodic noise of the crowd yelling the lyrics back to them, a familiar melody that dove from the surface to the depths where bones lay white on the seabed. The hair lifted off the back of her neck; she might not be able to see them, but there were adults watching. These children were as protected as any Gale child.

The fiddler in her head returned with "Ma, Ma, Come Let's Dance."

Charlie leaned a little closer to the kids. "Do you hear fiddle music?"

The boy pointed toward the stage.

"Right. So, where did your mum find my phone?"

The girl shrugged skinny shoulders. "Mum says Aunt Roswen found it." She drew her hand back when Charlie took the phone, showing a crescent of webbing between her thumb and forefinger. Charlie wondered if it had been Aunt Roswen she'd run into during her swim.

"Thank you."

They glanced at each other, had the kind of silent conversation Charlie remembered from when her twin sisters were small, then turned and ran.

The phone looked none the worse for its adventure, but then, it never did. It rang as Charlie slid it into her pocket. Allie's ring.

Allie skipped right past hello. "Oh, good, you're still awake!"

"It's a three-hour time difference, Allie-cat; it's only nine forty. What's up?"

"It's Jack . . ."

Right. Jack. Charlie made a mental note to quit throwing away her phone until after Jack landed in Halifax. It suddenly occurred to her that given how crowded the van and Shelly's car already were, they were going to need a bigger vehicle. Or another vehicle. Maybe a motorcycle. She could hear the roar of the engine nearly drowning out the classic rock soundtrack. The Cabot Trail on a bike would be amazing . . . except Jack carried a lot of metaphysical weight, and if he shifted that on the back of a bike, results would be spelled splat. Of course, he could always ride with the band while she . . .

"Charlie!"

"What do you think about Jack on the back of a motorcycle?"

"Ask me what I think about you on the front of a motorcycle."

"Okay . . ."

"You're too easily distracted. You'd see something shiny and game over."

Charlie traced a charm over a mosquito bite on her ankle. "You sound like your mother."

"Thank you. And speaking of transportation, we got Jack a plane ticket for the third. He's got a three hour layover in Toronto and . . ."

"Why?"

"Because that's what kept coming up," Allie answered pointedly. "Auntie Jane has offered to go and sit with him."

"Auntie Jane wants to talk to him."

"Duh."

The aunties considered airport security to be an indignity other people were forced to endure. As a plane carrying an auntie would be the safest plane in the sky, skipping the grope and grab was significantly safer for the airport employees. "Wait, this is the 29th. Why wait until the third? He's not old enough for ritual, so there's no point in keeping him over the 2nd."

"Yes, but Calgary has police helicopters . . ." Allie's tone suggested Charlie should have remembered that because of course Charlie kept track of security concerns in a city thousands of kilometers away. ". . . and we have only three aunties, all of whom will have their hands full of David. I want to keep Jack around for air support. I also want you to make sure he knows exactly what that means because Auntie Bea keeps getting all nostalgic about the Ka-32 Helix."

"The what?"

"It's a Russian helicopter."

"I don't think I want to know," Charlie muttered. And speaking of not knowing, should she tell Allie about the missing skins and her grandmother's possible involvement? No. Not until Auntie Catherine had a chance to mislead and manipulate in her own defense. Charlie'd be seeing Allie on the 2nd—it was a travel day for the band and there'd never really been much chance of her going to the ritual in Ontario—and she could tell her everything then.

"Charlie?"

"Sorry. Got a lot going on." Right on cue, the teenagers finished up to a roar of approval. "I'll see you Tuesday."

"Sure." She could hear Allie smile. "Go wild."

"Go Flames!"

"What?"

"Not important. See you Tuesday."

Her phone blipped as a pair of texts came in from the twins.

Tell mom 2 back off!

Stop tossing ur fcking phone!

Dealing with Auntie Catherine suddenly seemed like the lesser of two evils. Unfortunately, the call went straight to voice mail. "Hey, it's Charlie. We need to talk."

Short and sweet.

Nothing Auntie Catherine could use either as warning or threat.

The beer tent, however, was looking appealing.

Saturday morning, Charlie wandered out onto the front porch while Tim was making pancakes to find Eineen waiting for her with a slender, dark-eyed, dark-haired woman. This new woman was obviously family and apparently about ten years older—except Charlie could see the frayed edges of the glamour wrapped around her and the desperation the glamour didn't hide.

"This is Neela," Eineen announced.

"Yeah, and good morning to you two, too." Yawning, Charlie dropped into one of the Adirondack chairs and waved a hand in Neela's general direction. "Hers is one of the missing . . ."

"Yes." The wind off the water danced Eineen's hair around her head like it had been animated by Disney. Neela wore hers in a braid. A braid like Eineen had worn the first time Charlie had seen her, more beautiful than any other woman in the crowd of . . . "You said you might have a place to start looking." Eineen's voice snapped Charlie out of her reverie.

There'd been no promises made. Never were when there was an auntie involved. "I'm waiting for a phone call."

Eineen's right eyebrow rose—like the slender wing of black gull. Charlie couldn't seem to stop the overwrought description from popping into her head. Did gulls even come in black?

"A phone call. That's all?" Dark eyes narrowed. "Yesterday, you gave us a moment of hope, and now . . ."

Charlie'd had dark eyes narrowed at her for her entire life. The effect had worn thin. "And now, I'm waiting for a phone call. All I have are suspicions, I told you that yesterday. Neela, I hope you're not here because you thought I'd have found your . . ." She glanced over her shoulder at the screen door. About six feet on the other side of it, Mark was demanding Tim make at least some of the pancakes with chocolate chips. " . . . thing."

"No." Neela hugged her torso, hands wrapped around her elbows, the webbing between the fingers only visible because Charlie was looking for it. "I'm here because doing anything is better than doing nothing. And because I was here anyway; I'm married to Gavin Fitzgerald."

"Gavin Fitzgerald, the fiddler from Five on the Floor?" Five was one of the festival bands and Gavin was pushing fifty, so that explained the glamour—like Joe and Auntie Gwen, Neela had aged up. That she could easily be a few thousand years older than Gavin was moot. "Another fiddler? I thought your people usually hooked up with fishermen?"

Neela shrugged, the movement graceful in spite of her defensive position. "Not many working fishermen around these days, but you can't throw a rock on this island without hitting a fiddler. A lot of them play down on the shore. They're very . . ." Her mouth twitched, not quite managing a smile. ". . . alluring."

"Does he know?"

She nodded. "A marriage based on lies isn't likely to last."

The Gales had tried it both ways, but non-Gales who could cope with the family dynamic were rare on the ground. Auntie Ruby muttering *there's always the corn* tended to put a few off.

And speaking of the corn. "Traditionally, when your things go missing . . ."

"Gavin didn't take it. It was Carlson Oil." Neela slid a hand into the back pocket of her faded jeans and handed over a piece of plan white printer paper folded into quarters.

It had clearly been unfolded and folded again a number of times. The paper was slightly damp and the creases had softened. "*Support the well on Hay Island,*" Charlie read, "*and your skin will be returned when the wellhead is in place.* Yeah, that's pretty definitive." The writing had been done with a fine tip marker. Charlie rummaged through pockets in her shorts, found three guitar picks, an orange lollipop condom she had no memory of acquiring, and a piece of chewed gum wrapped in torn tissue, but nothing to write with.

Laziness being the mother of invention, she licked a charm over the writing, careful to stay away from the edges and potential paper cuts.

Auntie Catherine hadn't actually written the note. Which meant nothing at all. An auntie could get a perfect stranger to support the arts; convincing one to write a note wouldn't be a problem.

"It tastes like . . ."

"Alcohol? Dyes?"

"Formaldehyde?"

"No, it . . ." Charlie glanced up from the smeared ink and twisted around to stare at Mark who was standing on the other side of the screen. "Formaldehyde?"

"I heard they used it in some inks. You here for breakfast, Neela? Tim's made his magic pancakes."

"No, thanks, Mark."

Actually, it figured they knew each other.

"I left the kids with Harry," Neela continued, fighting so hard to make her voice sound normal it sounded as though it was about to shatter under the strain. "I need to get back before they all get matching tattoos and someone calls Children's Aid. We're in number four if you want to come by later." That to Charlie as much as Mark.

"The whole band?"

"Gavin and I brought the RV."

Mark stared at her for a long moment, then stepped out onto the porch. "Everything okay?"

Her smile had the same tattered edges as the glamour. "Not really, no."

"Can I help?"

"Not really, no."

Charlie could feel Mark's gaze against the top of her head. Finally, he sighed, shifted his attention to Neela's companion, and said, "So what about you . . ."

"Eineen," Charlie filled in wondering if Eineen did anything as mundane as eat pancakes.

". . . he's made blueberry *and* chocolate chip."

Cod flavored, maybe.

"Thank you, no." Eineen inclined her head and Charlie found herself mesmerized by the curve of her neck. "Come, cousin, I'll walk you home."

When Charlie held out the paper—the message smeared and feathering into the path of saliva—Neela shook her head. "You keep it."

They'd disappeared behind a clump of trees when Mark smacked her on the side of the head. "Come on, Chuck, there's pancakes calling our names."

Pancakes that contained nothing but calories. That sounded like a good idea to her.

"Your tongue is blue," he said as she wrestled gravity to get out of the chair. And, being Mark, he never asked why she'd licked a piece of paper in the first place.

At noon, when Auntie Catherine still hadn't called, Charlie called Allie.

"I haven't spoken to her since I ordered her away. Over a year ago." She still sounded angry. No one held a grudge like a Gale girl. To be strictly accurate, Charlie amended, no one held a grudge like Alysha Gale. "Why do you want to talk to her?"

"Because Auntie Catherine wanted me to meet her in Halifax, so she's here in Nova Scotia, and she might be screwing over some . . ." Not friends, however close Charlie wanted to get to Eineen. " . . . people I know."

"She's a vicious, manipulative harridan!"

"Yeah, I kno . . ." Wait . . . harridan? "She's a what?"

"She's a bitch, Charlie."

"Not arguing, but she's still your grandmother, and you know she'll answer if she sees it's you. You don't have to make nice, just ask her to call me." In the distance, over the sound of bands rehearsing and people packing cars to head over to the festival grounds, a single fiddler played the gentle roll of summer waves, the curl as they crested, and the white foam dancing over blue-green as they lapped against the shore. An actual fiddler, not an imaginary fiddler in her head. Charlie found that reassuring. "It's important, Allie, or I wouldn't ask."

After a long moment, Allie sighed. "Be careful."

*　　　*　　　*

At twelve seventeen, "Ride of the Valkyries."

"So, Charlotte, it seems I have you to thank for my granddaughter finally climbing down off her high horse and calling me. What can I do for you?"

"Why did you want me to meet you in Halifax, Auntie Catherine?"

"I wanted to talk to you."

"What about?"

"If I was willing to do it over the phone, Charlotte, I would have done so then. Join me for lunch and we'll talk."

Mark wanted the band together at two, so she had time. "Fine. Where are you?"

Even over the phone she could feel the edges on Auntie Catherine's smile. "Find me."

"The Trippers" followed her to the Wood but not into it, her fiddler falling silent in under the trees. Charlie folded her hands on top of her guitar, well away from the strings, calmed her breathing, and listened. Allie had been her touchstone since her third trip in; fifteen and cocky and completely lost with the Wood shifting into shadow around her, she'd followed the younger girl's song home. Now she dialed Allie's song back until it was no more than the faintest whisper drifting between the birches, the family harmonies rising to dominate. There, Auntie Jane, nearly Sousa. Her mother's gentle rise and fall. The twins' techno wail, threatening to escape but never quite making it out. Auntie Ruby's dissonant intervals that still worked in the context of the family melody. Under it all, Uncle Evan's steady bass. One by one, she let them drop out until only the aunties were left and then she began sifting through the layers until, of the aunties, only Auntie Catherine remained.

At twelve twenty, Charlie pushed aside a masking branch on an enormous weeping birch and stepped out into the Halifax Public Gardens. Shrugging out of her gig bag, she stowed her guitar and walked toward Spring Garden Road.

It took a moment for her eyes to readjust to the sun when she emerged out onto the rooftop patio at *Your Father's Mustache,* but when she finally blinked away the flares, she saw Auntie Catherine smiling up at a gorgeous young man with a brilliant white smile and broad shoulders that strained against the fabric of his uniform T-shirt. Although she assumed she'd be unnoticed until she reached the table, given the scenery, she'd barely moved a meter before Auntie Catherine glanced up and beckoned her over, silver bracelets chiming.

"Charlotte, so glad you could make it. This is Frank. He'll be our waiter."

He'll be our waiter sounded an awful lot like *he'll be our lunch.*

"Good luck," Charlie murmured as she passed him, set her gig bag next to the latticework railing, and slid into a seat.

"Frank says the lobster roll is to die for."

"I'm sure." Charlie shot a less predatory smile at him. "But I'm working the festival circuit out on the island and lobster rolls are thick on the ground. Can I get the mushroom and swiss burger, on the rare side of medium rare, with a garden salad—I know, two-fifty extra—roasted red pepper and Parmesan dressing, and an iced tea, please. I've done a lot of studio work in Halifax," she added as Auntie Catherine's lip began to curl. "This is not my first rodeo." The lip curled higher. "Sorry. Leftover cowboy shi . . . thing. I've been here before. I've played here before. Downstairs in the pub."

"Of course. It suits you."

Charlie attempted to work out if that was an insult as Auntie Catherine ordered an asparagus crepe, flustering Frank so badly by discussing the firmness she required in her asparagus—with accompanying hand gestures—that when he turned back to Charlie, she could see his blush even given the darkness of his skin.

"We don't actually have iced tea . . ."

"Not usually, but check the kitchen; you've got some today. However . . ." She raised a hand to cut off his protest. He had no way of knowing that if a Gale wanted iced tea, a Gale got iced tea. ". . . if you check, and I'm wrong, I'll have a ginger ale."

Frank backed away from the table before he turned. Credit where credit was due, he had a great ass.

"Evidently not his first rodeo either," Charlie observed. "So . . ."

Auntie Catherine's raised hand cut her off. "Not yet, dear. Now, we appreciate the view from this angle. Appreciate . . . Appreciate . . ." A sweeping gesture sped Frank on his way as he disappeared down the stairs. "You were saying?"

Charlie'd intended to slide sideways into the conversation, but the pause for Frank had given her time to reconsider. If Auntie Catherine appreciated it so much, why not be, well, frank. Charlie pushed her chair a little farther out, crossed her legs, tugged a fold out of her cargo pants, and said, "So, are you stealing Selkie skins in order to force them to support Carlson Oil drilling off Hay Island?"

Auntie Catherine blinked and Charlie gave herself a mental high five for coloring outside the lines. Oh, sure, any auntie could fold a simple yes or no question into shapes an origami master would envy, but points for throwing her off her game.

Momentarily.

Dark eyes gleaming, Auntie Catherine stroked the end of her braid, and said, "Yes."

"Yes?"

"Yes, I am stealing Selkie skins in order to get them to support Carlson Oil drilling off Hay Island."

"Okay, then." Down on Summer Garden Road, someone hit their horn. Under cover of the noise, Charlie gathered her thoughts. Thought. "Why?"

"Because they're paying me." Dropping her braid on her lap, her hair looking more like white gold than silver in the sun, she grinned. "In fact, they're paying me a great deal. As you'll recall, I handed my business over to Alysha so, as I don't want to return home, a sentiment I'm sure you understand, I needed an alternative income stream."

"An alternative . . ." Hands flat on the table, Charlie leaned forward and snarled, "The Selkies are pretty fucking upset!"

"That's the point, Charlotte. You can't blackmail someone with the potential loss of something they don't care about, now can you?"

"And that's not *my* point, Auntie Catherine. They're upset. Hysterical. Unhappy."

"Good, that was the intention. But why do you care? They're not family, they're Fey. This isn't even their world."

"I care because this is affecting the band and the band is a family, a type of family," she amended as Auntie Catherine's eyes narrowed. "And I'll be damned if I let you just fuck them over!"

"Yes, quite probably. Oh, look, they did have iced tea after all . . ."

The faked surprise set Charlie's teeth on edge. She stared down at her placemat until Frank was gone—poor bastard didn't need to deal with her mood as well as Auntie Catherine's salacious interest—then kept her eyes on the wet ring marking the table as she drained half the glass and took a deep breath. She'd been expecting jazz, each of them trying to lead the other through complex signatures. What she got was the big bass drum in the marching band. Bam. Bam. Bam. *Yes. I. Did.*

When she looked up, dark eyes were watching her with amusement. "When you called, when I was in Calgary, why did you want me to come to Halifax?

"I felt sorry for you."

"Well, I wouldn't help you . . . what?"

"You'd been domesticated." Auntie Catherine smiled an aspartame smile, likely to turn to formaldehyde at any moment. "You still believed yourself a wild child with your hair a dozen different, brilliant colors, but my grand-daughter would play out the leash, give you the illusion of freedom, and then tug you back to her side."

"I came back willingly . . ."

"I know, dear. And I'm not blaming you. After all, I designed my grand-daughter to be strong enough to defeat the Dragon Queen. It's no surprise you can't stand against her."

"And yet here I am."

"Here you are." And there was the formaldehyde. "Still wasting your potential."

"Because I'm not working with you?"

"Because you're dragging that guitar . . ."

Charlie reached back to touch the gig bag. "I'm a musician!"

"My point, exactly. You think you're a musician." She held up a hand for silence as Frank brought their orders, cut the end of her crepe off with the side of her fork, moaned around the mouthful of food and purred, "Exactly firm enough."

"Forget working for Carlson Oil," Charlie muttered, spearing a cherry tomato. "You should try porn."

"What, again?"

*   *   *

Charlie followed Mark's song back to Mabou, stepped out of the stand of Norfolk pines protecting the line of cottages from the north wind, and came face-to-face with Eineen. Literally, face-to-face. Their noses no more than a centimeter apart. Her breath smelled slightly salty and her lips, parted just enough to show the edges of perfect teeth, were slightly chapped. Charlie fought the urge to lean just a little closer and taste, taking the chance she'd probably never be offered again.

Two things stopped her.

One, she didn't want to be that girl.

Two, many of the Human-seeming Fey were significantly stronger than they looked. Charlie had no idea if the Selkies fell into that category and had no intention of finding out as a result of pissing Eineen off. As much as she wanted to know how Eineen's mouth would feel under hers, she was against pain on principle. Pain hurt.

"I was waiting for you to return."

"Yeah." Charlie took a step back, smacked herself in the head with a tree branch, and jerked forward, leaving a clump of hair attached to a gob of pine gum. "Ow! God fucking damn it! Yeah, I got that! What do you want?"

"You said you were waiting for a phone call."

"She called. And then we had lunch." Eyes watering, she rubbed the back of her head. "And—oh, joy—Auntie Catherine is stealing your skins to force your people to support Carlson Oil."

"That's more than we knew. We can use that to try and stop this."

Charlie figured *we* in that instance didn't involve her. She reached out and grabbed Eineen's arm as the Selkie turned. "What part of auntie were you missing there, babe? This is work for hire right now; it's nothing personal . . ."

"It's very . . ."

"On her part," Charlie cut Eineen's protest short. "And believe me, you don't want to piss her off."

"And yet, we can't leave things as they are."

"No, we can't."

Eineen stared at her for a long moment, long enough to realize the definition of *we* had changed. "So, what do we do?"

You think you're a musician.

It was nothing personal as far as the Selkies were concerned. Charlie, personally, was hoping she'd piss Auntie Catherine off to the point of spontaneous combustion. "We stop her."

"How?"

Realizing she'd been hanging onto Eineen's arm maybe a little too long, Charlie let go and started for the cottage. "First, we find out how she's getting to the skins, and we block her from getting any more." Eineen fell into step beside her. "Then we find the skins she's already taken, and we take them back. Or I will."

"So easy."

Okay, she did not deserve that level of sarcasm. "Not really. While I'm doing that, you and your people will pretend to play along so that Carlson Oil doesn't up the stakes because it's one small step from Auntie Catherine to nuking you from orbit and letting the gods sort things out."

The campsite was strangely quiet, or their footsteps as they reached the access road were strangely loud.

"I assume your auntie is getting to the pelts by . . ." Eineen waved both hands in random patterns.

"Semaphore?" Charlie guessed. "ASL? Wet nail polish?"

"Magic."

"Can't think why you'd believe that." At the far end of the road, down by cottage number one, two fiddlers were in an argument so intense, even at a distance, it looked as though their bows were about to be used as swords. "If we're going to find out how Auntie Catherine is doing it, I need to examine the crime scenes."

"UnderRealm CSI?" When Charlie turned to look, Eineen gave a soft bark of laughter. "What? I watch television. We should start in Neela's RV."

Charlie stepped over a Nerf crossbow as she stepped up into the trailer, pushed a half dozen tiny cars out of the way with her foot, and had to slide sideways as Eineen followed her in to keep from knocking a stack of dirty dishes into the tiny sink. The bed over the "sofa" hadn't been made, the tangle of sheets sprinkled with plastic building blocks. About four meters of orange track spilled down from the double bed up over the cab.

Seals and fiddlers. Not the best housekeepers in the worlds.

Eineen pointed past her shoulder. "Keep going back that way."

To the left, wet bathing suits had been piled in the bottom of the shower. To the right, a headless doll sprawled on the closed toilet seat like the crime scene for the latest hooker decapitation. Charlie had no idea why those dolls were so popular.

The hunter-green striped wallpaper and the burgundy carpet suggested the rear bedroom had been decorated in the early '90s. An empty violin case shared the unmade bed with piles of clothes and there were two closed cases stacked on the dresser—the lower one held together by strategically applied duct tape. There were no visible charms.

"Neela's was the first skin to go missing."

"How could she tell?" Charlie muttered, lifting a stack of sheet music off the dresser and steadying a trembling tower of DVD cases with her elbow as she scanned the newly exposed artificial walnut wood grain finish for charms. She sketched a quick charm of her own on the top case to prevent disaster before she lifted the DVDs.

"We always know where we put our skins." Eineen reached past her, brushing warm against Charlie's arm. "We keep them on us if we're walking around in daylight and somewhere safe if we're spending the night ashore."

"And Neela was spending every night ashore."

"Neela had a landlife so, yes. She kept her skin in this violin case."

"In that violin case?" Two Transformer stickers held down a worn edge of tape. "An entire sealskin?"

"They fit wherever *we* put them. In other hands they're larger, heavier . . ."

"Harder to move." Made sense. "For security reasons?"

"Not that it seems to be working, but yes."

Charlie took the case from Eineen's hands and opened it. No charms inside, but then there didn't need to be. By the time she opened the case, Auntie Catherine had found what she was looking for. "Okay, there isn't as much as a potted plant in the entire RV, so she must've come out of the Woods near where Gavin was parked and then charmed a lock open."

"It happened at night, while everyone was asleep."

"Yeah, well, the aunties like to wander around and check on things. If they don't want to be heard, they're not heard."

Eineen frowned. "That's seriously creepy."

"Tell me about it. One of the first charms we learn is how to block our doors." Charlie smacked herself in the forehead. "I'm an idiot. If I put that charm on the hiding places of every skin that belongs to a Selkie with a landlife, Auntie Catherine won't be able to get to them."

"But then you'll know where every Selkie with a landlife hides her skin."

"Only the room they're in."

"You're asking for an enormous amount of trust."

Charlie glanced at her reflection in the big mirror screwed to the wall over the dresser, shifted enough to see herself between the photos of Neela's kids stuck to the glass, picked a bit of pine tree out of her hair, and tried to look trustworthy. "I know."

"You're asking us to trust in a member of the same family who has stolen our skins."

"The aunties are a law unto themselves." The UN Security Council rumors were probably untrue.

"Blood tells."

"Yeah, well, when you put it that way . . ." Leaning forward, Charlie picked a picture of the girl who'd returned her phone off the floor and stuck it back where the tape marks suggested it went. "Think it over."

Auntie Catherine had left no charm on the bedroom door. Or on the window. As Eineen returned the violin case to its place, Charlie checked the rest of the trailer. Nothing.

"This looks like it's been washed recently." Squatting to check the outside bottom of the actual entrance, she looked up as Eineen descended the two steps to the ground and found herself momentarily mesmerized by the long line of her legs and the soft downy hair that covered them.

"It rained last Tuesday. Could rain wash a charm away?"

"Rain could wash a charm drawn in dirt away," Charlie admitted, straightening and shrugging her gig bag back up on her shoulders. "Well, this was time productively spent. Not. If Auntie Catherine's just walking in and your people won't let me close off the remaining skins, I can't stop her. If she's getting in another way, I don't know what the way is, and, I can't . . ."

Her phone rang; John Bonham's drum solo from Zeppelin's "Moby Dick." Proximity had gotten Mark a ringtone of his own.

"Chuck! Where the hell are you? It's two ten and we're waiting."

Shit. She'd forgotten about running through Mark's new song. "I'm at cottage four. I'll be there in five. No, three. I have to go," she told Eineen, sliding the phone back into her pocket. "I am one hundred percent on your side and I will get your skins back, but I have commitments and . . ."

"The music calls."

"The crazy drummer called, but yeah." To Charlie's surprise, Eineen fell into step beside her. "You're . . . uh . . . ?"

"Coming with you so I can take Tanis away for a while. Bo won't be able to give himself fully to the music while she's there."

"True that." It had to be hard to play with a lap full of weeping Selkie. "She's really taking this hard."

"No more than the rest, but Tanis isn't as able to hide her feelings. She's young and this is her first landlife."

How rude would it be to ask about Eineen's past? *How many landlives have you lived? Have you loved a Human? Would you like to? Give me a couple of days; I can learn to play the fiddle. Or I could play a symphony on you.* Before her train of thought degenerated further, Charlie settled for a neutral, "Ouch. Rough start."

"Yes, your people have made it memorable for her."

"Person, not people. Don't blame the whole family."

"I meant Humans." Charlie could feel Eineen's gaze on the side of her face.

"My people are Gales first. And moving past my people for the moment . . ." She stepped over a rut outside cottage seven. ". . . according to the note, Carlson Oil doesn't just want you to back off, they want you to actually support the drilling. Have you?"

"We spoke to a reporter from the *Post*, telling him we withdrew our opposition. I believe there was something said about new jobs."

"The *Cape Breton Post*? I suspect Amelia Carlson is going to think that's nothing more than a local paper."

Eineen shrugged. "We're a local group."

"A local group she brought out the big guns for. Why? I mean, it's not like you can march up and down in front of the legislature buildings carrying protest signs that say Selkies against offshore drilling. Although," she added after a moment's reflection, "that'd be pretty damned cool."

"My family has been in this area for a very long time, and we've made some canny investments."

"Bonus points for planning ahead, but you can't be able to throw the kind of money at the problem that'll worry an oil company."

"Perhaps not. But by approaching their leaders one on one, we *can* convince other environmental groups to protest with us and bring significant numbers to bear against local and provincial politicians. We stopped the Hay Island seal hunt, we had the effluent regulations tightened for Halifax Harbor, we forced new items onto the environmental protection act regarding the disposal of items other than bilge water at sea. And, as you well know, if those in power are male, we can attract their attention and influence their decisions."

"What if it's a woman?"

"No. My people cannot move outside rigidly defined gender norms."

Charlie snorted. "You *have* been here for a while. What about your males?"

"We use them if we have to, but our males seldom come out of the water. Their time on land is dangerously constrained."

Charlie waited for more as they turned in toward number ten cottage but that seemed to be all the information about Selkie males Eineen was offering. "Does Carlson Oil know what you can do?"

"They know what we are if they brought one of your aunties in. There's no way of knowing what specifics they're aware of."

"We should find out. It's not like Auntie Catherine had an ad on Craigslist. Scary older woman available for all your metaphysical ass-kicking needs." Charlie paused, one foot up on the porch step. "Actually, we should check into that."

"Tanis has a smart phone with an extensive data plan. I'll have her look it up." When Charlie turned, Eineen shrugged. "As I said, her first landlife. She's embracing the possibilities. What do you need to know?"

"I'm just curious how they contacted . . ." Charlie turned again to see Mark staring at her through the screen. Back to Eineen. "Mostly, I'm curious, but a few internet searches might distract Tanis long enough for Bo's shirts to dry out." Back to Mark. "I'm sorry I'm late and I . . ."

Her phone rang; "Evelyn Evelyn" by Amanda Palmer and Jason Webley.

The twins. Not answering would only mean they'd keep calling. "What?"

"Ever since Uncle Evan took over, the boys are showing horn most of the time. It's a good thing school's not in."

"Yeah, Kevin got sent home twice last year for fighting as it was."

"Andy broke Peter's cheek, but Peter stuck a tine into his shoulder."

"We didn't know they were that sharp."

"Did Mom tell you about Europe?"

"We're totally going."

This is why she preferred to keep her phone elsewhere. Like inside a whale. "Guys, I can't talk right now." She waved her other hand at Mark in the universal sign for *family shit*.

"Will you be home Tuesday?"

"Yes . . . I mean, no. I'll be in Calgary."

"Ha. Knew it!"

"You've totally switched to the Allie side of the force."

"Totally."

Charlie closed her phone without responding and handed it to Eineen. "Drop it mid Atlantic. I don't actually need it until Wednesday."

The fiddler in her head broke into a perky version of "Over the Waves."

"Charlotte?"

"Sorry." Concentrating brought the volume down, but it seemed as though the intermittent soundtrack her life had acquired was there to stay.

"The mid Atlantic? Are you sure?"

"Get it back to me Wednesday and I don't care what you do with it."

For the first time since they'd met, Eineen seemed honestly amused. "Go. The music calls."

"Yeah, Chuck, the music calls." Mark held the door open. "Let's answer it, shall we. We've got less than an hour before we have to head back to the festival, so chop chop. You remember the festival, right?" He stood aside as Tanis left the cottage, her eyes dry but her nose red. "We've put together a band for it and everything."

Muttering apologies to Mark, Charlie waved good-bye and went in to take her place in the circle.

"Play it acoustic today, but we'll plug in when we play the park."

Mark had written the lyrics to "Wild Road Beyond" a couple of years ago and had been messing with the melody ever since. The heartbeat of the bodhran stayed consistent, but every other part had been discarded and re-written at least twice. Other songs had come and gone—they had three of his originals on the set list—but this one had never been played in front of an audience. *"It's still missing something,"* was Mark's only explanation.

Because it meant so much to Mark, she blocked out everything else she had going on—Selkies and Auntie Catherine and Tuesday's ritual and her sisters and Jack and Allie—and when they finally put all the parts together . . .

"All right, people, let's put our grown-up pants on and get through this once without stopping as the actress said to the bishop."

. . . Charlie threw herself into the song. Her left hand flew up and down the fretboard, her right moved between dancing the pick over the strings and slamming out the chords. She slid effortlessly up into her falsetto for the descant harmony, winding her voice around Mark's lead. Shelly's rhythm throbbed in her blood and Tim's keyboard stitched them all together as Bo's fiddle called them to the wild side and took them home.

They were dripping wet and breathing hard as they finished.

Bo's last note wailed off into perfect silence . . .

. . . shattered into pieces by a crack of thunder.

"Holy shit!" Shelly jerked, flailed, and just managed to catch her bass before it hit the floor. "That sounded close."

They made the porch more or less together, Bo out in front still holding his instrument, Tim bringing up the rear, having gotten tangled in the accordion strap.

The sky to the northeast looked like a bruise, purple and green and likely to be painful if anyone could come into contact with it. A canvas beach chair tumbled past the cottage, rolled along the gravel by the wind. Thunder cracked again.

"It's moving fast."

"Too fast. What?" Bo demanded when Mark poked him with a stick. "It's what you say when someone says that."

"And besides," Shelly added, "that fucker is moving too damned fast. Storms don't come in like that, not from the northeast. Northwest maybe."

"We need to get to the festival. The festival," Charlie repeated when no one moved, "where they've got a crowd of people to get to safety, and a shit-load of stuff to batten down."

"Most of those people are from the island," Bo said, eyes locked on a line of distant lightning. "You really think they'll need our help?"

The thunder cracked before the lightning dimmed.

"Yes."

*　　*　　*

By the time they piled out of the van at the festival gate, the first drops of rain had started to fall. Although people were jostling for position, arms loaded down with blankets and coolers, trying to move en masse to their cars and avoid a soaking, no one had panicked yet.

But it wouldn't be long.

The potential for panic was there in every wide-eyed glance up at the sky. In the face of every parent who held their child closer than the current situation required. In the expressions of the locals who knew storms didn't come in like that.

The parking lot—field—required the patience of a saint to get out of at the best of times. Charlie shot a glance back over her shoulder at the roiling clouds. Which this wasn't.

"Tim! Mark!" She had to shout to be heard and even then the wind tried to snatch the words away. "One fender bender in that lot . . ."

"On it!"

Shelly grabbed her arm and together they ducked a plastic water bottle. "I'll head for the booths! They'll need extra hands!"

"Not you!" Charlie snagged a handful of Bo's shirt as he tried to follow Shelly. "You head for the stage." She dragged him around, shifted her grip to his left wrist, wet her fingertip and draw a charm on the polished wood of his violin.

He stared at it like he'd forgotten he was holding it. "What are you . . . ?"

"Doesn't matter. Get to the stage and play!"

"Play what?"

At least he hadn't asked why, knowing as well as she did that if anything would keep this particular crowd from panic, it'd be music. "Something familiar, something that'll stand against the storm."

He stood for a moment, frozen in place, then he nodded once and ran, fighting his way in against the exodus.

Charlie followed, hauled a small child up off the ground by one skinny arm and thrust her at her father, swore as an abandoned lawn chair slammed into her shins, saw a man with a fiddle case . . .

She reached him just as he settled a four-year-old boy on his hip. Recognized the two kids hanging onto Neela's hands. The family was a very small island of calm in the growing chaos.

"Gavin!" Had to be Gavin. "You're needed on stage!"

"What?"

She turned him until he could see Bo, bending to plug in. "If enough people pause to listen . . ."

"They'll get hit by lightning?" But he was already handing the boy to his mother and opening his case. He whipped his head around to glare at her when Charlie reached past him and drew the charm. His instrument was visibly older than Bo's; had been played harder.

"What do you think . . . ?"

"Gavin!" Neela's eyes flashed black, rim to rim. "Let it go. Just play."

He scowled, looked from his wife to Charlie and back again. "Is this . . . ?"

"Yes. Hurry!"

"You three stay with your mother. Help her!" Violin and bow in the same hand, he ruffled his other hand through his eldest's hair, kissed Neela quickly, and ran for the stage.

The rain seemed to be rolling off Neela's hair without being absorbed. Which was hardly surprising, all things considered. "Do you need . . . ?" Charlie began.

"You have other things to do, Charlotte Gale."

Someone screamed. And that was all it took for people to start charging toward the exit like the storm wouldn't hit them if they were off the festival grounds.

"It's not *that* the wind blows," she muttered, as a baseball cap smacked against the side of her head, "it's *what* the wind blows." It was the punchline of a joke about being out in hurricanes although, at the moment, Charlie didn't find it that funny.

Ducking debris, she cut another two fiddlers out of the crowd. No more time to draw charms, she realized, shoving her reinforcements toward the stage. Gavin and Bo would have to suffice if the power went out.

The rain had started to pound down. Each individual drop hitting hard, then they were hitting so close together it was like being pounded by a wet fist.

Up on the stage, pressed in against the back where the rain couldn't reach them. Five, no six, fiddlers played "Bandlings," one of the classic Cape Breton reels. Gavin must've grabbed a couple more musicians on his way up. The sound system, put together by people who understood maritime weather, continued to hold.

As the speakers crackled to life and the reel danced out on the wind, heads jerked toward the stage. And okay, maybe more people were thinking *are they fucking insane* than *let's stand together against the storm*, but hey, whatever worked.

Lightning/thunder.

Ears ringing, blinking away the afterimages, Charlie wondered why popular opinion was thunder/lightning when the lightning always came first.

Lightning/thunder.

Or came too close to call it.

Praying that last impact hadn't been with anything living, she found herself in front of one of the luthier's booths—still mostly standing. With the storm and the music sizzling together under her skin, she reached without thinking for the last of the unpacked guitars, pulling a pick from her pocket with the other hand.

Without a strap, she folded her legs and dropped cross-legged to the ground, water seeping immediately through her shorts. Chin tucked in to keep from drowning like a turkey, she played the two sounds together.

Music. Storm.

The song changed. "The Battle of Killicrankie."

The fiddler in her head took up the harmony line.

Should've grabbed a piper, she thought and swore under her breath as she lost her grip on the wet pick.

No time to find another. No choice but to dig her thumb against the strings.

The wind shifted and slapped a wall of water against her. If she'd been standing, it would have knocked her over. Her palm protecting the sound hole as much as possible, she kept playing, forcing the storm to the music's parameters. The four un-charmed instruments fought her almost as hard as the storm, but she pulled them in, pulled it all together, played it . . .

Played it.

Played it.

Stopped it.

Later, they said the storm blew back out to sea as quickly as it blew in. No one mentioned that storms didn't do that.

Or that as the soggy people started putting things back together, the sky was a brilliant blue as far as anyone could see, and the sea was so calm the seals looked like stepping stones bobbing in the water, all of them staring toward shore.

SIX

AS THOUGH TO MAKE UP for Saturday, Sunday's weather was beautiful. Sunny and warm, the sky looked as though it had been scrubbed.
With none of the Selkies about—Tanis had wiped her eyes and told Bo she
had family obligations and Neela had gone off with her kids—Charlie concentrated on the festival, making notes on the competition, jamming with
the competition, and explaining an infinite number of times why she had a
Band-aid on her right thumb. She hadn't even realized she'd strummed it
bloody playing the storm.

She bought the guitar.

Her bank account held twenty-two dollars more than the reduced asking
price and, given what it had been through, the odds were high no one else
would be able to play it anyway. Back on her hillock, listening to Five by Five
rock out to "Ghosts of Calico" by Enter the Haggis, Charlie changed the heavies
that had been on it for mediums—the luthier had set it up for bluegrass and,
evidently, storm calling. Although she'd changed strings thousands of times on
dozens of instruments, she drew blood with every string. Was it because the old
strings had been blooded and that was what the guitar now required or was she
just short on sleep, a little bit stoned, and three beers into the afternoon.

When she wandered away from the party at the campground that night
to stand on the beach, she could see the darker lines of seals hanging vertically in the water, watching the shore. No, watching her. She walked to the
right, their heads swiveled to follow. They didn't follow the couple holding
hands, trying to convince each other that what they felt was real and not a

result of the music. They didn't follow the four kids up way past their bed-time too buzzed on sugar to sleep anyway. They followed her. Only her.

It was impossible to tell at this distance, in the dark, if they were merely seals but swimming out to check seemed like a very bad idea. As Aston had discovered, seals bit.

And Selkies . . .

Now she couldn't stop wondering if Eineen was a biter.

The fiddler in her head got out only the first three bars of "Haste to the Wedding" before Charlie shut it down.

Next morning, Shelly's cheerful whistling of the same tune jerked her out of a sound sleep.

"Good night?" Charlie yawned without lifting her head as the other woman bounced into the small room.

Shelly grinned. "Not bad." Then she frowned and sat on the edge of her unused bed, legs filling the minimal space between them, right knee pressed against Charlie's left elbow. "Tell me you didn't not hook up because you're not pining for Eineen. Because, sweetie, that's never going to happen."

"You know her?"

"Oh, yeah, you see her at the festivals all the time. Last year Mark thought she was one of the secret judges, but it seems she just really likes the music. And I saw her at the protests for stopping the seal hunt; she's part of some environmental watchdog group. Also, I think she introduced Tanis to Bo—they're related somehow. But my point is very, very straight."

"I know. It's . . ." Charlie flopped over on her back and sighed up at the ceiling. "It's complicated. I look at her and I want her, but I swear, I'm not pining. I just didn't feel like partying."

"Steve Morris was asking after you."

"Did he have the money he owes me for that session work?"

"I doubt it since he had a plan to make it up to you."

"Do another CD and he'll pay me for both?"

"It's like you know him." Straightening her leg, Shelly kicked her in the thigh. "Now get up. We have to be out of the cottage by eleven and it's nine forty-five."

*　　*　　*

Grinneal was off until Wednesday afternoon when they'd meet up at Cheticamp in the Cape Breton Highlands National Park for a paid gig. According to Mark, the Wednesday ceilidh was essentially a barn dance, but it made the tourists happy and that was all that mattered.

"I will not forget we have a sound check at three," Charlie insisted as Mark glared at her through two very bloodshot eyes. "I won't be even be late. I'm just going to help Tanis look for the heirloom she's lost."

Arms folded, holding a pair of sticks in both hands like Egyptian regalia, Mark's glare morphed into a puzzled frown. "Hadn't realized you two were so close, Chuck."

"We're not. But I've got some time to kill, and if she's happy, Bo's happy." They moved in unison to avoid being run down by Tim carrying three accordion cases and the coffeemaker. "A happy fiddler makes for a happy band."

"So you're doing it for the band?"

She grasped his shoulder, cupping the spider tat, and drew a small, reassuring charm on damp skin with the edge of her thumb as she squeezed. "I'm selfless that way."

Unwilling to chance the Wood with a passenger and a new, and potentially dangerous guitar, Charlie left it and her clean clothes with Shelly, borrowed a backpack for her dirty clothes, and went out to meet Tanis and Bo. Bo continued to take the *world is wider than you imagine* remarkably well although Charlie was beginning to think it had as much to do with Tanis not allowing enough oxygen into his system as it did with Selkie brainwashing.

Watching her rub the soft curve of her hip against Bo's groin, Charlie had to admit it was an effective way of keeping Bo distracted.

"Bo? There's a familiar truck approaching."

He moved his lips far enough from Tanis' mouth to say, "My brother's picking me up."

Charlie recognized the driver. "Your brother have a bad '70s pornstache?"

Impossible to pucker while smiling that broadly. "No such thing as a good one."

"Hey, dipshit!" The mustache didn't seem to affect his volume. "Stop molesting that woman and get in the truck. Your audition's at two fifteen, and Dad'll want to see you first. Hey, Tanis, still not interested in trading up?"

"Audition?" Charlie asked as Tanis went to the driver's window.

"Symphony Nova Scotia. Dad's Assistant Principal Cello and Feroz is

Second Bassoon." When Charlie lifted a brow, he snickered. "He shaves during the season. Mostly I audition to make my father happy, but I wouldn't turn down a steady job over the winter either."

"You go where the music calls," Tanis murmured, tucking back under his arm.

When he bent his head to kiss her, Charlie shared a look with Feroz and flicked Bo's ear. "Two fifteen audition," she reminded him. "Go. Call her when you're done."

"Do you need a lift . . . ?"

"No."

"Is it . . . ?" He widened his eyes and waggled his brows up and down.

"Yes, it's a bad Groucho Marx impersonation. Get in the truck. Tanis, get the door. You know," she sighed as the truck finally headed away from the cottages, and Tanis gave a weak sniffle, "nothing against Bo, he's a great guy and one hell of a fiddler, but you don't *have* to lock your landlife to a man."

"Actually . . ." she paused to blow her nose. ". . . we do."

"You do?"

Tanis smiled and spread her hands, the webbing evident. "We leave the sea to dance in the moonlight and fall in love. That's the Rule my people live by. Fortunately, we fall in love easily. With men," she added hurriedly. "Eineen can't . . ."

"I know."

"But you still want her."

Her personal soundtrack agreed with a spirited "Cherish the Ladies."

First Shelly, now Tanis; apparently, she'd been more obvious about her attraction to the Selkie than she'd thought. Charlie spread her hands as Tanis had, letting the gesture answer, then turned and headed behind the cottages, Tanis falling into step beside her.

"Have you tried wanting men?" she asked after a moment.

He'd been a strong man once, broad shoulders, large hands, skin browned by the wind and the sun and sea.

Charlie grinned. "Not since Friday," she said as the fiddler segued into "Boys of the Town."

Too innately graceful to trip, Tanis paused for a moment, then hurried to catch up. "But . . ."

"Human rules are less specific than the Rules of the Fey."

"You're not entirely Human," she pointed out.

"Gale rules are Gale specific." Charlie ducked in under the reaching branch of the big pine and stopped, settling her guitar into place. "Put your hand on my shoulder and I'll bring us out by those three birches behind your house."

Dark eyes widened in wonder. "How did you know?"

"Google Earth. You gave me your address, I borrowed Mark's laptop."

"Oh."

"Still magic of a sort."

"I suppose." Her fingers felt slightly damp against Charlie's skin. "Are you sure you can take all of what I am through the Wood?"

Charlie shushed the fiddler and checked. The missing skin left a gaping hole in Tanis' song, silence where there'd been both deepwater music and waves against the shore. Easy enough to fix. She wove the absence of the skin through the song—a wail of longing bending the treble strings. She didn't need to turn to know Tanis was crying again.

"Trust me," she said lightly, trying to lift the Selkie's mood before the Wood got wet. "I took a Dragon Lord through last year, and your other form can't possible weigh what he did."

"A Dragon Lord?" Damp interest.

"They were . . ." Hunting. Invading. Igniting. ". . . visiting in Calgary, and we went to Chicago for pizza. He weighed more on the way back. Those guys can eat."

Tanis' grip tightened and she sniffed, more in pique than sorrow. "I've always been told that we opened a gate to this world because of the Dragon Lords. That they found our other form . . . tasty."

Charlie snorted. "I get the impression they find pretty much everything tasty. Hang on."

Tanis lived in a small house on Grandfather's Cove outside Main-a-Dieu. "It's been in the family for generations," she said leading the way out of the brush and over the rough cut lawn to the back door. "Not our generations of course, yours. Actually, Humans. I'm the only one living here right now; the others with landlives live with their husbands. But my sisters and my cousins visit often, and I spend a lot of my time with Bo." She caught a handful of hair blown wild on the wind and twisted it into a braid. "Soon, I'll leave here to live with Bo. Until he betrays me."

"What?"

"It's how our story always ends. With betrayal." Her eyes went dark from lid to lid and a single tear fell to roll down the perfect curve of her cheek. "Mortal lives are so short."

The Fey were walking, talking clichés sometimes. "So they betray you by dying?"

"The ultimate betrayal." She shrugged, the glamour back, whites in her eyes again. "It's the only betrayal left, isn't it? These days, we choose the men we live a landlife with."

Is seemed as though the men so chosen couldn't decline. But then, the Fey tended to get what the Fey wanted and as long as none of them made a move on a Gale boy, not her problem. "So no one ever sees you doing the obligatory moonlight dancing and steals your skin instead of falling in love?"

"Please, most modern men wouldn't believe what they saw and the last man who did and then strutted around saying *I have your skin and you must be mine* got visited by half a dozen cousins who kicked the living shit out of him until he divulged the hiding place."

"Half a dozen cousins? Not one of your males?"

"A male would have killed him."

Seals bite.

Also, *divulged*? Who actually said divulged? Tanis' speech patterns were an interesting mix of Fey formal and twenty-first century casual.

"Mr. Alcock next door mows the lawn," Tanis continued, as though she hadn't just been talking about putting the boots to a modern application of Celtic myth. "And his wife comes in and cleans once a week as the Alcock family has done for generations. In return, the family are the most successful fishermen in the village. Actually, these days, they might be the only success-ful fishermen in the village. Over the last few months, the remaining fishing grounds have all but emptied. As though the fish are fleeing before Carlson Oil can destroy their homes."

"Good for them . . . but back to the kicking. If you could find that skin . . ."

"You weren't listening; we could only find the man who had it—not that it was hard, what with the strutting and bragging and all. He had to tell us where the skin was."

"Okay, but my point is, we *know* who has the four missing skins."

Tanis sighed and pulled a key for the back door out from under an up-turned clay flower pot. "Don't be ridiculous. We can't threaten an entire corporation. They have the skins, so we won't *be* a threat. Plus, the CEO is a woman; we can't even lure her somewhere secluded and point a male at her hoping she'll survive long enough to talk. Given the way she does business, she's probably taken that possibility into account. Her executive assistant is a man and he's usually the one getting his hands dirty, but even if we get these skins back, we can't stop them from getting more, and they'll definitely up the ante. I'm the only landlifer without kids and Carlson Oil has a rep for being hard-line and we're vulnerable now they know what we are. What?" she asked as Charlie stared at her. "Because we spend so little time in the water, those of us living a landlife are the core of the environmental group, and offshore drilling was on our radar even before Carlson filed for permits."

Of course it was. Turned out Tanis was pretty chatty when she wasn't sobbing or her lips weren't attached to Bo's. "So offshore drilling's innately evil?"

"If the Gulf spill taught us anything, it was that spills are inevitable. Even ignoring the flight of the fish stocks, Carlson wants to drill right next to a seal rookery. We have family there. Wipe your feet," she added as she opened the door.

There were no charms on or around the back door even though the birches would have been the easiest place for Auntie Catherine to emerge from the Wood.

The downstairs of the house had been simply furnished with the sort of heavy, handmade eighteenth century pieces that would cause the most stalwart antique dealer to have palpitations as he worked out his commission. Provided he could find buyers willing to ignore the slight scent of fish.

The decor in Tanis' bedroom jumped ahead a few centuries to come down in the land of online shopping. Comforter, sheets, shams, curtains, rug . . . everything matched. Bed, dressers, and bedside tables were MDF, shipped flat-pack and assembled. The art prints on the pale blue walls were generic landscapes. The room looked like it had been put together by someone not quite Human but trying hard. Personality showed only in the pile of

romantic comedies by the television in the corner, the brightly colored clothing piled and draped over every possible surface, and, the poster of George
Stroumboulopoulos on the plaster-and-lathe wall between the two dormer
windows. The CBC late night talk show host, who declared he was everyone's
boyfriend, had apparently not been told that Canadian celebrities, particularly those on the CBC, didn't smolder.

Charlie admired the poster a moment longer, then asked, "So where was
your skin?"

"In my underwear drawer. No, the other one," she added as Charlie
reached out.

If the skins could be the size the Selkies wanted, Tanis had obviously
wanted hers to not take up much room in a drawer crammed full of matching bra and panty sets. If that wasn't enough, and it looked like enough for
two or three women, a leopard print demi bra hung from one corner of
the dresser mirror, sharing space with a fuchsia cami and a lime-green
thong.

Charlie waited to see if her fiddler had anything to say, wasted another
moment imagining Eineen in a thong, then took a deep breath and set about
methodically searching the room for charms. Nothing.

"You were in the room when it was stolen?"

"Bo and I both were. Sound asleep."

Every other entrance into the house was as bare of charms as the back
door. Charlie even checked the chimney just to be on the safe side. Nothing.
Just like the RV.

Back in the bedroom, Tanis pulled the note from the drawer in the bedside table and handed it over.

*Support the well on Hay Island and your skin will be returned when the wellhead
is in place.*

The only difference between it and Neela's note was the entirely expected tearstains.

Leaning back against the big dresser, Charlie hit paper and ink with every
WTF? charm she knew and discovered nothing. Nada. Goose eggs all around.

But something nudged at her, twanged her subconscious like a familiar
song she could only just . . . barely . . . hear. Almost had it . . . nearly . . .

Distracted by the lime-green thong and its reflection, she lost it.

"What now?" Tanis asked as they went back downstairs.

"I have no idea. But I'm not giving up," she added hurriedly as Tanis started to sniffle. "Maybe I should talk to Amelia Carlson."

"She's the head of the second largest oil company in Atlantic Canada."

"And I'm Charlie Gale."

Tanis paused at the front door, brows raised. "Can you just walk up to her, then?"

Charlie shrugged. "Don't know. I've never tried."

The view at the front of the house was amazing. A flagstone path led to a gravel road, across the road a narrow band of beach grass, across that a tidal beach, and across that, the sea. Turquoise close to shore, darkening farther out, distant waves topped with white ruffles—only water separated that shore from Europe. One hell of a lot of water.

And a Selkie.

Eineen crossed the sand, her hair wet and flowing down over her body like a midnight veil, her face too narrow, her eyes too large and too dark, her proportions wrong. Every time her foot touched the sand, it added another note to the song wrapped around her . . . wild seas and drowning men and bones white against the seabed. She met Charlie's gaze and held it and between one step and the next was still beautiful but no longer *other*.

Except for the sealskin she held in her right hand. That was pretty freakin' other, Charlie amended.

"We all keep some clothes here," Tanis explained, pouring boiling water into a teapot as Eineen showered off the salt. "Between you and me? Given how much time Eineen's spending at the festivals and working with the environmental group, I think she's ready for another landlife." Her mouth made a perfect O of dismay. "I don't mean with you," she added. "I mean, you're nice and you're helping and all, but . . ."

"But she's not really helping, is she?" Eineen had thrown on a purple tank and black cotton skirt. Her hair was still wet but merely hair rather than unearthly tresses. "Or have you found something here?"

"Not a thing," Charlie admitted, sniffing a homemade cookie for traces of cod. "To paraphrase Dr. McCoy, I'm a musician, not a detective. There isn't a mark on either site. There isn't even a place where a charm's been removed. I have no idea how Auntie Catherine is getting in and getting the pelts out."

Wrapping her hands around a mug of tea, Eineen looked thoughtful. "Maybe you're asking the wrong question. Before you ask how, you should ask where."

"What?"

"How did your Auntie Catherine know *where* to look? How did she know there was a pelt in this house? In Glera's house? In Seanan's boat? In Neela's trailer? How did she know where the skins were hidden?"

Charlie swallowed and sucked chocolate chips off her teeth. "Someone told her?"

The temperature in the room dropped about ten degrees. Eyes, face, webbing, teeth . . .

They had remarkably pointed teeth, Charlie realized. She spread her hands, thought of Aston, reconsidered, and tucked her fingers between her thighs and the stool. "According to Tanis, it always ends with betrayal. If that's true, then what's to say you haven't been betrayed?"

Eineen's features softened, and Tanis burst into tears. "Bo didn't betray me!"

"Oh, for . . ." Eineen sighed, stood, and gathered Tanis into her arms. "Hush, little one."

"Actually, I very much doubt Bo betrayed her." Charlie reached for another cookie. She appreciated baked goods that weren't layered in charms. "Gale girls know besotted and he's clearly, completely besotted."

This brought on a fresh burst of tears.

"Happy tears?" Charlie guessed.

Eineen shrugged, rubbing comforting circles on the small of Tanis' back. "The husbands of the other three know," she admitted. "One of them could have betrayed us."

"No. Not to Carlson Oil." Tanis lifted her head from Eineen's shoulder and wiped her nose on the back of her hand. "I worked with all of them when we stopped the seal hunt and while they might sell us out for a guarantee the drilling would never happen, they'd never do it get a well put in. Not so close to shore. Not so close to the rookery."

"Jobs . . ."

"They're fiddlers."

Charlie shrugged. "It's Cape Breton; who isn't?"

"And sure," Tanis continued, ignoring her, "Glera's brother-in-law works the oil fields out west . . ."

"Fort McMurray?"

"I don't know. Does it matter?"

"Evidence of a small world."

"This one," she agreed. "But he couldn't betray Seanan; he doesn't know about the boat."

They were almost at something. Charlie could hear all the notes now but not the tune. Not quite. "Auntie Catherine went straight to the underwear drawer. She had to have, because she wouldn't have bothered cleaning up after herself if she'd had to toss the place." It was a little harder to tell that Neela's trailer hadn't been tossed, given the mess, but the mess, in turn, helped support her theory. It would have taken hours to search through the scattering of toys. "Auntie Catherine has the Sight. Maybe she saw where the skins would be. She could have seen it years ago and only just found a use for the information. Now me, I'm not an auntie, not even second circle—they're all about connections—and I certainly don't have the Sight . . ." Charlie couldn't think of much worse than getting glimpses of the future and having to decide whether or not to interfere. Okay. Advance warning of Justin Beiber might have been worth it but not much else. ". . . so no, not a hope in hell I can find them the same way. But *this* is who *I* am." She picked up her guitar from where she'd leaned it against the wall, settled it on her lap, and barred her way up, and then down the fretboard before settling to play.

Eineen's song was deep and mysterious and dangerous, and Charlie couldn't so much play it as evoke it, letting the bass strings ring as she built the melody above them. Outside, across the road, across the beach, the waves beat out the percussion against the shore. With a wail of strings, her fiddler joined in.

Charlie stood and walked up the stairs, following the music, the stairwell barely wide enough for her to keep playing even with the guitar tipped. The second bedroom held a narrow bed and a lot of clothing; different styles, different sizes, different eras. She stopped in front of a line of brass hooks screwed into the wall behind the door. Stopped playing. Lifted a powder blue chenille dressing gown. Lifted a yellow windbreaker. Lifted a shawl . . .

And found herself holding a sealskin.

It was heavy, it smelled like fish, and the empty eyeholes were creeping her the hell out.

"I'll take that." Eineen reached past her, tugged the skin from her hand, and it was a shawl again. Then a fabric belt, wrapped around a narrow waist.

It was possible, likely even, that Auntie Catherine had been able to maintain the glamour. Somehow, Charlie couldn't see her dragging what looked like a skinned seal all over the province.

"I took Tanis through the Wood," she said, leaving the room. "I know her song and her skin is a part of it. It doesn't matter where Auntie Catherine has hidden it, I can track it the same way I found yours. It's not even tracking really; it's just joining the pieces. Second verse, follows the first."

"Now?" Staring up at her from the bottom of the stairs, Tanis' eyes were open painfully wide.

Charlie flexed her fingers. The Band-aid on her thumb made her grip on the pick uncertain, so she tugged it off with her teeth and then shoved it in the pocket of her shorts.

"I can get rid of that."

"Thanks, but I'll take care of it." Gales didn't leave their blood just lying around, not if they wanted to survive adolescence. Or, specifically, their siblings' adolescence. Those sorts of charms always went wrong. "Stand beside me, hand on my shoulder, like when we were traveling . . . and why are you crying now?"

"I just . . . it's almost over."

"Shouldn't you be outside? If you're going to be traveling," Eineen expanded as Charlie turned toward her.

"Not yet. First I have to find the missing piece of the song, the part that links Tanis to her sealskin. Once I have it, we ride that to the final chorus. Safer to fill in the blanks before we start moving."

Feet braced, Charlie relaxed her shoulders and played the opening notes. Listened. Built Tanis' song up from the touch on her shoulder, from the waves, from her tears, from the love on Bo's face when he looked down at her. She touched the absence of the skin and, this time, felt the shape of its absence, followed that shape out, away, and . . .

And. . . .

And. . . .

Eineen's fingers were cool around her wrist as she stopped the movement of Charlie's right hand. "You can't get there, can you? And you're bleeding again."

Charlie had no memory of losing the pick.

Tanis, predictably, was crying.

"Auntie Catherine knows I'm here," Charlie growled around the thumb in her mouth. "She's deliberately blocked me."

"So now what?"

"Now, I'm heading home." Early afternoon had become early evening while she played. The three-hour time difference was about to save her ass. "While I'm gone, you guys and your lifejacket group are going to set up a press conference, where you discuss how maybe possibly, a shallow water well wouldn't be such a bad thing."

"Why would anyone believe that?" Eineen demanded, arms folded.

"Talk about how many jobs it'll bring to Cape Breton, that's the usual 'get out of jail free card' around here. But don't talk to anyone one on one; you're not actually trying to change people's minds, you're just putting on a dog and pony show so Amelia Carlson thinks you're going along with her plans and doesn't grab another skin."

"She's not stupid."

"Clearly. But from what I've seen, she's all about the sound bite. She uses television spots to sway popular opinion without ever saying a damned thing. She'll think you're doing the same."

"All right . . ." Eineen nodded, acknowledging Charlie's analysis. ". . . while we're doing that, what will you be doing?"

"Amongst other things, talking to the family about what Auntie Catherine's been up to."

"And will they choose to support you over this older, more venerated member?"

"Some of them."

"Oh, that . . . she's just . . . I want to . . ." As the lights started to flicker, Allie forced herself to calm down. "Why is she doing it? Did she tell you that much?"

Charlie swallowed a mouthful of peach pie. "She says it's because they're paying her. You've got the Emporium; she needed an alternative income stream."

"Do you believe her?"

"The aunties don't tend to lie." The aunties believed in telling the truth and enjoying the fireworks.

"So she's stealing Selkie skins for an evil oil company?"

"I'm not sure it's evil . . ."

Allie spread her arms wide in the universal gesture for *are you kidding me?* "It hired my grandmother!"

"Yeah, okay, that doesn't look good, but that doesn't make it evil." Charlie, for one, had no intention of giving up cold beer, Belgian waffles, or amplified sound and all that required power. Power required oil companies. "Say, rather, unethical."

"Point of interest . . ." Graham raised his fork. ". . . Harvard business school only recently started teaching ethics. Graduates had previously been taught you do what you have to for the company."

"Which makes my point. Besides, we don't actually care about the company, we care about Auntie Catherine and on a scale of one to ten, based on what an auntie *could* do, blackmail barely makes a seven."

"Wait . . ." Jack swallowed a last enormous mouthful, licked a dribble of peach juice off his lip, and looked hopefully at the pie until Allie rolled her eyes and cut him another slice. ". . . there are Selkies here? In the MidRealm? Near where I'm going to be?"

"There are," Charlie replied, reaching for her ice tea. "And you can't eat them."

"But they're really good!"

"I don't doubt you, but on this side of the gate, Gale boys don't eat anyone they can have a conversation with unless . . . OW! Allie!"

"He's fourteen."

"And not stupid," Jack muttered, spewing crumbs. "I have an internet connection."

Allie folded her arms. "I'm seriously reconsidering sending you east."

That lifted Jack's attention from the pie, if only momentarily. "Graham?"

"Allie."

"Fine."

Wow. A whole conversation in three words. Charlie envied Allie that. A little. She definitely envied Graham's improved ability to read Allie's expressions because Charlie had no idea what her cousin was thinking as she cleared the table and stacked the dishes in the sink although she knew, from the set of Allie's shoulders, that something was up.

Up *right now*, she realized as Allie turned to face her.

"Jack, lets you and me go out and grab some more butter and maple syrup." Seemed like Graham realized it, too. "You know how many pancakes this family goes through post ritual."

"But we've got gallons of . . ." As Allie moved closer to the table, Jack's well honed sense of self-preservation kicked in before he finished the sentence. "Right. Good idea." He picked up his pie in one disproportionately large teenage hand, shot Charlie a sympathetic look, and nearly beat Graham to the door.

"Why didn't you tell me?" Allie asked as it closed behind them.

Charlie kept her voice level, matter-of-fact, refusing to turn this into a thing. "I just did."

"You've known for days."

"I didn't want to accuse your grandmother until I spoke to her."

"You spoke to her Saturday." Allie dropped into the chair next to Charlie's and closed her hand around Charlie's arm. "And why would I care about you accusing my grandmother of anything? She's probably guilty of a lot more than you've discovered. If I had to choose between you, it's not a choice."

"I know, but you had a ritual to put together. I didn't want to pump up your anger at her and distract you from what's really important."

"I almost believe that, except the ritual's tonight, so I still have to pull it together and you just told me. Try again."

"Look, Allie-cat, if you don't like my reasons . . ."

Allie's gaze never wavered. "I haven't heard your reasons."

She wasn't going to let it go, Charlie realized. She'd sit there at the table, right through the ritual if it came to it, solemn expression in place, waiting for Charlie to admit aloud the conclusion she'd already come to. It was a second circle thing, this connecting the dots and assembling a conclusion; Charlie's mother did it all the time. Allie was frighteningly good at it, considering she'd crossed not much more than a year ago. "Are you pregnant?"

"What? No! Stop trying to change the subject."

It had been a long shot. "I, uh . . . I have a fiddler in my head."

"And again: what?"

"Every now and then a lone fiddler shows up, plays a bit of music that's more or less relevant to what's going on and then buggers off until the next time."

"An actual fiddler shows up?" Allie held her thumb and forefinger about six centimeters apart. "In your head?"

"Not an actual fiddler, no, just the music."

"You've always heard music."

"This is a little specific."

"Then maybe it's trying to tell you something specific."

"You think?"

Allie looked smug. "I think you still haven't told me your reasons. Nice try, though."

With nothing left to deflect Allie's question, Charlie took a deep breath and looked deeper. Listened deeper. Listened to what her own song had to say. Then considered lying anyway. Didn't, but it was close. "This is mine," she said at last. "Mark and Tom and Shelly and Bo, and through Bo and Gavin . . ."

"Gavin?"

"Another fiddler, another band. The point is the band is mine, the music is mine, and, through the fiddlers, the Selkies are mine. Or their problems are mine. And Auntie Catherine is a Wild Power, so her interference makes this even more mine."

"And you thought I wouldn't understand that?"

"I don't . . ."

"You can't tame a Wild Power, so you have to meet her on her own ground. Like calls to like. This . . ." Releasing Charlie's wrist, her gesture took in the city. ". . . was about settling in. What you're doing is about setting free, and you know what the T-shirt says."

Charlie glanced down. "If we're attacked by zombies, I'm tripping you?"

"Not that T-shirt."

Grinning, Charlie blocked her swing. "I love you, but if you quote that at me, I'll teach Jack the lyrics to every filthy song I know while he's with me."

"Fine. No quoting. You know, Grandmother was one of the ones who told me I'd never tame you. She's a manipulative harpy, but that doesn't mean she's wrong. You do what you have to; just tell me how I can help. But first," she added before Charlie could speak, grin broadening, eyes gleaming. "Tell me what's up with Eineen. You glow when you talk about her."

"I don't glow."

"You do. Like a giant firefly."

"Male fireflies glow."

"Charlie."

"Nothing's up."

Allie leaned back and looked thoughtful. "It's more than a crush, then. Is it love?"

"It's not nearly that complicated. I just . . . want."

"You want?"

Charlie concentrated on the last of her pie.

"Oh. I thought the Selkie glamour didn't work on girls."

With an empty plate in front of her, Charlie sighed. "Am I the only one who didn't know that?"

"Possibly."

"It's not her. It's all me."

"Ego much?" Allie laced their hands together, and tugged Charlie around to face her. "You okay?"

"I'm not without options, Allie-cat."

"Tonight's third circle will . . ."

"No. Unless the aunties have moved another boy west in the last week, Cameron's the only third circle male out here. He's got the six off his list to deal with . . ."

"Seven counting Katie," Allie amended.

"And you're making my point. Jack and I will form a fourth circle and guard the perimeter."

Nose Hill Park felt like an empty stage as the family began arriving.

Embracing her cousins, Charlie noted that the males were already showing full racks. Probably in reaction to Uncle Edward's death—distance wouldn't have stopped them feeling it—but possibly only in response to David who was waiting for them, silhouetted at the peak. Roland, Randy, and Dave, all second circle, wore their horns with an easy grace, but Cameron shifted under the weight of his, eyes wide and nostrils flared as he drew in deep lungfuls of air and forced them back out again, obviously ready to begin.

"Dude!" Charlie cuffed him on the side of the head as he passed, already out of his shirt and working on his shorts. "Pace yourself! It's twenty minutes to midnight and this isn't your first ritual."

He spun around, looking for a fight, and deflated with no other male visible.

Not Charlie's first ritual either. She'd timed it so the others were already most of the way up the hill and out of his line of sight.

"Are we anchoring third?" he asked, working his lower lip between his teeth.

"Not this time, Cam. It'll be Katie, although she might give way to Melissa if asked nicely."

He shrugged, muscles moving prettily under smooth skin—although she knew he had a scar along his right side where he and Dmitri had gotten into it a couple of years ago. "Don't care who anchors, really. It's not like I'm choosing."

"Good. You choose now and the aunties'll go off the deep end when they're forced to relocate another third circle male." And that would be fun for no one. The aunties believed in tossing others into the deep end with them. It was how most Gale girls learned how to swim. "But don't worry. If it happens, it'll be Melissa doing the asking. Now, get going before they start without you." When he was about ten feet away, she sat back against the hood of her car and said, "You can come out now, Jack."

A double image moved out of the shadows, Dragon Prince absorbed into the Gale boy. "How did you know I was there?"

"Your song got louder."

"Really?"

"No. There's a lingering scent of scorched gravel."

He sat as far away as the narrow hood of the car allowed. The August night was warm, but Charlie could still feel the heat radiating off him. "So what do we do?" he asked. He was fourteen, a little less than a year too young for ritual, old enough he couldn't stay still.

"I take care of the perimeter on the ground, you're the air support. Calgary has police helicopters and while they don't generally patrol at night, they do come out if they think something's up."

She glanced up to the top of the hill where she could just barely make out Allie standing in the circle of Graham's arms. Even if her gaze hadn't been drawn to them as they began to pull power, she'd have been able to pick them out of the small crowd. Graham was the only male on the hill without antlers. They'd all gotten used to that over the last year and it certainly hadn't hurt to see him take Roland down without benefit of horn last spring. Next to David, he was the most potent male in the park. "Allie's so connected the city responds, and ritual pulled the police out at midsummer. Drew them to her. You were off eating a buffalo, so Auntie Gwen had to deal with it."

"Ow."

"Little bit. Auntie Bea wants this one." The three aunties stood around David, one at his head, two at his flanks. Although he wouldn't change until it started, the four of them were already becoming difficult to see. If he was nervous about having their hands on him, given what had just happened back in Ontario, it didn't show. "Auntie Bea," Charlie continued, "is definitely an ow. I need you to get into the air and if the police show up, lead them away— preferably before anyone on the ground notices. Don't let them see you, as you, but otherwise do whatever you think will work that comes with plausible deniability and no one getting hurt. Butterflies are not plausibly deniable, but in case I didn't say it before . . ." She reached out and punched his arm. ". . . way to think on the wing."

He snorted, the smoke nearly obscuring his face. "Everyone was mad."

"Worried."

"They sounded mad."

"It's a tricky distinction." She stood and walked around to the backseat, pulling out her guitar. "But now it's almost time. So, wings out and get high enough you won't be distracted by what's happening on the ground."

Jack changed in a sheet of flame, emerging at his full size, and Charlie's car shifted three meters back, tires dragging trenches in the gravel.

An enormous golden dragon looking sheepish was actually kind of adorable, but Charlie buried her reaction because an enormous *sulky* dragon was not. "No harm no foul; front tires missed my toes by whole centimeters." Feeling the power starting to build, she jerked a thumb toward the sky. "Move it!"

The backwash from Jack's wings nearly knocked her on her ass, but she played a D flat minor 7th against it and managed to stay standing. She watched him rise until he covered a patch of stars no larger than her hand, then turned her full attention to the ritual. Either she trusted Jack to do what was necessary or she didn't, and if she didn't, he had no business being up there.

Charlie felt the moment David changed and the family anchored itself deeper in its chosen home. Felt Allie begin to gather power as Graham stabilized her. Felt the other members of the family join in—Katie muting Cameron's metaphysical yell. Gathered it all up and directed it, through her music, into a ring of protection around the park.

Part of the ritual but not in it.

An insider voluntarily on the outside.

A necessary difference to keep the family safe.

All right, she told the universe as she fed more power into the surrounding fourth circle, stretched it up to include Jack, *I get it.*

After ritual, the family always ended up at Jonathon Samuel Gale's house out in Mount Royal. It hadn't actually been his house since Jack had eaten him, but the name had stuck. When he'd molted, back in the winter, Jack had curled up in the enormous room in the basement where his father had once displayed magical artifacts. With a four-year-old in the house, the artifacts had been prudently locked in the vault.

"Because the last thing we need is for Lyra to get her hands on the cross section of the thigh bone of the last True Hero, that's why!"

Jack could think of plenty of things Lyra could grab that'd be worse, but he'd tucked his tail under his body and kept his mouth shut.

There were three green plastic garbage bags of his shed scales in the vault now, too.

The thing he liked best about the house was the huge yard. Even with the pool/hot tub combo, enough open grass remained for him to land at full size. And Lucy'd said she wanted that tree down, so he'd really just done her a favor.

Charlie, smelling like sex, sprawled on one of the lounge chairs by the pool, and looked up as he stepped onto the stone edging although she had to have heard him land. "Where have you been?"

"Grabbed a bite before I came back."

"Do I want to know?"

He shrugged. "It had a sore hoof and the heat was just going to make it worse and there were so many, he'd never miss one."

"And would be unlikely to blame a dragon if he did."

Jack shrugged again, shoved her feet aside, and sat down on the end of the lounger. Charlie's attitude toward his meals was totally better than Allie's. "What're you doing out here?"

"Thinking. With you coming east, I'm going to need my car."

He couldn't see how it could have taken her very long to come to that decision. He couldn't exactly fly around after her; that was the kind of thing people eventually noticed. "Okay."

"And you need to not spend three hours in Toronto with Auntie Jane."

Without even trying, Auntie Jane was as scary as Auntie Carmen and Auntie Gwen and Auntie Bea put together. Although Auntie Bea could be pretty scary on her own.

"So," she continued, "I was thinking of alternative ways to get you and the car to Nova Scotia."

"Drive."

"I need to be there by tomorrow afternoon."

"Drive really fast."

"Tempting, but still impossible. I thought I'd try taking it through the Wood."

"It?"

"The car. And you."

"You can't get me through the Wood. Size matters."

"But you'll be in the car and the car is mostly steel and steel is mostly iron and surrounded by iron, you'll be diminished. Metaphysically speaking."

He poked the bottom of one bare foot, adding just enough heat that she jerked away. "You're totally bullshitting."

"Yes, I am. But it should still work. And watch your language, Allie doesn't like you swearing."

"Bullshit isn't a swear. It's what comes out of a bull." When Charlie continued to hold his gaze, he sighed. "Fine. But if a car is mostly iron, you can't move it through the Wood."

"I'm not Fey, you are. And the car'll be moving on its own, I'll just be steering."

"Still something that comes out of a bull."

"Still not arguing. Should still work.

"But you've never done it."

"I used to think about doing it with *Dun Good*'s bus."

"But you've never done it."

She grinned. "First time for everything."

Jack studied her grin and suddenly missed not knowing if he'd live until dark. It was a weird feeling; he hadn't been that homesick for months. "Okay, then, let's do it." He glanced at the house. The smell of sausages and pancakes wafting out of the enormous kitchen covered the scent of who was up. "And let's do it before Allie stops us," he added.

"You think she can stop me?"

He rolled his eyes. "Duh."

"Yeah, you're probably right. But we'll go tomorrow morning. Two reasons," she added before he could protest. "One, I'm starving and two, there's stuff to sort out after ritual and I don't want to leave it all to Allie. Oh, and nice work with the helicopters, by the way. The UFO thing was inspired." Surging up onto her feet, Charlie grabbed the pool net and started fishing her clothes out of the water.

"Why are . . . never mind."

"Did you charm them?" Jack whispered as Charlie closed the apartment door and locked it.

"Nope. I wore them out." She gestured with the bulging plastic bag stuffed full of jeans and sweaters and he started down the stairs. "It's a good thing they're used to you slipping out for an early flight because you can't sneak for shit. What did you do? Raid the refrigerator?"

The tips of his ears, all the skin she could actually see from three steps up, flushed pink. "Aunt Mary sent another peach pie."

"And you wanted one last piece." Understandable, Allie's mother made great peach pie with a minimum of charms. *Have a good day. Stay safe. A few grandchildren would be nice before I'm too old to enjoy them.* Fortunately, that last one was aimed specifically at Allie. "Maybe I should go back and get . . ."

The pink darkened.

"You ate the whole pie?"

"I was hungry, and she's not going to be sending peach pies to . . . That's weird." Jack paused and stared at his reflection, moving his head closer to the glass then away again.

"Your pigeon impression? Is weird?" she added when he shot her a look dripping with teenage scorn.

"No, this!" He made the move again as Charlie stopped beside him.

She rolled her eyes. "Ah yeah, the 3D thing again. Hate it."

"I've never seen it do this before." Stepping back as far as the narrow hall allowed, he made a few of the martial arts moves that seemed to be hardwired into the teenage boy genome, then charged forward. "Cool. It's like I'm coming out of the glass."

Charlie grinned. "The fact that you're so easily amused will probably come in handy later." Crossing behind him, she opened the door leading into the store—she'd parked out front, knowing they couldn't sneak past the loft and Auntie Gwen. She stepped out into the Emporium, stopped cold, and stepped back. "Say that again."

Jack shrugged, grabbed for his hockey bag as the strap slid off his shoulder, and said, "It's like I'm coming out of the glass."

"It's like you're coming out of the glass," Charlie repeated. Her fiddler ran through the first few bars of "Smash the Windows" but only because "It's About Fucking Time" had never been put to music. She pushed past Jack, back to the mirror, where fireworks were going off around her reflection. "I'm an idiot."

"Okay."

"Not talking to you." Leaning forward, she exhaled against the glass and drew a charm in the condensation. "Thank you. I'm sorry I was so slow."

"You just apologized to an inanimate object," Jack pointed out as she turned.

"Auntie Catherine is coming in through the mirrors when she goes after the sealskins. That's why I couldn't find any evidence of charms; they're all on the other side of the glass. The mirror, this mirror, has been trying to tell me that since she started, but I didn't get it."

"You are an idiot."

Charlie cuffed him on the back of the head. "Come on, kid, we're going to be heroes."

*   *   *

"You ready?" Charlie flexed her fingers over the strings and angled the headstock a little more toward the roof of the car giving her better coverage over the sound hole and making it less likely she'd clip Jack in the ear at an incredibly inopportune moment.

"Not really."

"Loosen up on the steering wheel, I can smell burning plastic."

"This is crazy."

"Three hours with Auntie Jane."

"Okay." Jack drew in a deep breath.

"Ease off the clutch as you give it a little gas."

"I know!"

Of course he did. Teenagers knew everything.

The car jerked forward.

"A little more gas."

"I know!"

They roared down the street toward the riverbank, the car demanding a higher gear.

"Now, into second." Charlie'd covered the car with the necessary charms—where necessary meant every charm she could think of that might work. "You're doing great. Now, third." She braced herself against the dashboard just in time. "Okay, that was first, not third. Remember the H shape."

Unfortunately, when she'd come up with the idea of taking the car through the Wood, she'd forgotten she wouldn't be able to drive it. Still, how hard could it be for a Dragon Prince/Sorcerer/Gale to master a crash course in driving a standard shift?

"That's good." Right knee against the door holding her steady, Charlie played an arpeggio in G. G minor. G minor seventh. "Now give it more gas and drive it straight into those trees."

Crash course being the operative words.

*   *   *

"Brake! Brake!"

The back of the Selkie's house on Grandfather's Cove was coming up fast.

Really fast.

Too fast.

"Jack, that's the clutch! Off the gas and on the bra . . ."

The car bucked up on its front wheels and stalled.

". . . ke," Charlie finished as it bounced to a stop. A slightly singed birch branch slid down the windshield, bounced off the hood, and fell to the ground. Steam rose up through the front vents. Hopefully steam. Smoke would be bad.

Breathing would be good, too, she realized.

Turning to Jack, she poked him in the side and he exhaled explosively.

Good news: compared to what now filled the car, that was definitely steam coming off the engine.

"That was still better than three hours with Auntie Jane." She couldn't see his face, but Jack sounded fine. Of course he was fine. He was a Gale.

They got out of the car more or less in unison. Guitar swinging from the strap, Charlie coughed, waved away the smoke, and stared at the ruts crossing the backyard. As she reached out and patted the back of the house, not actually needing to completely straighten her arm, her G string broke.

"End of the summer, we might take the long way home," she said thoughtfully, jerking her head away from the flailing wire.

"Yeah . . ." Jack was still smoking on every exhale but the volume had started to taper off a bit. ". . . I'm down with that. You think they've noticed we're gone?"

A phone rang inside the house, Allie's ringtone clearly audible through the open window.

Charlie'd given her phone to Eineen. Who'd evidently left it here. Nearly seven Calgary time, nearly eleven in Nova Scotia, and no one was answering. So no one was home. "Well, that sucks. Here we are, bearing the knowledge of how to keep Auntie Catherine from playing bogeyman— and there's no one to tell. Wait!" Jack jerked and she hid a smile. "I can use your phone!"

"I'm not fifteen, remember. But Auntie Jane said she'd give me a phone early when we talked in Toronto."

Possibly. Charlie was sticking to her original theory that Auntie Jane didn't want Jack running Wild.

"I can get through that door," Jack offered. "Easy."

If she had her phone, she could call Tanis—who couldn't go into the water without her skin so was probably weeping on Bo's shoulder.

"The door isn't a problem, but we have to time it right."

"Time it? Charlie, it's a . . ."

The phone stopped ringing.

"Now!"

Charging across the kitchen, slamming her thumb into the edge of the table as she snatched up her phone, Charlie managed to dial out before anyone else dialed in.

"It's like on *Stargate*," Jack said as she waited for Tanis to answer.

"The TV show? I think they got that idea from Auntie . . . Tanis? Auntie Catherine is coming through the mirrors. That's how she's taking the skins. What? Please stop crying, you sound like you're talking underwater." She waved Jack toward the door and mouthed, *you broke it, you fix it.*

He leaned the door against the kitchen cabinets. "How?"

"Hello? Sorcery."

"Sorcery!"

"No, Tanis, Auntie Catherine is not using sorcery; it's a Wild Power thing, like going through the Woods, only shinier." She waited while Tanis told Bo, then added, "Tell everyone to cover their mirrors, that'll keep her out."

"All their mirrors? Even the small ones?"

"Even the small ones. This may be the one time size *doesn't* . . ." Tires squealed. Charlie winced. "Tanis? Tanis?" Given the volume of the shouting, both Tanis and Bo were fine, but they sounded liked they had some things to work out. Charlie tossed her phone back down onto the table. "Tanis ripped off the rearview mirror and threw it out the window. Come on, let's go."

Jack jerked a thumb back over his shoulder. "The door's still a little wonky."

Both the door and the space it filled were no longer exactly rectangular. But they weren't butterflies, so Charlie counted it as a win. "Does it lock?"

It did.

"Good enough."

"I thought I wasn't supposed to do sorcery?"

"You're not supposed to be a sorcerer," Charlie told him, sliding in behind the wheel. "Not the same thing. Now, if we're going to make sound check . . ." Fingers crossed, she settled her left hand in the undulations Jack had melted, and turned the key with the right. The engine grumbled for a moment but started. ". . . we're going to have to drive fast."

"Cool." Jack rolled down his window. "Can we stop for food, though? I'm starving."

Inside the house, the phone began playing "Ride of the Valkyries."

SEVEN

"SO, YOU'RE COUSIN JACK." The weird guy in the skirt straightened, and peered at Jack over the top edge of his sunglasses. "You seem to be a good influence on Chuck since she's actually here on time. Mark." He stuck out his right hand.

Jack looked at the tangle of cables Mark held and then over at Charlie, who shrugged. Maybe this was a test. After a little initial confusion, he'd learned that when people held out their hand in the MidRealm, it was a greeting not a threat. While Allie'd applied first aid, Graham had explained that it used to mean, *See, my hand is empty. I'm not likely to kill you in the next few moments.* Was Mark saying, *I can strangle you with these cables, you decide how this interaction is going to go?* Or had he just forgotten he was holding them? Given what Jack could see of Mark's expression behind all the hair, he was betting on the later. Tugging the cables free of a surprisingly strong grip, he shook the guy's hand, then handed the cables back.

Seemed to have been the right thing to do, but he supposed it could come back to take a bite from his tail later.

"I like him, Chuck. You know why you're here, Cousin Jack?"

"As far as Mark's concerned," Charlie said before Jack could answer, "you're here to be a roadie for the band. That's as far as his interest extends."

Her expression said, *He doesn't have to know all you are.*

Well, duh. Who did?

"Bullshit. I have extended interests." Mark seemed harmless. Jack didn't trust that. "Anything you need to know, Cousin Jack?"

He shrugged. "Charlie's got it covered. But . . ."

"Yes?"

"Why the skirt?"

"It's a kilt."

"Okay." He waited. Glanced over at Charlie, then back at Mark.

After a moment, Mark's brows rose—barely visible between the sunglasses and the hair. "Oh, you really wanted to know. I thought you were just being a smart-ass, you know, given the fourteen and all. I wear a kilt . . ." He ran his empty hand down over the pleats. ". . . because I find it more comfortable to let the boys hang free."

"Genitals," Charlie said quickly. "Don't give me that look," she added more quickly still as Jack closed his mouth so emphatically his teeth clacked. "You know you were about to ask how he got boys under his kilt and you . . ." Turning to Mark. ". . . were going to say a six-pack usually works, so . . ." She mimed a rim shot. ". . . moving on."

"No one appreciates the classics," Mark muttered. "Can you lift an amp, Cousin Jack?"

Jack shrugged. He could lift a buffalo. "I'm stronger than I look."

Stepping away from the van, Mark made a sweeping gesture at a black box thing with fabric and dials. Jack guessed that must be an amp. Charlie'd never brought one home, so he'd never seen one up close and personal. They looked fuzzier on YouTube. He leaned in, lifted the box thing up, and said, "Where do you want it?"

"Get it to the stage. Tim'll place it."

Even in this form he could probably carry two, three if they weren't such an awkward size, but he suspected, given the question, Humans couldn't.

"Ah, the energy of youth," he head Mark say as he headed for the stage. "Anything else I should know about him? You said his parents were dead?"

"Father's dead, mother's not around. He's strong-minded, independent, easy to feed, and . . ."

"And I can still hear you!" Jack yelled without turning.

". . . picks his nose with his tailtip when he thinks no one's looking!"

Jack flushed.

"Of course we tell the truth," Auntie Bea sniffed. "We're hardly responsible for what people believe."

It hadn't taken him long to realize that it wasn't what a Gale said, it was how they said it.

Listening to Mark laugh, Jack wondered if Charlie knew that basic rule applied to every word out of her mouth.

It figured that in front of a crowd of tourists, most of whom couldn't tell a jig from a reel, Grinneal had never sounded better. At the last minute, Mark decided not to play "Wild Road Beyond."

"Wasted on this lot," he'd said. "Too many Tilleys in the crowd."

His song, his decision, but Charlie couldn't see that the hats made much of a difference. Everyone was on their feet from the second song, and when they knew the words—international crowds meant American covers—they roared the chorus back at the stage like they'd been raised to the sound of the fiddle.

By nine thirty, the hats were white blobs in the gathering darkness and the smell of sweat had overwhelmed the scent of mosquito repellent. Ignoring the teenagers employed by Parks Canada, who were attempting to herd everyone back to their campsites, the crowd demanded one last song.

Mark's eyes gleamed. Charlie tightened her grip on her pick as he slammed them into "Mari Mac." Eight verses later, the band finished the song at Mach 10 and the crowd, wrung dry, finally surrendered the field.

"Figures this wasn't a festival show," Shelly gasped, tossing Charlie a bottle of water and cracking one for herself. "We were on fucking fire!"

"Damn right," Charlie agreed, stretching her T-shirt up to wipe her forehead. "So we just do it again. And again. And again." She emptied the bottle as Shelly laughed.

"You think it's going to be that easy?"

"Please. If it was easy, everybody'd be doing it. We, however, are amazing."

"We are."

"We not only rock and roll, we Celt."

"I don't think you can use that as a verb," Shelly pointed out, bending to unplug her electric upright bass.

"I can use anything I want as a . . ." Charlie couldn't see what Tanis was looking at, but, even at a distance, it seemed as though Bo's arm was the only thing keeping her vertical. Swinging her guitar back around in front of her body, although she had no idea what she'd do should Auntie Catherine have decided to get up close and personal now the mirrors were blocked, Charlie ran from the grandstand to where the fiddle player and the Selkie were standing at the end of the trampled grass.

Not Auntie Catherine.

Jack.

And his eyes were gold.

"Tanis, Bo, I see you met my cousin Jack. Jack, this is Bomen Deol, our fiddle player and Tanis, his girlfriend." Squirming past Tanis, she moved in beside Jack and elbowed him hard in the ribs. "Remember the food rule." Her presence had stopped Bo's constant demands to know what was wrong and Tanis, at least, wasn't crying. Of course it didn't look like she was breathing either. "Tanis! Snap out of it!"

The Selkie blinked, her eyes welled up with tears, and she sank to her knees—sliding out of Bo's relaxed grip. "Highness."

Oh, right. Dragon *Prince.* Usually the dragon part was the more relevant. "Jack!"

"I didn't do anything!" His eyes hazel again, he waved a hand at Tanis who shuddered and leaned away. "She's just . . ."

"Tanis, get up." Eineen did not sound happy. Or look particularly Human as she appeared out of the darkness. "Highness." She inclined her head to Jack, then turned on Charlie, lips pulled back from pointed teeth. "What is he doing here?"

"He's my cousin."

"He is also . . ."

"I know. But he's my cousin."

"And that cancels out the rest, does it?"

Charlie shrugged and slung an arm around Jack's shoulders. It wasn't particularly comfortable, given how much taller he'd gotten, but she didn't want anyone, especially Jack, coming to the wrong conclusion. She felt him begin to relax under her touch. "Trumps the rest, at any rate. He's family. He's a Gale."

"Your Auntie Catherine is family and a Gale."

"Never said the family didn't disagree."

"And if His Highness decides to disagree?"

"Like I said, he's a Gale. That makes it our business, not yours."

"This is not the UnderRealm. He does not rule here. He does not feed where he wishes."

"He knows that."

"He's not deaf," Jack muttered. "Look, there's lots to eat here that's not going to get bent out of shape about it, right? So get a grip. I'm just spending the summer with Charlie and carrying amps and stuff."

"And yet you remain who you are."

He sighed, only smoking a little. "And I'm a Gale, like Charlie says."

"We shall see. Tanis."

Tanis blinked, the tears finally rolling down her face as Eineen took her arm.

"I think tonight you had best come home. Tomorrow morning, we hold the press conference to discuss the shallow water well." Her gaze swept over Jack before it came to rest on Charlie. "The press conference *you* suggested. I sincerely hope you know what you are doing."

"I do." She did. Sort of. "You hold a press conference; I speak to Amelia Carlson while she's lulled into a false sense of security and find out where the skins are."

"And a false sense of security is your plan to gain access?"

"Please." Apparently, Selkies didn't recognize that as a dismissal. Fine, if she needed a plan . . . "Grinneal is taking part in a major festival. Majorish," she amended, "and if I have to talk my way past a secretary or something, I can say I'm there asking for a corporate sponsorship."

Eineen's eyes narrowed and her lips thinned.

"It's a lie to get in the door," Charlie reminded her. "It's not like we'll actually use her evil oil money."

"So you say." Arm around Tanis' shoulder, much as Charlie's was still around Jack's, Eineen led the younger Selkie off toward the water.

"Hey!" Charlie took a step away from Jack then stopped. She wasn't going to go running after them. "Did you fix the mirrors?"

Eineen paused at edge of shadow. "We have passed on the message."

"Yeah, well, you're welcome," Charlie muttered as they disappeared.

"What the hell just happened?" Bo demanded.

"You heard her," Charlie told him. "Press conference tomorrow morning."

"Charlotte!" Eineen's voice came out of the darkness. Followed by Charlie's phone.

Jack snatched it out of the air.

Bo continued to look confused. "Okay, so Tanis is spending the night with Eineen, right? I have no idea what's happening anymore." He peered at Jack, and Charlie realized that of the people involved in the confrontation, only Bo couldn't see in the dark. "You're a prince?"

Jack shrugged. "Sometimes."

"I find it helps to concentrate on the music," Charlie told him, waving Jack off when he tried to hand her the phone.

The lines in Bo's forehead smoothed out. "The music, yeah, I guess that's the smart thing to do. So, I think I'll start by helping Shelly pack her gear up and move straight to beer after that."

"Sorry about messing things up with you and Eineen," Jack muttered when they were alone.

"How do you know . . . ?"

"No contractions." He snorted. "Like that doesn't give everything away."

"Well, since there wasn't anything actually between me and Eineen, no harm no foul. Also, no snacking."

"I got that the first seven million times."

"Bears repeating."

"It really doesn't."

Charlie had a sudden memory of her mother going on and on and on at her about her hair falling out if she dyed it again. "You're right. You're fourteen, not four. Go help Bo and Shelly load the car."

"Where are you going to be?"

"Right here." She took the phone from his hand. It rang. "Reminding Allie what Wild means."

The Two Seventy-five N press conference took place in Halifax, in one of the Halifax Film Company studios. The room was surprisingly full; Charlie saw cameras from CBC, CTV, and Global as well as all two dozen of the province's newspapers from the daily *Chronicle-Herald* to the monthly *Tatamagouche Light*. Standing at the back of the room, watching the male members of the press swarm around Tanis, Eineen, and one of Tanis' sisters like moths to a flame, she wondered how many of them had already been burned. That whole seal-wife thing might place the Selkies among the more passive aggressive of the UnderRealm immigrants, but all the Fey played hard with their toys.

Of the four men at the front of the room, two were fiddlers, Kevin and Ian Markham who played together in The Brothers Markham Mayhem—usually referred to as Mayhem—the other two Charlie didn't know but assumed they were representing the fishermen who wanted an oil spill as little as the Selkies did.

As the press corps settled, Eineen smiled and said, "Thank you all for coming."

Charlie mimed a rim shot, although she was probably the only one who got the joke, then turned and slipped out the door. As much as she'd like to stay and watch very pretty people do what she'd told them to—and honestly, who wouldn't?—she had plans of her own.

Attendance at press conferences given by local environmental groups opposed to a Carlson Oil project was not generally a part of Paul's job description as Amelia Carlson's executive assistant. Under normal circumstances, any one of the summer interns cluttering up the place would be sent along as a place holder.

None of the circumstances surrounding this latest project even came close to resembling normal.

Seated on the outside aisle about halfway up the room where he could either make himself noticed for a sound bite or slip away unseen, Paul watched the press milling around the seven members of Two Seventy-five N in attendance and had to admit that for whacked-out environmental activists, they were a good-looking bunch. The price of every single article of clothing they wore all added together probably cost less than Paul's linen jacket, but they wore their tatty shirts and faded jeans and plastic sandals with more confidence than he'd been able to pay for. Paul had never been a both sides of the street kind of guy, so he didn't have much of an opinion on the men, but something about the women drew his attention and kept it.

They had a similarity about them that suggested family—not just matching dark hair and dark eyes but the way they moved and smiled. As it happened, he'd run identity checks on everyone connected with the group and most of the unmarried women shared a surname: Seulaich. It was an old Cape Breton family—the name went back as far as the records did—and the odds were good that these three were cousins if not sisters.

As they took their seats, the tallest of the women swept her gaze around the room gathering everyone's attention, and said, "Thank you all for coming. We'll begin with a prepared statement concerning Carlson Oil's proposed shallow water well just off Hay Island and then take questions."

She didn't read the statement, one of the other women did, but Paul continued to watch her as he listened. She barely moved, sitting composed and still, the lights painting highlights across her hair and faint shadows below the dark fringe of her eyelashes. He barely registered the contents of the statement, distracted by the smooth curve of her arm at the edge of her sleeve.

When she announced they'd take questions, he couldn't take his eyes off the movement of her mouth.

"You say that upon consideration you're supporting Carlson Oil's bid for drilling permits; what *exactly* are those considerations?" Lisa Dixon from CTV.com asked aggressively. Paul knew from experience that Ms. Dixon asked everything aggressively, as the website tried to prove itself separate from the network.

The big blond guy at the end of the table smiled before he answered and from the coquettish change in posture, Paul was willing to bet Ms. Dixon wasn't going to argue with a word of his response. And the response was . . .

Dark eyes met his.

It was like looking off the side of his father's boat into deep water, feeling himself falling even while his boots remained on the deck and his fingers stayed clamped tight around the rails.

He was holding a copy of Two Seventy-five N's prepared statement. Print reporters were milling about, cameras were being packed up, web reporters were already filing. He'd missed . . .

There hadn't been . . .

He was having a little trouble remembering.

"Hello."

She was even more beautiful up close, nearly as tall as he was, and . . . was that fiddle music?

"Eineen Seulaich."

"What?"

"It's my name. I thought that since you spent the entire press conference staring at me, you might have missed a few things and we should probably talk."

"Talk?" He could feel the sea surging through his veins, his pulse the crash of the waves on the shore.

Her smile made it difficult to breathe. "You're going to need something to file besides my description."

"File?" Confusion helped him focus. "No, I'm not a reporter. I work for Amelia Carlson, of Carlson Oil."

The disappearance of her smile made it even harder to breathe. "Do you now? Well, then . . ." Her fingers were cool against his cheek. " . . . you'll have to work a little harder for me."

"I don't . . ."

"Yes, you do." She fell in beside the others as they passed.

Frozen in place, Paul watched the doors close behind them and found himself alone in the room with a few reporters and the certain knowledge that his life had just changed.

Or was about to change.

Or would change, if he could just figure out how.

It hadn't been difficult to find Carlson Oil's Sydney office: the address was on their website.

It wasn't the sort of business where people walked in off the street—if a person was in the building, that person had a reason to be in the building. Charlie probably would have remained unquestioned as she checked out the first floor even if she hadn't been hiding behind the pleasant little melody she was strumming.

The most interesting thing on the first floor was a big room filled with maps and rocks and a table covered in a model of the drilling rig off Hay Island and the proposed refinery on Scatarie. The water of the painted sea was a uniform and unrealistic blue everywhere but under the model of the rig where it was a purplish/greenish/black, like a bruise, the edges feathering out into the blue as though both colors of paint were still wet. Although they weren't. Why would an oil company paint in an oil spill under their own rig? Either it was a weirdly artistic bit of corporate sabotage, or one of Amelia Carlson's employees had a warped sense of humor.

Other than the model, the first floor held only a few worker bees in worker bee cubicles. The queen would be on the second floor.

A glance left at the top of the stairs showed nothing but a hallway and doors. To the right, behind a set of open glass doors, an office that smelled faintly of fresh paint. On the far wall, another solid door, slightly ajar.

This was where Charlie'd planned to use the corporate sponsor story, fast talking her way past the assistant who should have been guarding the door. Looked like she could save the story for another day.

Hands by the strings but not actually playing, she crossed the office, paused, and slowly pushed open the inner door. The woman behind the desk looked up, obviously expected to see someone else, and clearly would have frowned had her forehead been capable of movement. Amelia Carlson's attempt to remain at her media-inspired peak was a lot more obvious in the flesh. Charlie'd never seen anyone dig their artificial fingernails so desperately into their youth, although, she silently admitted, she didn't travel in the kind of circles where it might be a common behavior. Gale girls knew where the real power lay.

"Amelia Carlson?"

The woman behind the desk ignored the question which, Charlie figured, answered the question. "And who are you?"

"I'm working for some people whose property you've taken."

"I own the land in Pictou County free and clear. Now get out."

"Not that property."

"Oh, for . . . I gave Brandt a fair price for that warehouse. If you want to discuss it further, make an appointment with my assistant."

She clearly hadn't been acting out of character when she'd paid Auntie Catherine to steal from the Selkies. "Not that property either."

"Then what . . . ?" Her lip curled, enough disdain to move the collagen. "You're not a lawyer."

Charlie glanced down at her guitar. "No, I'm not."

Eyes narrowed, Amelia Carlson looked past Charlie to the door.

Considering how little of her face moved, Charlie had to guess what she was thinking. *If I tell you to go, you won't. As I can't make you, that would weaken my position. In order to remain in control, I must control the conversation and that means I issue the definitive statements, not you.*

Of course, it was equally likely she was thinking: *Oh, good, the half a dozen burly miners I employ to kick ass are on their way down the hall.*

All right, maybe not as likely, but possible.

"Fine." She sounded bored. "Why are you here?"

So much for the burly miners, Charlie thought a little sadly. She'd have known how to deal with those. "I want the sealskins back."

Leaning back in a chair that looked like it should be on an episode of *Star Trek*, Carlson steepled her fingers and looked intrigued. "I assumed you'd be older."

"What?"

"You're the one working for them, aren't you? You're like her."

"Her?" Oh. Auntie Catherine. "I'm not like her."

"Please." Carlson waved the protest off with a manicure that probably cost more than Charlie made in a week playing with *Grinneal*. "She already told us you were like her."

"She's wrong."

"You're very young."

"I'm almost thirty."

"Really?" A slow sweep took in Charlie's flip flops, shorts, and Disneyland 2011 T-shirt.

Teeth closed on a verbal response, Charlie exhaled slowly and then ghosted her fingers over the strings.

Carlson shuddered and leaned a little farther away although she tried to make it look like she hadn't. "All right. Fine. I don't know what they're paying you, but I can pay you more."

"I don't want your money, I want the sealskins. You must have seen the press conference; you don't need them anymore. You've won."

"Do I look stupid?" Relaxing back to her previous position, Carlson's lip curled again. Something had clearly changed, but Charlie didn't know what. "When they say public opinion changes like the tides," Carlson continued, "they literally mean that twelve hours is the length of time people will hold an opinion without reinforcement. If I give you the pelts, I have no leverage. Next thing I know, that little environmental group is back at it and we go through it all again. So no, you can't have the pelts. You'll have to go to the police. Oh, wait, you can't go to the police. It's all up to you." Her lip curled higher into a nasty smile. She spread her hands. "All right, then, smite me."

"Say what?"

"Torture me for their location. Threaten me with retribution." To Charlie's surprise, she laughed. "You don't have it in you. You showed me what you were, but not what you could do. You're right. You're not like her. The one of whatever you are that *I* have, she could smite and torture and threaten, but that's not you. I've looked across my desk at politicians and the competition and my own board members and, in order to survive, I've had to know what I'm looking at. Do you know what I see when I look at you? I see someone who likes to hang out with her friends, have a few beers, play a few tunes. You have a good relationship with your family, but you don't take their concerns seriously. I believe the word is: slacker. Play me a protest song, if you want, but you're not getting those pelts."

Charlie pressed the fingers of her left hand down on the strings so hard she felt the wire dig into the bone, as though the calluses weren't even there. She could read her audience as well and right now she knew she could play the pain the Selkies felt and Amelia Carlson would feel it, but she wouldn't care. She'd consider it evidence her blackmail was succeeding.

If making her *feel* wouldn't work . . .

Grabbing her, taking her through the Wood, and abandoning her—*Give me the sealskins or I'll leave you here* —would only piss her off.

The charms Charlie used most were to ease her way, some specially so she didn't die in a fiery car crash, but usually just to make the world a more convenient place. She didn't know how to say, *"Do what I want you to do,"* and mean it.

"You've got nothing, do you?" Carlson smiled. "Get out."

The important thing to remember about slackers wasn't that they spent their time lounging about doing nothing. If lounging was all they were capable of, they wouldn't be *slacking.* No, the thing to remember about slackers was that, by definition, they weren't living up to their potential. Amelia liked to think she had a good eye for potential. It was why she'd hired Paul. He'd wanted away from his working class background so badly that he'd accomplish the impossible to do it.

She'd seen potential in the woman with the guitar; the seeds of the same certainty that made Catherine Gale so terrifying. Catherine Gale had shown up in her office and announced she had a way of getting the worst of the environmental groups to back off, allowing the government to issue permits for the well off Hay Island with a clear conscience. At that point, with the news of the well about to break in the media, Amelia would have listened to a dwarf announcing he could spin straw into government influence.

The deal had been for cash. No paper trail linking Carlson Oil to Catherine Gale. Amelia had been told to leave four equal payments overnight in a locked desk drawer—one on July 26th, one on July 29th, one on August 1st, and one tonight on August 4th. Maybe Catherine Gale hadn't wanted to make a suspiciously large, lump sum cash deposit. Maybe there was some sort of ritual in four payments three days apart. Amelia didn't know and didn't particularly care. Although the drawer had still been locked when she returned to her office every morning after having left the money as agreed, the money had been gone. It felt as though she were paying protection to the shoemaker's elves or leaving one hell of a snack for Santa.

Amelia pulled the two stacks of cash from her top drawer, stared at the fifty dollar bill on the top of each stack for a moment, then she pulled out a piece of paper and wrote, *Two Seventy-five N sent her to my office. I saw on her face the curve of your cheek, the angle of your nose. We need to talk.*

"Why didn't you just make her do what you wanted?" Jack asked, peering suspiciously into his hamburger.

"What? Throw a charm at her that made her tell me everything? Because she'd have told me *everything*." On the other side of the table, Charlie jabbed the ice at the bottom of her glass with her straw. "Tell me where you've hidden the Selkie skins that you had stolen in order to blackmail Two Seventy-five N into supporting you is just a little more specific than charms are."

"I didn't mean with a charm."

"Yeah, well, I could have sung the Selkie pain at her, but she wouldn't have given a shit."

Frowning, Jack set the upper bun to one side wondering if Charlie was being deliberately stupid. "You could have just asked her," he muttered. When Charlie rolled her eyes, he added, "Okay, fine, if you aren't going to *make* her talk, I could."

"You could make her pee herself, but I don't think she'd tell you anything. What are you doing to that burger?"

"It has onions. I don't like onions."

"You ate your father."

"Not with onions." He reassembled his burger. "So if you weren't going to make her talk, why did you go see her?"

Charlie snagged one of the rejected rings. "I thought she'd think she was winning and she'd tell me where the skins were."

"Seriously?" Jack sputtered, spraying the table with sesame seeds. "You've never actually had enemies, have you?"

She thought about growing up surrounded by family, by people who loved her completely, unconditionally, fiercely. About discovering her way through the Wood and how her family had stepped back and let her go, let find her own path. About Allie who had been hers in all the ways that mattered since she was fifteen and about Graham who trusted her. "No," she said at last, "I haven't."

"Duh. Enemies don't defeat themselves for you; not even if you're a Gale. You're going to have to put a little effort in."

"I don't . . ."

"And again, duh. And next time, before you try stupid shit, talk to me. Twelve uncles, remember?" His eyes flared gold. "I know about having enemies. You going to eat those?" When Charlie shook her head, he dragged the last of her fries over to his side of the table. "So, what're you doing tonight?"

"Practice, with the band. It's a festival stage this weekend in Louisburg." She flicked sesame seeds back toward him. Not like she could do anything for the Selkies, not without knowing where the skins were. "We need to scoop some points."

"Playing in the Fort? I read the pamphlet when you were in the can," he added nodding toward the tourist brochures tucked in between the stainless steel napkin holder and the wall.

"Just outside the Fort by the visitor's center, I think. But we can go inside the Fort if you want."

He shrugged, suddenly too teenage to admit he wanted. "Do I need to be there tonight?"

"Depends, what are you likely to do instead?"

"Fly." He shrugged again. "Scout out the lay of the land, you know, in case I need to get somewhere quick because you have . . ." Teeth more Dragon than Human bit a french fry in half with cheerful overemphasis. ". . . an enemy."

"Who can't do anything to me, you know that right?"

"Rules have changed. You've agreed to be a Hero."

Yeah right. A Hero. So far her only contribution had been all about locking the barn door after the skins were stolen. But since Jack seemed to be waiting for a response, she growled, "Shut up."

"And I may eat a deer."

It took Charlie a moment to rewind that back to context. "Just don't fall asleep in a cave someplace. That'd be a little hard to explain to the band."

Jack snorted. "Not for you."

"You want dessert?" The diner's single waitress frowned at the dissipating smoke as she tapped her order pad with what looked like a bowling alley pencil.

"Do you have pie?" Jack's grin was all Human. Well, all Gale, Charlie amended and the waitress couldn't help but respond.

Her gaze softened and the tension in her shoulders relaxed as she turned to face him. "We've got the best pie in Cape Breton, hon. Blueberry, raspberry, peach, lemon meringue, and coconut cream."

"Uncharmed?"

Charlie kicked him under the table.

"I mean, yes, please!"

His enthusiasm chased her confusion away. "Well, which do you want?"

Charlie held up two fingers and Jack sighed with such force the blast of warm air curled the edges of the paper placemats. "Blueberry and coconut cream."

"They won't be as good as what you get at home," Charlie warned him when they were alone again.

"Yeah, but pie. Uncharmed pie!"

He had a point.

Paul had no idea why he was sitting tucked out of the wind with his back against a jumbled pile of rock, staring out at the barely visible waves of the North Atlantic slapping against the shore. His day after the press conference had been like a thousand others. He'd been on the phone most of the 398-kilometer drive back to Sydney, booking appointments, touching base with Captain Bonner who commanded the leased barge already loaded with the pylons for the drilling platform, and speaking to three people in the ministry of natural resources office although not to the actual minister. He'd arrived at the office at 4:35 PM then had gotten immediately back into his car and driven Ms. Carlson to the Sydney airport so she could fly to Halifax and attend a dinner for the Nova Scotia Professional Women's Association along with the four female members of the provincial cabinet and seven Members of the House of Assembly.

The Minister of Natural Resources might issue the permits, but he was as susceptible to peer pressure as anyone.

They did the debrief about the press conference on the road.

"Were they convincing?"

"Stunning. I mean, yes. Convincing. Very convincing."

After seeing her off, he'd returned to the office and analyzed the minister's schedule for any leverage they could exert, then gone over the simplified seismic surveys for the Hay Island well, making sure the PR department had covered all the bases. He'd dealt with a list of problems left on his desk in Ms. Carlson's nearly illegible scrawl about her leased accommodations, brought her appointment with the dermatologist ahead two days because of a television interview, checked that her pale pink linen suit was back from the dry cleaners then, around 9:05, he'd cleared his desk, turned out the lights, and been, as usual, the last man out of the building.

He'd picked up some fast food on the way back to his hotel.

Then he'd driven past his hotel.

He hadn't intended to head for the coast, but somehow, forty minutes later as the long summer twilight had started to deepen into actual darkness, he'd found himself testing his car's suspension on a set of ruts leading east off 255 toward the ocean. He'd driven until he'd run out of even the semblance of a road, then he'd walked, then he'd sat, and watched the last of the light disappear and the water turn from gray to black.

He didn't know why he was here.

"The sea gets in your blood," his father had told him and had listened patiently to a ten year old's explanation of how blood was, evolutionarily speaking, not much different than the seawater that had surrounded the original, single-celled life destined to eventually climb up out of the oceans. It wasn't poetry, but science.

It seemed science had his heart pounding in time to the steady rhythm of the waves against the shore. The tide had turned and was on its way back in, but a lot of the rocky beach remained exposed. There wasn't much of a moon—more than a crescent but not quite half. Paul didn't know what to call it, but the sky was clear and the moon seemed to be shedding light out of proportion to its size. Each wave had been edged with silver. The rocks glistened. He could see the gleam of shells polished white . . .

Like bone.

Where the hell had *that* come from? Like bone?

"Men who die at sea," his father had told him, *"die alone."*

Who said that kind of shit to a kid? Really? And he wasn't *alone;* he was by himself. Not the same thing. Even if he'd had time to meet women, he didn't have time for a relationship. He didn't have time to wake up next to someone, to fight over the last bagel, to unlock the door again so he could kiss them good-bye. He didn't have time to explain the difference between offside and icing to a warm body curled up beside him on the couch. He didn't have time to forget anniversaries, remember birthdays, and share ownership of a small brown dog with a curly tail.

But he wasted a moment in *want.*

This is ridiculous. He shrugged back into his suit jacket and paused, a line of cold stroking down his spine, as he saw a dark oval out in the water. Grown men with two degrees and workplace responsibilities didn't spend their time thinking of bones and bodies and dying alone. Then the oval became a head. A seal head framed by a silver vee as it moved closer to the shore.

Four seal pelts tucked away in a mine.

Just stay still. It won't even know you're here. The odds of it coming up on shore are . . .

It reached the shallows, reared back, and stood, the pelt sliding down over moonlight-gilded skin, flapping for a moment in a grotesque semblance of life, then caught up and becoming . . .

. . . a scarf knotted around slender hips.

Long dark hair flowed across the curve of shoulders, the bell of breasts, dusky nipples exposed, then covered, then exposed again. The eyes were seal's eyes, too large and too dark. The dance was too graceful for land; flesh needed the support that water offered to move so freely.

Paul didn't remember standing.

Or clambering down to the water's edge.

He remember stumbling across the wet rock but only because he fell and drove a sharp edge of storm-split stone into his knee.

The dancer ignored him so obviously it was clear she considered herself alone on this stretch of beach and yet, she danced away every time he tried to move closer.

Finally, as the beach grew smaller and blood ran down his leg to mix with the seawater destroying his shoes, she let him catch up. He reached out and, as she spun, managed to hook one finger behind the scarf around her hips.

The slightest pressure tugged it free and it slapped into his injured leg, wet and heavy and smelling of fish, empty eye sockets starting up at him.

Five pelts.

She stopped dancing and turned.

"Eineen?"

Her smile was as dangerous as deep water and his reaction as unstoppable as the tide.

Careful to keep from crossing the moon and giving himself away, Jack glided away from the drama being played out on the shore below. He'd never paid much attention to the seal-folk back home; they were tasty if caught but had nothing in common with a life of air and fire. They sure were a presence here, though. Every group of seals he'd passed had one or two or half a dozen bright spots of *other* visible to his sight and most of the seals had at least a touch of shine. No surprise. According to his Uncle Adam, things that tasted good had a strong urge to reproduce and an UnderRealm bull would be dominant in any MidRealm herd.

Did they sense him, he wondered? Did they feel him flying overhead and dive for deep water? Or did they realize he was different and they were safe?

He was a Gale. *With wings and scales.Wings and scales, teeth and tail. Sorcery that never failed.* Lips pursed, he blew out short blasts of flame instead of the mouth beats—dragon mouths not so much made for rap—and wondered if any of the bands in Charlie's festival ever played anything good. *Gale. Scales. Never failed. In your face; I got a family place!*

Wheeling inland toward the sound of a large body moving through the underbrush, he used his shadow to herd the deer into a clearing large enough for him to strike. He used to wonder why the family got totally bent out of shape about Pixies—and no one, not even other Pixies cared about Pixies—but he could chow down on does and fawns and stags and no one blinked an eye. Not even David.

He used to wonder.

He didn't anymore.

When he finally landed behind the church, he could hear Charlie's band still playing in the basement. Charlie probably wouldn't have carried through on her threat to play only bagpipe music in the car if he was late but only a total moron would risk it. Who listened to music that sounded like Naiads being tortured?

Actually, at least half the Courts back home would probably love it.

He remade his clothes from grass clippings and fallen leaves—if he forgot to undress, they burned off when he changed—and pulled them on leaning against Charlie's car. Head half through the neck of the Green Lantern T-shirt, he froze. Somewhere close, a phone was ringing. It wasn't loud, but that wasn't because of distance it was because it was . . .

. . . coming from inside the car. Charlie's phone, then, but just ringing, not playing a signature song.

Someday he'd make her change the ringtone she'd put on for him. Puff was a stupid name for a dragon.

But a plain ring, that meant it was someone Charlie'd never given a song to. Or maybe, they weren't calling for Charlie. Maybe they were calling for him. The family knew where he was and he didn't even have a lame phone that did only voice and texting—although Charlie was probably right about Auntie Jane's ulterior motives—and he hadn't talked to Allie since they'd left Calgary. The ring was so faint only someone who could hear a mouse fart under their flight path would be able to hear it.

Jack unlocked the car and, head cocked, tracked the ring to the glove compartment. Unlocked the glove compartment. Used a claw to cut through the duct tape sealing it shut. Pulled out the wad of dirty laundry. Opened the *Where the Wild Things Are* movie lunch box. Unwrapped the kaiser roll. Pulled the phone out from inside the kaiser roll, ate the kaiser roll, and answered the phone.

"Who are you? Put Charlotte on immediately."

Okay. Not for him. "Can't." He watched the fiddle music stream by, joining the streams always in the air. "She's at band practice."

"Band practice."

It was more of an insult than a question, but he answered anyway. "Uh-huh."

"Tell her to call me when she gets it right!"

"I don't think that means . . . Hello?" He snapped the phone closed and tossed it on the driver's seat. If Charlie'd wanted it to stay hidden, she shouldn't have made it so easy to find.

He told Charlie about the call after they'd loaded all the equipment back into the vehicles and were on the way to Shelly's brother-in-law's cousin where they were spending the weekend.

"No promises," the brother-in-law's cousin had snorted, *"but the missus, she's been buying boxes and boxes of dry cereal against the chance of a zombie apocalypse and I can probably convince her to let go her hold on a couple, maybe even throw in a bag of milk come breakfast time."*

"You're sure it was an auntie?" Charlie asked, turning onto Beatrice Street.

"All the hair on my body stood on end, and if that wasn't creepy enough . . ." He rubbed the back of his neck where goose bumps lingered. ". . . she called you Charlotte and that seal-girl you like is the only other person I ever heard do that. And she was kind of mad at you. They're kind of obvious when they're mad."

"But why wouldn't an auntie know you?"

"Don't know." He was impressed Charlie didn't care about a mad auntie. Angry auntie. Probably. "I thought the aunties had that cool da da DA-da ringtone?"

"Not an auntie trying to fake me out and get me to answer the phone—which would normally mean Auntie Jane."

"She'd know me."

"She doesn't actually know everything. Don't tell her I said that," Charlie added after a moment.

They were stopped behind Mark's van at the bridge when he remembered. "So that seal-girl you like? I was flying up the coast and I saw her come out of the water on legs and dance. And there was a guy there and he grabbed her skin. Her sealskin," he added in case Charlie'd missed the point even though there'd been other grabbing going on. "You know what that means." After a minute, when the silence gained weight, he added, "Sorry."

Charlie sighed. "It wasn't going anywhere, me and her."

"I know. But you liked her."

She sighed again as they started moving. "Yeah, I did. But what can you do."

"Lots of stuff. If I was your prince instead of your cousin and you came to me, I could get the skin back and tell the seal-girl she wasn't allowed to make you unhappy. Even if she couldn't make you happy." When Charlie turned to look at him, he shrugged. "I would, if you wanted."

"If you were my prince?" He braced himself for the lecture on how Gales didn't have princes no matter how spoiled some of the boys got—it was one of Auntie Carmen's favorites—but all Charlie said was, "Need to be a prince very often these days?"

He shrugged again. "Sometimes the lesser folk like that I'm here. This is . . ." He waved a hand out the open window, ". . . messy."

"Confusing?"

"No. And I know the difference."

"Sorry."

"They just like that I could make order even if I don't, you know?"

"I think so."

"But I don't think the Courts know how many of the lesser folk have come through. That's got to be weakening the border." A little of the dashboard melted under his grip. "Look at the road now, okay?"

The brother-in-law's cousin's rec room was crowded with all five of them in there, but he didn't realize how bad it was going to get until Shelly waved him toward the sofa bed, saying, "Charlie and I have shared before, and I know teenage boys need their own space."

"I can't!" He turned to stare at Charlie. The music might've made the band her other family, but carrying some of their equipment didn't make them his family and things happened at night he couldn't control. There were scorch marks on the ceiling of his bedroom to prove it. And *this* ceiling, it looked flammable.

"You can, but you don't have to." Charlie tossed him a pillow. "If you want, you can take your sleeping bag out to the backyard. It's August, it's not going to rain, and I doubt Shelly's brother-in-law's cousin will care."

"Really?"

"Sure. You're fourteen, not four. You can sleep without adult supervision."

"There's bugs, though," Shelly added. "They'll eat you alive."

"I ate a bowl of roasted grasshoppers once," Mark said thoughtfully. "Tasted like peanuts."

Tim's snort suggested *tasted like peanuts* was a relative term.

Bugs didn't bother him. "I can sleep outside?" He checked with Charlie. "Like this?"

She knew what he meant; in skin, not scales. "Why not? Stay in the yard. Come inside if you have to use the bathroom; don't pee against the fence."

"Hadn't occurred to him until you mentioned it," Mark snickered.

"Hey."

His tail nearly ripped its way out of the sleeping bag before he realized Charlie was sitting cross-legged on the grass beside him. "Don't sneak up on a guy!" he snapped, trying not to sound like he'd nearly changed. He hadn't changed without meaning to for years.

"Sorry."

Total lie. "And I don't need you checking up on me."

"I wanted to ask you a question."

He squirmed down in the sleeping bag, muttering, "Yeah, it's proportional."

Charlie snickered. "Your cousins?"

"Duh."

The girls who'd come West with Cameron had stared wide-eyed at his dragon form, then all made a point of drawing him aside to ask. Cameron had patted him on the shoulder and said, *"Take my advice, dude; until you're fifteen just tell them to piss off. They'll be running your life soon enough."*

"Well, I am way outside your seven-year break, so not my problem. Although . . ." She frowned as she broke off blades of grass and flicked them off her fingertips onto the breeze. ". . . your first ritual had better be with one of the older girls. You burn when you're stressed and she's going to need to keep control."

"Over me?"

"Duh." Grinning, Charlie sprinkled bits of grass over his face. "Which brings me to my question. Given that worrying about burning the place down is more likely to cause you to burn the place down, why haven't you ever asked Allie if you could sleep in the courtyard or on the roof?"

"As if. There's no way up to the roof in skin."

"Please. Like she wouldn't jump at the chance to have Michael visit and do that architecture thing. Also, I know for a fact she's always wanted a spiral staircase."

"Why?"

"I have no idea. Now, answer the question."

He turned the next sprinkle of grass into ash before it hit him. "Because people, Gales, sleep in bedrooms."

"Where am I sleeping tonight?"

"In a basement."

"And last night?"

"In a tent, yeah, I get it you're a Gale and you don't sleep in bedrooms, but you're different."

"And we have a winner."

Jack stared at her for a long moment, allowing his vision to sharpen until he could see her as clearly by starlight as he would have in daylight. The charms on her eyelids were freaky, but the rest of her face seemed to be triumphant rather than concerned. That was new. These kinds of conversations with Allie always ended up with her looking like he was a lost sheep or something equally useless and unable to be a Gale.

"Different." She patted her chest. "Different." She smacked his.

"Obvious much," he muttered unable to get his arms out of the sleeping bag to swat her hand away.

"Apparently not." Bending at the waist, she leaned forward and kissed his forehead. "My bad. I should have noticed and done something about it sooner."

"So you're my new mommy?"When her eyes widened, he sighed. "Fourteen, not four. And as Auntie Bea keeps reminding me, when I'm fifteen, and I'm not a child and I'm not protected by being a child, I'll still be a sorcerer and you know what they do to sorcerers."

"You'll also still be half dragon and that makes you unique, unique powers are Wild Powers, that makes *you* a Wild Power, and Wild Powers play by different rules."

"Gale boys aren't Wild Powers."

"Yeah, that's what the aunties said. But Gale boys aren't dragons. Or, technically, princes. First time for everything."

About to tell her that just because she said something that didn't make it so, Jack realized that this was Charlie and all he said was, "Okay."

"Okay?"

"You know, sleeping outside is going to be a nonevent if you don't go away."

"Point." She stood and smiled down at him. "Firm the ground when you get up. Shelly's brother-in-law's cousin won't want a chunk of his yard feeling like a mattress."

"I was *going* to."

"Sleep sweet, Jack."

He rolled his eyes, closed them, and faked a snore. She let him hear her walk away.

First time for everything. Charlie said so.

But it was probably still a good idea to try and do something amazing enough they'd want to keep him around.

EIGHT

AMELIA CARLSON'S CELL PHONE rang at 9:02. Her private number. The one very few people had.

Catherine Gale's last payment and the note had been gone when she got to the office that morning, having already spent an hour with her personal trainer and what felt like twice as long trying to choke down a wheat grass/banana/blueberry smoothie—anti-oxidants and potassium and she had no idea what the hell the wheat grass was in aid of, but considering what she'd paid for it, it had better work.

Her cell phone rang again. And a third time.

Paul appeared in the open doorway. For the first time since she'd hired him, he looked like he hadn't gotten enough sleep. On one level, she approved; overworked assistants gave a person credibility. On another level, bags under anyone's eyes weren't attractive.

Four rings.

"Boss?"

"I've got it." Always three rings to show she wasn't at anyone's beck and call. "Close the door on your way out." She had no idea why she'd waited for four. "Hello."

"The fourth ring is just self-indulgent," a familiar voice said. "What is it we need to talk about?"

Amelia took a deep breath and reminded herself that Sister Benedict was long dead. "I don't care what the relationship is between you and the woman

Two Seventy-five N has hired to find those pelts, but I will not have her walking into my office like she owns the place."

"You won't?"

She could hear Catherine Gale's smile, and only years of practice in boardrooms and at drill sites surrounded by the good ol' boys of the oil industry kept her tone level. "No, I won't. It appears my people can't keep her away any more than they can prevent your coming and going." Contrary to common opinion, flattery was not a universal motivator, but subtle flattery could prime the pump. "I dealt with her yesterday, but I have no doubt she'll regroup and try again."

"You dealt with her?"

The question sounded disappointed, but Amelia had no idea if it was because she'd been able to deal or because Catherine Gale had wanted to do it herself. "Yes. I dealt with her, and I'd appreciate it if you could keep your relatives from wasting my time."

"I am not responsible for my relatives."

"You are responsible for this one showing up in my office."

"How so?"

The longer any conversation continued without a discussion of payment rearing its head, the less likely payment would be required. She would much prefer not having to pay Catherine Gale to deal with this. "You came to me."

"You had a problem I could solve."

"And now I have another one. The difference being, you caused this problem." Amelia had a certain skill at reading silences and this one, this one sounded amused.

"All right, here's what I'll do." Catherine Gale sounded more amused than the silence had. "I'll throw some distractions her way. If she can handle them with time enough left over to bother you, well, you're on your own."

Trying to make one last point while people were hanging up looked desperate. Amelia waited until the dial tone made Catherine Gale's final statement before placing her phone on the desk. She wanted to have Paul set up a meeting with Dr. Hardy, but that wouldn't move the wellhead fifty feet out of the Atlantic or move the Minister of the Environment off his fence.

"Ms. Carlson? The Honorable Cal Westbrook called. Personally. He wants to set up a lunch date."

"Isn't one of his responsibilities the Sydney tar ponds agency?"

"Yes, it is."

"Come up with a believable excuse."

"On it."

On the one hand, it wouldn't hurt to have another cabinet minister on her side. On the other hand, a perceived association between Carlson Oil and Cape Breton's enduring environmental disaster was not something she wanted to encourage.

"Ms. Carlson? Since Two Seventy-five N's press conference supporting the Hay Island well has gotten excellent coverage—I've sent you the list, current as of eleven minutes ago," he added before she could ask, "have you considered returning the pelts?"

"Returning the pelts?" First Catherine Gale's pale reflection, now this.

"Because they've done what you requested."

"And they'll maintain that as long as we have the pelts. Is there anything else?"

"It's just, I got the impression, from the press conference, that I was at . . ."

"Are you drunk?"

He looked startled. "No, of course not."

He wasn't lying. "Then get to the point."

"The owners of these pelts have an emotional attachment to them."

Amelia rolled her eyes. "Of course they do. That's what makes this effective blackmail."

"So you won't . . ." He stared at her for a moment, then shook his head. "Of course not. You have a manicure scheduled for eleven and there'll be a reporter from CBC Halifax outside the building when you leave for lunch. He'll be looking for a spontaneous response to the press conference. I've prepared your statement. And the CRA has opened a docket on Mathew Burke."

"Should I know a Mathew Burke?"

"The union rep you wanted dealt with."

"Of course."

He paused halfway out the door, looking almost judgmental, shook his head, and kept moving.

Amelia rethought her position on Paul and sleep deprivation. It seemed as though baggy eyes were the least of the effects.

Charlie woke up to the sounds of Mark and Tim in the bathroom, saving water. The fiddler in her head played "Never was Piping so Gay" and given the whole piping/plumbing thing, Charlie supposed she would have done the same had their positions been reversed. Closer, she could hear Shelly up on the sofa bed, snoring softly. The light against her eyelids said it was close to noon, and she could smell grass fires as her uncles burned off the thatch in the ditches.

Wait . . .

Opening her eyes, she came face-to-face with Jack, cocooned in his sleeping bag, mouth open, a smudge of ash on his cheek.

Someone would've screamed by now if it was serious, she reminded herself and poked his forehead.

His eyes snapped open instantly, flared gold, then softened to annoyed teenage hazel. "What?"

"You came in."

"Too light too early," he muttered, flopped over, and went back to sleep.

Charlie ticked off another fact on her Jack-as-teenager list—*doesn't stress about burning the house down if he wants to sleep in.* Since it would clearly be a while before she got to use the bathroom, or would want to use the bathroom if she'd matched up the correct actions to the sounds, she joined him.

Paul had never felt this way about anyone. He thought he'd been in love before—Janis Rinscind in grade six, who'd shoved him off the end of the pier and he'd had to ditch his jacket and shoes to make it back to shore, and Bonnie O'Neill in the summer between first and second year university who'd lost her hat at Peggy's Cove and he'd almost been swept away getting it back—but what he felt now, what he felt for Eineen Seulaich, was the difference between looking at a puddle and looking at the ocean.

Janis and Bonnie, they'd been puddles.

Eineen was like the ocean—deep, mysterious, too beautiful to describe. *The sea is a harsh mistress* had been one of his father's more persistent homilies. Paul had never understood it. The sea had always been nothing more than a large body of salt water containing rapidly depleting fish stocks that some men chose to risk their lives for.

He understood it now. Palm sweaty against the plastic case, he waited for Eineen to answer the phone.

"Hello?"

It wasn't her voice. "Is Eineen . . . She gave me . . ." The words got stuck behind his need to speak with Eineen. His need to know nothing had happened to her since he'd left her at dawn. His need to know the entire night hadn't been a dream no matter how much the bruises on his knees suggested it had been very real. Pebble beach; not his first pick for that kind of activity although at the time, he hadn't noticed the rocks.

"Paul, right? Hang on, I'll get her."

"Thank you." Sitting in his car in the dry cleaner's parking lot, he remembered how his name in her mouth had sounded like a storm at sea, sweeping up and shattering everything in its path.

"Paul." Today, it was like waves sliding up over the shore, quiet and welcoming.

"Where are you?"

"With my cousin in Louisburg."

"I need to see you."

"I know."

"Ms. Carlson won't give the pelts back until the drilling has begun."

"I told you."

"I had to ask."

She sighed, and Paul swore he felt her breath against his cheek. "I know."

He thought she'd tell him they'd have to take them back themselves, steal them back, but she said nothing. He listened to his engine purr and his air conditioner hum and thought about the gas he was using and the oil that gas had come from and how there was better than ninety percent chance there were billions of barrels of it under the sea by Hay Island—even if only 500 million were recoverable with today's technology, and said, "I know where they're hidden. We can get them tonight. We can't get them now," he added quickly before she could protest. "I have meetings all afternoon and three calls to Fort McMurray I can't make until after five, but then I'll pick you up and we'll get them, I promise."

"You would turn against your company for me?"

His lips twitched into what was almost a smile. "You told me to."

"You could have refused me."

"No . . ." He ran his thumb along the leather seat, thought of the soft skin of her inner thighs, remembered the empty eyes of her seal pelt, and started talking again before things got weird. Weirder. "How could I? You're the reason I'm breathing." It was quite possibly the most ridiculous thing he'd ever said. And the truest.

"But only after your day's work is done."

He could call the office, tell Ms. Carlson something had come up he had to deal with personally. She'd assume it was to do with his job, with her, and it wasn't like he couldn't—didn't—do a good portion of his job in the car. No, wait, he couldn't, he had to deliver her dry cleaning so she could wear her favorite silk blouse to dinner with Mac Reynolds from the Canadian Environmental Law Association. The blouse was the perfect blend of professional and might-be-interested and he'd been on the lookout for a couple more like it, but for now . . .

"Paul."

"Don't ask me to walk away from this job. It's . . ." It wasn't his father's job. It wasn't up before dawn, and a body destroyed by the cold and the wet, and still not enough money to make ends meet.

"I haven't. I won't."

He believed her. And he chose to ignore the subtext that said she wouldn't have to.

The Louisburg stage for the Samhradh Ceol Feill was a solid seasonal structure near the Fort's Visitor's Center that took advantage of the Fort's parking. It had a backstage area actually large enough for the bands to transition smoothly and a stage manager who seemed to know what she was doing. Although Grinneal had drawn a Saturday evening spot, the entire band had taken advantage of their all access passes to check it out. When Tim didn't swear at the electrical, and Mark approved of the roadies who'd be helping Jack, Charlie figured they were set.

Actually, some of the roadies looked familiar.

"Those two played in Mabou," Shelly told her, pointing at a couple of scrawny teenagers staggering past with cases of bottled water. "They volunteer and get a chance to go on stage between bands. Most of them are solos, but they can have up to three in a group. Their names go into a lottery; winners sit out the next draw but go back in the draw after. The festival stage offers a lot of exposure."

"Sure," Charlie snorted, "if you want to be an itinerant musician dependent on the kindness of strangers, which I'm not saying is a bad thing," she continued as Shelly's brows went up. She spread her arms. "I mean, hello, knowing of what I speak."

"It's not a bad life." Shelly grinned. "In fact, it's a fine life."

"No show tunes!" Mark snapped, swinging around to face them, sunlight glinting on his holographic Sharon, Lois, and Bram medallion. "I end up in one more drunken ode to Rodgers and Hammerstein and I will put my head through my floor tom."

"It's three in the afternoon. Who's drinking?"

As Shelly began naming names, Jack poked Charlie in the side. "Ow."

"Yeah. Whatever. The seal-girl, I mean the fiddler's girlfriend, is trying to get your attention."

"Tanis? Is she crying?"

Jack leaned out to the right, and squinted. "I don't think so."

"Wonder of wonders." Charlie turned and Tanis waved. "Come on."

"I don't . . ."

Jack's arm was warm when she grabbed it but more like *car parked in the sun* than *burn the flesh from your bones*. "This may be about what happened last night. You're my distraction."

"From what?"

"I don't know if you've noticed, but Tanis is a bit emotional. Tanis, hi. What's up? Don't kneel!"

Tanis wobbled but stayed standing and compromised by so obviously not looking at Jack she might as well have been staring. "Eineen . . ."

"Has hooked up. I heard. I'm happy for her."

"Who told you . . . ?" Her gaze flicked over to Jack for a millisecond then locked back onto Charlie's face, eyes moist. "The Dragons are wise and all knowing."

"Know-it-alls, maybe," Charlie grunted as Jack elbowed her in the ribs.

"I wouldn't say . . ."

"You didn't." She got him in a headlock but knew she'd never get him to say auntie before he raised his body temperature from sun-warmed to deep-fried. "Was that all?"

"No . . ." Tanis watched them, confused, but that was a huge improvement over moist. "The man she joined with, he works for Carlson Oil."

Suddenly released, Jack hit the ground on his hands and knees. Swearing under his breath, he slapped out a small grass fire.

Charlie kicked him lightly with the side of her leg. "Watch your language, Your Highness. So Eineen's with a man from Carlson Oil? That's interesting."

"More than interesting; he's the personal assistant of Amelia Carlson."

"Not a fiddler, then?"

Tanis searched out Bo in the crowd of musicians. "He says his father was a fisherman."

"He?"

"Paul."

"Okay." Charlie waved a hand in front of Tanis' face until the Selkie stopped staring at her boyfriend. "Did Eineen plan this?"

"We don't plan the dance."

Jack made a rude noise that morphed into a squawk when Charlie smacked the back of his head. "If it was a plan, it's pretty clever. If it wasn't . . ." She glanced up at a cloudless blue sky and wondered if the gods were laughing. ". . . it looks like the universe is sticking its oar in again. It's a seagoing reference," she added when Tanis looked confused. "Is Paul giving your sealskins back?"

"He doesn't have them, but he knows where they're hidden. Eineen says they're going to pick them up tonight."

"They are?" Charlie looked up at the sky again. "So, I wonder why I'm even here . . ."

The fiddler in her head broke into a reprise of "I Won't Do the Work."

"I didn't say I wouldn't do it. I just said I didn't know what needed to be done."

"Uh, Charlie?" Jack poked her arm. Hard. "You're talking to yourself."

"I have a fiddler in my head," she sighed.

"Is that like one of those things that means something else?" he asked. "Because if it isn't, you're officially the weirdest person I'm related to."

"I'm officially the weirdest person you're related to."

"Okay, then."

And the fiddler played "Farewell to Decorum."

When Paul walked out of the office at 7:22, the earliest he'd ever left voluntarily, Eineen was waiting for him by his car. She wore a purple tank and faded, low-cut jeans held over the sweet arc of her hips by a worn leather belt. On her feet, cheap department store sneakers. She looked like the girls he'd grown up with in Dartmouth except that her hair flowed over bare shoulders like water from the darkest, deepest part of the ocean and the curve of those shoulders was the perfect curve of a wave heading for shore. He cupped her face with both hands and realized, as he caressed her cheeks with his thumbs, that her skin felt like water sun-warmed in tidal pools. Her eyes promised him everything, unconditionally.

He felt as though he was being swept away by all she offered, so he anchored his mouth to hers and . . .

. . . remembered he was in the parking lot outside of Carlson Oil's Sydney office.

Licking lips that tasted of salt, he pulled away. "I can't do this here."

"But you're doing it so well." She yanked him back against her by his belt loops.

"No, I work here. It's unprofessional." He shifted slightly, changing the angle of contact while he was still able.

"To have a life?"

"I was going to pick you up in Louisburg."

Her shrug moved their bodies together in interesting ways. Goose bumps rose on his scalp under the cool paths her fingertips stroked over the side of his head. He didn't realize she'd removed his earpiece until she handed it to him. "It was faster for me to come to you."

"How . . . ?"

"I took a taxi."

"But money . . ."

"Dead men's bones can't stop us claiming treasures from the ocean floor. Also," she added, allowing him to step away, "about forty years ago one of my cousins danced for an investment banker. We have a comprehensive portfolio."

"An investment banker?"

Eineen smiled. "His father was *also* a fisherman. And he was a better than average fiddle player, if only at ceilidhs."

She spoke like she'd known him.

Paul remembered seeing her change, he remembered seeing the pelt fall empty-eyed to the rock, and while he knew it had happened only the night before, it felt as though it happened to someone else a long time ago, everything that had happened overshadowed by the crystal clear memory of how she'd danced to the rhythm of his heart. He knew what she was. He didn't care. Hell, if she didn't care what he was, he had no grounds for complaint. She was tall enough, he barely had to bend when he stepped back in and kissed her. "Let's go make this right."

She licked her lower lip as though chasing his taste, but she didn't look happy. "Returning the skins won't make it right."

"But it's a start?"

"Yes, it's a start."

He knew he should put his earpiece back in. The greater part of his job involved being available when Ms. Carlson needed him. The plastic housing was warm and slightly greasy in his hand. He slipped it into his jacket pocket.

"Yeah, I had a call you were coming, Mr. Belleveau." The guard at the gate frowned, but it looked more like concern than suspicion. "It's kind of late and it's going to be dark soon. Are you sure you don't want to do this tomorrow?"

Paul fought to keep his grip on the steering wheel loose. He'd been pleased to see a different guard than the one who'd let him in before although a repeat of the first man's disinterest would have been a bonus. "I'm here tonight."

"Pardon me for saying this, but you're not exactly dressed for . . ."

"I came straight from the office."

"Well, okay, but . . ." He pushed his cap back and rubbed at the red dent in his forehead. ". . . you shouldn't be going in alone. What if something happened?"

"You know where I am."

"Well, yeah, but . . ."

"If I'm not back in three hours, assume something has happened."

"Three hours is . . ."

"I have no intention of rushing an inspection."

"I guess that'll . . ."

"Good. Thank you." Paul stepped on the gas just emphatically enough for instinct to move the guard away from the car. He drove as fast as he thought was unremarkable to the other side of the wellhead and parked. And exhaled.

"He didn't see you."

"I told you he wouldn't. He saw your jacket and your briefcase." Eineen lifted them both off her lap, twisting gracefully to drop them in the backseat.

"That's amazing. You're amazing."

"I just wasn't the droid he was looking for." When he frowned, she shook her head. "Never mind. Come on."

Paul hadn't even considered going back to the *Duke* alone, although had Eineen not been able to do whatever she'd done to the guard, getting her in would have been complicated. In all honesty, he had trouble thinking about doing anything alone. Every thought of the future, from ten minutes to ten years, involved Eineen. There were whole blocks of time, minutes stacked on minutes, when he didn't think about work at all.

She looked incredible in the hardhat. As the cage descended down the hoist shaft, he wrapped his hands around her waist and kissed a line up one side of her throat, along her jaw, and down the other while she murmured his name and held onto his arms tight enough to leave bruises.

When the cage jerked to a halt at Canaveral, Paul pulled away and fixed his shirt before opening the gate. The corner of Eineen's mouth twitched and he knew she was laughing at him but there was nothing wrong with looking good even one hundred and fifty meters underground. He was still who he was, and who he was did not wander about with a dress shirt untucked and rumpled.

"It's this way, down C tunnel. We can grab the cart I used the last time; it's just inside the tunnel."

When he turned his helmet light on, Eineen reached up and turned it off again. "It might be best," she said quietly, "if the shadows weren't moving."

There were *more* shadows with the only illumination coming from the tunnel lights, but Eineen was right. They stayed put and that was a huge improvement over his last trip when fear had seeded the deserted mine with imaginary dangers.

Pulling his phone from his pocket, Paul called up the schematic as they walked. Without it, he'd never recognize the correct cross corridor. In all honesty, he hadn't tried very hard to mark the place where he'd left the pelts. That wasn't like him, and he wondered if it had been guilt, already present but buried under his obligations to his job.

The cart rolled effortlessly along the tracks, easy enough to push one-handed. They walked silently, Eineen close enough to his side he could feel the turbulence her movement caused in the still air.

"We're under the sea . . ." Cool fingers pressed down on his mouth, stopping the words. When he turned toward her, she shook her head, reached out, and pulled the cart to a stop. Pulled it to a stop before he stopped pushing. He looked at his hand on the crossbar, on her hand beside his, and decided *beside his* was the important thing to remember.

As the last of the noise chased itself down the tunnel—metal on metal, his leather soles on the stone—she leaned close and whispered, "There's something down here."

And all at once he remembered the sound of claws against rock.

"Where . . . ?"

She shook her head, but whether she wanted him to stop talking or because she didn't know where, he couldn't tell.

The cross tunnel, the first cross tunnel out under the sea where he'd left the pelts, was still about ten meters away. Paul pointed and jerked his thumb to the left.

Eineen nodded, came out from behind the cart, and started forward slowly.

Completely silently.

Sweat dribbling down his sides, he followed. Not quite so silently.

It was a deserted mine. It had been deserted for years.

There was nothing down here with them.

They were granting the dark and the quiet and the heat and the oppressive weight of rock and water too much influence.

They were allowing their imaginations to . . .

He missed his footing on a bit of uneven rock, brought his right foot down a little too hard.

It wasn't much of a sound. Anywhere else, it would have gone unnoticed, lost in the ambient noise. Anywhere else, there would have *been* ambient noise.

He froze. Eineen froze, then slowly reached back toward him. Paul caught her hand and laced their fingers together, breathing shallowly, trying to hear past the blood roaring in his ears.

It sounded like rats at first, rats in the distance.

Claws skittering against stone.

He remembered that sound.

It grew louder and sounded less like the random movement of animals.

Still claws against stone, but moving purposefully.

Behind that sound another sound, harder to hear. A rough burr. Stone scraping against stone? As if whatever moved slowly up from the lower tunnels dragged a rock. A large rock. Under the scraping, he could hear a slow thud. Slow but steady. His heart began to match the rhythm.

Eineen's grip tightened as she turned. Her voice bypassed Paul's ears and jabbed straight into his brain, overriding the rhythm that held him in place. "Run!"

They abandoned the cart, and when Eineen's hardhat fell off, crashing and rolling behind them, they abandoned that, too.

Slick soles slipped against the rock. These were not the shoes he would have worn if he'd known he was going to be running for his life. He'd been a runner in high school, quit in university when someone had made a crack about Kenyans, making it a race thing, but he was barely keeping up and he could tell Eineen had slowed her pace.

He wanted to tell her to go on without him.

He didn't.

He hung on, let her yank him forward, keep him from falling, keep him moving faster than he could've gone on his own.

He tasted iron at the back of his throat.

His lungs fought to suck in enough hot, humid air. Then fought to force it out. In. Out.

Don't think of what might be following.

Just run.

Eineen reached the cage first, out in front by the length of their stretched arms. She ran in through the open gate and turned, staring past him. Her eyes were too large. Too dark. Her face the wrong shape. Nostrils flared too wide. He could see her chest, rising and falling. Her shoulders were too broad. Her torso out of proportion. Then he touched the steel and she was Eineen again. Stronger than him; he couldn't have turned to look behind them. Not for anything.

Panting, he keyed in the code with his free hand.

Nothing happened.

The hoist wouldn't work with the gate open.

He'd have to turn.

He spun on the ball of one foot. Grabbed the bar. Yanked it sideways. Swore as it bounced back.

The skittering scraped over his skin, rubbed nerves raw. The boom boom boom slipped into a more primal place.

Eineen's hand beside his, he slammed the bar home again.

This time, it caught.

No, latched. *This time it latched. Don't think caught.*

He input the code again.

Smacked the green button.

The cage jerked up. He staggered back, Eineen steadying him as the cables groaned and the elevator began to rise steadily toward the surface.

Then something hit the bottom of the cage, slamming into the metal grating hard enough they both grabbed for the safety bars to keep from falling.

"Don't look down!" Eineen made it a command.

Paul wanted to obey, but he'd already ducked his head.

Clinging to the cable, the claws of one hand stuffed through the grate, was something out of nightmare. Huge eyes. Like a lemur's. An evil lemur's. Bulging and glistening. Too many teeth. Too many sharp pointed yellow teeth in a mouth too wide. Small ears, small and round and tight against its head. Paul couldn't help thinking they should have been pointed. Not much of a nose. Black skin. Really black. Not black like he was black. He was medium brown at best. These guys were black like the coal that had come out of the *Duke* back in the day. Purple iridescent highlights—the whole nine yards.

And the thing on the cable wasn't alone. Seven, eight, ten . . . They spilled into Canaveral like cockroaches. As the cage rose past the roof, they crowded to the edge of the hoist shaft.

"Do you have any salt?"

"Do I *what?*"

"Have any salt!"

"No! But I have sugar substitute." Not every coffee shop had the brand Ms. Carlson liked.

"Sugar substitute?" She was laughing at him, but it wiped the look of horror from her face and that was all that mattered. And looking at her was better than looking down. She cupped his cheek, leaned in . . .

Steel screamed as claws gouged deep lines in the grate.

. . . and she snatched the hardhat off his head.

"The light!" Dropping to her knees, she flicked the headlamp on and aimed the beam right into the creature's face.

It screamed, much as the steel had, and dropped away. The light glinted off its flailing hands. The creatures it passed as it fell screamed with it.

"Rings."

"What?"

"It's wearing rings!" Paul expanded, not sure he recognized his own voice. "It's not an animal."

"Of course not." Eineen rocked back up onto her feet, impossibly grace-fully, still pointing the headlamp down the shaft. "It's a Goblin. A type of Goblin, anyway. And they shouldn't be here."

"No shit!"

"A gate has been opened."

Paul sagged against the side of the elevator, only barely managing to stop himself from clinging, raising both feet up into the air. The air still seemed fine. The sea had hidden depths and the earth wanted to kill him, but the air, it hadn't changed. That was comforting.

Eineen leaned against him, her back against his chest. He wrapped his arms around her and anchored himself in the one thing that really mattered. Laid his cheek against her hair and breathed in the faint scent of fish.

When they were outside, when the system had been shut down and the lights turned off and all the doors locked behind them, when the stars were shining overhead and he was standing drenched in sweat beside the very normal, very solid bulk of his car, he asked the other question. "What was the big thing coming behind them?"

Eineen shrugged. "Demons. Demons in the dark."

"Demons? Are you serious?" At this point, he had no trouble believing in demons.

"Shhh. It's okay!" Her voice calmed him enough he could remember to breathe. "I meant I didn't know. It's a movie quote, from *The Two Towers*."

"The what?"

She tucked herself up against him, one arm around his neck, head on his shoulder and murmured, "I think I've spent more time out of the water than you have these last few years."

Her sympathy almost undid him. "My job keeps me busy."

"I know."

They stood there for a moment, regrouping, then he lifted his head and said, "What now?"

Her body moved against him as she sighed. "We're not fighters . . ."

Paul wasn't sure if she meant him and her or her people. Didn't matter, he supposed. He'd never been in a physical fight in his life.

"I know someone who is, though."

"Will they help?"

"That depends on how I ask him."

The festival had reserved a section for the bands off to the left of the stage. Some of them used it, but more of them sat with their families.

"Where is everyone?" Jack asked as Charlie handed him a wrapped package of fish and chips.

"Shelly's trading out her current A for a jazz string, for what I'm sure are very good reasons, Mark and Tim are in the beer tent . . ." Stacking two cans of cola on top of the second package and holding them in place with her chin, she dropped to the ground between Jack and her guitar case. ". . . and Bo is trying to get Tanis to stop crying."

"Again?"

"Still."

"I kind of feel like we should do something about that. You know?"

"I know, but they don't need us." Charlie'd thought she'd been called/sent/annoyed east to help the Selkies, but she'd started to believe that Jack learning how to be *of* the family rather than within it was the primary not the secondary reason. She tossed him a cola. Hers had been charmed to keep it from spraying after the hazardous journey from the United Church W.I. trailer. Jack's had not.

His eyes narrowed. Then he opened the can, took a long swallow, and sighed the long-suffering sigh of the put-upon teenager. "You're watching me."

"You used sorcery to keep your soda from exploding. Last night you used it to soften the ground."

"Yeah, but that's . . ."

"It's not a problem, Jack." Holding onto his ear, she shook his head until he swatted her arm away. "You use sorcery the same way the rest of the family uses charms. To smooth out life's little bumps. It's not a big scary different thing, it's just a 'remove the middleman' thing."

"The aunties say I could use it to take over the world."

"Do you want to?"

"Do I want to what?"

"Take over the world. They've never asked you, have they? They just assume you're going to."

"Yeah, well, I'm not going to and I don't want to. When you take over the world, you have to *run* the world and that's way too much work plus everyone else who wants to run the world tries to take you out." The can dimpled in his grip. "I had enough of that back ho . . . back in the Under-Realm."

Charlie watched him cram a half a piece of fried cod into his mouth and wondered if they could keep Gale boys with too much power from going darkside by trying to kill and eat them in their formative years. Jack's early upbringing certainly seemed to have created a perspective that the indulgent life the Gale boys lived did not.

The aunties would probably be all for it.

"Charlie?"

"Yeah?"

"Why don't the aunties try to take over the world?"

"You're not the first to ask this, young Padawan." She stretched out her legs, kicked off her flip flops, and crossed her ankles. "We all ask."

He waved a french fry at her. "And the answer?"

"The aunties are all about family. As long as the world leaves the family alone, they leave the world alone. Something interferes with the family, they cut a metaphorical willow switch and deal." After a moment's thought, she added, "Usually metaphorical anyway." Auntie Catherine had thrown Allie at Jack's mother in an entirely actual way.

They'd lost the light by the time Captain Wedderbrun, the second festival band, took the stage, but it was a Friday night and no one was in a hurry. Although it had to be past their bedtime by Charlie's nonmaternal estimate, kids still ran around the grounds watched over by extended family—she saw Neela's charge past in a crowd and then back again in a different crowd. A soccer ball slammed into Jack's side and when Charlie nodded, he took off to join the game. All through the audience, friends and family stood shoulder to shoulder, music moving feet and hands and smiles. Even the tourists were starting to relax.

If this were a Stephen King book, this is when the monsters would attack, Charlie thought. An old friend from another band kicked her legs as he passed, and they exchanged genial and complex insults.

Captain Wedderburn was good and, more importantly, knew how to play to the crowd. Their fiddler subscribed to the Natalie McMaster school of step-and-play and their keyboard player—an older woman no more than five feet tall—perpetually appeared to be about to join in. Nine members strong, they were the largest band in the festival and likely to be one of the top three.

At 11:09, the crowd demanded and got the single encore the competing bands were allowed. At 11:21, they were still screaming for more.

Then they were just screaming.

At one end of the field, the stage rocked back and forth as though subjected to its own personalized earthquake. A couple members of the band jumped free, but it looked like the keyboard player and the drummer were caught in their gear. Or refusing to leave their gear.

Charlie could see small dark figures shaking the supports under the stage but it appeared no one else could.

"No way! Boggarts!"

No one else but Jack.

At the other end of the field, a food trailer crashed over onto its side and went up in flames.

Grabbing Jack's arm, Charlie pointed toward the fire. "I'll get the ones under the stage, you put that out."

"How?"

"Hello! Sorcery!"

"Hello! Dragon!" He twisted out of her grip. "Not big on putting fires *out*. I could . . . I don't know. Drop a whole bunch of water on it?"

"Yeah, and a random water bomb would be a little hard to explain. Contain it. Keep it from spreading. If the grass catches . . ."

"It'd be big trouble, right!" He squared his shoulders. "I got it."

"Jack, do it in skin! And plausibly deniable if you can!"

He turned to stare at her. "I don't even know what that *means*."

"If you have to lie, make sure it's one they'll believe."

"Right." A quick thumbs up, then he turned and ran.

Charlie scooped her guitar out of the case and wrestled the strap over her head as she pushed through people running the other way. Besides being squat, hairy, and smelly even at a distance, evidence suggested the Boggarts were among those Fey who were disproportionately strong. There were only three of them, all just under a meter tall, but they were rocking a stage built to hold up under multiple dancers with more enthusiasm than skill. Music may have charms to sooth the savage breast, but it seemed unlikely these three would be soothed quickly enough to keep those members of *Captain Wedderburn* being flung about on the stage from injury.

As Charlie rocked to a stop, the left side of the stage buckled, nails ripping free, plywood cracking. A two by four snapped. The front corner of the roof dropped half a meter, shaking free a light that smashed against the corner of the stage, spraying glass and sparks. The immediate area plunged into shadow.

No time for anything but quick and dirty.

Eyes narrowed, Charlie put her fingers to the strings.

Music could empty a room as fast as fill it.

Bagpipes could empty whole neighborhoods.

Charlie wished she could play Jack's song on the bagpipes—it'd serve the destructive little shits right—but, as she couldn't, she hit the top E so hard it buzzed against the frets like an angry wasp. Then she bent the buzz.

Heads turned.

At least, she thought they turned. In all honesty, there wasn't much to choose from between the back and the front.

She didn't so much play Jack's song as wield it like a club.

Hey, Boggarts! Don't make me go Draconis on your ass! I have a dragon in my pocket, and I'm not afraid to use him. Okay, not actually in my pocket because he's way too big. And hungry. Big and hungry!

Mouths open, eyes wide—or if not mouths and eyes then facial features in approximately the same position—the Boggarts shrieked like middle-aged women at an Adam Lambert concert, and ran for it. Charlie closed the last two meters between her and the stage, reached out as the corner began to collapse and sketched a quick charm in the dust. Timbers creaked but held.

It wouldn't hold long, but the keyboard player had gotten her foot out from under her pedals and Captain Wedderburn's fiddler was hauling the drummer, clutching his bass drum, down to the grass.

Stage secured, Charlie spun around, hoisted her guitar up under her right arm, and ran for the other end of the field. She'd taken no more than a dozen strides when something exploded.

Those who'd been unsure of how to personally take part in the growing panic suddenly decided, charging away from the column of fire now rising ten to fifteen meters into the night sky. Half a dozen Boggarts ran with them, shoving, pinching, and spraying beer around.

Charlie pivoted without breaking stride. If she could plug into the sound system, she could clear the Boggarts off the . . .

The empty stage shuddered as a dangling cable scraped across the charm, then the whole thing fell in toward the collapsing corner. Cables ripped free. The sound system gave one last bleat of protest, and died, taking the stage lights with it.

"Okay, then." Another pivot. Dodging through a dark mass of hysterical tourists, Charlie ran for Jack. "Plan B."

Having spent the evening watching the action on a well-lit stage, she hadn't bothered with night-sight charms. If she had it to do over, she'd say screw the ambiance and sketch them on. At least the Canadians apologized as they careened off her.

She finally got close enough to see it was the Lions Club chip wagon that had gone over; the three double deep fat fryers the genesis of the blaze. Charlie couldn't see bodies and she couldn't smell pork so, since the food court had closed at ten, it seemed the club's volunteers had been long gone before the Boggarts showed up. The good news: it was *only* the Lions Club chip wagon burning. *Papa Dog*, previously tucked up snug to the left, was now about six meters away. Given that the paint on the side closest to the fire had blistered and peeled, it looked like Jack had stepped in and shoved it clear. A dozen or so people worked to carry everything even vaguely portable away from the heat, and a dozen or so more had their phones up, recording. The beer tent continued doing brisk business.

Charlie didn't see Jack until a second explosion slammed the shadows back.

"Propane tanks," he said as she stopped, coughing, beside him. "I fixed it so they shoot up into the air and any bits of metal fall straight back down into the fire. Is that okay?"

"That's great." His T-shirt had started to scorch. She licked her finger and charmed it cool. "Now roar!" The remaining Boggarts were still working the crowd. So far, in spite of the shrieking and the swearing, it didn't look as if anyone had gotten seriously hurt, but as long as the Boggarts kept ramping up the levels of hysteria, that wouldn't last. "If you can talk while you control this, you can roar. We need to let the Boggarts know you're here!"

She'd told the Boggarts to run. To be afraid. Very afraid even. Hopefully, since Jack couldn't roar for the Boggarts' ears alone, Human brains would refuse to acknowledge the information as he announced his presence with authority. Where the *authority* came from being a dragon.

When Jack opened his mouth, Charlies stuffed her fingers in her ears and watched the crowd split into three. The Boggarts and the pureblood Selkies ran. Humans with Selkie wives and Humans with Selkie blood turned to stare—and a lot of the locals had a touch of Fey. Seemed the Selkies had been getting busy over the last couple hundred years. Those in the crowd who were nothing more or less than Human, froze as their hindbrains screamed, OMG DRAGON! and an instant later carried on running and shouting as their forebrains added, NO SUCH THING AS DRAGONS, DUMBASS! FIRE, THOUGH, THAT'S REAL!

When Jack closed his mouth, Charlie unplugged her ears. Her bones were still vibrating, and she had a certain amount of sympathy for the Fey who'd run. Half of her wanted to get the hell out of Dodge before scaled death arrived to rend and tear, the other half muttered, P*lease, it's a Gale boy. What's he going to do, sulk at you?*

"How . . . ?" Oh, great, she was deaf. She'd formed the word. Said the word. Couldn't hear the word.

Another propane tank exploded, and her ears popped.

I'm not sure it works that way . . . She swallowed hard, then forced a yawn . . . *but what the hell.* "How many more tanks in there?"

"How should I know?" Jack rolled golden eyes. "It's not like I have propane sense or something."

"Fair enough. Listen, when the last tank blows, you need to go after those Boggarts. Catch one alive if you can."

"Why?"

"They're small scale. They can't open a gate, so someone invited them in; I want to know who."

Jack cocked his head, frowning. "You think it was Auntie Catherine, don't you?"

"Yeah, well, she's here." Charlie flicked up a finger. Then another. "She's already screwing the Selkies." And a third. "And you know what Chekhov says."

"Um . . . Wictor, wictor, seven?"

"If you hang an auntie on the wall in act one, she'll be a pain in the ass by act three."

"Is that in the extras? Because I didn't watch the deleted scenes."

"That was . . . never mind."

"Whatever." He shrugged and waved a bit of flame back into the bulk of the burn. "Charlie, why didn't the Boggarts know I was here? I mean, before I told them."

"They weren't ignoring you, Your Highness. You're wearing skin, surrounded by skin, and they can't have had a lot of experience with Humans. Also, you were close to the fire; it was probably masking your innate dragonness. Plus . . ." She bumped his shoulder with hers. ". . . they would have been able to tell that I'm a Gale and they didn't seem to care. That makes them not too smart."

Another tank blew, then one more immediately after it.

Charlie tried to count to ten, got to seven, and said, "Okay, I think that's it." Some of the lingering ringing in her ears turned out to be sirens in the distance. At least they'd gotten rid of the Boggarts before the Louisburg Fire Department had shown. The whole thing—encore to roar—had taken just under fifteen minutes. Auntie Catherine—and where the aunties were concerned, Charlie believed in guilty until proven innocent—had to have known how the Boggarts would run from a Dragon, so why had she gone to all the trouble of opening a gate for such a minor bit of vandalism?

"You need to catch one of those little shits and find out why they attacked the festival." She shoved Jack past the burning trailer toward the darkness on the other side and the masking bulk of the Visitor's Center. He could change behind it, so she wouldn't have to spend the rest of the night saying, *What dragon?* "And you need to do it before they run wee wee wee all the way home." If she were Auntie Catherine, she'd have left the gate in place but set it so it only worked one way, allowing the Boggarts to return to the Under-Realm on their own, but preventing anything else from coming through. However, given that she wasn't Auntie Catherine and Auntie Catherine was at best unpredictable and at worse really fucking unpredictable, the gate could just as easily be swinging wide for anything who wanted to come visiting. "Find out where the gate is so we can close it."

"Couldn't you just sing your way to it?"

"Probably. But the last time Auntie Catherine didn't want me to get somewhere, I ended up in Brazil. And, if the gate is guarded, I'd rather the large, fire-breathing, nearly indestructible dragon discovered that first." Another shove. "Now go."

"You want a coffee, too?"

"No, I'm good. Fly, my pretty!"

Jack dug in his heels.

Given how far they were dug in, Charlie suspected he was using dragon weight. The sweat on his T-shirt was drying out fast in the heat rising off his skin. "I'm sorry I called you pretty."

He folded his arms, smoke trickling out of his nose.

"And referred to you like you were a flying monkey. Now please get your golden ass in the air before our answers take a powder."

"What are you going to be doing?"

Good question. She stopped applying pressure between his shoulder blades and glanced around at the festival grounds—at the smoldering chip wagon, at the clusters of babbling people, at the crying children, at the half dozen musicians still sitting in the beer tent, at the fire truck and the EMTs. The excitement was over and the professionals were here. Hysteria would rewrite what had happened, editing the Boggarts out.

Reaching under her guitar, she pulled her phone from the pocket of her shorts. Jack turned and tracked the movement. Aunties didn't lie. And aunties loved messing with people more than Gales loved pie. If Auntie Catherine answered . . .

Auntie Catherine didn't.

Charlie put the phone back in her pocket.

"You going to go find her?" Jack asked.

"No."

"Are you scared of her?"

"Wary. Careful. Confronting an auntie has been known to end in gingerbread."

"I like gingerbread," Jack pointed out.

"As a career choice?"

"Oh."

"Besides, if she intended to tell me what was going on, she'd have answered the phone. Face-to-face, the best I'd get would be, "My business is none of your business, Charlotte." And I'd say, "Your having the Boggarts attack the festival makes it my business." And she'd say, "Did the Boggarts tell you I told them to attack the festival?" There's no point in talking to her until after you talk to the Boggarts. So . . ." Charlie took a deep breath and shook off the anger she'd felt since the stage started to shake. "I'm going to make sure the band is safe, retrieve my guitar case, and then I'm going to wait until you bring me some answers. You find the gate; I close it. You find out what Auntie Catherine told the Boggarts; we decide what we're going to do next."

We decide . . .

He's fourteen, Charlie! Yeah, he's more than that, but he's that, too.

Damn.

She took a step back, giving him space. "This is more than you signed on for. You can head back to Calgary tomorrow: no harm, no foul."

"Calgary is boring. Besides," he continued, his voice coming from inside a sudden cloud of smoke, "all you asked me to do is catch a Boggart. I can do that in my sleep." The smoke cleared, and he didn't look disgusted by the thought of going back to Calgary and boredom; he looked like someone had just killed his puppy. "Okay, not in my sleep but almost. It's easy. I'm sorry I didn't fly after them right away. Don't send me back, okay? I thought you wanted me here."

Charlie pushed her guitar out of the way and pulled him into a hug. "I want you here," she told him as he fought her grip, but she knew she couldn't have held him if he didn't want to be held. "You decide if you go back. I just want you to realize it could get dangerous."

"Yeah, the gingerbread crack kind of gave that away." He squirmed, suddenly very fourteen about being hugged, and she let him go. When they were far enough apart, he grinned. "You met my uncles, right? So far, this world is pretty much not dangerous."

"So far, the aunties have left you alone."

"So far, I'm still fourteen."

"That was my point. Fine." She held up her hand. "Fist bump. Wild Powers activate. Enough time wasted on mushy shit."

Jack's knuckles sizzled against hers. "Weirdest person I'm related to."

"Pot, kettle, cuz."

A few moments later, Charlie watched him rise from behind the shed like a shooting star in reverse, easy enough to explain away as a spark against the night sky to people already staring at a fire. She started back to the festival grounds and realized she was walking across bare earth. An arc about two meters wide had been completely cleared of grass out in back of the burning chip wagon. Jack had removed the grass. Since she couldn't see a pile of it, she hoped he'd just tossed it onto the fire. The day he first arrived, he'd made a pair of jeans out of fabric ripped from the interior of a rental car, so all that grass could have become a couple dozen . . .

She frowned, sighed, and muttered, "I got nothin'."

"Little Burned Potato," her fiddler suggested.

"Dude, trust me, you've got nothing either."

"A gang of teenagers on drugs?" Charlie stared at Mark in disbelief. "Seriously?"

Mark shrugged. He had a smear of ash on one cheek, and his sporran looked singed. "You got a better explanation, Chuck? That chip wagon didn't take a dive all on its own. Of course, Marty . . ."

"Piper from Hallelujah Frog?"

"That'd be the Marty. He seems to think it's a plot by the other bands to keep the Frog from winning."

"How much had Marty had to drink?"

"Funny, that's what the Horseman asked him. Looks like Tim's ready to go; I guess the festival committee doesn't want our help rebuilding." Mark jumped down off the picnic table and flipped his kilt into place. "You heading back to Shelly's brother-in-law's cousin's place?"

"No." She stood her guitar case on end between her feet, crossed her hands on the top, and rested her chin on them. "I'm waiting for Jack."

"Jesus, Jack!" Mark whirled in place as if he expected to find Jack standing behind him. "Where the hell has the kid gone?"

"He's fine. He's . . . gone off with someone." After, not with, but otherwise, not exactly a lie.

"A friend?"

"A *friend*."

"Ah." Mark nodded sagely. "Adrenaline rush. It's a statistical truth that more people get laid after horror movies than . . . Wait a minute. I thought you said he was fourteen! I mean, I was precocious, but . . ."

"They're talking," Charlie sighed. "Not fucking."

"Are you sure?"

"I'm sure." Not that it was immediately relevant, but did Boggarts even have a gender? Although, she considered as she watched Tim wipe the ash off Mark's face with some spit and the hem of his T-shirt, little Boggarts had to come from somewhere.

Charlie had no idea how Jack's hunt was going, but the rest of Grinneal hadn't been hard to locate. She'd found Shelly helping a cousin deal with three terrified kids and, in reaction to the growing *no court in the land would convict me* expressions on both adults' faces, had strummed a charm onto each child. Shelly's cousin had burst into tears of relief when all three kids had simultaneously calmed down and cheered up. Tanis had fled toward the Fort and the water when Jack roared, and one of the pipers had seen Bo go after her, upset for her sake but fine on his own account. Turned out that Mark and Tim had been among those helping to haul stuff away from the burning chip wagon and had been thanked and then chased off by the fire department. When Charlie had retrieved her case and caught up to them, Tim was on his way to see if he could help rebuild the stage, so Charlie and Mark had claimed a picnic table between the parking lot and the temporary fencing, sitting in a circle of illumination under one of the pole lights.

Although the stage remained dark, the perimeter lights hadn't gone out. Small mercies.

"Right, Chuck?" Mark's question jerked Charlie's wandering mind back to the here and now. He grinned and elbowed Tim. "I told you she wasn't listening."

Eyes open wide, she faked a look of rapt attention. "I'm listening now."

"Good. Because this is your leader speaking. I want to run through the set list tomorrow morning. The fine people in paid attendance at Samhradh Ceol Feill deserve a band that's got its musical shit together after tonight's excitement."

"And it won't hurt our standing with the judges either."

"That's what Tim said. So . . ." He gripped her knee, his palm warm and dry. "Don't stay out too late. There'll be a thermos of my secret recipe honey/lemon tea left on the stairs, so drink it before bed for your voice. You've been sucking smoke and we don't need another baritone. And maybe think about changing your two." A nod toward the guitar case. "It's sounding a bit harsh."

"Anything else, Mom?"

He nodded. "Yeah. Think about dying your hair. You walking around all natural and blonde is freaking me the hell out."

There weren't many cars left in the parking lot when Tim and Mark pulled out: her wagon, a few vehicles close to the stage she assumed belonged to the volunteers doing the rebuild, and a bus from Sydney that seemed short a few passengers.

More to have something to do with her hands than in any expectation of an answer, Charlie pulled out her phone and called Auntie Catherine again. Five rings. Nine. Thirteen. Charlie cut the connection.

The phone rang.

"Hey, Mom."

"Your sisters . . ."

Charlie balanced her chin on the top of her guitar case, letting the words literally flow in one ear and out the other, listening past the sounds of construction and profanity for the sound of wings. At the first pause in the monologue, she straightened and said, "Mom, they're going to Paris, not spending seven years in the UnderRealm. Let it go."

"But they'll be alone!"

"Everyone has to go it alone sometime, Mom. Even Gales. And there's two of them," she sighed to herself as she hung up.

Hanging up would come back and bite her on the ass later, but right now, hip-deep in family drama, she didn't have the patience for family sitcoms. She thought about calling to see if Allie was still mad, but a glossy black penis-mobile turning into the parking lot caught her eye. At first she thought the driver was a family member arriving late to rescue loved ones from the chaos, but then she realized it wasn't so much heading toward her in a general sort of way as it was aiming right at her.

She wouldn't have let that go on a good night. Tonight . . .

Time spent touring the prairies on the Dun Good bus had taught her a lot about vehicular charming, and these assholes with their size-fourteen carbon footprint were about to find out what happened when Charlie Gale played a country song backward.

Then the car stopped, parked diagonally across two spaces. Okay, maybe she'd overreacted a bit to their sense of direction, but given how much she hated people who didn't know the definition of parallel, she was half inclined to charm their manifold off just on principle.

She had her guitar out of the case when the passenger door slammed open, and Eineen emerged looking gorgeous and determined. Charlie froze, the strap held over her head. She hadn't seen Eineen in jeans before. She had an amazing ass.

"I need to speak to the Prince."

And suddenly the finger was off the pause button. "Hello to you, too," Charlie muttered settling the strap over her shoulders. "Yeah, we had a bit of an incident tonight; stage fell down, chip wagon burned, but everyone's fine, thanks for asking."

Eineen glanced over at the festival grounds and the smoke rising from the remains of the fire. "What happened?"

"We had Boggarts."

"We had Goblins."

Charlie opened her mouth. Closed it again. Finally slid off the picnic table onto her feet and said, "Okay, you win." Goblins wouldn't have stopped at malicious vandalism; they'd have gone straight to rending and tearing. Jack would've had to change to deal with them, and Charlie would've had to call in the aunties to deal with the fallout. She shuddered. Fun, wow.

Speaking of aunties . . . Boggarts fell into the general shit-disturbing category, but why would Auntie Catherine bring Goblins over?

Wait a minute.

"We?"

The driver's door opened, and a tall young man emerged. In his own way, he was just as gorgeous as Eineen. Beautiful dark skin, that sexy shaved head and goatee combo, slim but in good shape. He looked vaguely familiar, so Charlie leaned out for a better angle as he walked around the car to stand beside the Selkie. His suit pants clung to the curves of an equally great ass and the sleeves of his pale blue dress shirt had been meticulously folded to expose an expensive watch. On his feet, he wore a pair of scuffed and dusty shoes that probably cost more than the combined value of every piece of clothing Charlie'd brought with her to Nova Scotia.

"Paul Belleveau." Eineen's voice laid overtones of possession on the name. "Charlotte Gale."

Paul visibly paled. Considering the lack of light and his skin tone, it was an impressive reaction.

NINE

"CHARLOTTE *GALE*?" Paul took a step that put him between her and Eineen, although Charlie doubted he knew he'd done it. "Carlson Oil paid a *Catherine* Gale to take the pelts."

"Whose idea was it?"

"Hers." He'd responded without thinking and was obviously not happy about it. Too bad.

"That's interesting." Charlie let her guitar swing around until it hung down her back à la Johnny Cash. She folded her arms but kept her expression neutral. "And when I say interesting, I don't mean it's interesting that it was her idea; it's interesting that you knew it was her idea. I saw you at the press conference, but you're not a reporter, not in those shoes, and you're not a low-level flunky either." The items on the desk outside Amelia Carlson's office had been arranged with the same anal attention to detail that marked the roll of Paul Belleveau's shirtsleeves. He couldn't have gotten the fold more precise even if he'd measured it, and Charlie wasn't ruling that out. "Amelia Carlson's assistant, I presume?"

They didn't need to know Tanis had already told her who Eineen's new boy toy was. They could remain in awe of her powers of deduction.

Paul ignored her, turning to Eineen. "I don't think it's coincidence that they have the same last name."

"It isn't." Eineen took his hand, lacing her fingers through his. "They're family. But it's not important."

"You've never met Catherine Gale." From his tone, Paul had. The aunties left a lasting impression. "Trust me, it's important."

"We're not on the same side," Charlie told him, still neutral, stating a fact. She didn't owe him reassurance. Not that there was a lot she could say about Catherine Gale any sane man would find reassuring. "What Auntie Catherine did, well, that messed up our fiddler's girlfriend and that messed up our fiddler. I don't want our fiddler messed up, that messes with the music. That puts Auntie Catherine and me on opposite sides." It was the first time she'd made a definitive declaration. It hung in the air for a moment, waiting for Charlie to deny it, or qualify it, or freak out about it, but Charlie picked none of the above. Auntie Catherine had messed with the music. Turned out, it was as simple as that.

Dum dum dum DUM.

"So . . ." She shifted her gaze past Paul to Eineen and moved on to the next bit of business. ". . . of all the seashores in all the world, who'd have thought Amelia Carlson's assistant would show up on yours. Bad ballads get written about those kinds of coincidences."

"Not coincidence, destiny." Eineen breathed the word.

The fiddler kicked in with the first few bars of "Wha Can Help It."

Charlie rolled her eyes. "Useful."

Proportions shifted as the Selkie's glamour flickered. "Not mutually exclusive."

Holding up both hands in the universal sign for, *dial it down, sweetheart, I'm not dissing your bright and shiny new relationship,* Charlie murmured, "Fair enough." Not a surrender as much as an acknowledgment that it was none of her business. It wasn't like she'd ever actually had a chance of Eineen showing up on her seashore.

Paul shook his head. "You can't trust . . ." he began, but his voice trailed off when Eineen stroked his arm with pale fingers.

"Don't worry about it," she murmured soothingly.

And he didn't.

In the old days, when a man saw a Selkie dance in the moonlight and lost his heart, he grabbed her sealskin and hid it. As long as he had the skin, he held all the cards. The seal-wives did as they were told in fear of being trapped forever in a Human life—the same blackmail Carlson Oil had perpetuated, only they hadn't gone so far as to demand regular sex and housekeeping. Maybe a few of them fell in love with their captors in some kind of weird

Pinnipedia Stockholm syndrome—Charlie wasn't judging—but they sure weren't there by choice.

In this new age, although the Selkies remained bound by ancient Rules, they followed only the letter of the law. They danced in the moonlight and ensnared the hearts of men, but they did it now without handing over control. Paul may have gotten his hands on Eineen's skin, but Charlie doubted he'd held onto it for long.

On the surface, Selkies seemed to still be all about the traditional relationship. One man, one woman, two point five kids, all four and a half of them living happily ever after. Well, happily ever after until the tears and betrayal if Tanis could be believed, but the point was, all the attention on the seal-wife thing, on the little woman in the kitchen sliding the fish and chips into the oven with a bun or two in the oven herself, masked a fundamental point of the relationship. The Selkies were Fey and the Fey considered Humans more playthings than partners. And not playthings in a fun and kinky kind of feathers and whipped cream sort of way, playthings in a cat with a catnip mouse kind of way—it's all fun and games until the stuffing comes out.

Without the protection gained from holding her skin, modern man didn't so much get a beautiful and compliant wife as a wild ride with teeth and claws and attitude. Tanis had Bo wrapped around her little finger although Charlie had missed the full extent, masked as it was by the constant weeping. Eineen didn't bother to hide that she called the tune Paul would dance to.

In spite of their adherence to outdated gender roles, Charlie had to admit she admired the way the Selkies played the system.

"Just out of curiosity," she said, ignoring Paul and watching Eineen, "where did you have Goblins? And how did you get away? That's not the sort of infestation you can clear up with a few antibiotics."

"We ran. And we got lucky." Her fingers tightened on Paul's arm, dimpling the skin. Goblins weren't very big, but they swarmed their prey, overwhelming larger creatures with numbers. "They were in the mine where the skins are hidden."

"No." Charlie shook her head, thinking back to the blank verses in Tanis' song. "I could have found them in a mine."

"The tunnel they're in goes out under the bay."

"Under the water?" The Gales had their roots sunk deep in the Earth. They didn't do water and, until Jack, barely did air. Auntie Ruby's attempts at skywriting aside. "That might be enough to do it." *Had been* enough to do it. Obviously. "So you were trying to get the skins back. Mr. Belleveau's switched teams?"

"I'm not gay!"

Charlie and Eineen turned together to stare at Paul.

"And I've got news for you, caring about personal grooming has nothing to do with sexual orientation." He brushed a bit of dust or something equally invisible off his shirt. "I know gay men who wear flannel for God's sake."

"Okay. Not those teams. I meant you've switched from supporting the evil oil company to throwing in with Two Seventy-five N's protest."

"Oh." Paul squared his shoulders. "No."

"No?" Eineen's reaction cut Charlie's off, so Charlie waited. He couldn't refuse to answer Eineen. She wondered if he could lie to her.

"Taking the pelts, well, that was wrong." Paul turned to stare lovingly into Eineen's eyes, their fingers laced again. "It was wrong even though it was in the best interests of the company and I am truly sorry that we caused so much grief to your family." His free hand rose to cup her cheek. "But the well, there's nothing wrong with that well. There's a substantial oil field off Hay Island, and it only makes sense to exploit it. It's deep, sure, but the rock's stable and unlike deepwater wells, it'll be easy to sink, remarkably safe in comparison, and entirely profitable as it's so close to shore it'll make transportation costs negligible. We're in talks about a pipeline to a processing center on Scatarie Island and we'll be bringing significant numbers of jobs to Cape Breton."

Charlie really wished she had a camera. The expression on Eineen's face was priceless. "I'm guessing you two lovebirds didn't talk about this."

"There's nothing to talk about!" Eineen jerked back until she was standing far enough from Paul to work up the volume. "Scatarie Island is a protected wilderness area! If, no, *when* there's a spill, it'll destroy entire ecosystems. If it happens during storm season, and that's likely when it'll happen . . ."

"Because of the storms," Charlie added helpfully. "Being in the North Atlantic and all."

"A spill during storm season will be impossible to contain," Eineen continued, ignoring her. "Impossible. Not difficult! And that's not even mentioning the disruption of a protected seal rockery just putting the damned thing in! And," she added, cutting Paul off as he opened his mouth, "deep or shallow, all water wells leak. We're raising children in those waters."

"We?" he managed.

"Not you and I, personally!"

He didn't look reassured.

When Charlie pointed that out, Eineen told her to shut up and locked eyes with Paul. "If you are with me, you are not working for Carlson Oil. If you are with me, you are not supporting a company that wants to destroy my family's home."

No contractions, Charlie noted as the proportions of Eineen's face shifted between Human and not.

Reaching out, she pressed her palm over Paul's heart. "Are you with me or are you with Amelia Carlson?"

When a full thirty seconds passed, Charlie realized he was actually thinking about it. She was impressed. He had bigger cajones than it appeared. And he'd need them if the expression on Eineen's face was anything to go by.

"We are together," she growled.

"I know. But I worked hard to get this job. I'm good at it and I'm paid well for doing it. I mean really well." He held out his wrist. "This watch cost me eight hundred dollars. My father never owned a watch that cost more than twenty."

"You are not your father!"

His smile looked more like a snarl. "That's my point. My father wore thrift shop clothes and smelled of fish. At forty, his arthritis was so bad he could barely open his hands. When he died at forty-three, we had to sell the car to pay for the funeral. I'm not going back to just getting by."

"Daddy issues much?" Charlie muttered under her breath.

Eineen closed her eyes and visibly composed herself. When she opened them, she was more Human than Fey and the line of Paul's shoulders visibly eased. "I told you, but you didn't listen. Ships uncounted litter the floor of the sea," she said. "Some are coffins only, some are wrecks of no value, but some have spilled silver and gold from between rotting timbers. My people harvest dead men's treasure from the sea and then invest it. Our holdings are about seventy/thirty low-risk/high-return funds. We're loaded."

"Seriously?" Charlie didn't expect an answer, but to her surprise, Eineen flashed her a triumphant smile.

"Seriously. How do you think Two Seventy-five N can afford such kick-ass lawyers?"

"Hadn't actually thought about it."

"Wait." Paul seemed to be having a little trouble finding the right words. "You said there were investment bankers. You never said you were *rich*."

"I have as much as I need, or want, but if you need or want more, it's there. And there's a job for you taking care of it, making more of it if you want that. Strangers manage it now. It's been years since one of us has ended up with a mate who wasn't a fiddler or a fisherman. Or a German tourist, but we're fairly certain that was an accident; they own a lot of land on the island."

"Wait," Paul said again. "I'd work for you?"

"You'd work for the money. You need give up no material pleasures for love. That leads, in the end, only to resentment." She closed the fingers of the hand pressed over his heart and tugged on his shirt. "You'd have power of your own. Power I wouldn't interfere with."

Somehow, Charlie managed to keep her response behind her teeth.

"I'd need to think about it . . ."

"Of course. And while you think about it . . ." Human features slipping, Eineen twisted to face Charlie. "Call His Highness."

"Excuse me?"

"We need to speak with the Dragon Prince. Call him."

Charlie raised a brow. Eineen seemed a little confused as to just who she'd danced for.

"The Goblins," she continued, as though it explained her tone, "are guarding the skins. Until they're removed, we can't get them out of the mine. The Goblins might not obey his command, but the Prince is what he is and he is terrifying."

"Yeah, well, right now Jack's off terrifying answers out of Boggarts. So, sorry. No prince."

"Boggarts are vandals. Irritants. Cowards." Eineen dismissed them with a wave. "They're probably heading straight back to the gate. Chasing them is a pointless waste of time."

"Chasing them will find the gate and get us—that would be me and Jack—information on who opened it."

"You know who opened it. Your Auntie Catherine opened the gates and forced the Goblins through so they could guard the pelts."

"She convinced me they'd be safer in the mine." Paul answered the question Charlie hadn't asked. "Who else could add that kind of security?"

"Carlson Oil didn't pay her to add it?"

"To add *Goblins*?"

Charlie nodded at the woman beside him. "Selkie."

He acknowledged the point. "No, we didn't pay her to add Goblins."

"Well, trust me, she certainly didn't do it out of the kindness of her heart. Why would she throw her support so vehemently behind stopping Two Seventy-five N and getting this well in?"

"She's your auntie," Eineen snarled. "Why don't *you* ask her?"

"That was rhetorical, right? Or do you want to stand here all night while I tell you?"

"I want you to call the Dragon Prince." Eineen glanced up at the sky, drawing Paul's gaze with hers. Charlie didn't look. Wings the size of Jack's made a distinctive sound; he wasn't up there.

"You're a Gale," Paul said. "We only have your word for it that you aren't working with her. For her."

"Why would I toss Boggarts at a festival I'm trying to win?"

"An accident," Eineen sneered. "One gate would have done for both the Goblins and the Boggarts. Boggarts often hang around the edges of Goblin gangs trying to look tough, too stupid to realize it only puts them in danger from the Goblins as well as larger predators."

"And the reason for their appearance here tonight?"

"If you opened the gate, they'd be drawn to you."

"If I opened the gate, they'd *know* I could kick their collective asses, and Boggarts, as you pointed out, are cowards. Auntie Catherine is a Wild Power. That makes her a wild card. That means if there's high-level shit disturbing going on and she's in the neighborhood, she's probably behind it. Plus we already *know* she was the one who took the skins. We just don't know *why!*"

"Everything okay over here?"

Charlie turned toward the police officer, suddenly aware she'd been shouting. And waving her arms. And stamping her foot. "Everything's fine."

"I was asking Eineen."

She smiled. "Everything's fine. A night like tonight . . ." She waved in the general direction of the burned chip wagon and, for all Charlie knew, the mine. ". . . nerves are on edge. That's all."

"If you're sure. So I hear Seanan's not well."

Seanan had been one of the Selkies whose sealskin had been stolen.

"She's a bit under the weather, yes, but I'm sure she'll be fine soon." Eineen glanced pointedly at Charlie. Who gave serious thought to throwing a charm on the cop just because she could.

"Well, tell her I was asking after her when you're talking next. And you," he turned back to Charlie. "You keep it down, okay? I think there's been enough shouting in these parts for one night. Eineen."

"Brayden. Seanan's husband is his cousin's brother-in-law," Eineen added as he joined the other officers by the Visitor's Center.

Like a small town, Charlie reminded herself.

"If Seanan's going to be fine soon," Eineen began.

"You need to get the skins, yeah, I got it." None of the Fey were subtle. They thought they were, but no. "I need proof I can confront Auntie Catherine with, and that means I'm not calling Jack back from hunting Boggarts. Plus . . ." She held up a hand, cutting Eineen's protest off. ". . . the Boggarts attacked a crowd of innocent people. When your people decided to join the environmental movement, not to mention put lawyers on retainer, you joined the game. You're players now, and there's risk involved in throwing yourself in front of corporate planning. Sure, it sucks that it bit you on the ass, but these people tonight, they came to listen to music. They're not playing; they don't even know there's a game going on. So we deal with the Boggarts first. Then, for chosen family's sake, and through Bo for Tanis, we deal with the Goblins."

"With the Dragon Prince's help, we could retrieve our skins tonight!"

Charlie half turned, and gestured at the smoking ruin of the chip wagon. "Seems his dance card's full tonight. But thanks for playing."

"Call him!"

She turned back, swinging the guitar around into place. "Or you'll what?"

Paul moved to put himself between them, but Eineen pulled him back and stepped forward in his place. He looked confused and unhappy but stayed where she'd shoved him.

"If Tanis asks him . . ." Her lips were drawn back off her teeth, her glamour so shaky she looked like a flip book. ". . . and Tanis will ask him if she's told to, Bo will stop playing for you."

"You think what you do to them . . ." Charlie waved a hand between Eineen and Paul. ". . . is stronger than what the music does? I'll take that chance." Cue a background chorus of what sounded very much like "I Lost My Love," and Charlie gave the fiddler in her head points for the title while not entirely convinced the situation called for a jig.

Eineen stared at her for a long moment, fierce and Fey. The moment passed. "You don't understand," she wailed, all unlikely angles and uncomfortable beauty. "I was so close to getting them back." Then she dropped her head, her hair flowing forward to hide the defeat Charlie'd glimpsed on her face.

She was Fey, so mind games were a given, but Charlie didn't think anyone could fake that kind of grief.

Paul wrapped her in his arms and glared over the top of her head.

Oh, yeah. Like I'm worried about you.

On one hand, there was no real reason she couldn't deal with the Goblins herself. If Jack could find her wherever she was, she didn't need to hang around here, and she'd never been good at waiting patiently. On the other hand, the pelts were completely safe, and Eineen knew where they were. It wasn't like they were still missing, exactly. On yet another hand, there was a chance that the Goblins had slipped through with or behind the Boggarts if they hung out together and then had been drawn to the pelts on their own because they were something of the UnderRealm buried in the dark places they loved, and that meant the Goblins had nothing to do with the Gales. On still another hand, if Charlie caved to Eineen's demands without argument, she was as enthralled as Paul, only she wasn't getting laid as a reward for good behavior.

Of course, she *had* argued. And shouted. And stamped. She'd made her point. Won her point. It was time to be gracious in victory.

Hand number five for the win.

Charlie sucked in a deep breath and jackknifed forward as her lungs filled with a lingering wisp of smoke. "Fine," she wheezed after a moment spent coughing up what felt like smoke and lungs and french fries. "I'll help."

"You?" Eineen lifted her head, her hair moving away from her face without being touched. "You can deal with the Goblins?"

"They can hear me, I can deal with them."

"They're in a mine."

"So you've said. The acoustics don't actually matter; I won't be giving a concert. They just have to hear me."

Eineen's lip curled. "And the Boggarts?"

"I can deal with your problem while Jack deals with them. And this isn't going to take long. All I'm going to do is keep the Goblins away while you retrieve the skins."

"They need to go back."

"Not tonight."

"The Dragon Prince . . ."

"Look, do you want the Goblins dealt with or not? Because I do have other things I could be doing. Apparently, I have a string that needs changing."

Paul shifted his grip, wrapping his arms around Eineen's waist. To Charlie's surprise, Eineen relaxed back against his body. "Are the pelts safe from the Goblins?" he asked. "Because they didn't look like the sort of creatures who play nicely with their toys."

He seemed to be handling the whole Goblin thing well. It was Bo's reaction, or nonreaction, to an expanded reality all over again. Which pretty much confirmed that sex with Selkies, fully aware that at least part of the time the hottie in their arms packed on a hundred pounds of blubber and ate raw fish that didn't come with saki, opened the door far enough that anything weird or wonderful could wander in. As for his question . . .

"If Auntie Catherine brought them over, and yes," Charlie sighed, "I'm pretty sure she did, and if she told them to leave the pelts alone, they would."

He nodded. "If. What are the odds?"

Charlie shrugged. "Honestly, about fifty/fifty." The family didn't play nicely with other people's toys either.

"I think," he said to Eineen, stroking his finger along the curve of her cheek, "we should let her help. Catherine Gale created this mess when she stole the pelts; who better than another Gale to deal with it?"

He had a point. It was a family problem from a couple of different angles.

Eineen turned her head and pressed a kiss into his palm. "All right. She can help."

"Don't do me any favors," Charlie muttered, heading back to the picnic table for her guitar case. She thought about calling Mark, but it was late and she'd be back in plenty of time to deal with whatever Jack found and make the run through of the set list. It wasn't as if she was going to ride the penis-mobile *back* from the mine.

When she turned, Eineen and Paul were in a clinch so cliché the fiddler slid into "Natalie and Donnel's Wedding."

"Could you two try and tone down the displays of blatant heterosexuality during this little adventure?" she sighed, walking over to the car.

As she opened the door, she heard Paul say, "Is she . . . ?"

And Eineen answer, "She's a Gale."

As if that explained it.

Which it did.

Hunting Boggarts wasn't as easy as Jack had pretended while talking to Charlie. When they were on the run, all that hair flapping about drew shadows that changed their shape, blending them into the landscape. If that David Suzuki guy on television could be trusted, then it worked the way a tiger's stripes did, hiding an orange-and-black animal in green-and-gold grass. It didn't help that he didn't know which way they'd fled. Probably inland, but just because he'd never dragged a Boggart dripping and shrieking out of the water didn't mean they couldn't swim.

Once he got into the air, he began a low, slow spiral out from the festival grounds. He was a good swimmer—his Uncle Viktor had tried to drown him more than once—and the night was warm enough he hoped the Boggarts had run to the sea.

They hadn't. His life sucked.

Inland. Figured.

He picked up their trail just before they reached this really skinny lake and stayed high while they crossed a bridge he vaguely remembered Charlie driving over on the way to Louisburg. One of them nearly got nailed by a monster truck but scrambled up onto the guardrail at the last minute. What would they know about trucks?

They knew about dragons, though. He circled around and came in so that his shadow on the ground didn't give the game away.

The last Boggart in the pack of nine wasn't guarding the rear, it was the slowest and if it couldn't keep up, the others would leave it behind without a second thought. It squealed when Jack's claws closed around its fur.

Or beside its fur. Or something.

The Boggart could've rolled sideways to freedom but, propelled by blind panic, it tried to run faster and catch up to the pack disappearing into the underbrush at the side of the road. With the two of them on the same trajectory, Jack had time to poke through the illusion and get a good enough hold to haul the shrieking creature into the air. Afraid it might thrash its way free, Jack gave a quick squeeze and then worried he'd crushed it beyond conversation all the way to the clearing where he landed.

Masked from Human notice by surrounding trees and the night itself, he dropped the Boggart on the dormant grass and bent to check it was still alive. On the bright side, he'd found the pack, so it wouldn't be hard to grab another if he had to.

The Boggart lay on its side like road kill already beginning to bloat.

Jack took a long sniff, close enough he sucked a hair up into his nose, and sat back on his haunches when the Boggart jumped up and ran for the trees.

Ran right into the cage of Jack's claws.

It flipped upside down, spun around on what might have been shoulders, head bent at an awkward angle, then decided to play dead again and flopped flat.

Jack sighed.

Coughing and choking, the Boggart flailed its arms and legs, trying to wave the smoke away. Once it had cleared enough for Jack to see its face, he said, "Look, you answer some questions, and I won't eat you. You keep dicking me around, I'll have a snack and catch up to the pack."

Flat black eyes narrowed. "Am cheated! Not said You Highness here!"

"Who didn't say?"

"Scary!"

"Yeah, I'm gonna need a little more than that."

"Scary not all Human!"

"Little more." Although that wasn't a bad definition of an auntie.

The Boggart waved an arm, hair flapping. "Rock hair! Night eyes! Power like dirt! Smell like dirt!"

"Dirt?"

It smacked the ground. "Dirt!"

"Earth?"

"Earth. Dirt." The Boggart made gesture that clearly meant *whatever*, and stood. "Go now?"

"Not yet." Jack translated rock hair and night eyes to gray hair and black eyes but the important part of the description was the smell. All the Gales smelled a little like earth to him. Charlie smelled like wherever she was—in Calgary a bit like the mountains, in Cape Breton a bit like the shore. Allie smelled like growing things. But the aunties smelled like the dark, rotting places deep in the oldest part of the forest. "Did the scary not all Human tell you to attack the festival?"

"No. Attack music place!"

"Yeah, that's what a festival . . . never mind."

"Said young scary not all Human there! Said not hurt!" It folded its arms. "Not said You Highness there!"

"Did the scary not all Human open the gate?"

It blew foam from between rubbery lips. Jack decided to take that as a *duh*.

"And the scary not all Human called you?"

"Called all."

"I didn't mean *just* you. What did she promise you if you attacked the music place?"

"Not to hurt. Do thing. Go home."

"So the gate's open?"

"Go home, not come back."

"The gate's open one way," Jack translated. "You can get back to the UnderRealm but you can't turn around and return to the MidRealm."

"Goblins stay. Big nasty."

"What?"

"Goblins stay. Big nasty." It was clearly wondering what Jack hadn't understood about that.

"There's Goblins here? In the MidRealm, and they're staying? Goblins came through when you did?" Goblins were mean. And kind of gross tasting, but right now that wasn't important. Boggarts hung around on the edges of Goblin packs trying to seem tough, so he guessed they'd be *the* big nasty to the Boggarts. "Where are they now?"

The Boggart made a noise that could have meant it didn't know.

Jack singed the grass at its feet.

"Goblins not here!"

"I know that!"

It flattened under the sudden blast of smoke, hugging the ground. "Goblins do for scary not all Human!"

"Do what? Never mind, they're Goblins." Goblins were thugs, vicious, nasty thugs. His Uncle Ryan had been attacked by about fifty of them once. Taking down a Dragon Lord would have made them top dog in more than just the low-level circles they ran in, but it would have worked out better for them if they'd been less flammable. Afterward, Uncle Ryan had lit up any Goblin he ran into—or flew over—as a kind of a hobby. If the Goblins were doing something for Auntie Catherine, it was something unpleasant. "Did you hear where she sent the Goblins?"

"No. Truth to Highness." It rolled back onto its feet and held up both hands. One hand had three fingers. One had six. "Truth to Highness," it repeated. "Go home now?"

"Yeah. Sure." Jack shifted back on his haunches, giving the Boggart a clear run to the trees. It looked up at him suspiciously for a moment, then took off, using its hands as well as its feet to gain speed. As soon as it was out of the clearing, Jack surged up into the sky. He'd follow it to the gate and see if he could pick up the Goblins' trail. They wouldn't be far from the gate. Not even Auntie Catherine would allow a pack of Goblins to run loose in the MidRealm.

He hoped.

"Why are we stopping?" Charlie leaned forward and peered out the front window as Paul pulled over to the side of the road. She could see lights through the trees but nothing near enough to the car to explain them stopping.

"There's a guard at the gate. If I go back in again, at this hour . . ." Paul's voice trailed off.

Charlie sighed. "So your entire plan was to ask Jack to help and wing it? Great. And I'm guessing Eineen can't do that whole Selkie seduction thing now you two lovebirds have paired up."

"Expecting Eineen to seduce the guard isn't only demeaning, it's cliché."

"You use the skills you've got, dude. But never mind . . ." She opened the back door. "I'm on it."

"Planning to seduce the guard?" Eineen asked.

Charlie settled the guitar strap over her shoulder and grinned. "Depends on the guard. How far are we from the gate?"

Paul glanced at his GPS. "About half a kilometer."

"Give me fifteen minutes and come on in."

It was a pleasant walk. The night had cooled a little but was still warm with just enough breeze to lift damp hair off her forehead. She could hear the two part percussion of waves against rock in the distance while, closer at hand, an owl mournfully demanded her identity from the trees. Directly over the road, half a dozen bats created shadow patterns between her and the stars. Then the owl swooped out of the trees and nailed one of the bats, snatching it out of the air with a twist of its head and snap of its beak. The bat squeaked once, and died.

Allie would have called it an omen. Charlie wanted a second opinion before she jumped to any conclusions. Sure, the whole experience had sucked for the bat, but the owl got dinner.

The gates leading onto the mine property were locked on the inside. No surprise.

The lights were on in the trailer. She could just see the top of the guard's head and a lot of messy dark hair through the open window. About to play him out and up to the gate, she realized she had no idea how close the Goblins were or how well they could hear. Given their reputation, it didn't seem too smart to give them a heads up and time to plan an ambush.

"Hey! Hello in there!" When the guard looked out the window, Charlie smiled at him and waved. "Hi! My car broke down and my phone's dead. I need some help!"

The thing was, most men wanted to be heroes.

"Are you lost?" he called, coming down the stairs. He'd clearly attempted to tame his hair by running his hands through it and he was tugging wrinkles out of his shirt as he hurried to the gate.

In spite of Joss Whedon, most men didn't see danger when they saw a pretty blonde.

"I'm just in Cape Breton for the music festival and I guess I took a wrong turn and then my car made this grunch noise and just stopped."

"A grunch noise?" His smile slid toward patronizing, and Charlie absolved herself of any guilt in advance. "So you're a musician?" He gestured at the guitar with the hand holding the lock as he pulled the gate open with the other. "You going to play something for me?"

"Actually, I am." Charlie put her fingers to her strings.

When Paul's penis-mobile pulled up seven minutes later, the gate was open and the guard was on the ground, propped up against the fence.

Paul's eyes widened. "You killed him!"

"Don't get your y-fronts in a twist," Charlie sighed, getting into the car. "He's having a nap."

"There? On the ground?"

"Interestingly enough, I can do a lot of really cool things—including getting in and out of a D minor 7th add 9—but carrying a sleeping man significantly heavier than I am across six meters of grass and up four crappy stairs to his comfy chair is a bit beyond me. He'll be fine," she added when Paul continued to stare and the car continued to stay exactly where it was. "I'll give him a poke when we leave. Now, can we get on with this? It's late and I'm tired."

"Paul." Eineen's voice drew his attention off the guard. "We should get this done."

"It's like I'm not even talking," Charlie muttered as Paul finally got them moving in the right direction.

When she got out of the car, she scuffed through the thin layer of gravel to the dirt below and paused for a moment, sifting the night for the out-of-place. If there were Goblins in the mine, then the gate had to be close. Goblin herding made cat herding look like a smart idea; not even Auntie Catherine would be able to control them over any great distance.

She couldn't sense the gate, but she honestly hadn't expected to. Like she'd said to Jack, Auntie Catherine, knowing she was in the province and working with the Selkies, had probably hidden it.

Paul had unlocked and opened half of the big double doors. Eineen waited on the threshold. "Are you coming?"

Charlie grinned. "Not even breathing hard."

The contrast between the night and the light in the room that led to the elevator and the shaft down into the Duke made Charlie's eyes water. She blinked rapidly, trying to speed the adaptation. Mines, particularly empty mines, should be dark and spooky not lit by harsh industrial fluorescents. By the time all the retinal flares had died down, Paul had the elevator open and was handing out hard hats. She couldn't see Goblin sign in the room, but just in case, she asked Eineen what she saw.

The Selkie's eyes went black from lid to lid. "No blood, no gouges from tooth or claw. They have not been this high."

Charlie spun her hardhat on one finger. "I was kind of hoping for no empty beer cans, no used condoms, and no graffiti saying *UnderRealm rules! MidRealm drools!* but I'll take no blood or claw gouges." She paused at the elevator and leaned out over the shaft, peering down through the grates on the floor. "I see why they call it a cage. You're sure this is safe?"

"I would worry more about what you'll face at the bottom," Eineen told her.

"Yeah, I think I'll worry about getting to the bottom first." She took a deep breath and stepped into the elevator, grate cutting into the bottoms of her flip flops.

When Eineen moved to follow, Paul stopped her. "You should wait up here. I can bring the pelts up. There's no need for us both to go into danger," he added quickly.

Charlie snickered. "You know she can probably kick your ass, right?"

They ignored her.

"The skins belong to members of my family. I will retrieve them. We . . ." She reached out and touched his cheek. ". . . we will retrieve them, together."

"Yeah, that's sweet." Balanced on her right foot, butt against the safety bar, Charlie sketched a charm on the bottom of her left flip flop to make it a little sturdier. "But none of the skins are yours. Why not grab Tanis or Neela—they're somewhere around the festival—and let them retrieve their own skins?"

"Because they're distraught!" Hair fanning out in an ebony wave, Eineen spun around to face Charlie. "They would have no consideration for their lives."

"Okay, I'll give you Tanis, but Neela barely cracked upset, and yeah, I'm sure she's repressing for the sake of the kids. Mental states aside, they deserve to be here."

"With their skins so close, they'd be easy prey for the Goblins and what-ever else is down there!"

The gate clanged shut.

"Excuse me?" Charlie dropped her shoe to the floor and slid her foot into it without taking her eyes off Eineen—and not for the usual reason. "And whatever *else* is down there? It's funny but I don't recall you mentioning anything but Goblins."

"It was more a feeling," Paul told her. Eyes still locked on Eineen, Char-lie could see him in her peripheral vision, standing with his hand over the big green button.

"We didn't see anything but we heard . . . thudding. Kind of drumlike. Um . . . booming."

"Booming?"

"And scraping."

"Scraping? Booming and scraping," she repeated, but they didn't sound any better lumped together. Call her paranoid, but Eineen's complete lack of expression suggested she hadn't mentioned both the booming and the scrap-ing on purpose. "There is no way those sounds can be good."

"Whatever it was, it was deeper than the skins," Eineen pointed out. "If you keep the Goblins away, we can grab the skins and be out before it rises from the depths. Do it!"

About to ask what she expected done, Charlie realized, as Paul's hand slapped down on the go switch, the command hadn't been to her. The eleva-tor shuddered and dropped about six inches. Reflexes honed growing up in a large family only just kept the bottom curve of her guitar from impacting against the metal grid as the sudden movement slammed her to one knee. "Fucking, ow!" Small mercies, the edges of the metal had been worn smooth by men in hard-soled boots, shuffling in place as they rode up and down and down and up and down again, but the grid still dug into her knee and it hurt! "That's definitely going to leave a . . ." She frowned and touched a gleaming line where the paint had been scored from the metal. "Last time you were here, did a Goblin grab on to the bottom of the elevator as you left?"

"Yes, but Eineen aimed the beam from my hardhat light into its eyes and it fell away."

"Thanks for mentioning that, too." One section of the grate had been nearly cut through. "It looks like the Goblins are staying in the mine even though they could climb the walls or the cables or, from the looks of this, cut their way through the rock to the surface. Eineen, what are the odds they're staying down there because that's the job they were hired to do?"

"You don't hire Goblins," Eineen sniffed. "You bully them or you black-mail them or bribe them and even then you don't expect them to keep their word."

"Yeah. So why are they staying in the mine?"

"They can't get out."

Charlie twisted and pointed at Paul. "That's right. They can't get out." Eyes narrowed, she shifted her guitar against her thigh, strummed a simple chord progression with her thumbnail, then scanned the inside of the eleva-tor. "Paul. One step to the right."

"You don't tell me . . ."

"Now!" She played again as he moved. "There it is."

"There what is?"

Right. They couldn't see it. "It's a Gale charm. And since I didn't put it there, that pretty much guarantees Auntie Catherine did." The charm had been worked in and around the blank spaces on the instrument panel. "The Goblins aren't leaving because they've been charmed in. She's charmed the elevator so they can't use it, they may not be able to even get into it. Since they're still down there, she had to have also charmed the cables and the walls of the shaft. I don't know why they're not digging their way out, maybe they are, maybe she specifically told them not to and they're so afraid of her they're not going to try. But she missed a spot." The aunties were not omni-scient, no matter what they, personally believed. "They can ride out on the bottom of the elevator."

"But when they get to the top, the cage will be blocking the shaft."

Charlie scraped her fingernail over the deepest gouge. "They'll go through the elevator."

Paul folded his arms. "You said they couldn't get in."

"Through isn't in. Those degrees of yours, not in English, are they?" Gripping the safety bar, she rolled back on her heels and stood. Then bent and took a look at her knee. The grate had pressed purpling dents into her skin but not broken it. On the one hand, good. On the other hand, a blood charm painted across the floor would keep anything out.

Overkill for Goblins, she supposed, but the thought of a pack of them running loose sent a shiver up her back. People would die before they were rounded up again. And, yeah, the Gales didn't interfere with the Fey; she'd heard that her entire life. Apparently Auntie Catherine hadn't been listening—the proof of her involvement was right there on a pitted piece of painted steel. Charlie settled her guitar into place, took a deep breath . . .

And nearly fell again when the elevator jerked to a stop.

"Warn a person!" she snarled at Paul.

He shifted to stand behind Eineen. Quite possibly, the smartest thing he'd done in the limited time Charlie had known him.

The elevator opened into some kind of central depot. Considering it was nothing more than a large room carved out of the rock to be a tunnel terminal, it was well lit. The five tunnels Charlie could see from where she was standing were not.

"We didn't turn the lights off in C tunnel when we left," Paul said quietly.

"Goblins don't like the light, remember?"

"They figured out how to turn the lights off?" He sounded horrified.

"Didn't have to," Charlie told him, sketching night-sight charms on her eyelids. "They probably ripped down the wiring and smashed the fixtures." She hadn't needed night sight at the festival, hadn't bothered with it on the road, but here and now, it seemed like a good idea. Not that it helped much. Beyond the first two meters, the tunnels weren't so much dark as filled with an absence of light, and the charms, like cat's eyes, needed minimal illumination to work.

"Why aren't they waiting for us," Eineen murmured, close enough that her breath lifted the hair off the back of Charlie's neck. "They must have heard the cage descend."

In a just world, Charlie would have refused to shiver. In this world, her body went with it. "Were they waiting for you the last time?"

"No. We heard them approaching when we got close to the skins."

"Best guess, they're exploring. If Auntie Catherine left them to guard the skins, then they've set up wards and your proximity called them back." Locked into the mine, easy to find, they wouldn't want to fail at the task Auntie Catherine had set them. Charlie covered a yawn with the back of her hand. She needed to get this over with and grab some sleep. "Okay, which way?"

Paul moved out in front, and Eineen let him. Given how close she stayed behind Charlie's right shoulder as they made their way through the open area, her position remaining constant as they stepped around abandoned carts and over the tracks they ran on, Charlie figured it had less to do with giving Paul a chance to man up and more to do with being terrified. Paul feared the Goblins because they were outside his experience. And okay, because they were freaky little not! Humans who'd tried to claw their way through steel to get to him. Eineen feared them because she knew exactly what the freaky little not!Humans were capable of.

When Paul began to maneuver one of the flat carts onto the rails heading for tunnel C, Eineen stopped him and said, "We won't need it."

"Four pelts weigh . . ."

"As much as four lives, as little as I need them to."

"But the last time . . ."

"I didn't realize that was why you were taking the cart."

Charlie could tell he wanted to ask Eineen just what she'd thought he was going to use the cart for, but, in the end, he only shook his head and moved toward the tunnel. Given that he hadn't had the sense to run when Eineen came out of the water to dance, he'd better learn to cope with confusion.

Unfortunately, no matter how many times Paul flicked the breaker, the lights remained off in tunnel C.

Charlie put her hand over Paul's and stopped the obsessive working at the switch. "I think they're broken. I'll go out in front from here on, okay?"

For a moment she thought he was going to protest. Give her some involuntary testosterone-produced crap about being the man, but all he said was, "Okay."

Enchanted. Not stupid. Good to know.

About to draw a charm on the wall with a wet finger, Charlie squinted as a light bulb came on above her head.

"Sometimes the helmet lamps take a while to warm up," Paul explained. "And there's no absolute guarantee that, in spite of regulations, the batteries are 100% full." He laughed, nervously. "Still, there's no absolute guarantee for anything, is there?"

"I thought you met Auntie Catherine," Charlie muttered, scanning the rocks for . . . "There you are. Come to Mama, baby." The piece of coal was about the size of a chocolate truffle and soft enough it ran easily over the rock wall as she sketched a charm at the point where the light from the big open area gave up and quit. Leaning forward, she huffed a breath at the wall. The black lines sparkled, then gleamed, then glowed white. The charm didn't throw a lot of light, but it created a small oasis in the darkness. Charlie'd learned it in Auntie Claire's outhouse, the charm written so that closing and latching the door completed it.

Oh, great. Now I have to pee.

"What would happen if I drew that mark?" Paul asked speculatively.

"Think you can remember it?" The lines of the charm had been washed out by the light.

"Of course, I . . ."

Leading the way down the tunnel, Charlie grinned at the frown in his voice. "Let it go, dude."

"Do you know how much energy could be saved if everyone could draw on the wall, or the on ceiling, and light their houses?"

"Do you know how boring music would be if everyone sang in the same range?"

"What?"

"To each their own, Mr. Belleveau." About two meters past the light from the first charm, she drew and activated another. If she'd been using spit, she wouldn't have needed to activate, but breathing took a lot less time than having to constantly wet her finger. She was pretty sure there was a dirty joke buried in that statement, but she was too tired to bother digging it out.

As time passed, she fell into what Mark would've referred to as a Zen state and Charlie thought might be closer to bored stupid. Walk and charm, walk and charm. Half circle of tunnel; curved roof, flat floor. Walk and charm, walk and charm. Rough roof, smooth floor. Walk and charm, walk and charm. Sound of her footsteps, sound of Paul's footsteps, silence of Eineen's footsteps. Walk and charm. When Eineen touched her shoulder, she jumped and made a noise she had every intention of denying later.

"We're nearly at the skins," the Selkie murmured. "The next side tunnel to the left."

"So far, no Goblins," Paul added.

Eineen made a nearly inaudible sound of protest.

"What?"

Charlie rolled her eyes as the unmistakable sound of claws against stone drifted up from the lower tunnels. Two degrees and the man had no understanding of what *not* to say in this kind of a situation. "And at least it's not raining," she sighed, finished one last charm, and dropped what was left of the coal. "Little bastards are fast." The sound of the claws had already come notably closer.

"We can hear them," Paul pointed out.

Kind of pointlessly, Charlie thought. The Goblins weren't trying for a stealth attack.

"So they can hear *you*," he added.

Oh. "I want them close enough the sound doesn't distort. You knew the job was dangerous when you took it," she added before he could protest.

"Without the Dragon Prince, what can you play that will make a Goblin run?" Eineen asked.

"Okay, first . . ." Charlie ran her thumbnail over the strings checking the acoustics. " . . . if you thought I had nothing to offer without Jack, *this* is not the time to bring that up. And, second, they've met Auntie Catherine." She squared her shoulders, settled the guitar into place, and wrapped the fingers of her left hand around the fretboard. "I'm going to point out the relationship."

When the darkness began to break into pieces, pieces that gleamed and glittered like eyes and teeth, she began to play.

Auntie Catherine's song. Her song. The song of the Gale women who hunted down Uncle Edward, tore him to pieces, and devoured him. Wild songs.

The gleaming and the glittering got no brighter.

Then it faded, and there was only the darkness.

Charlie played a moment more, then stilled the strings. The silence in the tunnel was oppressive. *Calm before the storm,* she noted silently. Because unlike certain executive assistants who'd been recently saved from the dark-side by the love of a good sea mammal, she knew better than to poke at fate.

"Did they look like they were running scared to you?" Paul took another poke. "They didn't look like they were running scared to me."

"The point is," Charlie reminded him, "they ran. Let's get the skins, make like a tree, and get the hell out of . . ."

Eineen raced past her.

". . . here," she finished as Paul ran to catch up. Speeding up a little, although she was not going to run, Charlie watched him reach the side tunnel and smack at a switch on the wall.

These lights were still working.

Paul glanced suspiciously up at the ceiling.

"You didn't get this far the last time, so the Goblins had no idea there *were* lights. They understand destruction," Charlie added, falling into step beside him. "They don't understand electricity."

"You say your family doesn't get involved with the business of the Fey, but you seem to know a fair bit about them."

"You'd be surprised how many people consider neutrality to be weakness."

"MBA; no, I wouldn't." He ran to join Eineen at the skins.

Charlie was just as glad three of them were in what looked like garment bags because the whole collapsed face, empty eyehole thing on the fourth was a little gross.

Her hair flowing around her in midnight currents in spite of the lack of any kind of a breeze, Eineen picked the top skin off the pile as though it weighed nothing at all and flung it into the air—kind of like Auntie Jane flicking the crumbs off a tablecloth. Except the tablecloths stay tablecloths while the pelt shimmered in midair and then became a beige scarf Eineen looped around her neck. She bent to the pile again and the sound of reinforced nylon tearing suggested she hadn't bothered with the zipper.

Skin two became a dark brown sweater with black patterning.

Charlie saw Paul open his mouth as Eineen shrugged the sweater over her shoulders, but she didn't hear what he said over the sudden sound in the main tunnel.

Thud.

Thud.

Thud.

Steadily growing closer, claws on stone playing melody over percussion.

"If whatever that is traps us in here, we're done. Pick up the pace!" Holding her guitar tight against her body, she ran to the tunnel mouth. Looking back toward the elevator, the charms were circles of light like pearls spaced along a black silk cord. Looking the other way, she almost thought she saw the darkness tremble with each heavy . . .

Thud.

Thud.

A piece of the wall broke way and skittered down the stone face to the floor.

Thud.

"Oh, shit."

She knew drums. Bodhrans. Tom toms. Snares. Steel. Taiko. Darbuka. Kpanlogo. Basic big bass drums.

Thud.

That wasn't a drum.

Thud.

That was a footstep. What had feet that would make that kind of an impact and still fit in the tunnels?

"They have a cave troll," she sighed as Paul and Eineen rocked to a stop behind her.

"Really?" From his tone, Paul didn't get the quote.

"You don't get out much, do you?" She reached back, snagged a handful of fabric—Paul's shirt—and yanked him past her into the main tunnel. "Now, move it. And no, not really," she added as Paul grabbed for Eineen's hand and all three of them started to run. "It's a regular troll; I just always wanted to say that."

"Catherine Gale brought a troll in with the Goblins and the . . . uh . . ."

"Boggarts. And, again, no. He's probably been here for years." Paul's slick-soled shoes had crappy traction, Charlie realized as Eineen kept him from falling. Her flip flops were no better, though, so it wasn't like she could call him on it. "Trolls are like living earth, they just *seep* through the barrier, but I wouldn't bet against Auntie Catherine using his seepage to anchor the gate."

"It would have hidden it on the other side," Eineen allowed.

"Yeah, like the Courts care." The Goblins had to have found the Troll when they were exploring the mine. Found it, woke it, got it moving. Trolls were nearly mindless and mindlessly vicious if provoked. Kind of like an avalanche. Sounded like the Goblins had provoked it and then aimed it.

"Why don't you do your thing and get rid of it?" Paul demanded.

"Living earth, remember?"

They were nearly past the last of the side tunnels, when the scrabbling of claws grew suddenly louder.

Charlie grabbed Eineen's arm and dragged her to a stop. Eineen's grip on Paul's hand stopped him. "There's Goblins between us and the big open area."

"It's called Canaveral," Paul whispered.

"Okay. There's Goblins between us and Canaveral."

"Are you sure?"

Something hissed in the darkness between the last two charms.

"Pretty sure, yeah." Fishing a pick from her pocket, Charlie slammed out fifteen seconds of power chords.

"Sister Mary Benedict," Paul gasped as the sound rolled away from them. "She terrified me in grade two. I haven't thought of her in years. What . . . ?"

"Basically, *don't make me come up there*," Charlie told him, pick sliding from sweat-slicked fingers. "Now run!"

THUD.

THUD.

BOOM.

"Boom?" Charlie demanded of the universe.

"Why is it so close?" Paul gasped and tripped over a rail. Eineen kept him upright until he regained his footing.

"Inertia." Charlie dodged around a row of empty carts. They probably weighed a couple hundred kilos each, but they were trembling. Not a good sign. "Once it gets moving, it keeps moving faster until something stops it."

"What the hell's an equal and opposite reaction to a Troll?"

Good question.

"If we get the elevator high enough, it'll fall down the shaft." Eineen could have been inside the elevator and halfway to the surface by now, but she held her pace to Paul's. More or less. Could be true love, could be because she didn't know how to work the machinery.

Not really the time to speculate, Charlie reminded herself running out of a flip flop and leaving it behind. Faster to kick the other one off.

Eineen reached the cage first, still dragging Paul behind her.

Charlie pushed past as they began to drag the gate closed.

BOOM.

BOOM.

BOOM!

She turned. It felt like she was turning underwater, moving against the pressure exerted on reality by the creature coming out of the tunnel.

It walked like a gorilla, massive body bent forward, the impact of its fists against the floor making the carts shimmy off the rails. Its half circle of a head sat directly on shoulders that scraped the sides of the tunnel as it emerged.

The darkness behind it splintered into glittering and gleaming, although the Goblins stayed prudently back. Waiting to see if the right side won.

Speed of the elevator. Speed of the troll. Charlie sucked at math, but it was obvious they weren't going to get the cage far enough up the shaft.

The Troll would hit the steel.

Reach up. Grab hold.

If it went over the edge, it would drag the crushed cage down the shaft with it.

Simple choice, really: Die in the elevator.

Or take a chance.

"What are you doing?" Eineen shrieked as Charlie slipped out past the closing gate.

"I have no idea." She was a Gale. They had roots sunk deep in the earth. The Troll was living earth.

And she was about to try and stop an avalanche with a song.

Fun, wow.

She'd dropped her only pick so it was back to her thumbnail and blood on the strings.

What stopped moving earth?

Heavy metal.

She remembered asking a guy in a different elevator if he knew the weight of the battery pack it took to run a portable amp. Not the sort of thing she wanted to schlep around with her. Here and now, it suddenly seemed worth the effort. A wah wah pedal wouldn't have hurt either.

The Troll reared back when the sound hit it, the ceiling of Canaveral just barely high enough to contain it. Its fists came off the floor and spread into three-fingered hands—thumbs and fingers the same length.

Its legs seemed too short to be jointed. Upright, it moved slower, but it kept moving.

Bare foot stomping the beat into the rock, Charlie screamed defiance over the chords. Metal didn't have to sound pretty, or melodic, but it had to be loud. The music bounced off a hundred different hard surfaces and ricocheted, creating a discordant harmony.

Behind and around, filling in the spaces, her fiddler threw in "Devil in the Kitchen."

The Troll ignored the shower of dislodged rock that fell from the ceiling and bounced off head and shoulders. It shoved one of the heavy steel carts out of the way and kept coming.

Slower though. Definitely slower.

That was good.

It'd stop before it got to her.

It would stop . . .

It grabbed the guitar, grazing Charlie with one finger and knocking the wind out of her. As it lifted the guitar and her by the strap now jammed painfully up under her arm, the ricochets of sound continued, but she couldn't reach the strings to pull them into a whole. Time slowed as the guitar splintered. Strings lost tension in the collapse. Sighed in defeat.

Without an instrument . . .

With no way to bend the music . . .

Keep playing, Charlie begged the fiddler, but silence answered.

The tension on the guitar strap gave way. Charlie braced one foot against the Troll's torso, clutched at its shoulder, dug her fingers into the ridges of living rock, and looked it in the eye.

Its eyes were the same slate gray as its body. Wild eyes. Truly wild. No allegiances.

Living earth.

The Gales had their roots sunk deep in the earth, but no one, nothing, had ever rooted in the Troll.

And doesn't that sound ridiculously smutty, Charlie thought.

It flicked away the ruined guitar—Charlie heard the pieces hit the ground even if she couldn't, wouldn't look—and closed a hand around Charlie's body.

Fuck my life. Should've stayed in Calgary.

Time continued moving slowly as her ribs began to crack.

The Troll's eyes widened at the sound, and for the first time, it actually saw her. If she had to guess, Charlie'd say it didn't like what it saw.

This was Wild. It answered to no one and nothing but itself. It didn't need music to form and direct its power; it was power. The look in its eyes said, *I know you. And I'm not impressed.*

As the pain started to catch up, Charlie frowned. The Troll's eyes weren't slate gray. They were Gale gray.

And Gales didn't care if walking slag heaps were unimpressed.

Gales knew what Wild meant. They knew it had to be contained, controlled, before it became all there was. Sure, the aunties could take Uncle Edward down, but they were tied to place. Allie had slapped the Dragon Queen home, but she couldn't leave the city. Gales who could do little damage were free to wander as they would—in spite of what her mother thought, Paris would survive the twins—but Gales who could change the very nature of reality were shackled.

And no one had shackled them. The certain knowledge of her own death lending clarity, Charlie knew they'd limited themselves. One day an auntie had looked out at the carnage, folded her arms, and said, *That'll be quite enough of that.* But every now and then, a bit broke free. A Wild Power. Untied. Because every now and then, something too big to ignore bellied up to the bar and declared it could take all comers.

Her frown deepened. Pain might have mixed a few too many metaphors there, but the point was, the power wasn't in the guitar, or she'd never have been able to pick up a guitar she'd never seen before and play away the storm. The instruments focused the power. The power was in her.

Another rib cracked.

Charlie didn't have breath enough to scream.

Pain wasn't *focusing*. It was distracting.

You think love hurts? She didn't have breath enough to snicker either. *Try having your ribs crushed by a Troll.*

Her phone rang.

You have got to be kidding me.

"Charlotte Marie Gale!" Auntie Jane's voice was tinny but remarkably clear considering it came from Charlie's pocket. On an unanswered phone. "A little less smart-ass and a little more focus. I will not have you killed in such an embarrassing manner."

Right. Let's not embarrass Auntie Jane . . .

Charlie squinted the Troll's eyes back into focus, sucked in as much air as she could, and hissed with everything she had left, "Piss off."

As she hit the floor, and it felt like a hot iron spike jammed up through her chest, she realized she should have told it to put her down first.

TEN

J ACK SPLIT THE DIFFERENCE between keeping an eye on the Boggart and not giving himself away, but that still put him high enough he had to keep one eye out for planes. Although he'd never admit it to a Gale, who were in lots of ways just as narrow-minded as his family on the other side, planes were one of the reasons he wanted to stay. Beings without flight had claimed the sky. How cool was that? No one in the UnderRealm had ever tried it. Sure, his uncles would have taken them apart the first time they got off the ground, but that wasn't the point—they hadn't even tried.

Humans were pretty cool.

He was a lot less pissed off at his father than he used to be.

The Boggart squirmed under a fence that guarded three sides of a property—a cliff and the Atlantic guarding the fourth—and headed straight for the cluster of buildings over by the edge of the cliff. There was a car by the building and a guy asleep over by the fence, but Jack couldn't see anything that said there was a gate around. He circled, and as he came in from over the ocean, saw the Boggart squirm through a square hole in the roof of one of the buildings and disappear inside.

Adjusting his size so as not to bring the building down, Jack landed and stuck his head in the hole. The Boggarts, all the Boggarts, not just his, had definitely gone down there. The smell was unmistakable; old damp sofa cushion mixed with ash. No, old damp sofa cushion mixed with the inside of the vacuum.

If he was going to follow, he'd have to get smaller still. Deep breath and . . . clench.

The breeze off the ocean blew the smoke inland as he snickered. Good thing he couldn't change size in skin, he'd fall into the toilet. Digging his claws into the tiles, he reminded himself to repeat that observation to Charlie later.

Deep breath and . . . clench.

All that time he'd spent messing around with the mail delivery person was about to pay off. It wasn't easy compressing himself into hawk size; none of his uncles could get this small, and he was bigger than all of them. But then, none of his uncles were sorcerers. Or Gales.

It didn't matter that he was smaller than the Boggarts now. He was finding the gate—not heading for a fight. Besides, at this size, his flame would cut like a blowtorch, and if he had to get bigger, too bad for the building.

Finally small enough, he turned on the diagonal so his wings would fit, and dropped into the hole.

It was fun following the shaft through the building, the Boggarts' trail easy to follow. Too easy with a side order of maximum gross-out at one point. He'd have fried the damp pile as he passed to kill the stink, but he was afraid of cutting through the thin metal under it and Human buildings were weirdly flammable.

There were twelve Dragon Lords, so most of the UnderRealm built in stone.

When he reached a shaft that descended down into the earth with Boggart-scented cables running from enormous pulleys, he knew where he was. Back home, Dwarves mined the mountains near his mother's cave. Cameron had laughed when he'd told him, but Dwarves weren't a cliché where Jack came from and anyone who got along that well with his mother had balls out of proportion to their hei . . .

Music? Charlie.

He hadn't been hurrying, but now he folded his wings close in to his body and dove, snapping them out as he emerged into a huge room carved out of the rock.

Snapping them out further to their full width when he saw what the rock had hold of.

Clutching the bar on elevator's gate so hard the metal cut into his palms, Paul stared at the creature hauling Charlotte Gale into the air. Enormous arms were attached to massive shoulders that tapered down to stumpy legs. It had a head, and Paul thought he saw a face before it was blocked by the Gale woman's body.

It looked like living rock.

Except rock wasn't alive.

"Living earth, remember?"

Wasn't alive.

Wasn't.

"I have the skins." Eineen's hand closed around his arm, warm, grounding. Something in her touch pushed the terror back. "We need to get out of here."

He still couldn't get his fingers to unclench, but he nodded toward the . . . the Troll. The gesture turned into a flinch as it flung the pieces of the smashed guitar aside. "We can't."

"We can't do anything."

"We can't leave her."

"She's a Gale. She'll be fine."

Catherine Gale would have been fine. Paul wouldn't have worried for a moment about Catherine Gale. Had he not been running for his life, he might have worried about the Troll. But the Troll wasn't crushing Catherine Gale and Paul realized that nothing could have convinced him of the differences between the two women more than the terror he now felt *for* her younger relative. Even Eineen's reassurances came in a distant second.

"We have to do . . ."

A horde of small furry creatures swarmed down over the elevator, swerved wide around the Troll, spotted the Goblins at the last minute, shrieked, swerved again, and disappeared down a different tunnel.

"What the hell?"

"Boggarts." Eineen's grip tightened slightly, but the calming effect had definitely lessened. "The gate is in these tunnels."

Paul looked at the Troll, past it to the Goblins, then turned just far enough to look at Eineen. "You think?"

Something hit the top of the elevator, bounced, and a single Boggart scrambled across the open area and after the rest.

The Troll didn't seem to notice.

Or had noticed everything and not reacted. What the hell did Paul know about Tro . . .

At first he thought it was bird, maybe a big golden gull—not that gulls came in gold but what did he know about b . . .

"Dragon! Oh, my fucking God, that's a DRAGON!"

The tail slammed the elevator, rocking it, knocking him back. The wings, half folded, filled Canaveral. The head dipped low on a long, sinuous neck. Steel screeched as carts were crushed under enormous clawed feet or flung to crumple against the wall.

The space filled with fire, a heartbeat of searing heat that didn't burn, and a boy in his mid-teens with pale blond hair, crouched over Charlotte Gale's body next to a pile of stone. He was naked, but, other than that, he looked absurdly normal. He turned. Wild, golden eyes locked on Paul's face as he wailed, "Help me! I don't know enough about Humans!"

So much for normal.

Smacked by the dragon's tail, the cage door had buckled.

Paul dragged at it. He'd never move it. "I can't . . ."

The boy's eyes flared. The door unbuckled and snapped open so fast Paul nearly lost a finger. He stepped forward, but Eineen still had hold of his arm.

Eineen was on her knees, face hidden behind her hair.

"Hey!" He couldn't get free of Eineen's grip. Trying hurt. "Eineen!"

She shook her head, her hair waving like kelp at low tide. "The Prince."

Which was when Paul connected the dots. In his own defense, this was his first dragon. The boy *was* the dragon. The dragon was the prince Eineen had been going to ask for help. And none of that mattered.

"Get up." He tucked his free hand under her other arm and hauled her up onto her feet. "We have to help him. He doesn't know enough about Humans."

Something he said, or maybe because it was him saying it, got through. Eineen tossed her hair back and stared past him at the boy. At the woman on the floor.

And then they were moving, Eineen dropping back to her knees beside the body.

No, not the *body*. Blood still bubbled between parted lips. It wasn't a body until she stopped breathing.

"Did you do this, Highness?"

Jack glanced over at the Selkie touching the pile of rubble that had been the Troll and shook his head. "No, Charlie did. But she's hurt. She's hurt bad and she won't wake up and I don't know what to do." He couldn't control the smoke that puffed out with every word. He waved it away from Charlie's face and bit his lip until he tasted blood. He wasn't going to cry. Crying was weakness. Weakness was death.

A drop of water splashed onto Charlie's arm and rolled off.

"You have to take her home, Highness. Her people can heal her."

The Selkie's voice was soft but insistent. Jack rubbed his nose on his wrist and said, "How? Home is too far away and . . ." He looked over the rubble at the empty tunnel where the Goblins had been. They'd fled when he'd arrived, but he'd seen them. "The gate is down here. Stupid! I'm so stupid! I followed the Boggart to find the gate, so of course the gate is down here. I can take her through the gate, cut through the UnderRealm, and out again by Allie. Allie can fix anything."

"If you move her, she'll die."

Jack glared up at the man standing by the Selkie. "I have to move her, or she'll die!"

"The blood, in her mouth . . . there's internal damage. Broken ribs, for sure. If the ends haven't punctured a lung yet . . ." The man's voice trailed off and he shook his head. He looked really upset, like he cared, so Jack didn't kill him for what he'd said. For stopping him from taking Charlie home.

"Okay." He touched Charlie's hair because that wouldn't hurt her. He just had to think about this. He was a dragon, but a dragon would eat her, and he didn't want to do that even if he could have. He was a Gale and a Gale would take her home, but he couldn't do that. He was a sorcerer and he could turn her into butterflies, but butterflies died so easily. He could move things without touching them. He could . . .

He could make clothes out of nothing.

First day he'd been here, right after he'd followed his father's blood through from the UnderRealm, he made clothes out of parts of David's rental car so he'd look like everyone else. David had been really, really pissed, but that didn't matter now. Point was, he could make *things* out of other *things*.

He could make a *thing* so he could move Charlie.

There were bits of the Troll broken up under her so Jack started with those, smoothing them out and connecting them together. They weren't Troll anymore. Whatever Charlie had done, they were only rock. Then he shoved the Selkie out of the way and brought more bits over and started to curl them up and around, just barely touching Charlie's skin.

"She's not dead! You can't . . ."

The Selkie stopped the Human male before Jack did. That was good because Jack didn't want to split his attention, but he totally would have fried that guy if he tried to tell him what he could or couldn't do.

He was especially careful around Charlie's head, but he might have caught a bit of hair anyway.

Then he sat back, took a deep breath and looked.

Except for a circle over her mouth and nose, he'd totally encased her in rock. The troll had hurt her and now it would keep her safe while he got her home.

"As long as I don't whack her on anything, I can move her."

He stood, changed, and realized that if he stayed small enough to get through the tunnels to the gate, he'd be too small to carry the rock and Charlie.

Paul had watched the rock flow and change and feared for a moment the boy—dragon—was building a coffin, but it soon became clear he was using the rock to immobilize Charlotte Gale's injuries. Casting her in stone, as it were. He'd have laid her out were he building a coffin, not taken such care to wrap her where she lay.

When the boy stood and became a dragon again, the problem he faced was obvious to anyone with eyes. "We can lift her into one of the carts." If they could find a cart the Troll and then the dragon-boy hadn't crushed. "And then we can roll her to the gate."

Another flash of fire and a naked teenage boy stared at him, wide-eyed. "How did you . . . ?"

"The rock has made the . . . has made Charlotte Gale not only heavy, but bulky. You've got to stay small to fit through the tunnels. It's just a matter of putting the information together and coming up with a solution. It's what I do."

The dragon-boy's smile made Paul feel as though he'd just—well, slain a dragon wasn't the best analogy under the circumstances, but he felt like he'd finally done something important with his life. The feelings Amelia Carlson had evoked for a job well done weren't even close.

He stepped away to find a working cart and realized Eineen had remained on her knees, once again locked in place, staring at the dragon-boy.

When Paul touched her shoulder, she said, "Your people do not do such things."

Since he had no idea what she meant, he turned his attention to the dragon-boy who shrugged, light catching the scatter of golden scales on his chest. "I'm unique."

"You're impossible."

His teeth were almost Human when he grinned. "Sometimes."

"You're . . ."

"I'm in a hurry! Get up and help, Seal-girl!"

She stood as if she were a puppet and he'd pulled her strings. Paul didn't like the look of that, but since the dragon-boy then ignored her, he decided it was a problem that could be temporarily forgotten. Kind of like the whole naked issue.

They found a high-sided cart with a dent in one side that still rolled. Unfortunately, they could only roll it about a meter before a tangle of crushed carts blocked the tracks. Paul glanced around Canaveral. This was a staging area. With any luck, a working forklift had been left behind when the mine had closed. Just because he hadn't seen one . . .

"Seal-girl!"

"My name is Eineen, Highness," she snapped as she pushed past Paul. Seemed she wasn't happy about the puppet experience either.

The dragon-boy rolled his eyes. "And mine's Jack. Now help me push!"

"You can't," Paul began, but it seemed they could. Eineen put her hands next to the dra . . . to Jack's on a piece of buckled metal and the two of them shoved what was probably half a ton of crushed steel out of the way. Jack's eyes flashed gold again, and forced the cart over a section of flattened track and rolled it up beside Charlotte Gale's body.

"Wait!" Paul swallowed as Jack turned glowing golden eyes toward him. Had to swallow again before he could continue. "You've immobilized her injuries, but you've got to be careful moving her. Her insides could shift." *Contents could shift during shipping.* He shook the thought away. "If you can lift her on your own, Eineen can get into the cart and steady her as she's lowered. We can stay in the cart with her to steady her as you roll her to the gate." Although given Charlotte Gale's current weight . . . "Try not to make any sudden turns."

"I don't," Eineen began.

Paul cut her off. He understood her protest. Thought he understood anyway. She'd gotten away from this kind of hierarchy when she'd left Faerie or whatever they called it when they were home and she didn't want to go back, but the hierarchy wasn't the issue here. A woman's life was. Charlotte Gale's life. "He'll be able to move faster with our help."

"Okay." Jack nodded. "Great. Get in the . . ."

Eineen raised a hand. "Do not make it a command." She climbed over and into the cart, then turned, hands up. "Lift her in, Highness. Slowly."

The best Paul could do was stay out of the way. He watched as Jack, the dragon-boy, and the woman he loved, who just happened to be a seal part of the time, lifted and settled Charlotte Gale, wrapped in re-engineered Troll, up and into a mine cart. His job with Carlson Oil seemed to have happened in another life. Here and now, he couldn't call to mind why he'd been so proud of it.

With Charlotte Gale settled in the bottom of the cart, he climbed in beside Eineen. He couldn't lift a body wrapped in rock, but he could help brace it.

"We were meant to have a life as close to normal as I could make it," Eineen murmured as Jack pushed the cart into the tunnels.

"We were meant to have a life together," Paul told her, taking her hand and placing a kiss in her palm. "As long as I have you, I don't care about the rest."

"Trolls and Goblins and Boggarts and Dragon Princes . . ."

"And Amelia Carlson and Carlson Oil and thousand-dollar suits." Another kiss. "They don't matter. We do." He was almost surprised to find he meant it. Something had changed over the last few hours—or maybe it was him who'd changed on a deep and basic level. He was done with the job and what he was expected to do in order to keep it. Monday morning, he'd walk into the office and say . . . "This isn't the tunnel we went down before!"

The only light came from the headlamps he and Eineen were still wearing. There were no magical lights on the tunnel walls.

"This is the tunnel the Boggarts went down," Jack told him, his breathing level and unlabored as he pushed the cart at a full run. "Little cowards were heading straight for the gate."

"The Goblins?"

Jack snorted out a cloud of smoke. "They won't come near when I'm around. I'll fry their asses."

It sounded like teenage bragging. In a way, Paul supposed it was, but that didn't make it any less true.

It seemed the Goblins knew that because there was no sign of them as they moved farther and farther into the mine. As near as Paul could determine without the schematics, the tunnel they were in followed the line of the bay to the southwest. He watched Charlotte Gale breathe because it was less disconcerting than watching the tunnel walls speed by.

"We're close," Eineen said as Jack dug in his heels and slowed the cart.

Braced against the rusting steel, Paul checked his watch. It was 2:37 AM.

"It's that side tunnel," Jack grunted. "The next one."

As far as Paul was concerned, the next side tunnel looked no different than any of the others they'd passed. And they were going to pass this one, too. Bare feet and a teenage boy, no matter what else he was, couldn't stop the forward momentum of steel and rock and two adults, no, three adults and . . .

The cart stopped with the front edge about six centimeters beyond the tunnel in question, the rear edge buckled under Jack's grip, the steel hot to the touch.

Jack and Eineen reversed positions to get Charlotte Gale out of the cart. Nostrils streaming smoke, Jack lifted her over the edge, and with Eineen steadying her, tipped her carefully onto feet—or the rock over her feet. Eineen kept her upright until Jack jumped out and took possession.

"You can carry her like that?" Paul asked. "As a person?"

"I'm always a person, dude!" Jack glared over a stone shoulder, his eyes flashing gold. "But yeah, for a little ways. Long enough to carry her through . . ." He shuffled forward three steps and vanished. Not into the darkness.

Not there.

Paul shone his headlamp down the tunnel. It looked like a tunnel, no different than any other they'd passed. He stepped forward and a grip on his belt jerked him back, Eineen suddenly between him and the tunnel.

"You don't want to do that," she said, wrapping her arms around his waist and laying her head on his shoulder. "It's dark and bloody on the other side."

"It's where you come from . . ." Her hair smelled like the wind coming down the eastern passage carrying the scent of the sea and the knowledge that the world was wide and wonderful. And a little like fish. ". . . so it can't be all bad."

He felt her smile. "We were the best, and we left centuries ago."

"Jack . . ."

"Isn't like the other Dragon Lords."

"I gathered. He's . . ."

Claws skittered against rock. The sound was between them and the way out.

"*They won't come near when I'm around . . .*"

Jack flew low, following the contours of the land. It was harder work, but he hoped that by staying close to the ground his uncles would miss his return. The last thing he needed—the last thing Charlie needed—was for him to have to play their stupid power games. Actually, the last thing he *really* needed was for his mother to notice he was back in the UnderRealm.

It smelled wrong.

He'd gotten used to the smell of people and engines and industry.

Wings spread, he bent his head and sniffed at Charlie, cradled safely in the claws of his right foot. He'd gotten used to the smell of family.

She was still alive.

He'd get her home and Allie would keep her alive.

If he could find the other gate.

He couldn't feel a blood link to his father anywhere. *I'm so stupid!* He should've known there wouldn't be a blood link to the gate in Fort Calgary, or his mother would've gone through it and not followed *his* blood over the weirdly twisty path he'd had to take to get to the MidRealm.

He could take that path again; at least he thought he could. He'd done it once and then his mother had done it and Allie had sent his mother and his uncles back along it and that many dragons marked a route. If they hadn't destroyed the path completely.

Didn't matter. Charlie didn't have time for him to go that way.

Charlie needed him to get her home.

Hit with a sudden wave of homesickness, his stroke wavered and he ended up a lot closer to the ground than he'd intended. He knocked something over with his tail, heard it crash, and struggled to gain altitude without looking back.

He wanted Allie to tell him everything would be all right.

He wanted Graham to explain how.

He wanted Joe to translate the explanation.

He wanted Auntie Gwen to roll her eyes and then fix things.

He wanted Charlie to . . . to do anything. Open her eyes. Sit up. Survive.

He was too old to cry.

He missed his room. He missed his stuff. He missed pie. He missed . . .

The landscape in front of him had shifted.

If he flew straight and true, he'd make it home. The gate in Fort Calgary had left a weak spot in the border within the territory the Gales claimed, and he could feel home through it.

Easy.

He flew a little higher. A little faster.

"Home again, home again, jiggedy jog." The red Dragon Lord came out of the sun and matched Jack's pace. Uncle Viktor was the only one of his uncles who could still keep up to him at his full speed. He couldn't do it for long, but he made the most of every opportunity. "I can't remember if it ends with them eating a hog or a dog and don't care. We missed you around here, Nephew."

"Piss off."

"Well, they didn't teach you manners, your squishy relatives." His voice faded and Jack thought he'd outflown the older dragon but a sudden sharp pain in his left wing membrane told him where his uncle had gone. Given their difference in size, it was the one place he could do significant damage. He always went for the wing membrane. Jack knew that, but the need to get Charlie home had distracted him.

"Running away again? Running away like you're just out of the egg and your scales are soft and you're too scared to fight. What's that you're carrying? Is it precious?" Viktor sneered. "Can I make you drop it?"

Jack whipped his neck out to the side and snapped.

Uncle Viktor laughed. He knew how close he could fly to Jack and remain safe.

But Jack had grown while he was gone.

Blood hot in his mouth, Jack spat out the wing. Let it flutter to the ground. They were flying low enough Uncle Viktor might survive both the injury and the impact with the ground. He didn't care either way.

And he was still too old to cry.

By the time he could sense the weak spot in the border between two trees up ahead, his wing sent ripples of pain up into his back and through his whole body with every downstroke. He'd never flown so fast for so long

When he landed, he had to drop forward and brace himself on his hands. Fortunately, the grass was too damp to burn. His foot had cramped holding Charlie for so long. Breathing heavily, shaking his head to clear the smoke, he forced it open, his claws dragging trenches through the dirt so Charlie could be set directly onto the ground. He had to change in order to fit through the gate, but he didn't have the energy for clothes no matter what Allie said about clothes inside the city limits.

If anyone other than his Uncle Viktor had noticed he was home and had gotten ahead of him, this was when they'd attack. He wasn't worried about someone finding Uncle Viktor and coming after him—at the speed he'd been moving, they'd still be eating. Slipping and sliding, he managed to get his arms around Charlie and tip her carefully up onto her feet.

She was still breathing. There was fresh blood on the dried blood covering her lips, so she had to still be breathing. Right?

If it hadn't been so silent, if everyone and everything that lived near the gate hadn't hidden at his approach, he'd have never heard the wings.

He ducked behind Charlie and nearly dropped her in the backwash from the black dragon's dive.

"Knew you'd be heading here, Nephew." Uncle Adam sounded amused. "But the gate is closed. What do you intend to do now?"

Open it. He intended to open it, but he wasn't about to tell his Uncle Adam that. Of all his uncles, Adam seemed to want him dead the least, but wanting him dead the least didn't mean wanting him alive. Dragging Charlie between the trees, Jack put his hand against the weak spot and pushed.

It gave. Not enough. He didn't break through.

Jack had no idea of how to open a gate. He just knew he had to.

"You're not your father, Nephew." The ground shook when Uncle Adam landed. And that was just showing off because Jack was twice his size and the ground hadn't shook when he'd landed.

He pushed against the weak spot again as Adam furled his wings.

"What have you got there? It smells like blood. Like . . ."

Jack didn't turn to look but he knew Uncle Adam was frowning.

"Like Gale blood. Familiar . . . Well, if it isn't the Wild One. What have you done, Nephew?"

"I haven't done anything. I'm taking her home!"

"Are you?"

He could feel home. So close he should be able to touch it.

"No, I don't think so."

Uncle Adam had moved closer and if he got hold of Charlie, Jack didn't doubt for a moment he'd use her. And she'd die from it.

"Still trying, Jack? I admire that I suppose, but there's no gate there now. Alysha Gale slammed it out of existence, and you can't make something from nothing."

Yeah. He could. He slapped his hand again the space again and screamed, "Be a GATE!"

The only thing that got him and Charlie through was that Uncle Adam clearly didn't believe he could do it and was still just far enough away.

He fell with Charlie through the gateway into Fort Calgary, softening her impact with the ground as much as he could. She made a sound that hurt his heart as he twisted and yelled, "Stop being a gate!" before his Uncle Adam decided to follow.

He could hear the water and the traffic and smell people and engines and he was so close, but he couldn't pick Charlie up. He just couldn't. He was so tired and the rock was so heavy . . .

Inside the rock, Charlie's phone rang.

And rang.

And rang.

He found enough energy for claws and dug the rock away above the sound then ripped Charlie's pocket getting the phone out.

"Allie?"

"Jack?"

"Help . . ."

Turned out he wasn't too old to cry after all.

The fiddler in her head was playing "Homeward Bound." Charlie'd had enough fiddle music to last her a while so, in an effort to get it to shut the hell up, she opened her eyes.

"Her eyes are black!"

Allie.

"Don't worry, Catherine's used to go black off and on for years before the change."

Auntie Bea.

"That's not reassuring!"

Allie again. She sounded upset. Charlie wanted to say something reassuring, but she just didn't have it in her. The fiddler had stopped, though. Taking advantage of the silence while it lasted, she drifted off to sleep.

Next time she opened her eyes, Auntie Gwen seemed to be wiping her face with a warm cloth. Seemed to be. It was always best not to take the aunties for granted, especially when laid out flat feeling like overcooked pasta.

"So, you're back with us, are you? Don't answer that," she added as Charlie scraped a dry tongue over cracked lips. "Let me get you some water first."

The water, in a sippy cup shaped like an elephant, was room temperature and the best thing Charlie could ever remember drinking. "What happened?" she managed after half a dozen careful swallows.

"You took out a Troll, the Troll nearly reciprocated, and Jack brought you home through the UnderRealm having remade the Troll into a kind of a cast. He saved your life. We laid you out on the hill, called a ritual, and put your pieces back together. Allie insisted on you returning to the apartment, so Jack gave up his room although you'd hardly know it since he's been in here most of the time. Congratulations on accepting the responsibilities of a Wild Power, and don't ever do anything like that again." Auntie Gwen's dark eyes glistened. She brushed angrily at the single tear that rolled down her cheek and added, "Call your mother. She nearly broke the second circle apart trying to get to you and, apparently, your sisters are displacing their teenage angst by hunting vampires in the catacombs under Paris."

"There's vampires under Paris?"

Auntie Gwen sniffed. "Not for much longer if your mother is to be believed."

"How long?" Charlie asked. Nothing hurt, but the sheet seemed to weigh a hundred kilos, holding her flat.

"Since Jack brought you home?" Auntie Gwen helped her sit up, jerking the pillows up with her as support. "Nine days."

"Nine days! I've got to call Mark! Wait . . ." Her mistake; frowning hurt. "He has my number, why hasn't he called me?"

"Jack crushed your phone."

"He what? Why?"

"The poor boy was a bit upset. Did you miss the part about nearly dying, Charlotte?" She stepped back and folded her arms. "You'll just have to write off your little festival group in exchange for being alive. The injuries you had don't heal overnight. Wouldn't have healed overnight even if we'd allowed Jane to bully us into sending you back to Ontario. This is where . . ."

"Charlie!"

That Allie stopped her charge before she threw herself into Charlie's arms told Charlie more about how badly she'd been hurt than anything Auntie Gwen had said. Up to and including *nine days* and *nearly dying*. She opened her arms. "It's okay, Allie-kitten."

Well, relatively okay, Charlie thought as Allie clung to her and cried. But breathing was highly overrated anyway.

Allie had said Jack could go in first, but Jack liked Graham too much to put him through that. The poor guy'd been cried on pretty much twenty-four/ seven from the moment Charlie'd been brought from the hill. Allie'd held it together until then, but the moment Charlie'd been moved into his room, she'd stopped being the Gale who led the second circle, who anchored the family in Calgary, who'd kicked his mother's tail—and the rest of her—back to the UnderRealm, and became kind of impressively weepy. Her and that seal-girl back east could have a weep off.

Allie'd wanted Charlie in the big bedroom with her and Graham, so Jack offered his before the aunties could move her out of the apartment altogether. There was more room and more family at his father's old house, but Allie moving in would have shifted the power dynamics and who could get better with all that going on?

It was weird that Allie knew Charlie was going to be all right, but still couldn't stop crying. Jack had totally stopped worrying the moment the ritual was over. He let the aunties fuss over him, scrubbing down his scales and fixing his wing and then, once Charlie was settled, he'd changed, flown north, snatched up a buffalo from a ranch herd, and carried it into the mountains to eat. Then he'd slept for three days.

When he got home and Charlie was still asleep, he still didn't worry. An injured Dragon Lord found a safe place to hole up and sleep until he recovered, and Gales were almost as hard to kill as dragons.

No one could get to Charlie, but they could get to him and, for the first time, there was no question he was a Gale boy with all the indulgences that entailed.

Now that Charlie was awake, he was a little worried about how long Allie was staying in there with the door closed after Auntie Gwen had left. If they were having sex in his bed, that would be just too creepy. When the door finally opened, he breathed a sigh of relief and turned to Graham who seemed likely to pace his way through the floor. "You go. I can wait."

"You're sure?"

"I've got things to do." Jack used his fork to gesture at the line of pies on the kitchen counter. Seemed like every member of the family in Calgary had shown up with two or three every day since Charlie'd come home. The charms were pretty basic—*get better, don't be sad, we're in all in this together*. The Gales who'd baked then may have called the charms something else, but that's how Jack read them. Aunt Judith had been making meat pies, figuring that even Gales couldn't live indefinitely on lemon meringue. Aunt Judith was currently Jack's favorite aunt. And given all the pie he'd been eating, he felt great. Very reassured.

Even David had been in and out, although he hadn't brought pie. He had the changes mostly under control now. Jack liked to think he'd helped with that.

When Graham went into the bedroom, he left the door open.

Jack appreciated the gesture. Not that he'd been feeling excluded or anything.

The last slice of strawberry ice cream pie and a half a slice of peach pie later, Graham stuck his head out of the room. "She's wondering where the hell you are."

"I'm right here." He licked his fork.

"Missing the point, kid. Get your ass in here."

Jack sighed and stood. He stretched, scratched under the edge of his T-shirt, and padded barefoot across the room. When he paused at the door, Graham reached out and gripped his shoulder.

"She's fine. A little damp, given Allie's reaction, but fine."

"I know." Jack shook himself free. "I was there when they fixed her. She's just been sleeping."

"Okay."

Okay? He had no idea what Graham meant by that. He pushed past, ignored whatever Allie had to say as she moved to join her mate, man, Graham at the door, and stopped at the foot of the bed.

Charlie was sitting up against a pile of pillows. Her hair was sticking out and needed washing and she had purple shadows under eyes although he didn't know why because she'd been asleep for nine days. She was drinking out of one of Richard's sippy cups that Aunt Judith had brought over even though she was sitting up.

And she was fine.

"Hey." She put the cup down and held open her arms. "Come here."

Jack didn't remember crossing the rest of the room. There was a damp spot on the T-shirt Charlie was wearing, but he hadn't made it.

"I'm okay."

"I know." When he'd seen her last, they'd said she was fixed, but she'd been all limp . . .

"Hey, you saved me."

"I know. I bit Uncle Viktor's wing off." He felt her laugh. He liked that she laughed about it because it was pretty cool.

"For what it's worth, if they try to send you back or make you do anything you don't want when you're fifteen, they'll have to go through me first. Actually," she added as he sat up and wiped his eyes that had totally gotten wet off the mess Allie'd left on Charlie's shirt because he wasn't crying, "I'd have had your back regardless, but I have a feeling it means a little more now."

Her eyes were black. Then she blinked and they were gray again.

Jack took a deep breath and waved the smoke away as he exhaled. "There's pie."

Charlie shifted Graham's hand from her hip to Allie's, slid out from under Allie's arm, and got out of bed without waking either of them. Years of bands and bars and leaving town early the next morning, had given her mad skills in slipping away, no fuss, no muss. Although, after nine days, it should surprise no one that she couldn't sleep.

Grabbing a robe on her way out of the bedroom, she thought about looking in on Jack, but he was fourteen, not four or forty, so she kept going out of the apartment and down the stairs to the store. Or the hall behind the store.

The mirror shimmered in the light coming through the courtyard windows.

Her reflection, dressed in the red-and-black-checked dressing gown, appeared to be wrapped in silver bands.

She leaned in, cheek pressed against the cool glass, hands lightly gripping opposite sides of the frame. "I'm glad to see you again, too." Straightening, she rubbed at the smudge her face had left with the sleeve of the robe. "Enough of this mushy stuff, though. I'm fine. What've you got for me?"

What it had was her, still in the robe, eating sushi with Jack. As she watched, he picked up a piece of octopus with his fingers and dropped it into his mouth, the golden armor he wore moving with the sinuous grace of scales.

"Jack is my knight in shining armor and I should take him out to dinner?"

Her reflection's hair turned turquoise.

"And my look could use updating. With you there, dude."

There were little bears on the dressing gown at each intersection of red and black. Charlie'd never noticed that before. As she checked to see if the actual robe matched up with its reflection, she heard the door to the loft open out in the courtyard.

The hinges needed oiling.

Or, more likely, given that Auntie Gwen was knocking boots with a leprechaun and he'd never have let that go, the noise was just to get her attention.

Charlie glanced into the store on her way by. She'd never noticed before, but the metaphysical items gave off a green glow in the dark. Given the absence of light behind the counter, the signed photo of Boris was enough to cover the glow of the nail. The nail that lost the horseshoe, the horse, and the war. *"Lose it,"* Allie's voice said, in memory, *"and you lose everything."* Seemed like the nail couldn't be all it was cracked up to be if a hot shot of a minotaur could block its light. Even the painting of Elvis on black velvet shone brighter. She could feel its eyes following her as she went out the back door.

Auntie Gwen waited by the tiny shrubbery wearing one of Joe's shirts. She folded her arms, yawned, and said, "So, ask."

"I don't . . ." Actually, she did. "You congratulated me on accepting the responsibilities of being a Wild Power."

"That's not a question," Auntie Gwen pointed out after a moment.

Pointless to argue she'd known what Charlie'd meant as it was pointless to argue with an auntie just generally. "What does that mean?"

"Congratulations is an expression of pleasure at the good fortune of another."

"Auntie Gwen . . ."

She yawned again. "It's three in the morning, Charlotte, and you hauled me out of a warm bed. You're lucky I'm still grateful you're alive. Okay . . ." She drew in a deep breath and let it out slowly, reminding Charlie of Shelly and her early morning yoga. Reminding Charlie she still hadn't called Mark. "Charlotte!"

"Sorry." Her broken commitment to *Grinneal* would have to be dealt with, but for now, she aimed an expression of rapt attention at Auntie Gwen. "Go on."

"You're sure?"

Charlie nodded, fully aware it had not been a rhetorical question.

"All right, then, at some point, and I assume it was during your struggle with the Troll, you had an epiphany."

Point was, the power wasn't in the guitar . . . the power was in her.

Because every now and then, something too big to ignore just had to belly up to the bar and declare it could take all comers.

When Charlie opened her mouth, Auntie Gwen cut her off. "I don't need to hear what it was. It's always a variation on a theme. You don't get this kind of power in order to charm strangers in bars or rack up frequent flier miles going through the Wood. With great power comes great responsibility, a responsibility someone decided generations ago that not everyone in the family can be trusted with. You, Charlotte Gale, are a free electron, able to affect what you will. A warm body between this world and all the metaphysical shit that comes down the pike."

"Because I'm responsible enough to handle it?"

"Because until you were put in a position where you needed to use it, you had no interest in it. People who want this kind of power . . ." Her dark eyes gleamed. ". . . should never have it."

"Jack?"

Auntie Gwen looked like she'd eaten something that disagreed with her. "There could be an argument made that Jack also accepted his responsibilities."

"There could be an argument made that Jack has always accepted his responsibilities," Charlie pointed out. "Being the Gale formerly known as Prince."

"Yes, well, you can make that argument to Jane because I'm certainly not looking forward to it. You know that in spite of his saving your life, she's still going to be suspicious of his power. Given that it's *his* power."

"I handled a Troll. I think I can face Auntie Jane."

"Really?"

Charlie thought about it for a moment. "No. Not really. So what about Auntie Catherine?"

"Catherine is a Seer, as you are a Bard."

"Not what I was asking."

"Yes, well, no one said the system was perfect or that any one of us is fully aware of the whole. And now that I've gifted you with pearls of wisdom you'll probably ignore . . ." She yawned again. " . . . I'm going back to bed."

"Wait! What do I do?" Charlie asked as Auntie Gwen turned back toward her, one eyebrow raised.

"What has to be done."

"What has to be done?" Charlie repeated watching the door to the loft close behind Joe's shirt tail with a definitive snap. "Thank you, Yoda."

She'd left a mess behind in Cape Breton, that was for sure. Eineen had the skins back, so Carlson Oil had been stopped and the Selkie rookery saved, but making it right with the band was going to take a little work.

Three AM in Calgary. Seven in the Maritimes. No way would Mark be up. But it was six in Ontario, and Auntie Jane never missed a sunrise.

Charlie pulled her new phone out of the robe's pocket, a little disgusted by the used tissue wrapped around it. Still, she hadn't put the phone *in* the robe's pocket, so dealing with crunchy mucus wasn't entirely unreasonable.

"Good morning, Charlotte."

"Good morning, Auntie Jane. I just called . . ." Except there wasn't any *just* about it. "I called to say thank you."

"For what, Charlotte?"

"A little less smart-ass and a little more focus. I will not have you killed in such an embarrassing manner."

"For being there when I needed you."

The pause extended. Charlie figured it took time for Auntie Jane to remember how to smile.

"You're welcome. I'm pleased you survived."

"Me, too."

"Of course you are. Is there anything else you wanted to discuss?"

Jack. Jack's future. "No, I'm good."

"That, Charlotte, is still open to debate." The dial tone punctuated Auntie Jane getting the last word.

As usual.

Feeling eyes on her, Charlie looked up to see Allie standing in the window. She slipped the phone back in her pocket and headed indoors. It wasn't like the situation back east could get worse in the next few hours.

The entire family—minus David, who reverted to hooves and horns in crowds—descended on the apartment for breakfast. The center of a talking, laughing mass of adults and teenagers and babies, all happy to see her up and about, Charlie figured Mark could wait a little longer. Chased away from the kitchen—there were benefits in being the only living Gale girl who couldn't cook—Charlie settled in one of the big armchairs, Wendy and Jennifer tucked in beside her, and told the story of the Selkies and going after their sealskins, and fighting the Troll. She stopped when she hit the floor of the mine, got Jack in a headlock, and noogied him until he agreed to continue.

She noted how no one looked concerned by her roughhousing, the awareness of Jack being both a Dragon and a sorcerer buried under their knowledge he was a Gale. The kids cheered when he bit his Uncle Viktor's wing off. He finished his part of the story just as platters of French toast and sausages were set out on the big table and he blushed, just a little, as Cameron took the time for a fist bump in the rush for food.

Cameron was nearly twenty. To a fourteen-year-old boy, that made him more relevant than anyone else in the room. Auntie Jane aside, it looked like Jack's place in the family was secure.

French toast left fewer opportunities for charms than pancakes so, except for baby Richard trying to inhale the sausage he'd been happily gumming, breakfast was uneventful by Gale standards.

After, having been hugged hard enough to rebreak her ribs as people left, Charlie settled into washing the final sink full of dishes.

"So," she said, scrubbing coffee stains out of a mug as Jack dried a plate, "what happened to Eineen and Paul? The Selkie and her new boyfriend," she added when Jack looked confused.

He shrugged. "I don't know. I left them in the mine."

"In the mine?"

"Duh. That's where the gate was."

Charlie replayed the events in the mine as she washed another mug. "Jack, did the Goblins go through the gate?"

"I don't know." He paused, one arm stretched over his head to put a plate on the pile. "I don't think so." He was frowning when he stepped back from the cupboard. "I followed the Boggart trail to the gate, but I don't remember seeing any Goblin sign. Nothing new, anyway."

"Okay, that's bad."

"He was a little distracted," Allie put in from where she was curled up on the sofa with Graham.

"Not what I meant." Grabbing Jack's dish towel to dry her hands, Charlie turned from the sink. "The gate was pretty deep in the mine, right? If the Goblins didn't go through the gate," she continued when Jack nodded, "then it's very likely that they were between Eineen and Paul and the exit."

"I thought she was Fey," Graham began.

"She's a Selkie. That's basically a serial monogamist with debatable taste in men and a fully fish diet. She's stronger than your average bear, sure, but unless she's facing a cod not very scary. And Paul had recently had a manicure." Charlie sagged back until her ass was supported by the edge of the sink. "I got the impression he'd suck big-time in a fight."

"You don't ever fight one Goblin," Jack said, sagging against the counter, his movement as near an exact copy of Charlie's as differing physiognomy allowed. "They'll come at you all at once, figuring numbers beats size."

"So unless they got very, very lucky, like winning a multimillion lottery level of luck, Eineen and Paul are dead."

"I can find out." Graham stood, ignoring a muffled protest from Allie as she toppled over. He walked over to the computer desk by the front windows. "I'll e-mail a friend at the *Herald*," he said, crossing to where his phone sat in the charger. "If she doesn't know off the top of her head, she'll be able to pull the stories. Bodies found in a mine . . ."

"Not enough left to be *bodies*," Jack interrupted.

"Body parts found in a mine," Graham amended, "will be news."

"It'd be national news." Charlie swept a gaze around the room. "Did no one watch the National while I was out?"

Jack shrugged. "I never watch the National."

"We were a little a distracted," Allie said, sitting up and retrieving her mug from the coffee table. "Particularly during the first forty-eight hours when the story would have been . . ."

"Graham, stop! Sorry, Allie," Charlie waved an apology in Allie's general direction. "I don't want to know. It's better *we* don't know."

"They aren't family," Allie agreed.

"No, it's better we don't know because I'm going to fix it."

"Fix death?" Graham asked putting his phone back on the charger.

About to snap out the kind of reply that kind of smart-ass question required, Charlie paused and thought about what she intended to do. After a moment, she said, "I'm not going to fix death, I'm going to make sure no one dies."

Charlie let Allie and Graham shout at her for a few minutes. She had lots of time. When they began to wind down, she said, "Allie, remember how you always said I could get you home through the Wood before you left?"

"Yes, but . . ."

"I'm going to go back to the mine before I left."

ELEVEN

CHARLIE CAME OUT of the Wood just inside the perimeter fence, facing the mine-head.

"All I need is a definitive moment in time. Something that resonates so loudly, I'll have no trouble following its song out of the Wood."

Allie folded her arms. "What if you're wrong?"

"Then it doesn't work and I end up where, not when."

"And if you get lost?"

Charlie sighed. "Get lost once your first time in and no one ever lets you forget it."

The landscape told her absolutely nothing about when she was. She'd followed the stirring anthem "Charlie Kicks Troll Ass" which should have brought her out just as the Charlie of ten days ago realized how things worked. Unfortunately, all that had happened / was happening deep in the mine leaving no impression on the surface. There was always a chance she'd followed an echo, a chance the song had been so powerful it would resonate through the Wood for years leading travelers astray. Well, travelers attuned to that sort of thing. Okay, her.

If it had worked, here and now Jack was chasing a Boggart down the elevator shaft and she was just about to hit the floor.

"What about paradoxes?" Graham had demanded.

"Chill. What happened, happened. And we don't know what happened after that happened, so anything can happen." When he seemed about to protest, she kissed him, kissed Allie, hugged Jack, and walked through the shrubbery in the courtyard into the Wood.

As Charlie emerged from an annoyingly dense bit of dog willow, she spotted Paul's penis-mobile. No way would it still be sitting there ten days after Paul had disappeared or been discovered disemboweled. Either way, it'd be in a police impound lot.

Punching the air seemed entirely justified.

"Holy shit, I traveled in time. I'm like freakin' Dr. Who, and the cute redheaded companion should turn up right about . . . now." A quick look around. "Or not." Apparently time travel was fine, but a cute redheaded companion was too much to ask of the universe.

She patted the penis-mobile's shiny black roof as she jogged by. Kept jogging past the big double doors they'd left unlocked ten days earlier, and charmed open a standard-sized door in the next building. The big elevator was down in the mine, but a little research had turned up three smaller ones.

"*Machinery breaks,*" Graham pointed out. "*If the big elevator is fried and they absolutely have to, they can get the miners out the coal shaft, let them ride the belt up, but better to spread their eggs over a few baskets and get them out one or two at a time in smaller, supplemental shafts.*"

Much smaller, Charlie realized peering through the grating as the motor powered up. This cage would hold two people, three if they were willing to be very friendly and if Graham hadn't printed up the schematics of the building for her and marked a big X on the spot, it would have been easy to miss. The steel door said only, *no unauthorized personnel beyond this point* not *open me to find an elevator you can use to save the day.*

She glanced at her watch. Jack would have finished wrapping her in the Troll by now and started pushing the cart toward the Gate.

"*Jack, I'm sorry, but you're still too heavy to get through the Wood.*"

"*The car . . .*"

"*I'm pretty sure . . . absolutely sure,*" she corrected because certainty was at least half of making this work, "*that I can get myself when I need to go, but I have no idea how much I can take with me. I'd hate to lose the car and you somewhere between now and then.*"

"*That would suck,*" Jack admitted reluctantly. "*What are you going to tell the guys and Shelly about me not being there?*"

"*That your guardian got freaked by news of the violence at the festival and made me send you home.*"

"*In the middle of the night?*"

"Don't worry, they'll believe me."

"Yeah," Jack snorted. *"Totally not worried about that."*

The tiny elevator smelled like heated dust and every once in a while gave a grinding hiccup that made Charlie think she should have just climbed down the metal rungs she could see passing outside the cage.

This elevator only went down as far as the Canaveral level.

"Don't need to go any farther," Charlie muttered, stepping out into a dark and empty tunnel. Pulling out a dozen plastic bracelets, she cracked them and slid six on each wrist.

"Magic?" Jack asked as she filled her pockets in the Emporium.

"Nope. Chemistry."

A vigorous shake and she was bathed in the soft glow of dibutyl phthalate, the multicolored bands of light just enough to activate the night-sight charm on her lids. She couldn't see much, but she could see enough to keep from slamming into random carts or the tunnel walls. Running full out, she followed a song of shattered stone to Canaveral where she'd fought the Troll.

"And won," she muttered, stepping around a crushed cart, squinting under the overhead lights.

No sign of Eineen or Paul or the Goblins, but if the Goblins had let their prey get more than three meters from the gate, she'd be very surprised.

Another song sent her after Eineen and Paul. Circumstances dictated it be a love song—boy meets seal, seal enchants boy, boy and seal have children who make the Canadian Olympic swimming team. As she followed it, Charlie made a mental note to check if previous gold medal winners had ancestors from Cape Breton.

Given that it would be pretty pointless to arrive after the Goblins attacked, she concentrated on speed rather than stealth, leaping debris and not bothering to muffle the sound of her sneakers against the stone. Refocusing the Goblins' attention on her was the point of the trip.

"How long will the batteries powering the headlamps last?" Eineen whispered.

"I don't know. They're supposed to be fully charged at all times, but there's often large variables between supposed to be and are." He was amazed by how calm he sounded. Forty-eight hours ago if someone had told him he was going to find himself deep in the *Duke* with a girlfriend who became a seal—or possibly a seal who'd become his girlfriend—backed up against a gate to a fairytale realm, and under attack by Goblins, he'd have suggested they were off their meds. He was terrified, sure, but Eineen was a warm weight against his side, her arms wrapped around his waist, and he had to hold it together for her.

The same way she was holding it together for him. He could feel her trembling, but her voice was steady, the question had been matter-of-fact. He'd never loved her more.

Pushed into the light by its companions, a Goblin hissed, and spit, and howled out a one-man catfight as it scrambled back into the dark.

"That sounded insulting."

"They use very inventive profanity," Eineen agreed.

"You can understand them?" The noise hadn't sounded like words.

"A little. But it's been a long time since I've heard Goblin."

He thought of asking her how long, but if time spent with Amelia Carlson had taught him anything, it was never ask a woman her age.

"This has all been for nothing," she sighed. "When they attack, the four skins Catherine Gale took will be destroyed with me."

"You're not going to be destroyed."

"Destroyed. Eaten. Same thing. They don't like the light, but it doesn't hurt them. Eventually, the taunting will drive one of them out to attack and at first blood—ours or theirs, it doesn't matter—the rest will follow."

"Well, I'd never thought about going through a Goblin's digestive tract with you, but as long as we're together, there's worse ways to end up."

She twisted in his arms to look up at him—twisted the headlamp back toward the Goblins, setting off another storm of hissing—and said, "You actually mean that, don't you?"

"I actually do." Paul would have kissed her except dipping his head would turn the light away from the Goblins. "However, are you sure that going through the gate . . ."

"Even if they didn't follow us, what's on the other side is worse."

"Jack, the dragon-boy . . ."

"Dragon Prince. And he's long gone."

Paul had already tried the breaker that was supposed to turn the lights on in the side tunnel. He didn't know if it wasn't working because of the gate or the Goblins, but in the end, it didn't matter. His pockets held his phone and some change. His belt buckle wasn't large enough to use as a weapon. He was out of ideas. When he'd thought about dying, he'd thought about wearing a pale gray Armani suit and having captains of industry cancel million-dollar meetings in order to attend. There might have been a wife weeping attractively in the background. Torn apart and eaten by Goblins in a mine had never come up. It was hard to believe it was real.

Then it was suddenly very easy.

Pushed from behind, another Goblin stumbled into the light. Head tucked in between its shoulders, it snarled softly. Tiny gold rings glinted along the curve of one rounded ear and two of the small teeth between the four-centimeter fangs were gold as well. It bent and scraped the claws of both hands against the tunnel floor, gouging out four parallel lines and proving that its claws were strong enough to cut through rock as well as steel.

Wonderful.

Paul hoped that the marks on its grimy leather tunic were a faded pattern, but they looked a lot like tattoos.

The hissing and howling from the darkness grew louder. Goblins crowded the edge of the light. Glistening. Gleaming.

"They're taunting it."

Paul licked dry lips. "It?" A stupid thing to worry about, but he suddenly had to know.

"Goblins are hermaphroditic."

"Okay, then." His heart was pounding so hard his whole body throbbed with every beat. He couldn't breathe. He couldn't swallow.

"So are salamanders and Sylphs."

"What?"

He felt Eineen shrug. "I didn't want you to think it was only an attribute of the vicious."

"Right."

The Goblin crouched, reminding Paul of a cat just before it pounced. He shoved Eineen behind him, felt her hands on the small of his back, brought up his fists. His eyes snapped closed. He forced them open.

The Goblin was in midair, its claws a meter from his face.

And then it exploded.

Ears ringing, Paul staggered back, Eineen steadying him.

From the mess seeping out into the light, more than the one Goblin had exploded.

It looked like every Goblin in a line between the one attacking them and . . .

Charlotte Gale.

She picked her way through the mess, glowing . . . no, not glowing just bracelets on her wrists glowing. Her face . . .

Actually, she looked disgusted and muttered a litany of "Eww" as she minced forward. When she cleared the worst of the wet chunks, she looked up and smiled. "You know how there's a note that shatters glass? Seems there's a note that shatters Goblins."

Those Goblins who'd been outside the line of fire were gone. Had disappeared back into the darkness.

Paul took a breath, gagged, swallowed so he wouldn't vomit, and realized at some point in the last few seconds when death in obscurity had been imminent, he'd pissed himself.

"I can take care of that." Charlotte nodded at Paul's hands—lovely large hands—now covering the spreading stain on his suit pants. "You play in enough bars, and someone you know is going to end up with a lap full of beer."

"No." Eineen pushed out from behind him, her voice shaky but her back rigid. "You're not putting a charm anywhere near his penis."

"Get over yourself, it'll be on his pants. Dries right through to the skin. It's perfectly harmless."

"No. I do not trust you with genitalia, Charlotte Gale!"

"How about we let Paul decide?" Paul was looking, well, stricken if Charlie had to put a word to it. Seemed like his last straw had been one of those crazy, bendy straws that leaked all over. "Hey. Boy-toy." When he blinked and focused on her, pulled out of his head by the insult, she smiled. "I'm not judging. You've handled all the shit that's come down the pike at you really well. Will you let me dry you off?"

He took a deep breath and said, "You have something on your shoe."

Charlie glanced down. There, just where the rubber of her sneaker gave way to canvas, was a large glob of glistening, greenish-gray Goblin guts. "Oh, gross." Holding the top of the cart, she scraped it off against the bottom edge. She'd barely worn those shoes and that was definitely going to stain.

When she looked back at Paul, Eineen had moved between them, his arms wrapped around her waist, her hands over his. Charlie didn't have anything against Eineen loudly, if nonverbally, shouting "*Mine!*" or even mistrusting a Gale's motives around her man, but making that man wear pee-soaked trousers because of that overly possessive lack of trust? That was mean.

Okay. Charlie could do mean. "So as I arrived, I noticed you were about to shove him at the Goblins, hoping they'd spend enough time eating him that you could haul ass and get away."

Eineen tossed her hair as much as her position allowed. "I'm carrying four skins that aren't mine. I have a responsibility to my family."

A little impressed she didn't deny it, and had stayed completely Human-seeming while doing so, Charlie spread her hands, the bracelets drawing streamers of light. "*I* get that," she said pointedly, looking at Paul.

He wet his lips, swallowed, and said, "I would have happily died if it meant Eineen survived."

"Happily?" When he nodded, Charlie surrendered. "I'm impressed; that's some enchantment. Walk in pee with my blessing. And while we're on the subject of walking, we should walk out of here."

"The Goblins?"

"Don't worry about them." She pointed back along the tunnel with enough emphasis the lovebirds finally got moving. "The Goblins won't come near when I'm around."

"That's what the Prince said," Eineen muttered, stepping over one of the sloppier piles of Goblin bits. "Then he left us."

"And I came back."

"You were gone for barely half an hour and you were near death."

"Yeah, well, I heal fast." She put enough edge on the words to discourage further questions.

"Why?"

Or maybe not. "Why what?" she asked.

Eineen turned her head far enough the beam from her headlamp swept across the side tunnel they were passing. The darkness screamed, *Keep moving, nothing here.* "Why did you come back? We are not your family and the Gales do not get involved in the business of the Fey."

Charlie snorted. "You lucked out, I decided to be one of the good guys."

"You can decide that?"

"Seems I'll be deciding that every moment of every day. Great power. Great responsibility. Yadda. Yadda."

"Sucks to be you," Paul said dryly.

Charlie laughed. "You're okay, Boy-toy."

It was clear he wasn't okay, not quite, not yet, but with every touch of Eineen's hand, or bump against his shoulder, or loving glance, he got a little better as the attitude adjustment that protected the Selkies in relationships distanced him from what had happened back at the gate. Walking behind them—mostly because they had the lights, but if they wanted to believe she was guarding the rear, she was good with that—Charlie could see the wobble in his movement firm up until he was moving as normally as his trousers allowed. When he half turned to help Eineen over a junction in the rails and she could see the edge of the stain, she sang the charm onto it.

Paul stopped walking, looked down, looked back at her, and said, "Thank you."

Eineen turned to glare. Charlie shrugged. "Saved your life, saved all four skins—five counting yours—don't need your permission anyway, only a line of sight, and you're welcome."

When they emerged out into the open area, Eineen and Paul ran for the elevator. Although the cage door had been left open and even a Goblin could figure out a big "press here" button, the elevator was right where they'd left it.

Charlie faced the tunnel. She didn't bother raising her voice; the Goblins would hear her. "Go home. Close and lock the gate behind you. If I come back down here and any of you are still around, I will make you watch the entire run of *Barney and Friends*. What?" she asked as she turned and found her companions staring at her. "It's not like they understand English. It just has to be a credible threat."

Given the destruction in Canaveral, it was a miracle the elevator had remained undamaged.

"Not a miracle," Paul told her when she made the observation aloud. "The dra . . . Jack. The door had crumpled, but his eyes glowed and he . . ." Jazz hands stood in when he lost the words.

"Good thing," Charlie allowed, closing the gate behind her. "I know another way out, but it'd be a tight ride up."

Although, given the way Eineen and Paul cuddled all the way to the surface, she doubted that they'd have minded.

Charlie, while appreciating that true love had inspired half her play list, was tempted to break into Newfoundland sealing songs if only to counteract the rising level of schmoop. Particularly since the schmoop wasn't being generated by true love but a Selkie enchantment. Still, they'd been through a lot and she supposed they deserved a bit of comfort. First word of baby talk, though, and she was responding with a rousing chorus of "Come All Ye Jolly Ice-Hunters."

The fiddler in her head threw in a few bars in clear agreement.

Half an hour or so later, standing by the car watching Paul lock up behind them, she finally couldn't take it anymore. "Are neither of you the slightest bit curious as to *how* I got back moments after I left, fully healed and wearing different clothes?"

Eineen shrugged, the movement impossibly graceful. "Fey with even the slightest sense of self-preservation don't get involved in the business of the Gales."

Okay. That made sense. "Paul?"

"You look like Catherine Gale." he said turning from the building.

"Well, sure, there's always been a family resemblance but . . ."

"I don't mean physically." Pulling his car keys out, he pointed the fob and unlocked the doors. "I don't know how to explain it." He frowned, obviously intending to try. "When you meet a wild animal, you have no way of knowing if they'll walk off and leave you alone, or attack. You and Catherine Gale share that same unpredictability. You didn't use to, but you do now."

"You used to be powerful because of who you were." Eineen slipped an arm around Paul's waist. "Now, you're dangerous because of what you are."

"Besides," Paul added before Charlie could figure out her reaction, "you might have wanted to be asked, but part of that was wanting to say *I can't tell you* when we did."

"That's . . . actually bang on," she admitted. No real reason *not* to admit it.

"I deal with power every day." He held the passenger door open for Eineen who wore the smug expression of a cat with cream. "The power may be different, but dealing with it isn't."

The fiddler in her head came in with a rousing rendition of "Princess Royal."

Charlie stopped Paul before he could open her door as well—manners devolved into chauvinism too often in her experience—but punched him lightly on the arm as he turned to head around the rear of the car to the driver's door. "I like you, Paul Belleveau. I didn't expect to, but you're okay."

"I'm thrilled."

"You should be. And you needn't look so smug," she added sliding into the backseat, and flicking Eineen in the back of the head. "It's not like you knew what kind of a man he was when he groped your sealskin." A short pause. An added rim shot. Because a sentence like that seemed to require one.

"You planning on using that ax this afternoon, Chuck?"

"Going to have to." Charlie finished tuning the six on her storm guitar and ran her thumb down the strings. "My other one got destroyed last night." Last night for the guitar, ten . . . nine . . . eleven nights ago for her. She'd be glad to see those days pass again, so she could call Allie, tell her it worked, and merge the timelines of her life back together. It suddenly occurred to her that no one was going to call her for the next ten, or eleven, or nine days and that was almost enough to make up for losing her guitar. Almost.

The unnatural silence drew her attention back to the basement. Shelly, Tim, and Mark were staring at her wearing varying expressions of horror.

"Ah, Jesus, Chuck, that sucks the big, hairy hard one." Crouching down, Mark braced himself on her knees and peered up at her through a messy fall of hair. "You okay?"

"I wasn't," she told him honestly. More or less honestly. "But I am now. When it comes right down to it, it was only a guitar. It could have been worse."

He tightened his grip. "That's a remarkably mature attitude, Chuck. If I'd lost my kit, I'd be lying on the floor, drumming my heels and screaming."

She'd done a little of that back in Calgary, but Jack's expression kept reminding her how much worse it *could* have been, so . . . "Yeah, well, you're wearing a *Hello Kitty* sporran. Where the hell did you get that, by the way?"

"Esty shop. It's a one off." He patted the pink leather bag hanging over his crotch. "You like?"

"Ignoring the innuendo because Tim's a foot taller than me, I'm just happy to discover they're not in mass production."

"I totally don't blame Jack's guardians for freaking," Shelly muttered, cradling her upright bass against her chest and rubbing her cheek along the smooth finish on the edge of the fingerboard. "I mean, terrorizing grannies and toddlers is one thing, but destroying instruments is a whole other level of fucked up."

"Aggie Forest, Captain Wedderburn's keys, got caught in her cables and nearly went down with the stage, talk about fu . . ." Mark paused, twisted back around to face Charlie and said, "You had your guitar when we saw you last night. Tim went to ask if we could help with the rebuild, and you and me were sitting on that picnic table. You had your guitar then, Chuck."

Oops.

"I had my guitar *case* then, Mark. Still have the case." It had been in the back of Paul's car. "Now this guitar is in it."

Mark frowned. Ran his thumb along a bit of flaking varnish. "It looks like it got caught out in the rain. How's it sound?"

Charlie picked out the first four bars of "Wildwood Flower," segued into "The Boy's Lament for his Dragon," finished up with Zeppelin's "Tangerine." "Sounds okay to me." She grinned at Mark's expression—he'd dropped back to sprawl at her feet when she started playing—and kicked him in the thigh. "For the love of . . . well, Tim, learn to sit like a lady."

He had his mouth open to answer when one of his sticks nailed him in the back of the head.

"Quite the hollow bonk," Shelly murmured.

"A little respect for your fearless leader," Mark commanded, scrambling up onto his feet. "But Tim's right. We need to get this run through moving; he's got a *Kids on Keyboards* workshop at one. Where the hell's Bo?"

Tanis had been one of the Selkies who'd got her sealskin back. It was entirely possible Bo wouldn't be able to walk for . . .

"Sorry, sorry, sorry." As if called by the question, Bo bounded down the stairs into the rec room. "Happy girlfriend, happy me, happy idiot in a pickup doing thirty in front of me all the way into town. Let's rock and roll in a Celtic sort of way that'll win us this shindig, get us a recording contract, fill our pockets, and cover us with the limited amount of glory available." He set his case down on the top of the sofa, pulled out his violin, and took a moment to look around the room. "What?"

Tim snickered.

Mark spread his hands. "Nothing." Hands still spread, he spun in place. "You heard the man, people, let's Celt and roll."

Charlie kept a tighter than usual grip on her tendency to throw a *you like me, you really like me* charm or two out. Today, this first day back playing, she had no idea if a slip would throw out more than just a joy in the music cranked up to eleven.

"Chuck . . ."

"Sorry." She needed to get some kind of barrier up to slow the seepage of . . . of *her* into the music so she could play without worrying.

Finally, three songs in—well, two because they took three runs at their cover of "And if Venice is Sinking" by Spirit of the West. Two with the erection, one without. Consensus after the fact kept the erection in. Point was, erection aside, by song three, she'd managed to work out a balance between putting her heart into her playing and throwing the rest of her in as well. It wasn't entirely comfortable and it felt so much like slacking that when they finally ran through Mark's "Wild Road Beyond," she let the barriers drop and just played. It seemed safe enough. Bo had the lead and Mark's insecurities ensured they'd never play the song in public, so she'd never be asked to repeat this performance on a stage.

When they finished, Bo's last note circled the basement half a dozen times before fading into silence.

Then someone sniffed and all five of them turned to stare at Shelly's brother-in-law's cousin and what looked like the entire extended family perched on the basement stairs. They looked at Grinneal. Grinneal looked at them. A burly older man wiped at his eyes with the hem of his T-shirt.

The applause when it came was loud enough Mark's cymbals shimmied with it.

Later, after all the women and half the men had come the rest of the way downstairs to hug Bo, Shelly sagged back against the sofa cushions, bass cradled between her legs, and bounced a finger up her E making it sound. "All in favor of adding 'Wild Road' to the set list?"

"No." Mark jumped in before anyone could answer. "It still isn't quite right."

"Dude, if it was any more right, it would ascend." She glanced around the room. "Little help, guys."

"Personally, I'm willing to play that song twenty-four/seven. I want it played at my fucking funeral. Hell, I'll come back from the dead to play it myself." Bo stripped off his sweat-soaked T-shirt and caught a dry one Tim tossed him. "But . . ." He sighed as his head emerged. ". . . it's Mark's song. His call."

"Charlie?"

Charlie grinned. "I'm sorry, I was distracted by Bo's happy trail. What was the question?"

"Charlie!"

"Mark's song. His call."

Shelly rolled her eyes. "And I don't even need to ask Tim, do I? He'll back Mark's play. Fine. But we could win with that song."

"Please," Charlie snorted before things got heated, "we've heard the competition. We could win with 'I's the B'ye.'"

"You bitch," Mark muttered as Tim filled the bellows of his accordion and began to play. "I should never have told you how much I hate that song."

That afternoon, they could've won with "Farewell to Nova Scotia." Charlie didn't have to keep herself from leaking into the music, there wasn't room. It leaked into her, thrumming through her body. The crowd fed off Grinneal's energy and bounced it back at them. Out and back. Out and back. Until they weren't a band and an audience, they were one musical organism.

When they finished, Shelly couldn't decide whether to laugh or cry as she stood shaking in the circle of Charlie's arms. Tim stared at Mark with equal parts awe and lust and Mark stared back wearing exactly the same expression. Charlie prudently stepped out from between them, taking Shelly with her. Bo beamed in the center of a circle of babbling fiddle fans until Tanis threw herself at him, shrieking his name and practically glowing.

Actually glowing.

Charlie threw a charm at her before anyone came far enough out of the music to notice.

Their performance bled off into the band after them and *Faic Tusan* kept the audience up on their feet, dancing and singing along.

Charlie wandered through the crowd, nursing a beer, and enjoying being told how amazing Grinneal's set had been. That never got old. She saw Eineen and Paul, waved but didn't go over. The Selkies' problems were solved—thanks to her, not that anyone except Paul had expressed any gratitude—it was time to leave the mine behind and enjoy the sunshine. She did notice that Paul was in a golf shirt, cargo pants, and deck shoes, but that was Eineen's problem.

She was a little surprised when Neela's husband Gavin found her later and asked if she thought Mark might be willing to share out the score for "Wild Road Beyond." By the end of the evening, nearly every fiddler at the festival, both performers and audience members, had spoken to her. Seemed like Bo had been talking. Fiddlers married to Selkies—and there were half a dozen in attendance—had come to her because of who she was. The rest had come to her because the other fiddlers had.

Charlie told them all the same thing. They had to talk to Mark.

No one could find Mark.

Or Tim.

And everyone apparently needed to follow that information with an enthusiastic *wink, wink, nudge, nudge.*

Sipping a glass of tolerable champagne, Amelia Carlson found herself enjoying the charity casino put on by the Multiple Sclerosis Society of Canada far out of proportion to the enjoyment actually available. Partly that was because she was there with Evan Damon, recently divorced, owner of the largest steel works in the Maritimes, and partly it was because his invitation had saved her from attending some sort of local music festival in Louisbourg. Wandering unprotected through crowds of tourists listening to fiddles and accordions extolling the virtues of a subsistence lifestyle was a little more "of the people" than she was interested in. Honestly, she employed "the people;" what more did they want?

As the MS Society was a particular charity of the Premier's, the entire cabinet plus wives, husbands, and children of legal age were in attendance. The Minister of Health was having remarkable luck at one of the roulette wheels, the Minister of Transportation had just successfully drawn to an inside straight, and the Minister of the Environment hadn't left the high stakes blackjack table all night.

Granted, the high stakes weren't all that high, but Richard Conway played with a focus Amelia found intriguing. She drained her glass, snagged another from a very attractive waiter, and wandered casually toward the blackjack table. Over the last few years, she had spent more time with the minister than with any other person in the room, including Evan, so it was only polite she spend a little social time in the honorable member's company.

Paul had never gone to work leaving a woman in his bed.

Not that there'd been a lot of women over the last few years; Amelia Carlson required one hundred and ten percent of his attention. Bad math, but standard business practice. The few women who'd stayed over, he'd taken out to breakfast and then home. Only one of them had stayed twice and, although she'd been determined to take their relationship to the next level, she hadn't been able to compete with his job.

His relationship with Eineen had no "next level" to go to; from the moment she'd come out of the sea Thursday night, she'd become everything to him. Sure, in the beginning, he'd believed he could have what he had with her and keep Carlson Oil, but their adventure Friday night had forced him to face up to the fact that working for Amelia Carlson had made him complicit in the Goblin attack that had nearly killed the woman he loved.

She lay on her side, facing away from him, one arm tucked up under the pillow, the sheets pleated in the hollow of her waist, rising to drape over the perfect curve of her hip. They were cheap motel sheets, not the twelve hundred thread count Egyptian cotton she'd be wrapped in if they were in his condo in Halifax instead of a Sydney motel room, but against the satin of her skin, they looked like finest silk.

"You're staring at me."

Paul could hear the smile in her voice so he smiled back. "You're the only thing in this room worth staring at."

"True." She rolled over, hair spilling across her breasts, and held out her hand.

"I have to get into the office," he told her, sitting on the edge of the bed and catching her hand up in both of his. He kissed along her knuckles, then turned her hand over and placed one last kiss in her palm. "I have to tell Ms. Carlson that blackmailing Two Seventy-five N is no longer on the table. I have to give her a chance to admit that it was the wrong thing to do. I have to try to make her see that if that's what it takes to get this well put in, then that alone is reason enough to find another field to tap."

Eineen traced the line of his jaw with the first two fingers of her other hand. "Why?"

"Because I gave her two years, five months, and . . ." He frowned. For the first time in two years, five months and whatever, he couldn't remember exactly how long he'd been Amelia Carlson's assistant. That was . . . freeing. "The point is, if she can be made to see she was wrong, then . . ." Reluctantly releasing Eineen's hand, he stood and tightened his tie. "Then I didn't flush that time down the toilet. If I can make her see she was wrong, I'll have begun to make amends."

"I don't need you to . . ."

"I do." He was wearing the khaki suit today. It was one of Ms. Carlson's favorites. He shrugged into the jacket, checked he had everything he needed in his briefcase, and walked to the door. "If this goes well, I may be a while."

"And if it goes badly . . ." Eineen patted the bed beside her. ". . . come right back to me."

Paul had not been in his office when Amelia arrived. The schedule for the day, printed out and left neatly centered on her desk, looked to be the same schedule sent to her phone. The same schedule Paul had drawn up Friday evening. There'd been no changes made as the oil industry and oil futures changed over the weekend. That was a first. Given where most of the world's producing deposits were, change was, as her third-year sociology professor had said, a constant.

Settling into her chair, she slid the printout off the desk and into the garbage. It was possible Paul hadn't been able to track any of the weekend's changes, but it would have been the first time that had happened in over two years. He'd be busy catching up when he finally got his very fine ass into the office, particularly given the news of certain changes she had to share with him.

So where the hell was he?

She'd been waiting for nearly thirteen minutes before she heard Paul's distinctive stride. "You're late," she snapped. "Get in here."

He wasn't carrying a green tea, soy latte. They'd have words about that later. He *was* wearing her favorite suit though, the one that made his shoulders and ass look amazing, weighting the scales back slightly in his favor.

"Ms. Carlson, I have something I need to tell you."

"Later. I have something I need to tell you." Smiling broadly caused crow's feet, but she couldn't stop herself. "I've never liked being involved in Catherine Gale's activities," she began. He looked relieved. Of course he did, he knew where she was coming from. She'd never had an assistant who understood her like Paul Belleveau did. Sitting back, she crossed her legs. "It wasn't that the whole thing was weird to the nth degree, I can deal with weird if it gets the job done, but I hated the lack of control. I hated being dependent on her. And yes, I know I was paying her, but we both know she's not the kind of woman to be dependent on those payments or to follow the golden rule—those who have the gold make the rules. But I've solved the problem."

"Ms. Carlson . . ."

He no longer looked relieved. Of course he didn't, he hated being out of the loop. It made it harder for him to take care of her. "Don't worry, things couldn't be better. It seems the honorable Richard Conway, the Minister of the Environment for Nova Scotia and Cape Breton, has a gambling problem."

"A gambling problem?"

If she kept smiling like this, Paul would be booking her an appointment with her esthetician the moment he reached his desk. "He can't stop playing, he can't count to twenty-one. He owes money to some very unsavory people. Or he did. Now, he owes me. Or he did." She glanced at her watch. "As of half an hour ago, the permits Carlson Oil needs are signed and a copy has been sent to this office by courier. An electronic copy was sent to both of us immediately after his signature was applied. They're calling for clear skies, I called Captain Bonner myself on the way in, and the barges can go out this afternoon."

"This afternoon?"

"Yes, this afternoon." Paul looked horrified. It wasn't a good look on him. Although she strongly disapproved, she was not adding to the damage she'd already done her face by frowning. "If you don't have press releases and potential scheduling in place, ready to go when we got the word, you're not the man I think you are. And if you're not, there's no real reason why I should be paying you." He didn't laugh with her, but then he'd always been a little sensitive about money. "As far as our more recent problems are concerned, Carlson Oil no longer requires Catherine Gale's assistance and Two Seventy-five N can test their flotation rating by taking a long walk off a short pier." She leaned back and crossed her legs. "Now, tell me how amazing I am and then I want to see the best case scenario for actually getting that rig up and working and finally getting oil out of that well."

He stood and stared at her for a moment, opening and closing his hands.

Amelia sighed. "For heaven's sake, Paul, spit it out so you can bring me a latte and then get some work done."

"Ms. Carlson . . ."

"That's my name."

"I quit."

"So, what're you planning for the next few days?"

"Nothing much." Charlie slid Shelly's tool box under her groping hand and went back to leaning on the back of the car. She had nine days' worth of sunlight to catch up on. "Probably head into Halifax and talk to some guys about maybe lining up studio work."

"Probably? Maybe?" Shelly's sneakers kicked twice, then she squirmed backward until she could drop her lower body off the tailgate and stand. "You don't sound very juiced about it."

"Honestly, I'm not." Charlie shrugged, her back sticking to the car around the ties of her halter. "But a girl's gotta make a living."

"Too bad Jack had to go home. He's a cool kid and you'd have had a blast showing him around." Flicking her sunglasses down off the top of her head, Shelly pulled Charlie into a hug. "If you get bored, head up to Dingwall. There's plenty of room and my gran loves company."

"If I get bored, you'll be the second to know." Charlie waited until Shelly got into the car, then sketched a *back off tailgaters* charm in the dust. It'd only last until the next rain, but the forecast was a week of clear skies.

"See you Friday morning in Ingonish!" She waved out the window and was gone.

It didn't seem to matter to Shelly's brother-in-law's cousin, who'd already left for work, that the rest of the band was still in residence.

Only in the Maritimes, Charlie mused, heading up the driveway, wincing a little as the gravel dug into her bare feet. Her gear was already in the back of the station wagon, but she figured she'd help Mark and Tim finish loading before she hit the road. After all, they had the amps, their roadie was back in Calgary, and she wasn't in any hurry to leave. Although lining up a few paying jobs wouldn't hurt, *probably, maybe* pretty much summed up her interest in studio work right at the moment.

The fiddler in her head decided to chime in with "I Won't Do the Work."

"Who asked you?"

Deciding to soak up a little more sun before breaking up the accordion/bodhran jam session she could hear going on in the basement, she leaned back against the rear of her car and closed her eyes. Having Wild Powers activated didn't seem to have changed much. Okay, sure, she was alive and ten days out of time, but other than that, she still had no idea of what she should do next.

A car screeched to a stop out on the street.

Charlie opened her eyes to see Paul and Eineen spilling out of his penis-mobile. "I still have no idea of what I'd do with a hundred thousand dollars," she murmured, glancing up at a cloudless sky. When no money appeared, she shrugged philosophically and, given the way Eineen's glamour was flickering, braced herself for yet more Selkie Sturm and Drang.

"Another skin missing?" Made sense for Amelia Carlson to have sent Auntie Catherine back out, and it was only Human nature to slack off covering the mirrors after a few days. Fey nature, too, it seemed.

"The barges are going out today!"

"Excuse me?" First she'd heard about barges.

"The Minister of the Environment signed off on Carlson Oil's permits for the shallow well," Paul explained. "Everything else was in place, waiting for the permit, so, this afternoon, Amelia Carlson is sending out the barges with the pieces of the production platform. She had a small army of men waiting to go to work building this thing; they'll have the piles driven before a protest can hit the courts and the platform constructed before a stop order can be issued."

"Succinct explanation. Also, nice suit." She sagged back against the car and tucked her thumbs behind the waistband of her shorts. "But what do you want me to do?"

"Stop the barges." Eineen was actually wringing her hands. Charlie'd never seen anyone do that before. "Save my people."

"Why?"

"Because you're the only one who can!"

Okay, so maybe it was a little childish to make Eineen pay for being entirely straight, but Charlie figured she was due a bit of self-indulgence.

"And because this is one of those decisions you'll be making every minute of every day," Paul added quietly.

Charlie blinked. "You're good." She'd had every intention of helping, but if she hadn't, that would have been the button pusher. "Fine. I'll stop the barges. Any idea of *how* I can stop the barges?" she added wiping the smile off Paul's face. "If you got me on board, I suppose I could get the captain to scuttle . . . scuttle?" She frowned. "That doesn't sound right. I suppose I could convince the captain to sink his ship, but then I'd be on board a sinking ship along with Amelia Carlson's small army of men. Not that far from shore, granted, but even if everyone survived, explanations would be tricky and I'm not throwing a perfectly innocent captain out as a scapegoat. "

"Couldn't you make it look like a natural disaster? Whip up the seas or something?"

"Okay, two points." Charlie flicked up a finger. "One, I'm still not up with drowning everyone on board the barge and you . . ." She pointed the finger at Paul. ". . . are being remarkably bloodthirsty which is probably your influence . . ." The finger moved to point at Eineen. The Fey seldom worried about Human lives. ". . . so cut it out. And two, did I not mention the whole land not sea thing last night?"

"There's land under the water," Eineen said.

And the fiddler in Charlie's head broke into "The Champion."

"That's very true." She squinted into the sun and swiped at a dribble of sweat running down her throat and over her collarbone, teasing out the bright beginning of a possible plan. "There's a lot of water over that land . . . I'm going to need a backup band." Blinking away spots, she refocused her attention on the two people standing in front of her. "Eineen, you need to find me as many fiddlers as you can, preferably men who've had contact with your people."

Eineen's brows rose up behind the fall of her hair. "By contact, you mean . . . ?"

"What are you, twelve? I mean I need fiddlers who won't freak at what I'm going to do, so I need fiddlers who've done the freaky with you lot. If we had another moonlit night, you could recruit a few more, but as it is, get in contact with as many as you can. Tell them we'll need them this afternoon and we'll send the location as soon as we get one. Paul, find me a location. I need the route the barge will be taking, the deepest water possible, and waterfront property without a vacation home built on it."

Paul pulled out his phone. "There's a very good chance Ms. Carlson hasn't informed the relevant parties I'm no longer working for her."

"And what will you be doing?" Eineen demanded.

"I will be finding a piece of music I can use to focus power. All right, fine." She held up her hand. "I know what I want to use, I'll be acquiring the rights. This isn't the sort of thing you can do with questionable authority."

The front door of the house opened behind her. "As Mark enters right on . . ." From the look on Paul's face, it wasn't Mark. Of course it wasn't Mark, Charlie could still hear the accordion and bodhran. This close to the harbor, there wasn't a decent sized shrubbery in sight, but every house had mirrors. Charlie grabbed Paul's phone, sketched a very fast charm, and shoved it back into his hands. "Go. Call me later."

Clutching Eineen's hand, he ran for the car.

Smart man.

"We need to talk, Charlotte."

Charlie turned. She didn't bother faking a smile. "I have nothing to say to you, Auntie Catherine."

"Not even a thank you for giving you the opportunity to embrace your full potential?" Auntie Catherine stepped off the porch and spread her hands, bracelets chiming. "I Saw your eyes when you came out of the mine after facing those Goblins."

"Really? Did you See my eyes when I faced the Troll? Enough broken blood vessels they looked like two balls of very lean bacon. Wasn't pretty." If she hadn't been glaring at the older woman's face so intently, she'd have missed it. "You didn't know, did you? You didn't know there was a Troll in the mine. Something that big, and you didn't See it."

"I don't need to tell you what I did or didn't See, Charlotte."

"Weak," Charlie snorted. "Very weak."

"The point is, you wouldn't have been in the mine without me, you wouldn't have fulfilled your potential without the mine, therefore, you owe me."

"Bite me."

"Don't push it, Charlotte." Dark eyes narrowed. "Potential is one thing. Actualizing it is another. You still have no idea of what's going on."

Charlie spread her hands in a mocking mirror image of Auntie Catherine's gesture. "If you're willing to be straight this time, enlighten me."

"The well must be drilled. Steel must be sunk deep into the seabed."

Gulls cried. Someone hit their horn in the tourist-clogged streets across the bridge.

After a moment, Charlie sighed. "Not so much with the enlightenment there. Because I said so isn't going to float this boat, Auntie Catherine. The way you've been dicking people around, I'm not taking your word for anything. You didn't have to convince Amelia Carlson that blackmailing the Selkies was the way to go—you could have figured out a number of ways to accomplish the same thing—you just like to fuck with people. Newsflash, you're not a nice person."

"Nice isn't required, Charlotte." The flash of teeth could not be called a smile by anyone sane. "Not for what I do."

Folding her arms, Charlie propped a hip against the porch railing. *What is it you do?* would slide the conversation into another key entirely, and so she waited. And waited. Two cars and a camper drove by. Gulls continued crying. The wind pushed a cloud over the sun, adjusting the glare but not affecting the temperature. The aunties didn't wait for what they wanted. Auntie Catherine was out of practice.

"Do not assume you are my equal," she snapped at last.

"If you could stop me, you wouldn't be talking to me."

Auntie Catherine sighed, the sort of sigh that said, *you are young and foolish and I don't know why I bother.* Which pretty much proved Charlie's point as far as Charlie was concerned. "If you stop this well from going in, something old and more dangerous than you can imagine will rise from beneath the sea. I have Seen it."

"You didn't See the Troll."

"That's an apples-and-oranges distinction, Charlotte."

Charlie shrugged. "They're both fruit."

"Oh, that's right, make a joke." Auntie Catherine pushed a strand of silver hair back off her face and snarled, "Fine, you want enlightenment? If you stop the well from going in, you'll be responsible for the end of the world. There's an enormous difference between one of the ancients rising and an oil spill or two!"

"Not if you're in the path of the oil spill. Besides, ancient gods rising from beneath the sea is so last millennium." She slid off the railing and planted her feet, peeling paint making the planks of the porch rough under her soles. "So here's what I'm going to do. I'm going to stop the well, then I'm going to stop the end of the world."

Auntie Catherine's lip curled. "What, with a Song?"

"Why not?"

"Because it won't work!" She took a deep breath, hands clutching the tangerine muslin of her skirt. "Let the pilings go in, then stop the well before there's any drilling."

"Why me? You stop the well."

"That's not what I've Seen."

"You've Seen me stop the drilling?"

"No, I've Seen the need for the pilings. The rest is incidental!"

"Okay." Charlie folded her arms. "How do I stop the drilling?"

"How else? With a Song!"

"Now you're mocking me." Not the words, but the clearly audible exclamation mark. "Nice talking to you, Auntie Catherine."

"Charlotte . . ."

Charlie made another of those minute-by-minute decisions. "You should leave now."

The aunties were used to getting their own way, leaving Auntie Catherine just as out of practice when it came to dealing with defiance. The audacity of a younger Gale standing so definitively against her had visibly thrown her. Her eyes were wide, her mouth slightly open, and her hands couldn't find a place to settle as she responded to Charlie's voice. Charlie suspected

this was entirely a one-shot deal as far as the aunties were concerned, but
here and now this was the only time she needed it to work.

"You will be sorry for what you have done this day, Charlotte Marie
Gale!" Unable to stop her march down the drive, Auntie Catherine turned at
the sidewalk to deliver the last word, then strode around the corner, skirt
swirling around her calves, phone in her hand.

Back on the porch, Charlie waited for *her* phone to ring.

Except . . . she was out of her time. As far as the aunties were concerned, the ones back home in both Calgary and Darsden East, Charlie was
still in a healing trance. Which was actually irrelevant because Auntie Catherine was certainly not going to call home to complain that Charlie was
disrespecting her and some other auntie needed to bring her in line. The
world would end first.

It came down to just the two of them.

And Charlie had proof that Auntie Catherine didn't See everything.

The fiddler in her head played "Mrs. McCarty, Have You a Daughter."

That was a little thematically obscure. "Say what?"

"I didn't say anything. Yet."

She could just make out Mark's expression through the screen door, and
Tim's bulk behind him. Not good. "How long have you been there?"

"Tim saw your Auntie Catherine come out of the big mirror in the hall.
He came and got me."

"Out of the mirror? Really?" She sent a silent apology to Tim. "And you
believed him?"

Mark's expression didn't change. "Tim's never lied to me."

Charlie bristled at the implication. "I've never lied to you. Okay, maybe
a few small lies and, at that, mostly lies of omission, but . . ."

"We want in."

"What?"

Mark opened the door and the two of them came out onto the porch.
"We want in."

"Into what?" Charlie asked in her best *Pie? What pie?* voice

"You're going to stop one of the ancient gods from rising."

"That's not . . ."

"Do you even read the paper? Have you seen what they're catching off
Scatarie? Look, we know you're different, Chuck." Mark shook his head, his

hair spilling out of the grimy Barbie bandana that secured his ponytail. "For fucksake, that first day you came east? You didn't even have a copy of the set list when you went out on stage and you never missed a note. Okay, you missed a couple, but I suspect that was a variation not a mistake. And," he continued before Charlie could argue, "your cousin's eyes glow gold."

If her experience with Auntie Catherine was any indication, she could make him, make both of them, believe whatever she wanted them to. "You noticed that?"

"In all fairness, I thought I was stoned, but Tim noticed, too. So, we want in."

"I could tell you that you don't and you'd believe me." No wonder Allie had let Jack come east. Charlie'd asked her to. With any luck, Allie'd never figure that out. "I could make you forget this conversation ever happened."

Tim shook his head. "You won't," he said.

"You're right. I won't." Because she'd made a decision not to fuck people around. Another minute-by-minute decision safely made. "Okay, you're in. But," she added cutting off Mark's triumphant smile, "there's one inarguable condition."

He spread his hands. "Anything."

"That's what I like to hear."

"The barge is coming out from Glace Bay, heading east around the headland then southeast around Scatarie Island. The closest point we can reach on shore to deep water is going to be out on South Head. Go up 255 to South Head Road, turn right. Cross the bridge and follow the road until it becomes Sailor Dan's Lane—there's tracks past the end of the lane, but they may require four wheel drive."

"I grew up in the country. Odds are they were made by a twenty-year-old rear wheel drive pickup full of teenagers." Phone tucked against her shoulder, Charlie scribbled directions. "Tracks are no problem."

"If you say so."

She bit off a laugh.

"If you're still in Louisbourg," Paul continued, "it's about fifty minutes."

"Leaving now. Have Eineen tell the fiddlers to meet us there."

*   *   *

For all it had been one of the first parts of Canada settled, empty places remained along the Nova Scotia coast where the rock was too close to the surface or the sea winds too harsh or the sea itself too unforgiving. Barely four hundred meters wide and about five kilometers long, South Head challenged the might of the Atlantic and, so far, seemed to be winning. The nearest cottage was back at South Port Morien and, although the day was hot and still, and the ocean was as calm as the Atlantic ever managed, they had the headland to themselves.

Charlie parked by Paul's car at the end of the track. "Second last chance to back out."

"Second last?" Mark asked from the backseat.

Her hands left damp smudges on the steering wheel. "We haven't started playing yet."

"We're in. All the way."

"Okay, then." Another time, the wind across the headland would have ripped the car door from her hand. Today, a gentle breeze pushed her hair back off her face. Mark and Tim fell into step behind her as she walked out to join Paul and Eineen on the edge of the cliff. She looked down into deep water. Then she looked west at a dot on the waves. "Is that it? Is that the barge?"

"That's the barge. It's due past here at precisely . . ." Paul checked his phone and frowned at the lack of signal.

Charlie pushed his hand down by his side. "We're not working with *precisely.*"

"What are they doing here?" Eineen asked, nodded toward Mark and Tim.

"Percussion." Lifting his drum, Mark answered for himself. Tim held Mark's second best bodhran.

"Wait, you play the bodhran, too?"

"He's a fucking show off, is what he is," Mark muttered, stuffing an extra tipper into his sporran. "I haven't found anything he can't play. Fortunately, he loves me enough to allow me the delusion of being the better drummer."

"What if they don't come?" Eineen stared out at the distant barge. Back at Charlie. Out at the barge. "What if the fiddlers don't come?"

Charlie listened to "Over the Cabot Trail" and smiled. "They'll come."

"My cousins reminded me yet again that the Gales don't get involved in the business of the Fey."

"This is my business, so this is Gale business," Charlie said. "Sounds like Bo borrowed his brother's truck."

The five of them turned to watch Bo park, Tanis hanging out of the window and waving. Neela and Gavin pulled in beside him.

Three more cars were coming down the track with four more following a little further back, nearly obscured by the clouds of dust.

Charlie drew in a deep breath of sea air and let it out slowly. "Nine's good."

The women, young and old, all had long black hair and skin like coffee and cream, and moved bodies inhumanly proportioned with an unnatural grace. They weren't working hard to hide what they were.

By the time the short explanation had ended and the nine fiddlers stood in a line along the cliffs, the dot was very definitely a barge. Close enough to shore they could see the cranes rising out of the pieces of platform like triangular masts, but too far to see details or people.

"How many on board?"

Paul looked down at his phone, sighed, and shoved it in his pocket. "Twenty-eight."

"Okay, that's a small army, but we only have ten . . ."

"We'll have enough," Eineen told her, pointing down at the water.

Charlie glanced over the cliff and saw another dozen . . . no, another two dozen . . . no . . . it was impossible to count the seals floating vertically in the water, noses and eyes all that were showing. "They know that the people on the barge aren't their enemies?"

Eineen's eyes flashed black from lid to lid.

"No one drowns," Charlie reminded her. "Not today." She stepped to her place in the middle of the line, Mark and Tim behind her. "Wild Road Beyond," she said to Bo at her right.

Bo shook his head. "They don't know it. I mean, Gavin might've played it through with me once or twice but . . ."

"Play it through once. The others will pick it up."

He glanced back at Tanis standing behind his left shoulder staring out at the distant waves and not crying for once, over at Mark scowling at Gavin, and then back at Charlie. "That's not . . ."

"Trust me. They'll pick it up." The fiddler in her head played "Rolling off a Log." *"Either put out or shut up,"* she told it, and then aloud, "Mark."

Mark and Tim laid the heartbeat down together.

Bo sighed, opened his mouth to protest again, but Tanis laid a hand on his arm. He raised it, kissed it, and put his bow to the strings.

Gavin came in two bars later.

By the end of the first chorus, they were all playing—all but the oldest fiddler standing at the end of the line. He frowned, tapped gnarled fingers against his thigh, then slowly raised his bow. A note. Another, extended. A soft run. Then he nodded slowly, changed his stance, and began to play an eerie harmony that lifted the hair on the back of Charlie's neck.

Grinneal had only ever played the song with a single fiddler. There'd never been a harmony before.

Three others joined him.

The Selkie behind the old man's left shoulder grinned and suddenly wasn't elderly but eldritch and beautiful. She leaned forward and kissed the back of his neck.

Charlie took a deep breath.

Music had blown the storm back out to sea. Had probably called it in, too, but that wasn't the point. Music had brought her back through time. Music could do this . . .

A sudden howling gust of wind nearly blew her off her feet.

She staggered three steps forward, felt the edge of the cliff begin to crumble under her foot, fought to turn, fell on her ass when the wind stopped as suddenly as it started, began to slide, gravity taking over . . .

As her left leg flopped off into air, strong fingers grabbed her arm and dragged her back. Then up onto her feet.

Charlie steadied herself on Eineen's shoulders, but her eyes were locked on the tableau back by the cars. Auntie Catherine lay crumpled on the ground, Paul standing over her, Charlie's guitar case in his hand. It was so quiet, they could hear orders shouted out on the barge.

"She came out of the side mirror," Paul said, blinking rapidly, as though his eyes were still trying to convince his brain. "She threw a piece of paper into the air and blew on it and you nearly went off the cliff, so I . . ." He glanced down at the case. "She's just . . . I've never hit a woman and . . ."

Charlie sang a fast E flat minor as Auntie Catherine tried to rise and she slumped back to the ground again. After a moment, when it became clear she was going to stay there, Charlie relaxed. "Okay. Good. And, if it makes you feel any better . . ." Charlie gave Eineen a little shove toward Paul. He looked like he needed an application of Selkie mellowing. ". . . if she'd seen you coming, she'd have found a cornfield."

"What?"

"Family thing. Never mind. Point is, you wouldn't have survived the experience. So . . ." Hands in her pockets to hide the trembling, Charlie turned back to the ocean. ". . . the barge is still moving, folks. Once more, with feeling."

Beyond the wild wood, the road. Beyond the road, the wild sea.

Mark let Tim hold the heartbeat and built a wild rhythm around it, in and out of the melody, over and around the harmony.

As the barge drew even with the cliff, and the music thrummed in blood and bone, and the fiddler in her head played the same song as the fiddlers on the cliff unless the fiddlers on the cliff were the fiddler in her head, Charlie drew in a deep breath, acknowledged that Auntie Catherine unconscious behind her was better than Auntie Catherine conscious pretty much anywhere for a while, and sang a single note.

And held it.

Sang to the land beneath the sea.

Eineen stepped to the edge of the cliff, naked, a belt wrapped around her waist. A woman stepped from behind every fiddler, stepped to the edge of the cliff, naked but for shawls or belts or scarves or sweaters. They were women in the air. They were women when they hit the water. They were seals when they surfaced.

The cliff trembled. Under the barge, the seabed dropped.

The sea dropped.

The barge dropped with it.

And the sea rushed in to fill the space, leaving a perfect oval in the water, the forged signature of a leviathan's dive.

Charlie changed notes. Mark changed the beat. Bo shook out his right arm, brought the bow back and began "Homeward Bound."

That, all nine fiddlers knew and had played a thousand times between them.

Out by the oval, the seals surfaced with coughing men clinging to their backs. They brought their living salvage in to shore about a kilometer from the cliff, swimming as close to the gravel beach as they could.

Once the last man staggered out of the waves, Charlie let the note die. When she closed her mouth, her lips stuck together.

One by one the fiddlers stopped.

Then Mark. Then, finally, Tim.

The waves continued to slap lazily against the cliff as the though the barge had never existed.

"Okay, I don't want to be a killjoy here, Chuck, because that was fucking amazing, but I think the science of this is off." Peering over his sunglasses, Mark scratched his head with his tipper. "I mean, you disrupted the seabed, shouldn't there be a tsunami or something?"

"We sank a barge with a song." Charlie dragged her tongue over her lips without improving the situation much. "Science isn't really a factor here."

"Point." He squinted along the coast to the saved men, some standing in groups, a few kneeling. "They're going to tell stories about this. Hell, they're going to write songs about this."

"No one will believe them."

"You don't know . . ."

"I do know. But the seals will get a legend out of it, and that oil field's not going anywhere, so good PR never hurts."

"Also point." He stared at her for a long moment, then grinned. "If you'll excuse me, Chuck, I think I've discovered what that song needs to be played in public." He hurried off along the cliff to the cluster of fiddlers. Tim rolled his eyes and followed.

Charlie felt something poke her in the arm, turned, and accepted a bottle of water from Paul. "I really do like you, Paul Belleveau. In spite of everything. If Eineen ever gets . . ." She glanced back at the fiddlers. Young and old and apparently happy with their choice. This really wasn't any of her business. "Never mind."

He gestured out at the water where the barge wasn't. "This won't stop Amelia Carlson."

"Doesn't have to." Best water Charlie had ever tasted. "It just has to delay her plans long enough for me to stop her."

"You *can* stop her?"

Charlie grinned. "I just sank a barge with a song."

Paul nodded, half turned . . . "What should we do about Catherine Gale?"

"Leave her."

"Leave her?"

"Trust me."

"She's going to be angry."

"Angry?" Charlie snickered and swayed a bit where she stood. "No. She's going to be wild."

Technically, she shouldn't be anywhere near the Emporium because technically she was upstairs recovering from being crushed by a Troll. However, given that she was, in point of fact, upstairs recovering from being crushed by a Troll, it was unlikely she'd be coming downstairs to run into herself. No harm. No foul.

Slipping in through the back door, the viburnum still quivering in the courtyard, Charlie headed straight into the store and behind the counter to where Boris' photo hung on a nail that glowed so brightly the light was visible six centimeters beyond the edges of the frame.

Amelia thought the young woman who brushed against her as she left the restaurant looked vaguely familiar, but the fuchsia hair was distracting, Ewan was being entertaining, the stars were enchanting, and the wine had been lovely so, honestly, who had time for vaguely familiar.

The sinking of the barge during the small earthquake off the coast of Cape Breton had opened inquires. She'd directed them all away from her to Captain Bonner and laid as much of the blame as possible on her ex-assistant. Nothing had stuck, but she'd crush Paul Belleveau in time.

This was a delay only. With the permit still in her possession, and the minister still in her pocket, the well would go in. No one stopped needing oil because a few sailors and ironworkers swallowed too much salt water.

Heroic seals. Honestly.

Since she never noticed the nail that had been slipped into one of the worn outside pockets of her Italian leather bag, she never noticed when half a centimeter of seam finally gave way and she lost it.

On the fall equinox, as gray-green clouds scudded across the sky and wind whipped the tops off the waves, the seabed by Hay Island cracked. The rock split across the site where the shallow water well would have been anchored by steel and iron had Carlson Oil not suddenly had to declare bankruptcy.

A tentacle emerged from the darkness below the rock and stretched toward the surface.

There were no seals in the water. Or on Hay island. Actually, given the enormous gold dragon perched on the rookery, there was no room for seals on the island. Fortunately, the Gales had always been a close family.

The seals were safely on Scatarie, their cousins standing behind them holding camera phones.

"You're on." Charlie braced herself against the downdraft as Jack took off. He'd grown since he'd left the UnderRealm. Grown, changed, matured a little although he was still, undeniably, a fourteen-year-old boy. He gave a whoop, or the dragon equivalent, when he hit the water.

Auntie Catherine hadn't Seen the Troll. She hadn't Seen Jack at the festival when she'd sent the Boggarts. She hadn't even known it was Jack answering when she'd called Charlie's phone. She hadn't Seen the obvious solution.

"Like I told you, Auntie Catherine, I've got this end-of-the-world thing covered."

Bracelets chimed as she tucked hair disturbed by Jack's flight back behind her ears. "No one likes a smart-ass, Charlotte."

Bottom line, it wasn't about forgiveness or understanding or working together for the greater good; it was about being a Gale.

". . . and although yesterday's small earthquake off the coast of Cape Breton was the second in as many months, both provincial and federal governments continue to

refuse to fund research. Acadia and Dalhousie Universities have announced they plan on sending geophysicists to the region with or without government funding."

Charlie reached over and turned off the car radio. "And geophysicists still on the shore at moonrise will suddenly find themselves in new relationships as Two Seventy-Five N adds to their resource base." Under Paul's leadership, the environmental group had begun to expand onto the international stage. Turned out that Eineen hadn't changed him, she'd just redirected his focus.

Feet on the dashboard of Charlie's car, Jack slouched as far as the seat belt would allow and belched.

"Oh, that's nice." The small fire on the dash burned out on its own.

"It's not my fault the old gods taste like a sneaker someone stored fish in."

Charlie grinned, swerved around a late season tourist, and tossed him a bag of nacho chips. "Remind me to take you out for good calamari some time."